C000177613

Dominic Dulley is a software developer with a passion for SF. His short fiction has been published widely in books, journals and magazines. *Shattermoon* and *Morhelion*, his first two novels, are the start of the fast-moving, action-packed space opera The Long Game. He lives with his wife and family in Warwick.

Also by Dominic Dulley

THE LONG GAME

Shattermoon

Morhelion

Residuum

DOMINIC DULLEY

Jo Fletcher

BOOKS

First published in Great Britain in 2021 by

Jo Fletcher Books, an imprint of
Quercus Editions Ltd
Carmelite House
50 Victoria Embankment
London EC4Y 0DZ

An Hachette UK company

A CIP catalogue record for this book is available
from the British Library

PB ISBN 978 1 52941 074 7

10 9 8 7 6 5 4 3 2 1

Typeset by CC Book Production

Printed and bound in Great Britain by Clays Ltd, Elcograf S.p.A.

For Hugo,
a much cooler nerd than I ever was

CONTENTS

1

NOT REALLY MY STYLE

'Was I right or was I right?' Ethan asked, his mouth full of lake shellfish. 'I was right, wasn't I?'

Orry Kent regarded her little brother with distaste. 'Don't speak with your mouth full.'

He grimaced and squeezed tender white flesh out between his teeth like he was five again.

She looked away, unamused.

'This place is even better than I expected,' he continued, cracking open another large claw and slathering it with melted butter, then stuffing it into his mouth. 'Can we stay here forever?'

'Not unless you've stashed a few million imperials somewhere you haven't told me about.'

A warm zephyr drifted across the crater lake, barely ruffling its calm surface. She turned her face to it and breathed in the exotic scent of mineral-rich waters. Halcyon was undoubtedly a beautiful planet. It was just so damned *dull*.

La Caldera was one of several al fresco restaurants lining this side of the lake, the canvas awnings that provided shade during the day now retracted so its patrons could look up at the stars. The place was busy, but by no means full, and a sudden burst of raucous laughter disturbed the low, contented murmur of conversation, causing some of the other diners to turn their heads in irritation. Orry ignored the disturbance; she'd already spotted the three young men a few tables away. She knew the type: Ruuz lordlings here to have a good time on family money. That was another thing she didn't like about Halcyon.

'What's up with you, anyway?' Ethan asked, breaking into her reverie.

'Nothing.' She pushed her grub salad around the plate with her fork.

'You don't like it here, do you?' he said, finally voicing what must have been obvious for days. 'But how can you *not* like Halcyon? *Everyone* likes Halcyon.' He laid down his knife. 'Even *Mender* likes Halcyon.'

She grunted; that *had* been unexpected. 'I don't know,' she told him. 'It was fine at first, but we've been here for weeks now. Aren't you bored?'

'*Bored?* Are you kidding me? This morning I swam with a school of great bluejacks – as close as we are now!'

'And what did you do this afternoon?'

He dropped his eyes and picked at his shellfish. 'I . . . er . . . fell asleep by the pool – but that's not the point—' He waved his fork at her. 'You're only bored because you don't *do* anything.

You need to chill, really get into this place. I mean, Sis, what are you even *wearing*?'

She looked down at her black tank top and red shorts. 'What's wrong with my clothes?'

She followed his gaze as he watched a lithe woman in a diaphanous gown sashaying past their table. He raised his eyebrows.

'Not really my style,' Orry said, suddenly very aware of her clumpy ship boots. She shifted her feet further under the table.

Two of the nearby lordlings were chanting something now, thumping the table enthusiastically and making the plates and cutlery clatter. There was a sudden shattering of glass and a harried waiter hurried over and attempted to calm the men. She noticed the third of them was watching his companions' antics with a mildly pained expression. He was a typical Ruuz, with a neatly waxed moustache and black hair rising like a wedge above angular cheekbones. He saw her looking and raised his glass to her as his friends sent the waiter packing, hurling insults at the poor fellow's departing back.

'Just ignore 'em,' Ethan advised, turning back to her and returning to his previous point. 'Look, if you're not happy here you might as well stay on board *Jane* with Quondam. There's no point shelling out for your lodge if you're not enjoying yourself, is there?'

'And I suppose you could use that money to stay in *your* lodge for an extra week?'

'Well, now that you come to mention it—'

'No, Ethan. I'm sorry, but we need to leave while we still have *something* left in the kitty.'

'Just one more week, Orry – *please*?'

She sighed at the thought of spending yet another week bored out of her skull, but they'd been through a lot on Morhelion and after all, her brother was still only a kid. She owed him this. 'I'll think about it,' she said, and Ethan rewarded her with a wide grin.

The put-upon waiter was returning with *La Caldera*'s maître d' in tow. The level of conversation in the restaurant dropped noticeably in expectation of a scene.

'Gentlemen,' the maître d' began, clasping his hands as if he was praying, 'could I please ask you to moderate the level of your conversation. There have been complaints.'

Orry felt for the man, caught between the Scylla of the entitled lordlings and Charybdis of his other wealthy, influential patrons, but she had her own worries.

'I spoke to *Jane* yesterday. She's worried about Mender – he's not answering her calls—'

'Why don't you stick your complaints up your arsehole!' the biggest of the young men said loudly. Very deliberately, he picked up a spoon and dug it into the ostentatiously large bowl of caviar in front of him. He smiled – and flicked the contents into the maître d's face.

Keeping his face schooled, the man produced a white handkerchief and wiped the oily black eggs from his cheek before saying calmly, 'This is a respectable establishment. If you cannot comport yourselves in a manner commensurate with your station, I will have no choice but to ask you to leave.'

At this, the second lordling, a painfully thin man with pale skin, started laughing hysterically. The big loud one tossed his still-lit cigar onto the linen tablecloth before rising unsteadily to his feet. The maître d' stiffened as he reached into a pocket, but all he produced was a wad of plastic notes, which he tossed in the man's face.

'Plenty more where that came from, you jumped-up little tit. Now, be a good fellow and fuck off, will you? Your face is making me want to punch it.'

The maître d' ignored the money fluttering to the ground around him. 'Please, gentlemen—'

'Right!' the big one said. His chair clattered to the floor as he took a step forwards, fists balled.

'Enough, Boris,' said the third man, rising smoothly to place himself between the two. 'I apologise for our behaviour,' he told the maître d'. 'I assure you we will be as quiet as mice from now on.'

Boris snorted at that, but he did pick up his fallen chair and sit down. Retrieving his cigar, which had scorched the heavy linen tablecloth, he puffed it back to life and grinned belligerently at the maître d'.

'Thank you, sir,' the man said, with evident relief. 'Can I get you anything?' he asked the peacemaker. 'Another bottle, sir? On the house, of course.'

'Nothing, thank you.'

The maître d' bowed and retreated. As he passed Orry she saw his face was tight with rage.

No wonder, she thought, throwing the lordlings a cold look. The one with the cheekbones inclined his head politely at her and she looked away in disgust.

'Pricks,' she muttered.

'What's new?' Ethan said, looking forlornly at the empty remains of his shellfish. 'Anyway, I'm sure Mender is fine. All on his own with as much booze as he can pour down his throat? He probably couldn't manage a coherent sentence even if he did answer.'

'I suppose you're right.' She grinned, reassured by his words. 'Just think of the unlucky bot stuck over there with him,' she said in mock horror. 'Can you imagine?'

He grimaced. 'Poor thing will need therapy.'

'They'll just scrap it,' she decided. 'The emotional scarring will be too deep.'

They both laughed.

'How's Quondam?' Ethan asked.

'He's happy enough on board – he and *Jane* spend a lot of time talking about the Ascendancy and history and stuff, I think. He was a chronicler on Kadir before the war, but he says there's a lot the Iron Council kept out of the history books. *Jane* sounds very interested.'

A waiter appeared at Orry's shoulder bearing a brightly coloured cocktail on a silver tray, which he set before her with a flourish. 'Compliments of His Lordship, miz,' he said.

Several tables away, Cheekbones raised his glass.

Orry scowled at him. *Arrogant bastard.* She glanced up at the waiter. 'Tell him I'm not—'

'Mmmm,' Ethan said, picking up the glass and downing half of it in one swallow.

'What are you doing?' she hissed. 'I was going to send that back.'

He licked his lips. 'Why?' He twisted in his seat to look at Cheekbones and raised the glass to him. The lordling appeared amused.

Orry hid her face in her hands.

'He looks all right,' Ethan informed her. 'Better than his mates, at least. You should go for it. Might be fun.'

She took the half-drained glass from his hand.

'Hey!' he protested, 'what are you doing?'

'You're only fifteen.'

'So what?'

'So you shouldn't—'

'Please don't say I'm too young to drink, because after everything that's happened to us, you're going to sound pretty stupid. You're not Dad, so stop trying to act like him.'

She closed her mouth and pushed the glass back towards him.

'Thank you,' he said. 'Now go and talk to him.'

'He's a self-important prig – and he's Ruuz.'

'So are we, technically. And that didn't bother you with Harry, did it?' He held up a hand to still her objection. 'I'm not saying you should *marry* him. You're on holiday. Just relax – who knows? You might actually enjoy yourself.'

She pushed her chair back and stood. 'As much as I enjoy receiving romantic advice from a teenager who's never had a girlfriend, I'm quite capable of running my own love life, thanks very much.'

'Of course you are,' he said.

She glared at him, remembering Vance Tyrell and what a fool he'd made of her. 'Oh, just . . . *shove it*,' she said, before marching away.

'Nice comeback,' he called after her.

She strode onto the beach, stopping only when the clear water was lapping at her boots, and gazed at the yachts moored out on the lake. Lights burned in some of them and she could hear laughter and muffled music drifting to shore. The resort of Laguna Alta extended halfway around the lake, which had formed within the vast caldera of an extinct volcano in Halcyon's temperate latitudes. The far side was rugged, full of steep cliffs and secluded coves, very different to the immaculately maintained beaches, edged by a ribbon of bars, shops and restaurants of the resort. The luxury lodges were dotted among the tall pines that covered the increasingly steep slope leading up the caldera's rocky rim.

Orry didn't deny the beauty of the place, but after enough time even the loveliest things could become mundane.

'It's all rather tedious, isn't it?' said a voice behind her.

She turned to see Cheekbones, a little way up the beach, eyes fixed on the view rather than on her.

'Most people would say it's beautiful,' she told him, irritated by his echoing of her thoughts.

He chuckled. 'But not you?'

'Why do you say that?'

'You don't strike me as the usual sort of Halcyon girl.'

'"Halcyon girl"?' she repeated coldly.

He looked at her and smiled. 'That's what I said.'

'And you would know, would you? A bit of an expert on "Halcyon girls", are you? Had a lot of experience?'

If her icy tone fazed him, he didn't show it. 'All I meant was that you seem to have a bit more about you than most of the women around here.'

She turned back to the view, wondering why she didn't just walk away.

He came to stand beside her. 'I'm Timofey.'

She opened her mouth to trot out an alias, then realised there was no need. 'Orry,' she said.

'You didn't like my drink?'

'No . . . well, I mean, yes, but . . .'

'Your friend seemed to enjoy it.'

'He's my brother.'

'Oh, you're here with family?'

His questions were making her uncomfortable. 'Not exactly. Look, I have to go.' She started to walk off.

'Wait . . . please.'

It was the second word that made her stop.

'I've handled this badly – I'm sorry,' he started. 'That thing with the drink, it was clumsy. I suppose I'm just used to . . .'

'Hitting on Halcyon girls?'

His sheepish look softened his angular features. 'Listen,' he said awkwardly, 'I know a little place nearby, if you'd like to . . . well, if you'd like to have a drink with me.'

She pursed her lips, cutting off her instinctive refusal and making herself at least consider his offer.

Maybe Ethan's right; maybe I should just relax and try to enjoy myself. This is Halcyon, after all.

Then she remembered the scene at the table and felt her face stiffen. 'I don't think so,' she said. 'If you'll excuse me, my brother is waiting.'

Timofey didn't protest. Giving her a formal bow, he stepped aside to let her pass. She felt his eyes on her all the way back to the restaurant.

'Can we go?' she asked Ethan as soon as she got to their table.

'I haven't finished my dessert – don't you want any?'

'I'm not hungry.'

The look of disappointment on his face annoyed her. Behind him, she could see Timofey had returned to his friends. She waited for the lordling to make some comment about her, but he just sat down and picked up his water glass.

'I'm going back to my lodge,' she told her brother and walked away, wondering what she was suddenly so angry about.

2

CALL ME BILL

Laguna Alta was a large resort but it never felt crowded. It helped, Orry reflected the next morning as she walked among the tall firs, that the guest lodges - the word 'lodge' was clearly designed to conjure images of the rugged outdoors living though they were really just luxury apartments - were scattered among the carefully curated forest that carpeted the inner slopes of the caldera. In fact, there was nothing rugged about hers, which was so comfortable that it was almost noon before she'd got up. That wasn't like her, and she decided she didn't care for the indolence this place was bringing out in her.

The bark chipping path was soft beneath her boots as she wended her way between the trees in search of a late breakfast. Birds trilled in the loose canopy above and the sun shone warm on her shoulders where it penetrated the leaves. The woods smelled of pine and mulch, tinged with the faintly mineral aroma of the nearby lake. She could see the waters now through the thinning trunks, a pale green expanse that filled the caldera, dotted with white pleasure craft gleaming in the sunshine. The path sloped gently down to the shore, where pale sand met the water. The beaches were far from crowded, though she could hear laughter and screams of delight and saw holidaymakers splashing happily in the water. She turned right and strolled along the road that separated the sands from the forest, heading towards the 'village' district where most of the restaurants and other leisure facilities were. She looked up as something buzzed overhead but it was only a small drone. It hovered for moment ahead of her, before spinning on its axis and zipping away towards the village.

She started to wish she'd thought to bring a headscarf or hat. The sun was hot out of the shade of the trees and sweat was prickling on her scalp and between her shoulder blades. She looked longingly at the cool water, but a hollow rumble from her stomach made her delay that particular pleasure until after breakfast. *Or perhaps it's lunch.* She couldn't be bothered to check her integuary for the time. *What's the point?* she thought, *when there's nothing to do anyway.*

Up ahead, a long pier stretched out over the lake. There were a couple of small craft moored on one side, but the boardwalk was crowded with people, mostly fishing or diving into the deeper water at the far end. As Orry came level, she heard a panicked scream from the water. The scream repeated and she saw someone in the water near one of the pier's stanchions, arms flailing frantically as their head disappeared beneath the surface, only to reappear briefly before sinking again. The people on the pier were crowding to the sides and pointing, but no one appeared to be actually trying to help the drowning person.

Orry started running, the sun-bleached boards thudding beneath her heavy boots. She was wondering whether she should kick them off before jumping in to help when she saw someone else had had the same idea; a young man was shoving his way through the spectators, tugging his shirt over his head as he went. Orry slowed, a little disappointed, as he dived expertly into the water and reached the struggling swimmer in a few strong strokes.

He managed to get behind and grip the person under the arms just as a red and white life ring slapped onto the water nearby. He ignored it and instead started towing his burden towards the beach. At least they'd stopped struggling, so he was making swift headway. Orry stopped halfway along the pier to watch – and realised she knew the rescuer: it was Cheekbones – no, Timofey – the Ruuz lordling from last night.

She took a couple of steps back so he wouldn't see her watching, but he was intent on getting his charge – who Orry could now see was a girl, a teenager – to the shore. As soon as they were able to stand, Timofey pulled her to her feet and helped her stagger from the water to collapse on the sand, where several resort staff bearing piles of thick towels were converging on them. The girl was smiling, Orry saw, and looking embarrassed as she scraped vibrant pink hair from her pretty face and waved away offers of help. Timofey, accepting a towel, which he draped round his shoulders, was quickly surrounded by staff and holidaymakers, all pressing close to shake his hand and congratulate him.

I bet he loves the attention, Orry thought sourly, then felt a stab of remorse. If anything, he was looking sheepish, embarrassed by the well-wishers.

'Harrumph,' she muttered, then realised with a shock that she sounded like Mender.

Scowling, she walked away to find some food.

Four hours later she still hadn't gone for a swim. The *Champagne Supernova* was set far enough back from the beach so as not to attract much passing afternoon trade, though she knew the place got lively enough after dark. Quiet was just fine, though; it gave her somewhere to brood. The incident with the drowning girl had somehow made everything worse. That sudden burst of adrenalin she'd felt – that was what was missing around here. It was how she felt when she was running a grift: alive, and on the edge.

She shifted on her stool and surveyed the bar's faux-rustic interior, idly looking for a likely mark. *Nothing complicated*, she promised herself, *and they can't know they've been had*. But the bar's patrons provided poor pickings: a trio of elderly gentlemen dozing over their wine glasses and a young couple too focused on consuming each other's faces to be interested in anything Orry might have to offer. She turned back to the bar with a grimace and tilting her head, sized up the barman.

He was a far cry from Sheng, the bartender at the *Rampant Cat* on Morhelion. Sheng had appreciated her bar tricks, but this guy ... well, he looked like all the staff did on Halcyon: prim and proper and so full of fawning respect it made her want to do something outrageous just to see how they would react.

Robots, she thought scornfully.

This man was a case in point, middle-aged and dressed impeccably in a white shirt and black necktie, his conservatively cut hair slicked into a razor-sharp side-parting. He saw her staring and came over.

'Can I help you, miz?'

She considered hurling her stool into the shelves of bottles behind the bar, but instead, she contented herself with draining her glass and pushing it towards him. 'Another one of those, please.'

'One more Maunderberry Eruption coming up.'

She watched him hand her empty glass to a stumpy little wash-bot below the bar and grab a clean one. 'What's your name?' she asked as he prepared the cocktail.

He looked up, clearly surprised by the question. 'Erik,' he said after a moment.

'I'm Orry.'

'Um, hi.' Erik cast a nervous look around the bar and went back to mixing her drink, focusing hard on the task in an obvious attempt to deter any further questions.

'Do you come from Halcyon?' she asked.

His shoulders slumped a little. 'Yes, I was born in Titus Bay.'

'Is that nearby?'

'No, a long way away.'

'Oh, so why are you here? I'd've thought there'd be work everywhere – Halcyon's a leisure world, after all.'

For a moment she thought he was going to say something, but then he just gave a slight shake of his head that could have meant anything, popped a little umbrella into the maunderberries piled on top and handed her the drink. His eyes slid over her shoulder to gaze at the entrance as he moved away to busy himself at the far end of the bar. She swung around in her seat and saw Timofey walking towards her, a broad smile on his angular face.

'Drinking alone?' he enquired lightly. 'Where's your brother?'

'No idea, but I'm sure he'll tell me in excruciating detail over dinner.'

He laughed, and she couldn't help but smile. 'I happen to be at a loose end as well,' he said. 'Would you mind if I joined you?'

Orry realised to her surprise that she'd been hoping he'd ask, which threw her. 'If you must,' she said, after a moment's hesitation.

He took the stool next to her and indicated her drink. 'What's that?'

She held the cocktail up to the light for his inspection. 'This? This is a Maunderberry Eruption.'

'Any good?'

'It's all right,' she admitted. 'I've had four of them.' She sniggered, and realised the four cocktails had snuck up on her.

He clicked his fingers at Erik. 'Two more of these, my man, and one for yourself.'

'Yes, sir, thank you, sir.'

Timofey leaned closer. 'He won't have a drink,' he told her in a quieter voice. 'They take it as tips.'

'"They"?' she said coldly.

'The staff.'

'I know what you meant. "They" are people too, you know. You don't have to treat them like dogs, clicking your fingers at them.'

In truth, she'd seen far worse behaviour. If anything, she was angrier at Erik, for letting Timofey talk to him that way. *The Ruuz wouldn't stay top of the pile for long if people stopped licking their arses and stood up to them*, she reflected as she sipped at her drink.

'Sorry,' Timofey said, 'you're absolutely right.'

She frowned, wondering if he was mocking her. 'I am?'

'Of course you are. Look, I . . .' He paused as Erik set the drinks in front of them. 'Thank you,' he said, sliding a plastic note across the bar.

The barman smiled his gratitude as he pocketed it and walked away; only then did the lordling turn to Orry, his face serious. 'I was born into money,' he said, 'but lately I've begun to have . . . well, doubts, really. My friends . . . I mean, you saw what they were like last night. That used to be me. We've done some pretty shitty things, to be honest – things I'm not very proud of.'

Orry was studying his face carefully. *If this is a line, he's a bloody good liar*, she concluded. 'Why are you telling me?' she asked.

He grinned, looking embarrassed. 'I don't know. I just . . . I guess I don't want you to think I'm like all the others. I'm trying to change, to be a better person.'

'Why does it matter what I think?'

'Um . . .' He reached for his drink and sipped at it, clearly reluctant to answer.

Taking pity on him, she said, 'I saw you save that girl today.'

'You did?'

'Was that part of you trying to be a better person?'

He laughed. 'No, anyone would have done that.'

'But *you* did,' she pointed out, thinking that no one else on the pier had tried to help.

'I suppose. Anyway, let's not talk about me. Tell me about you.'

This time it was her turn to take a drink while she thought about what to tell him. The tang of maunderberries was sharp on her tongue and whether it was because of the booze or the boredom, she found herself feeling mischievous.

'I,' she stated solemnly, 'am Princess Wilhelmina Katerina Quartz, eldest scion of House Quartz. You may kiss my hand.'

Trying not to smile, Timofey stood to accept her

outstretched hand, then brought his heels together in a formal bow, which ended with his lips brushing her knuckles. 'Your servant, Princess.'

She waved her hand airily. 'You may sit your, er, posterior, um, down.' *Nice.*

'Thank you, Highness.' He put on a puzzled expression, almost hiding his amusement. 'You know, I don't recall coming across House – um . . . ?'

'Quartz,' she reminded him.

'Quartz, just so. Is it a very large House?'

'Oh, the largest. I am, in fact the true heir to the Ascendancy, usurped and exiled by that beast Piotr.' She stopped, suddenly concerned that Timofey would take offence at even a light-hearted jibe at the Imperator, but the young man's eyes were sparkling with humour. 'By rights,' she continued gravely, 'I should of course be Imperatrix.'

He leaned back on his stool and blew out his cheeks, as if stunned by her revelation, then drained his glass and motioned for refills.

'If Your Highness would permit—?' he began.

'Call me Bill,' she said, enjoying herself. It was refreshing to play a role again, even as a joke.

He swallowed a laugh. 'As you wish . . . *Bill*. So tell me, what brings an exiled princess to Halcyon?'

'I am raising an army,' she declared loudly, 'in order to depose the pretender Piotr and restore myself to my rightful place on the—'

'Aaaaand perhaps we should stop there,' he interrupted quickly, glancing around the bar's few patrons, none of whom appeared to have overheard. 'You never know who might be listening,' he explained with a wince.

Orry felt her cheeks flush. Annoyed with herself, she turned to face the bar. She reached for one of her drinks, then changed her mind and pushed it away. *I think you've had enough,* she told herself sternly.

'Shit,' Timofey said, then chuckled, shaking his head ruefully. 'How are you not in prison?' he enquired.

She tried to stay cross, but his laughter was infectious. Perhaps she *should* have been a little more discreet, even though she knew Piotr would have found her game entertaining. She turned back to Timofey, who was watching her anxiously.

'I shall appoint you my Minister of Telling Me When to Shut the Hell Up in Bars,' she said.

He smiled with relief and raised his drink. 'I gladly accept the honour.' Setting the glass down, he looked thoughtful. 'Imperatrix? Is that really what you'd be called?'

'I think so. It's the female form of Imperator, at any rate, not that it matters. I just like the sound of the word.'

'I suppose you could be called whatever you wanted if you were in charge. It's odd, isn't it, thinking about the Ascendancy without the Imperator? He can't live for ever, though.'

'No,' she said sadly, remembering how frail the old man had looked after the assassination attempt at Holbein's Folly.

Sensing her change of mood, Timofey indicated the glasses lined up in front of her. 'Drink up.'

'You know what, I think I've had enough for now.'

'I can respect that,' he said, pushing his own away. 'I like a girl who knows her limits.'

She laughed wryly. 'Unlike some of your friends, I imagine?'

'Yes,' he said with a grimace. 'So, what are you doing next?'

An all-too-familiar wave of melancholy swept back in as she remembered where she was. Talking to Timofey had been a pleasant distraction and she rather regretted it was coming to a close.

'Oh, nothing much.'

He laughed.

'What?' she demanded.

'Well, it's just . . . you sounded so forlorn.' He placed the back of his hand against his forehead and pretended to wilt like a lady with the vapours. 'Oh . . . *nothing much.*' He gave a deep, theatrical sigh.

Orry slapped his arm. 'Shut *up!*'

'I sympathise . . . I really do.' His grin faded as he lapsed into a thoughtful silence. 'You know . . .' he began, then stopped.

'What?' she prompted.

He hesitated, then leaned in closer. 'There can be more to Halcyon than water sports and shellfish – if you want.'

'Like what?' she said dismissively. 'Saunas and massages?'

'Let's just say you won't find it listed in the entertainments directory. It's a bit more . . . edgy.' His clear blue eyes were gazing intently at her now, but then he shook his head. 'No, I don't think you'd have the stomach for it . . . *Princess.*'

Suddenly her playfulness was gone. She did her best to hide her annoyance with a shrug. 'Whatever. I can do without watching you and your chinless mates in a spanking circle.'

'It's nothing like that.'

'Then what?'

He shook his head. 'No spoilers. If you want to find out, meet me down by the pier at eleven tonight.'

She snorted. 'I don't think so.' She stood. 'Thanks for the drinks.'

'You're going?'

'Looks like it.'

'Wait.' He grabbed her arm, then quickly dropped it as she shot him a glare. 'Look, just consider it, will you? You won't be bored, I promise.'

She narrowed her eyes, not wanting him to see she was a little curious. 'Don't get your hopes up,' she informed him, and walked away.

3

LIKE A TUMOUR

Orry's bed was supremely comfortable, but she was anything but sleepy. In the darkness outside her bedroom window she could make out the nearest trees, which had been rendered silver by the light from the three of Halcyon's seven moons that were currently visible above the high caldera wall. She reached the end of the paragraph she was reading and realised she hadn't taken any of it in. Rather than try for the third time, she set down her reader and shifted position, bouncing around until she was lying flat on her back, staring up at the thick wooden beams supporting the roof. She stayed there for a minute, arms at her sides, then sighed and rolled into a foetal position, which she maintained for another minute before reverting to her back.

At last she sat up and using her integuary, opened a private channel to *Dainty Jane*.

Hi, she sent, forming the word in her mind.

Hello, Orry, the ship replied.

What's up?

I am currently playing a game with the resort's entertainment substrate.

Oh yeah? What sort of game?

It is a 5-dimensional strategy simulation. Quite enthralling, actually. Is everything all right?

Sure, sure. Just, you know . . . chilling. Orry grimaced; she sounded like Ethan.

I can terminate the game by forfeiting if you would like to talk.

No, no, don't do that. It's all good here. Cool-cool-cool. She winced at that. *Just, uh, checking in. I'll see you later.*

Very well. I am here if you need me.

Sweet. Bye, then.

She closed the channel and muttered, '*Sweet?* What is this bloody place doing to me?'

She considered calling Ethan but couldn't face the sheer levels of enthusiasm that would involve, so instead she tried Mender, someone who could never be described as enthusiastic, fully expecting him to ignore her. Which he did. *Comatose, probably*, she thought grumpily, then smiled. *I suppose that's one way to deal with this place.*

She dropped her arms to her side and stared up at the roof beams, clenching and unclenching her fists. Accessing her integuary again, she checked the time. *Ten-forty.* She glanced at her boots, standing by the bed, then back at the ceiling. Another minute crawled by.

'Sod it,' she said, and reached for her clothes.

*

The pier was pretty at night, strung with fairy lights, the water beneath it floodlit from the stanchions. Orry was humming happily to herself as she stepped from the shore road onto the wooden boards, but fell silent when she saw not one but three figures waiting at the far end: Timofey had his obnoxious friends from the previous night with him. She stopped and considered returning to her lodge, but he had seen her and was already running over, pursued by catcalls and kissing noises from the other two.

'You came!' he said, delighted.

'I didn't realise you were bringing your friends,' she said sourly, and he looked suitably crestfallen.

'I did try to get rid of them, but we'd already made the arrangements . . .'

'And you didn't want to upset them over a girl? I understand.'

He looked relieved, entirely missing her sarcasm. 'I knew you would. Anyway, it's only a short flight and they're not *too* awful. Well, Boris can be a handful, but Lev's all right – although he's pretty out of it.' Behind him, the bigger one was pretending – at least, Orry assumed he was pretending – to throw the other into the lake.

Timofey frowned and yelled, 'Boris! Pack it in!' The big man raised his middle finger and continued struggling. 'They grow on you,' he finished lamely.

'Like a tumour?'

He smiled uncomfortably, then looked relieved as a thrumming sound reached them from across the water. 'There's our transport.' He pointed at the flyer streaking across the lake towards the pier, low enough to leave a white scar of churning water in its wake.

'Where are we going?' she asked.

'To a spot up on the caldera's inner wall – out of sight of the tourists.'

'But—'

'Come on – that's our ride.' He moved to grab her arm, then thought better of it, instead making a flamboyant gesture towards the vehicle hovering off the end of the pier.

Orry chewed on her lower lip as she watched Boris and Lev climb into the rear compartment. She didn't much relish being shut up in a box with those two idiots, however plushly appointed it might be, but her curiosity was overcoming her misgivings.

'Are you lovebirds coming?' Boris called from the open gullwing door, and Timofey looked hopefully at her.

'I'd better not regret this,' she muttered, and clambered inside.

He squeezed into the leather seat beside her and the door swung closed. Her stomach sank as the flyer lifted and she felt herself pressed gently back into her seat as they accelerated away.

Timofey reached up to touch a button on the ceiling and the flyer's interior instantly evaporated, leaving them speeding across the lake, apparently suspended in mid-air.

'You like it?' he asked.

'It's all right,' she said, curbing her enthusiasm. She'd never experienced full-prospect technology, although it had been around for a while – in truth, it was thrilling; as close to actually flying as she'd ever come – but no way was she going to let the lordlings know that.

Lev, the smaller man, was sitting opposite her in the cabin. He'd had his eyes closed since she came aboard, but now he opened them – and squealed in terror when he saw nothing but clear air where he'd expected the inside of a flyer to be. He tried to crawl further up onto the ghost of his seat as Boris, beside him, roared with laughter.

'Everything's fine!' Timofey yelled at him. 'Lev, calm down! It's just full-prospect.'

'Wh-what?'

Timofey rolled his eyes at Orry and deactivated, then reactivated the effect a couple of times until Lev lowered his legs and placed his feet firmly on the unseen carpeted floor. He looked sheepish, she thought.

'What have you taken, anyway?' Timofey asked him.

'Just some j-ludes.'

'And two bottles of champagne,' Boris added, punching Lev hard in the upper arm. 'Twat.'

'Hey, quit it!' The smaller man flailed back at Boris, who effortlessly blocked the feeble blows.

'Please stop,' Timofey said, sounding pained and glancing pointedly at Orry.

A wide grin spread over Boris' fleshy face. He leaned forward in his seat and when he spoke she could smell meat and alcohol on his breath.

'Timo wants to fuck you,' he said. 'Don't you, Timo?'

Lev, beside him, gave a high-pitched giggle.

'Rama, Boris!' Timofey turned to her, his pale cheeks flushed red. 'I'm so sorry, he's *such* an arsehole.'

Having said his piece, Boris sank back in his seat, but Orry beckoned him close again.

Grinning, he obliged her. 'What?'

With their faces centimetres apart, she sniffed and gave a shudder. 'Ever hear of mouthwash?' she enquired, then turned to admire the view.

Lev sniggered again, louder this time, but Orry could practically feel the fury coming off Boris. She made herself watch the lake waters flashing past until he muttered 'Cow!' and settled back in his seat.

'Is it much further?' she asked, more to break the silence than because she wanted to know. They were climbing now, and slowing over the wooded slopes replacing the water beneath them.

'Uh, no,' Timofey said. He sounded surprised she was even speaking to him.

She turned to him and he pointed up ahead. Peering between Boris and Lev, one of them scowling and the other grinning like an idiot, she spotted what looked like bonfires among the trees.

The flyer banked to the right and descended, Timofey

deactivated the full-prospect view and she lost sight of the fires, but a moment later she saw trees out of the windows and the flyer settled gently onto the ground.

The doors opened and Timofey extended a hand. 'Shall we?' he asked.

4

RED RUN

Orry took Timofey's hand, more to annoy Boris than because she wanted to, and allowed him to help her out of the vehicle. She looked around a wide clearing; there were several other flyers parked there. Through the trees she could see the glint of even more, gleaming orange in flickering firelight. She could hear loud music playing somewhere nearby, and the sounds of people enjoying themselves.

'All this intrigue for a party?' she asked, thoroughly disappointed, but Timofey was shaking his head.

'Oh no, much more than that. Come and see!'

Keeping hold of her hand, he led her through the trees. They emerged into a much larger clearing packed with people.

'Timo!' A cold beer was thrust into her hand as a group of partygoers immediately surrounded them. They were all young and beautiful, men and women alike, and several conversations started up simultaneously around her, impossible to follow over the thudding beat.

Drinking, she surveyed the mass of swaying people, illuminated by the strobing lights strung among the trees around the edge of the clearing, where ornate iron braziers belched flames. Party-people were pressing in around a huge metal framework dominating the centre of the clearing. She assumed it was a stage at first, but it was long and narrow, almost as if it were for channelling livestock. A figure was dancing manically on a platform that moved along the top of the structure, but the flashing lights and fountains of multicoloured sparks prevented her from seeing any details. The crowd near the framework roared its approval of something she couldn't make out, and moments later a ball of flame belched into the sky.

Timofey grabbed her elbow. Leaning in to be heard, he yelled in her ear, 'Let's go closer!'

She allowed him to lead her through the crowd, followed by Boris and Lev, whose eyes looked huge as he gazed open-mouthed at the dazzling lights ahead of them.

When they reached the front, Orry could see that the cage was actually twin parallel tunnels formed of irregularly spaced metal arches over gridded metal walkways. The whole thing was probably a hundred metres long, with narrow walkways rising and falling over several levels as they threaded their way from one end of the framework to the other. She squinted at the nearest arch and her beer bottle stopped halfway to her mouth as she saw what appeared to be blades fixed to its inner surface like a shark's teeth. Lowering her hand, she tried to get a look at the next arch along. This one had no teeth, but was surrounded by a mass of pipes which led to nozzles aimed inwards at the walkway.

'What is this thing?' she demanded.

'That's the Red Run!' Timofey answered enthusiastically. 'It's what we've come to see.'

On the other side of the run and halfway along its length, she caught a glimpse of a woman wearing the white tunic of a medic who looked to be assisting someone in skin-tight running gear with several rips in it. She was pretty sure she could see blood and blackened scorch marks through the tears.

Before she could demand further explanation, the moving platform with its dancing occupant arrived back at the start of the arches and settled between a pair of tall, fluttering banners. The dancer was wearing a blood-red frockcoat and black top hat, which she swept from her head and used to make an elaborate bow to the cheering crowd. The woman's face was underlit by actinic spotlights which gave it a ghastly cast. Her eyes glazed for a moment and the bass-heavy music reduced in volume from mind-numbing to merely deafening.

'All right, *motherfuckers!*' she screamed. 'Are you ready for the next run?' The crowd howled its agreement and her teeth flashed white as she threw back her head and laughed insanely. 'I *said,*' she yelled, her voice distorting into a demonic howl, '*are you ready for the next run?*'

Orry winced as Boris bellowed wordlessly beside her.

'She's the configurator,' Timofey explained, shouting in her ear.

Below the configurator's mobile platform, Orry spotted a man and a woman being led to the Red Run's twin entrances. They wore the same brightly coloured, skin-tight running suits as the injured person she'd seen being led away by the medic, but these two looked anything but athletic. One was a man, large and powerful-looking, but he sported a prodigious belly and was well into middle age. The other, a woman of a similar age, was thinner. *Too thin*, Orry thought. She could practically see her skeleton through the woman's suit.

'This will be a two-horse race,' the configurator continued, her amplified voice booming through the clearing, 'at setting number *seven*!'

There were appreciative *oohs* and *aahs* from some of the crowd at the announcement, while as many again booed in displeasure. Laughing, the configurator's eyes glazed once again as she accessed her integuary and the Red Run began to reconfigure itself. Some of the existing arches folded themselves away while metallic limbs appearing from below like scorpion tails added new arches deploying an alarming array of weaponry. The walkways were moving too, adjusting the heights of some sections to allow for the reconfigured run.

'The settings go all the way up to eleven,' Timofey said loudly, 'but no one has ever survived a run at anything over nine.'

The two runners were attempting to limber up directly in front of them, much to the crowd's amusement. *They look terrified*, Orry thought. All around her, gilt chips were changing hands as people bet on the outcome. Boris in particular was taking bets from everyone, offering odds in a chillingly competent manner.

She pulled Timofey close enough to shout in his ear, 'Who *are* those two people? Why are they doing this?'

Before he could answer, the configurator's voice boomed out again, 'No more bets now, mizzes and misters, the run . . . is about . . . to . . . BEGIN!'

The thudding background beat morphed into dramatic music as the two contestants stepped up nervously. Pyrotechnics erupted from the framework and they flung themselves forward: charging down the metal runs.

Orry gasped as a metal bar swept out, forcing the male runner to leap clumsily over it to avoid shattered ankles. She watched with her hand over her mouth as the two were forced to dodge hazards that were becoming increasingly deadly the closer they got to the finish line. Bars were replaced with blades, jets of fire shot out and spiked pendulums swung across the walkways. Her horror grew as both contestants suffered lacerations and burns, until finally a two-metre hammer caught the man's side and sent him cartwheeling out of the framework and into the screaming crowd. The female runner, unaware of his fate, managed to make it the final metres to the finish line where she collapsed, gasping for air.

Boris let out a roar of approval and punched the air with a fist full of gilt chips.

'I told you!' Timofey exclaimed. 'Bet you're not bored now!'

He stepped closer, as if to put an arm around her waist, but she shoved him away hard, then pushed her way through the crowd, aiming for the far side of the run. By the time she got there the white-coated medic was helping the losing runner to his feet. Orry quickly went to the man's other side and helped support his considerable weight.

'Are you sure it's safe to move him?' she asked the medic. 'He took a hell of a hit.'

The woman scowled at her and indicated the baying crowd all around them. 'You want me to treat him here, genius? Help me get him back to the holding area.'

Together they half-dragged the injured man through the crowd to the edge of the clearing and on into the trees. It was a relief to get away from the press of bodies and the unbearably loud music.

They passed another woman in running gear who was being led back down the increasingly steep slope of the inner caldera wall towards the crowd, but Orry had no breath to say anything. Her thighs were burning and she was panting heavily by the time they reached an area where basic cots had been set up among the trees. Several of the beds were occupied by runners with a variety of injuries, while yet more contestants sat with their backs against the trees; some were staring gloomily at the ground while others were visibly trembling. Orry guessed it was fear making them shake rather than exhilaration.

They laid the man down on an empty cot and she stepped

back with relief to allow the medic to examine him. While she poked and prodded him, the runner looked up at Orry.

'Thanks,' he said.

'No problem. Are you okay?'

He winced as the medic touched his side. 'Rama, Doc, take it easy, will ya?'

'Stop whining, Sal,' the woman said. 'You have a couple of cracked ribs is all. You'll live.'

She opened a medical pack, selected a biomesh dressing and applied it to his injured side. The patient gritted his teeth as she did so, but didn't make a sound.

'I'm Orry,' she said when the dressing was in place and the woman was poking through her bag once more.

'Salvatore Santoro. Everyone calls me Sal.'

Orry looked round the clearing at the other injured competitors. From down the slope came the roar of the crowd. 'Can I ask you something, Sal?' she said.

'Sure.'

'Why are you all risking your lives on that . . . that *thing*?'

'For the money,' he answered slowly, as if she was an idiot. 'Why else would we do it?'

'But you could be killed! Do you need money that badly? On *Halcyon*?'

'Yes, on Halcyon,' he agreed, and gave a humourless laugh.

'What does that mean?'

'You're a guest here, right? Come to sample the pleasures of the galaxy's most exclusive leisure world?'

'A reluctant guest,' she admitted.

He frowned at that, as if 'reluctance' was a concept he'd never come across before, then said, 'I have a wife and two kids. Sonny is six and Maria is four. They mean everything to me, but they're in Silvertide – that's clear on the other side of the planet – and I haven't seen them in over a year. What I make serving you lot barely keeps a roof over their heads, and trust me, it's a pretty shitty roof, not like your luxurious top-of-the-range all-mod-cons lodge.'

'Hold still,' the medic interrupted. 'This will help with the pain.' She gave him the shot and some of the tension left his face.

'Thanks, Doc.'

She patted him gently on the shoulder and gathered up her bag. Other runners needed her attention.

'Can't you find a job nearer your family?' Orry asked. 'There are resorts everywhere on Halcyon, aren't there?'

'There are a lot,' he agreed, 'but most are fully staffed – you have to go where the work is.' Wincing, he adjusted his position on the cot. 'I'm pretty lucky, actually. At least the customer-facing jobs are all above ground.'

'What do you mean?'

'I mean, how do you think Halcyon is kept so pristine for people like you? What about all the support infrastructure? The power, manufacturing, maintenance? It's all done under-ground so you precious guests don't have to see it. Conditions down there are pretty bad, and the pay is even worse.'

'But . . . but this is ridiculous – everyone knows Halcyon is *awash* in gilt.'

'So I hear,' he said drily.

'If it's so bad, why don't you leave?'

'We can barely pay for food – how the hell do you think we can afford tickets offworld? Besides, Halcyon is my home: I was born here and I'll be damned if I'm driven out by the goddamn Ruuz!' His anger made him stiffen and he groaned in pain before slumping back on the cot. 'When Halcyon was first settled a hundred years ago it really was a paradise,' he told her, back in control of himself. 'My parents were among the first colonists, and they told me stories of what it was like here in the early years. But then some damn apparatchik in the Administrate decided it was too beautiful for *normal* colonists and redesignated us a leisure world. And as the Ruuz like to be waited on by *real* human beings, well, tada! We colonists became the staff. Job done.'

Orry said nothing, thinking about Erik the barman, and the other staff back at the resort. Earlier that very day she'd dismissed them as nothing more than robots. Guilt washed over her.

'Most of the food the guests eat is luxury shit produced offworld and shipped in,' Sal continued. 'The shipping cartels are in bed with the Great Houses who operate Halcyon, so of course the cost of food here is astronomical – and it's rising all the time. *That's* why we do the Red Run,' he finished bitterly. 'We need to make more money so we can eat.'

'This is outrageous,' she said. 'Isn't there *anything* you can do about it?'

Sal twisted his lips into a grim smile. 'We tried forming a union, even managed a couple of strikes a few years back, but the arbiters and Seventh Secretariat came down hard on us. They soon had agents riddling our ranks . . .' His voice tailed off.

'So how much do you get for doing a Red Run?' Orry asked after a moment's uncomfortable silence, feeling a familiar fury rising inside her.

'A fraction of what changes hands when those bastards bet on us,' Sal said angrily.

She was thinking now, channelling her anger into something more useful. 'And how dangerous *is* it?'

'There are a few deaths,' he admitted, 'mostly those who are absolutely desperate to win. They're logged as accidents, of course, but the big problem is the time we lose due to injury. I've been lucky tonight; I can still work with broken ribs. If you're out of action for more than a week, you're losing more than you got doing the run in the first place.'

'And the run itself, the machine – it's controlled by the woman in the red coat, is it? The configurator? She controls the settings?'

'Yes . . .'

'Using her integuary?'

He nodded, and grimaced at the pain.

'Hang on a minute, will you, Sal?'

He looked quizzically at her. 'I'm not going anywhere.'

She opened an integuary channel. *Ethan?*

It took him a moment to respond. *What's up?*

I need you to do something for me.

I'm kind of in the middle of something right now.

Well, you'll have to stop it. This is more important. I'm opening up my location to you. I need you to scan the surrounding area for integuary nodes.

Okay, wait a sec, he grumbled, and then, *what are you doing way out there, and . . . whoa! I'm seeing – like,* hundreds *of nodes. Where are you?*

Ignore personal nodes, she told him. *Can you see anything different – something like a machine would have?*

Um, hang on . . . yeah, I can see a load of flyers nearby and – got it. There's something different in the middle of the crowd. It's locked down tight.

That's the one. Can you get into it?

She could almost hear the smirk in his voice. *Sure, looks pretty vanilla. You want to tell me what this thing is and what you're about to do?*

In a minute. Get into it and ping me back.

Yes, sir!

Ignoring the sarcasm, Orry shut the connection and fumbled in a pocket for her gilt chip, which she handed to an increasingly mystified Sal.

'This has all my money on it,' she said, pressing the stud to show him the balance. She ignored the way his eyes widened and gave him his orders. 'I want you to talk to everyone you know and get them to transfer all their funds onto it as well – we're going to need as much as you can scrape together.'

He squinted suspiciously at her, holding the chip carefully between thumb and forefinger, almost as if he expected it to come alive and bite him. 'What is this?' he asked, 'some kind of con trick?' He frowned at the expression on her face. 'What's so funny?'

'Nothing,' she said. 'Look, I know you don't know anything about me, but please trust me – I hate these Ruuz bastards as much as you do. We could do this with just my money as a stake, but the more we have, the bigger you win.'

'You want to bet *all our money*? All *your* money? On what?'

A few people around, hearing his raised voice, were shuffling closer to listen.

Ethan's voice sounded in her head. *Sis? I'm in. What now? What are you up to?*

Good work, she sent back. *Hold on a sec, will you?*

'Okay, everybody,' she said aloud, 'gather around. I've had an idea . . .'

5

ELEVEN

Boris hadn't moved in the time Orry had been with Sal and the others. He didn't appear to notice the runners who had all followed her back to the clearing, those who could walk unaided supporting those who couldn't. They'd stopped when they reached the burning braziers at the edge of the trees.

'I thought you'd fucked off,' Boris shouted to be heard over the music. He graced her with a sour look, which she ignored.

'Just making some new friends,' she told him.

Timofey stepped towards her. 'Listen, Orry, I'm sorry about—'

'Shut up,' she snapped, and Boris laughed when he flinched as if she'd struck him. She held up the gilt chip, showing Boris the balance.

He whistled silently. 'That's a lot of gilt,' he said. 'What are you planning to do with it?'

'I plan to bet it.'

'On what?'

'On me – completing the Red Run.'

He ran his eyes over her. 'On what setting?' he sneered. 'One?'

'No, I thought I'd try it on eleven.'

Timofey laughed nervously, then paled as he took in the expression on her face. 'You can't be serious—'

'I thought I told you to shut up,' she said, not taking her eyes off Boris.

Boris looked amused as he considered her words. Then, coming to a decision, he raised his arms and waved at the configurator dancing madly on her platform, almost in time with the music. When she eventually spotted him, he indicated that she should turn down the music. When she'd done that with a command from her integuary, he pointed at Orry.

'This one says she'll do the run on eleven!' he bellowed – and the crowd went insane.

'I want a hundred to one,' Orry told him, shouting over the clamour of the watching elite.

Boris started to object, then he thought better of it. 'Whatever. You'll be dead before you're halfway round so it doesn't matter what the odds are, does it? Either way, it's your funeral.'

'He's giving me a hundred to one!' she yelled up at the configurator, who gave a double thumbs up as Orry handed Boris the gilt chip. The crowd cheered and began placing bets as well.

Timofey plucked at her arm. 'Don't do this, *please* – I could never forgive myself if anything happens to you—'

'But it's fine for them to risk their lives?' she said, indicating the staff gathered at the edge of the clearing. 'You make me sick.'

'I'm sorry! I told you, I'm trying to change. Really – don't do this – help me to see things the way you do instead, to be a better person—'

'Rama, you're *unbelievable*. It's not difficult! How about this for starters: treat everyone the way you expect to be treated yourself. Don't take advantage of folks just because they can't stick up for themselves. I have a friend who sums up his whole philosophy in four words: *Don't take the piss.* Stick to that and you won't go far wrong.'

'Don't take the piss?'

She couldn't believe she was having to explain something so bloody simple. 'Deep down, everyone knows when the thing they're about to do will ultimately harm someone else. What matters is whether or not you go ahead and do it anyway.'

As she was speaking, one of Timofey's entourage caught her eye. It took a moment to realise where she'd seen the pretty teenager with pink hair before. 'New friend?' she asked, pointing at the girl Timofey had saved from the lake.

The look on his face told her everything she needed to know.

'*Honestly?*' she asked, remembering the drone she'd spotted as she was walking to the pier that morning 'You staged all that, just to impress me?' He looked away, unable to meet her eye. 'You really are pathetic.'

She turned on her heel and strode towards the start of the Red Run, asking Ethan as she went, *Are you ready, little brother?*

Yeah, I think I've got a pretty good handle on this thing. Hold up, something's happening.

She stopped at the starting line, where the framework was reconfiguring itself again. *Turning itself up to eleven, I guess,* she thought, watching as additional arches locked into place along its length. Above her, the configurator was yelling at the baying crowd.

Remember, Orry sent, *no one can suspect what's really going on.*
I know, Sis. Good luck.

'Are you ready?' the configurator roared. 'Are you *r-r-r-ready?*' And as she capered more furiously and the crowd howled, 'ARE YOU READY? Then . . . let's . . . *GO!*'

A deafening explosion sounded and sparks shot high into the air on both sides of the starting line – but rather than launching herself forward at a mad run, Orry set off at a gentle jog.

Low bar from your right, Ethan sent, in control of the machine, *followed by a couple of spear things stabbing in from the left. You'll need to jump, then roll. Ready . . . and . . . now!*

She jumped the bar, then dived forward, hearing rather than seeing the spears as she rolled under them. The crowd responded as she recovered smoothly to her feet and hopped down into the next section of the course.

It was easy at first, with Ethan giving her plenty of warning for each hazard before he activated it, but as she moved through the run Orry could sense from the crowd's reactions that they weren't satisfied.

You'll have to step things up, she told Ethan. *We're losing the crowd – if it doesn't start to look more dangerous, someone will twig what we're up to.*

Okay, he replied cheerfully, *but just remember: you asked for it.*

Suddenly, it was a real challenge to keep up with the threats Ethan was throwing at her. As she neared the halfway point, she was tempted to ask him to back off a little, but the increasingly frantic cheers from the crowd stopped her.

Hammer right, hammer left, high blade, flame jet from above, Ethan sent, but the first hammer was already swinging in.

She managed to dodge it, felt the next one graze her backside, ducked under the blade and barely managed to leap past the flame as it ignited, feeling its heat on her back and smelling the stink of singed hair.

Oops! You okay?

Yeah, she sent back, shaken. *It just caught my hair. A little more warning next time, maybe?*

Do you want this to look realistic, or not?

Of course, but—

Roll right! he yelled.

She threw herself to one side as a whirring set of teeth sliced through the space where she'd just been crouching.

You need to keep moving, Ethan advised. *Stay right for the next bit.*

She set off again, her boots clanging on the metal walkway, which was now so narrow it was proving a real challenge just to stay on it as she went from jumping a gap from which a long spike shot upwards on her left to rolling under a spinning blade that whipped out at waist height.

You're more than halfway now, Ethan informed her. *You're doing well.*

Thanks, she sent back drily, panting for breath.

With Ethan calling out the timings, she navigated a series of what looked like giant mediaeval maces swinging across her path, but there was an unpleasant surprise in the middle when the walkway itself began to move like a travellator, increasing her forward speed – without Ethan's shouted warning in her head, her run would have ended there and then. The crowd were baying for blood now – of course no one had managed to survive setting eleven. Feeling a fresh stab of anger at the unfairness of it all, Orry risked a glance up at the configurator, whose platform had been keeping level with her progress through the run as she kept up her running commentary to her bloodthirsty audience. But the woman had stopped dancing and was wearing a puzzled frown.

Keep moving, Ethan urged her, *not much further now.*

The hazards of the run were beginning to blur into one another as she pounded on, sidestepping the blistering heat of dual flame-jets at one moment, then dodging through a shifting maze of razor-sharp scythes the next. For the first time she could see the fluttering flags that marked the end and she caught her breath for an instant as she waited for Ethan to tell her what to do next.

Instead of instructions, she just heard, *Shit.*

Shit? What's 'shit?' Don't say 'shit' to me, Ethan—

Sorry, Sis – there's someone else in here with me, messing with the settings . . .

Looking up at the configurator, Orry felt a deep chill. *Does she know you're in there?*

No, I don't think so – she seems to be checking the defaults – oh! Oh Rama! She's tweaking the bits you still have to get past!

What do you mean, tweaking? For the first time Orry felt panicked.

She's making it even more difficult. Rama, this is going to be impossible! You know what? I don't think she wants you to win.

Can you get me to the end without tipping her off that you're helping me?

I'll try.

You could sound a bit more confident.

Go . . . roll – now!

Orry felt something brush past her back as she dived forward into a front roll.

Left! Ethan yelled in her head.

She just dodged a crushing deadweight.

The crowd cheered.

Duck!

She dropped to her belly and – nothing happened.

Shit—

Stop saying that!

A vibration somewhere beneath her made her scramble

forward a second before a circular blade cut up through a slot that had opened in the walkway.

She activated that manually, Ethan sent. *I'm not going to be able to interfere without her realising I'm in here.*

Anything you can do to stop her? Orry asked, advancing cautiously, alert for the next threat. She could see the finish line just twenty metres away.

I'll see if I can spoof a glitch in her connection – kick her out, but make it look natural. Look out—!

Orry saw the blow-darts just in time and pressed herself flat to let them whizz past. *I can't stay still. You need to do it fast,* she told Ethan, and edged forward – just as a stabbing blade shot out from her right, catching her side as she twisted desperately away, drawing a line of fire. The crowd were baying for more and when she touched her side her palm came away red with blood.

She moved on cautiously, metre by metre, desperately wanting to run, but knowing that would likely be her death. A low whine warned her of an incipient flame jet – but where would it come from? Acting purely on instinct, she dropped, almost sobbing with relief as the flames roared over her head, scorching her back. Every movement made her side sting now, and she was moving more slowly. A glint of metal gave her an instant to dodge the next blade, which missed her by a hair's-breadth – and there was the exit, tantalisingly close . . .

But not close enough. There were still five arches, thick with weaponry.

The crowd jeered as she hesitated. *There's no way in hell I can get through that lot in one piece*, she told Ethan.

She twisted around at the sound of grinding metal: the walkway was rolling up behind her, obviously with the intention of forcing her onwards.

Ethan? she asked desperately, but there was no response. Rather than wait for the inevitable, she eyed the obstacles between her and the finish line. It wasn't the stuff she could see that worried her, but the unknown and hidden threats that would be shooting out of nowhere.

Not bored now, are you? she thought. *Idiot.*

She approached the first arch carefully, trying to stay light on her feet despite the increasing pain and weariness. A razor-wire swept downwards across the walkway, almost taking her nose off, and she took a quick step forward before it could whip back up again. A whine presaged a gout of flame; she leaped over it and tripped, mercifully avoiding a blade sweeping across at neck height. She dared not stop: there would be no safety now until the finish line.

She gasped as a metre-long section of walkway beneath her feet dropped away, grabbing for the side of the frame and shuddering as she saw the floor she'd been standing on vanish into a tank of some noxious green bubbling liquid.

The crowd were back on her side now, cheering as she jumped awkwardly over the gap, but when she landed, a sharp pain shot through her ankle.

The last few metres to the finish line looked suspiciously

clear of hazards – so who knew what she'd be facing. She limped forward, ready to move instantly.

So close, she thought. *if I could ju—*

Duck! Ethan yelled and she let herself drop, only to once again feel heat blistering her back, closer than it had ever been.

Roll right!

She rolled and a red laser beam sliced past, millimetres from her arm.

Wait . . . Ethan told her as another beam swept across the walkway in front of her. *Now – go, go, go—!*

She scrambled to her feet and raced toward the finish, teeth gritted against the pain in her ankle and her side.

Roll! Ethan screamed and she threw herself forward, feeling rather than seeing a scimitar passing over her.

She came out of the roll into a run – but there was nothing beneath her feet but thin air. She pitched forward, grunting as something hard slammed into her ribs – and ended up face-down amidst the needles of the forest floor.

The noise of the crowd was so loud it drowned out the music.

You're still alive! Ethan observed happily.

Better late than never, I suppose, she sent back, then, groaning in pain, she hauled herself to her feet. *Good job, Ethan.*

People were surrounding her now, yelling and clapping her painfully on the back. For a moment she thought they were going to hoist her onto their shoulders, but then the wall of revellers in front of her parted and Boris pushed his way through, Timofey trailing behind with a relieved look on his face.

'You cheated,' Boris said angrily, and the crowd quietened.

Orry limped over to him. 'Oh, really? And how exactly do you think I did that?' She winced and adjusted her arm so that the bleeding wound on her side was clearly visible.

Boris glanced up at the configurator but the woman just shrugged. Orry hid her relief. 'I don't know what you did,' Boris admitted, 'but I'm not fucking paying.'

Rumbles of discontent came from the crowd, but he just folded his thick arms and stared at her as she considered her options. Some of the audience were on her side at least; should she appeal to them? Or there was Timofey, who was looking mortified by Boris' refusal to pay up.

A commotion behind her made her turn and she saw Sal pushing his way towards them, leading the rest of the runners. He wore a grim expression as they formed a circle around Boris, whose look of puzzlement quickly changed to scorn.

'Oh, I'm *trembling*,' he said. 'What are you going to do, serve my vodka at room temperature?'

Sal stepped up to him. He was a little shorter than Boris but stockier and well-muscled, and Orry was pleased to see a flicker of doubt enter the lordling's eyes.

'You made a wager,' Sal said, loud enough for everyone to hear. 'We all heard it.' There were nods from some of the crowd and a general murmur of assent. 'This girl's just completed the Red Run on eleven, so you, *sir*' – he jabbed a blunt finger into Boris' chest – 'are going to pay her what you owe.'

Boris glanced at Timofey, then at the crowd. He put his face close to Sal's and said, 'Or what?'

Sal sank his fist into Boris' belly.

Gasping in pain, he staggered backwards – only to be caught by two of the runners standing behind him, who shoved him back towards Sal. The crowd fell silent, watching with evident discomfort, some starting to drift away to their flyers. The party was breaking up.

Boris remained doubled over for a moment, fumbling in his coat. When he straightened, he held a stubby pistol in his hand.

'Yeah, that's right,' he snarled, turning in a circle that made the runners surrounding him step back.

Orry heard a stifled scream from somewhere in the crowd, and people began leaving more quickly.

'Hey, man,' the configurator said from her platform, 'not cool, dude. *Not* cool.'

'Shut the fuck up!' Boris shouted, then, pointing the gun at Sal, 'I'm sorry . . . you were saying something?'

Orry stepped to Sal's side. 'This is ridiculous. Put that down before someone gets hurt.' Her stomach flipped as Boris turned the gun on her, his face twisting into a threatening leer.

'My father is a personal friend of Arbiter-Colonel Zaytsev,' he sneered. 'I could shoot you down right here and I wouldn't even have to give a statement.'

Timofey appeared at his friend's shoulder. 'This is stupid, Boris. Put it down and give her the damn money. It's not like we can't afford it.'

'That's not the point, *Timo*. She cheated.'

'She didn't!'

Boris snorted. 'You just want what's between her legs but you're too gutless to take it.'

Timofey's face reddened and he grabbed for the gun.

'Stop it!' Orry yelled, but neither man was listening as they struggled over the weapon.

The pistol was tucked in between their bodies and she gasped as a muffled shot sounded. Timofey stumbled back, clutched his side. He staggered for a moment, then his legs gave out and he collapsed into a sitting position, a look of confusion on his face.

Boris looked as shocked as his friend, staring at the smoking gun as if he'd never seen it before. Orry stepped forward and snatched it from his hand, tossing it back to Sal.

'I didn't . . .' Boris began, staring at Timofey.

The medic hurried up and crouched beside the wounded man, ignoring Timofey's cries of pain as she examined him. She turned to Orry and said, 'The bullet went through the fleshy part of his thigh. I need to stop the bleeding, but he'll be fine.'

'Orry,' Timofey said, 'I'm s—'

'Don't bother,' she snapped, then held out a hand to Boris. 'Money, now.'

He glanced at Sal, who was holding the gun. 'This isn't over,' Boris promised, giving her a look of loathing as he handed over a fistful of gilt chips.

'Thank you,' she said. Keeping only her initial stake, she gave the rest to Sal.

'All the winnings?' he said. 'You don't want any of it?'

'You need it more than me. Use it to help your families. I just wish I could do more.'

Flyers had been steadily rising from the forest and sweeping away for the last few minutes. The crowd was all but gone.

Sal pocketed the chips. 'Thank you,' he said awkwardly. 'If there's ever anything we can do for you, just ask.'

She squeezed his arm, then turned to look up at the configurator, who was watching silently from her platform.

'If I were you,' Orry called up to her, 'I'd get down from there pretty smartish.'

The woman in the red coat looked worried. 'Why? What are you going to do?'

'Don't say I didn't warn you.' She switched to integuary. *Ethan?*

Right here.

Do it, she told him.

With pleasure.

The configurator's head snapped round at the first sound of tortured metal. She watched in stark disbelief as the Red Run destroyed itself, cutting, slicing, battering and burning its own components. Metal shrieked, gears ground and the fresh smell of the woods was soon replaced with the stench of burning oil.

With a yelp, the configurator leaped from the platform,

landing in a heap at Orry's feet. When she looked up Orry could see tears in her eyes. 'What have you done?' she asked, as a whole length of the run collapsed in on itself in a burst of flame.

'You *did* cheat!' Boris yelled. 'Bastards! I was just going to have your jobs, but now . . .' He struggled to think of a fitting punishment. 'Now I'll have you all sent to Furina!'

'Oh, do shut up,' Orry told him, although in truth she was beginning to worry about the trouble Boris could cause for Sal and the others. They might not end up on the penal planet, but he could certainly make things a lot worse for them on Halcyon.

'Don't worry about us,' Sal said quietly, as if reading her thoughts. 'We've been letting those Ruuz bastards shit all over us for long enough. We're going to stick together from now on, no matter what it costs us.' A couple of runners who were near enough to overhear his remarks nodded grimly in agreement. Above them, the last of the departing flyers went whining away over the trees. 'It's probably time we left,' he said. 'Do you want a lift back to the resort?'

Boris, swearing vociferously, was striding away, followed more slowly by Lev, who had an arm around Timofey to support his weight. The dressing around his thigh was already staining red. He looked forlornly back over his shoulder at her as they approached the trees.

'Yeah, that would be great,' she told Sal. 'I think I may have lost my ride.'

6

A WALK IN THE WOODS

Orry didn't much care for the way Laguna Alta's lodges were deliberately isolated from each other by swathes of carefully cultivated woodland. She was following one of the many paths that snaked through the light woodland, illuminated by the soft glow of globes suspended from the branches above. The silence of the forest was broken only by the soft rustle of the treetops as they swayed in the breeze. It was the cultivation that was the problem, she decided – it was too perfect. Give her the tangled, insect-ridden jungles of Erlitz Shen any day.

She had waved away Sal's apologies that he couldn't drop her any closer, but after a five-minute walk from the beach she was starting to feel her injuries, even through the meds the doctor had given her after patching her up. She stopped for a moment to breathe in the scent of the needles underfoot and the earthiness of the rich soil, trying to decide which hurt worst, the shallow cut in her side or her twisted ankle.

A movement at the edge of her vision made her turn her

head and stare back along the path. Frowning, she accessed her integuary and shifted her vision into the infrared, zooming in on the area, but there was nothing, no heat source lurking in the treeline, no fading red splotches of footprints leading off the path. Returning her vision to normal, she let out a long breath. 'Getting jumpy,' she murmured, and gazed into the trees a moment longer before walking on, a little faster than before.

Had she seen something? Had Boris followed her, or sent someone to teach her a lesson? She wouldn't put it past him, but that didn't explain the lack of a heat signature. It wasn't likely that he had a mil-spec camo-suit lying around for just this sort of occasion—

She whirled without warning, knowing it was stupid but doing it anyway – and saw someone: a figure, dark against the trees bordering the path, unable to slip out of sight in time. They both froze.

'Shit,' she breathed, and broke into a clumsy run that set her ankle throbbing at every step. Risking a glance behind, she saw the figure was running too – and gaining on her. Whoever it was would be on her long before she reached anywhere populated. The meandering path took a turn up ahead and, sucking down the oxygen-rich air, she redoubled her pace, the pain from her ankle forgotten now. She followed the bend, taking a second to cast another swift look over her shoulder. Seeing her pursuer was momentarily out of sight, she swerved left, charging into the trees and continuing until the darkness closed around her before ducking down behind a wide trunk, trying to stifle her frantic breathing.

She opened a channel to the ship. *I may have a problem here,* Jane.

What's happened? replied *Dainty Jane* immediately. *Are you all right?*

Not sure. Can you get hold of Quondam? I could use him.

Of course. I'll—

The voice in Orry's head cut off.

Jane? Can you hear me? She swore and pressed against the rough bark, straining to hear any sound from the path. For a long time there was nothing but the branches moving far above her head, but after what seemed an age she made out the faint crunch of pine needles nearby. She shrank back, hardly breathing as the dark figure moved almost silently past her, her heart missing a beat when she spotted a slender pistol in a gloved hand.

She waited for as long as she dared, torn between her terror that they would turn and see her and an overwhelming urge to run. Eventually she crept around the tree and started to limp quietly back towards the path. Only when the dim light globes were visible up ahead did she chance a glance back into the darkness. She could still just see the figure in black, a shadow against the light bark of a tree. *Don't turn around,* she prayed, and took another step towards the path.

A twig cracked under her boot and the stalker whirled, pistol coming up.

Shit!

She ran, bursting onto the path – and right into the grasping arms of a second black-clad figure. Orry dropped instinctively, sliding under one arm and scrambling to her feet behind them. The way ahead was clear and she put her head down and focused on running as best she could. *If I can just get back to the beach – or anywhere there are people.*

She heard the thudding of boots close behind her and a weight crashed into her back, toppling her over. The wound in her side flared with pain and her face slammed into the path, but she immediately tried to rise, panicking, until a kick to her abdomen forced her back down. After a gasping moment, she rolled onto her back, spitting out bark chippings. The newcomer standing over her was dressed entirely in a black, mil-spec combat suit, a pistol pointed at Orry's chest. Reaching up, the figure pulled the black hood from her head to reveal a young woman with short, sandy hair, clammy with sweat.

'Nice dodge,' she said, then gestured with the pistol. 'Get up.'

'P-please,' Orry begged, playing for time as her mind raced. She forced tears into her eyes. 'Don't hurt me. I-I don't have any gilt on me.'

Who are these two? Certainly nothing to do with Boris, not dressed the way they were. She lifted herself onto her elbows to peer past the sandy-haired woman. Her partner was just emerging from the trees where Orry had broken out, twenty metres back. The woman standing over her had caught up to her in seconds; she had to be a gene-tweaked chimera.

The woman smiled, as if amused by Orry's play-acting. 'Get up,' she repeated.

'Wh-who are you? What are you going to do to me?'

'Very convincing,' she said, 'but I don't like repeating myself.' She pointed the pistol at Orry's face. 'Get . . . the fuck . . . up.'

'Problem?' Her partner, a man, Orry could now see, ambled up behind her.

'No problem.'

The sandy-haired woman fired her pistol. The movement was so unexpected that Orry had no time to react as the bullet smacked into the dirt an inch from her head. Terrified, she scrambled awkwardly to her feet.

'Now move,' the man told her, gesturing back the way they'd come.

'Listen, guys,' she said, dropping the terrified tourist act as she looked around for any means of escape, 'I don't know who you are, but you've got the wrong girl. My name is Amber Sphene. I'm here on holiday with my husband.'

'Let's just kill her,' the woman suggested. 'We can kick this bark shit around to hide the blood.'

'Do *you* want to carry a dead body back to the ship, 'cause I sure as hell don't.'

The woman grunted.

Orry activated her integuary. *Ethan?* Jane? *Mender! I could really do with some help here!*

'Don't bother calling for help,' the woman said. 'We're not amateurs.'

Her partner stepped out of Orry's path and motioned with his pistol for her to precede him. Out of options, she began limping back the way they'd come, holding her side.

'Where are we going?' she asked.

They didn't answer.

They'd been walking in silence for some time when Orry heard movement in the trees to her right.

'Stop,' the man said, clearly hearing it too. As his partner covered Orry, he edged closer to the treeline, peering into the gloom with his pistol held out in front of him. 'Fuck!' he snapped suddenly, and fired three times before stumbling fearfully backwards.

A massive shape burst from the trees and fell on him, one huge claw closing around his weapon, and Orry felt a rush of relief. Quondam yanked the man effortlessly from his feet and hurled him into a tree, which he struck with a sickening crunch before dropping limply to the ground.

Just as the sandy-haired woman fired at the Kadiran, Orry hurled herself forward, cannoning into the woman's side. The gun fell from her hand and they both scrabbled for it, but before either could reach it Quondam grabbed the woman by the ankle, hoisted her up with one slab-like hand, wrapped the other around her head – and twisted.

'No—!' Orry shouted, but it was too late.

Quondam looked curiously at her and released the woman, who crumpled to the ground, clearly dead.

Orry hurried to the man, but a quick check confirmed he was dead too. She was still shocked by how casually the Kadiran killed, but it was difficult to summon much remorse for her erstwhile captors when the only reason she was still alive was because they couldn't be bothered to carry her corpse back to their ship.

'I don't mean to sound ungrateful, Quon,' she said, 'but couldn't you have just disarmed them?'

'I was concerned for your welfare, Orry Kent. Was I wrong?'

She sighed. 'No, you weren't wrong. Thank you for saving me – but if you'd left them alive we might have found out who sent them, and why.'

He hung his head a little. 'This statement reflects the true state.'

She quickly searched the dead man's pouches and found a small device with a blue glowing light. She pressed a depression on its black surface and the light went out.

Jane? she sent.

I can hear you, Orry. Did Quondam find you? Are you all right?

I'm fine. Prep for take-off – we need to leave. Hang on. She switched to the common channel. *Ethan? Mender?*

What's up, Sis?

Where are you?

Why? What's—?

Where are you? she repeated sharply.

I'm at a little bistro near the pier. They have an amaz—

Are there other people there?

63

A few. Ethan's voice turned serious in her head. *Orry, what's going on?*

'Come on,' she told Quondam, and without further explanation, she started limping in the direction of the pier.

Someone just tried to kidnap me and they weren't fucking about. Stay in plain sight until we get to you.

Are you okay? Who were they?

I'm fine, Quon's with me. Stay where you are – we'll be there in a few minutes.

Okay, don't worry about me – I can look after myself.

She wasn't sure about that.

Mender? she sent. *Are you there?*

He's still not answering, Ethan told her.

Try to get hold of him, Jane, *will you?*

I will, Orry. Please be careful.

She closed the channel and told Quondam, '*Jane*'s on alert and Ethan's at the pier,' then concentrated on ignoring the pain as she limped as fast as she could manage towards her brother.

7

MENDER'S COVE

She spotted Ethan immediately, sitting at a table outside a bistro, his head bowed as he accessed his integuary.

Ethan! she sent, ignoring the guests recoiling from Quondam as he lumbered past. *Get your head out of your arse!*

He looked up, eyes clearing as she hurried over to him. 'You need to see this,' he told her before she could say anything.

'There isn't time. We need to get somewhere safe. Come on.'

He didn't move. 'I ran a broad-spectrum search to see if there was any reason someone was out to get you. You *really* need to see this.' His eyes glazed briefly and a link appeared in her vision.

She hesitated, focused on getting them all back to the safety of *Dainty Jane*, but something in her brother's voice made her pause. Quondam was standing beside her, surveying the terrified-looking guests with a baleful gaze, and she decided she could spare a moment. She opened the link.

It was security footage, overlaid with the digital watermark of the Halstaad-Mirnov Institute. Two figures were standing by large metal tanks covered in warning symbols lining one wall of what was clearly a laboratory. Orry recognised the man facing her immediately: Professor Rasmussen, Emeritus Professor of Exo-Culture at the institute. She'd heard the Kadiran Hierocracy had returned him as part of a prisoner exchange, but she hadn't seen him since. He looked older than she remembered, but that wasn't all that surprising for someone in their early hundreds. Orry felt a chill crawl up her spine as she looked at the second person, who had their back to the camera. The familiar red flight suit and sunburst orange hair were identical to her own.

The professor was speaking, but the feed had no embedded audio. He backed away as the woman dressed as her stepped closer to the lab bench that separated them. He looked scared now, and with good reason, it appeared, for the woman on the screen had produced a long pistol and was pointing it at him. He threw up his hands, clearly pleading – and Orry gasped aloud as the pistol jerked once and the professor clutched his chest and dropped from sight behind the bench.

She watched in horrified fascination as the fake her walked calmly to the metal tanks, set down the bag she was carrying and pulled out a slim, black oblong which she placed against the tank's curving side. It remained there when she removed her hands, and she swiftly repeated the process with the other three tanks before stepping back to survey her work.

The image switched suddenly to an external view of the

glass frontage of the institute at night. The woman-who-wasn't-Orry walked out of the building, stepping over the motionless body of a security guard as she left, glancing briefly up at the camera as she passed. Orry's breath caught in her throat: her own face was looking back at her.

A moment later the camera shook as the glass blew out-wards. Flames were belching from the building's shattered skeleton.

The image cut out.

'That wasn't me,' she said, numbness turning to anger.

Ethan rolled his eyes. '*I* know that, but the arbiters think different. I lifted that from a public repository before it was taken down. The Arbiter Corps has put out an arrest order for you.'

'Based on *that*? There's a dozen ways someone could have faked that footage: digital enhancement, a face-changer, um . . .'

'I know, and I'll figure out how they did it, but the institute was destroyed and it's all over the newsfeeds. At least the media haven't mentioned you by name yet.'

Orry's mind was whirling with a hundred questions, but this wasn't the time to stand around discussing it. 'Come on,' she said, glancing nervously about. 'We can figure it out later. This way.'

Ethan grabbed her sleeve. 'No – over here.'

He led her and Quondam past bars and restaurants, causing diners to stare open-mouthed at the Kadiran. One young woman screamed and stumbled back from her table, chair clattering to the ground. Next to her, a stout Ruuz with a fine set of white whiskers hurriedly drained his whisky and beckoned for another.

'I guess they don't get many other races visiting Halcyon,' Ethan muttered, offended for Quondam's sake, even though the Kadiran had barely noticed the scared interest he was attracting.

'Where are we going?' she asked. 'We have to get back to *Jane*, pick up Mender and get off this rock.'

'Trust me,' her brother replied as they arrived at one of the paved areas used as flyer pads.

One of the sleek vehicles was coming in now. It touched down gently in front of them, a gull-wing door swung open and Ethan motioned for her to climb in.

'I called a cab,' he said happily as he followed her into the sumptuously appointed flyer.

Without a word, Quondam squeezed his bulk in after him.

Ethan chuckled at Orry's face. 'Don't worry, I subverted it – it'll take us anywhere and no one will be able to track us.'

'Good thinking,' she said, impressed at his forethought. Whether she liked it or not, her little brother was growing up. 'In that case, it makes sense to pick up Mender before we head back to *Jane*. A flyer's a lot less conspicuous than a starship.'

'You got it. Any idea where the old bugger is, exactly?'

She tried the common channel again. *Mender? We have a situation here. Now would be a really good time for you to respond.*

It's no good, interrupted *Jane, I've been trying him since you called. He must be asleep.*

Passed out, more likely, Orry sent back angrily. *Do you have a fix on him?*

Of course. Transmitting coordinates now.

Mender's location popped up in her peripheral vision, but before she could say anything, Ethan had acted, sending the flyer lifting silently into the air.

Moonlight glistened from the mirror surface of the lake as they sped at close to the speed of sound towards a small cove on the far shore. Ethan was in an integuary-fugue; Orry wondered if he was already analysing the security footage. A wave of sadness swept over her as she thought about Professor Rasmussen's death. He'd been a difficult man at times, but she'd liked him. She tightened her jaw. *Why would someone want him dead – and why frame me for the murder? And why blow up the institute?* It had to be connected to the attempt to kidnap her, but she couldn't figure out why.

'Your safety will not be certain until you are aboard the ship and off this world,' Quondam said, as if reading her thoughts.

'I know,' she told him, watching the black water whip beneath them. 'But before we can go, we have to find Mender.'

'The rational course would be to depart immediately.'

'Not without Mender.'

'Captain Mender is not responding to your transmissions. If–'

69

She turned to him. 'I understand what you're saying, Quon, I do, and he's an idiot for not keeping in touch, but we're not leaving without him. It'll be fine, trust me.'

'Fine . . . ' he repeated doubtfully.

The flyer slowed as it approached the cove, little more than a strip of golden sand bordered by high cliffs, with a simple wooden hut squatting above the line of seaweed marking the high-tide line. As they got closer, they could all see a pair of skinny, pale legs poking out from beneath a large, colourful parasol near the water. A servitor bot was parked beside it. Orry nudged Ethan to get his attention as they swept down in a graceful curve to settle on the beach, just far enough from the parasol that their down-thrust didn't send it flying. If it had been Orry's choice, she'd have landed right next to the damn thing.

As soon as the doors opened, she jumped out and hurried over to the parasol. The legs belonged to Mender, who was comatose – which was probably something to do with the almost-empty bottle of some brown liquid lying on the sand next to him. His normal stubble had grown into a patchy white beard and his hair looked like it hadn't been brushed for a month.

The squat servitor bot suddenly shook itself into action, rolling forward on one large tyre. 'May I fetch you a drink, miz? Or a bite to eat?'

Ignoring it, she started shaking the old man. 'Mender?' she said, then, louder, '*Mender!*' She rounded on the bot. 'Just how much of this . . . *rotgut* has he had?' she demanded.

'I am not at liberty to discuss our guests' consumption. Would you like a cocktail?'

She slapped Mender's cheek, lightly at first, then much harder. He groaned, but still didn't waken, even when she lifted the lid of his one real eye. She gritted her teeth. 'We do *not* have time for this crap . . .'

She looked around, then shouted to Quondam, who was still in the flyer, 'Quon! Can you get him on board? *Jane* will be able to sober him up far more quickly than we can.'

The little bot came wheeling after her as she followed Quon and his insensate burden back to their taxi. 'Can I interest you in a snack from the bar?' it asked almost plaintively. 'Or a nice cup of tea?'

'Sorry, not now.' She climbed into the flyer and the servitor quickly reversed to get clear of the closing door. Sand blew around the little bot as they lifted into the air. It leaned back on its single wheel to watch them bank away towards the caldera's rim.

8

NOT A HAPPY BUNNY

Laguna Alta's airfield was located on the outside of the crater wall, several hundred metres down the mountainside and linked to the resort by a tunnel. The flyer took them up and over the rim, then shot out from the side of the mountain, across which a rainforest stretched, terminating in a distant body of water.

Orry's stomach flipped as the flyer plummeted downwards, turning back towards the craggy mountainside as it fell. 'Take it easy!' she snapped at Ethan.

'We're in a hurry, aren't we?' he fired back.

The airfield coming into view below them was a level area projecting out from the cliff-face and supported by a complex network of struts beneath it. Traffic was light at this time of night, just a couple of flyers picking up guests who'd ventured to other parts of Halcyon for the day. On the area reserved for larger craft there were several luxury yachts and a small commercial transport lined up alongside the large, shell-like shape of *Dainty Jane*.

Are you ready to go? she asked *Jane* as the flyer touched down nearby.

I'm ready, the ship confirmed.

While Ethan wiped their journey from the flyer's memory, Orry clambered out and hurried across the apron to *Dainty Jane*. The ship's twin nacelles were aimed downwards, the air beneath them shimmering in the heat from her rumbling drives. Quondam thudded after her into the cargo bay with Mender in his arms, Ethan hot on his heels.

'Get him sobered up, if you can,' she told Ethan, before climbing nimbly up through the galley to the cockpit. Once in her acceleration shell, she hooked the ship's engineering and avionics cores and confirmed that *Jane* was in launch configuration before opening a comm channel to the airfield's control tower, a glass construction protruding from the mountainside overhead. 'Laguna Alta Tower, merchant *Dainty Jane*.' She drummed her fingers as she waited for a reply. After an unusually long delay, even for a local field like this one, she got a response.

'Uh, go ahead, *Dainty Jane*.'

She re-checked the version of the data package the tower had sent over when the ship had requested engine start. 'Tower, *Dainty Jane* with information Gamma requests lift from hardstanding niner for trans-orbit and collapse out of system.'

'Wait one, *Dainty Jane*.'

Another delay? She looked out over the field, but there was still hardly any traffic. 'I don't like this,' she muttered.

'Orry,' *Jane* announced, 'I am picking up encrypted

communications between the tower and an incoming vehicle – correction: several vehicles.'

'What sort of vehicles?'

'Unknown. They are not broadcasting idents.'

'Go to active scan.'

'I've tried that, but I don't have line of sight from here. They are staying nap-of-the-earth, just above the treetops.'

Orry thought of the two men back at the resort. 'Could they be military vehicles?'

'Possibly – or law enforcement.'

She wasn't sure which would be worse. 'Tower, *Dainty Jane*. What's the hold-up? Can we lift or not?'

'Uh, just one more minute, *Dainty Jane*.' The controller's voice lacked the usual reassuring calmness of a controller. 'We're just experiencing some, uh . . . problems with the comm-link to Orbital Traffic. Should come back online any time. You are instructed to hold until then.'

'Screw this,' she told *Jane*, 'they're stalling. Clear the area – I'm taking us up.'

'If you're sure that's wise—'

'It's necessary.'

'Very well, Orry.'

The ship's warning klaxons blared and a moment later *Jane* reported, 'There is nobody near us. You're safe to lift.'

'Safe to lift,' she repeated, and fed power to the nacelles. The old ship shuddered as the mass-inversion drives thundered, but she rose steadily into the air.

'*Dainty Jane!*' The controller sounded panicked. 'You do not – I say again – you do *not* have clearance to lift. Return to the hardstanding immediately. Acknowledge.'

'Wilco Tower,' Orry responded with a smile, 'returning to the hardstanding.' The ship gathered speed.

A new voice broke into the channel. '*Dainty Jane*, this is Arbiter-Major Mayer. You are ordered to land immediately and await our arrival at your location.'

'Well, that answers one question,' Orry said to *Jane*. 'What are those incoming vehicles doing now?'

'They are climbing to intercept, but at their current velocity they will not be able to catch us before we reach the stratopause.'

'Can they follow us any higher?'

'It's doubtful. The data indicates they are small atmospheric craft. Even if they could follow us, it's unlikely they would be equipped with weapons heavy enough to damage me.'

'Nice. We're due some good news.'

They were well clear of the caldera now, the resort's scattered lodges falling rapidly away below them. Stars twinkled in the night sky, beckoning Orry on.

'*Dainty Jane*, return to the field immediately, by order of the Imper—!'

She muted the channel. 'What's the Arbiter Corps presence on Halcyon like?' she asked. 'Do they have anything in orbit that could intercept us?'

'I have no record of any Arbiter Corps vessels in-system. Their presence on Halcyon is entirely planet-side.'

'What about the Grand Fleet?'

'There is a training establishment on Vanat, a dwarf planet in this system's Kuiper belt. Last recorded complement was a small number of orbit defence craft.'

Orry relaxed a little. 'Looks like we've got away with it, then.'

'I hope you're right.'

The caldera was a tiny disk below them now, a black button dropped on a green carpet. She could see that the body of water she'd identified from the flyer was an ocean, the white whorl of a storm system halfway to the next continent. As the last vestiges of atmosphere thinned to nothing, she pointed the ship away from Halcyon. The faster they got clear of the planet's gravity well, the sooner they could leave this system. *And go where?* she wondered.

'*Jane*, plot a collapse to somewhere remote, will you? We need some time to figure out what's going on.'

'I've already programmed the navicom to take us to Vadik's Reach. We should be safe there for a while.'

'Perfect. Leaving Halcyon's atmosphere n—'

'Orry!' *Jane*'s voice was urgent. 'I'm picking up—'

The comm burst into life. 'Mercantile vessel *Dainty Jane*, this is Ascendancy destroyer *Ne Tron Menia*. Maintain your current attitude and thrust and prepare to be boarded.'

'Where the hell did they come from?' she said, hooking the sensor core and locating the destroyer: it was only fifteen thousand miles out and closing fast. She hauled *Jane* onto a course directly away from the approaching warship.

'Their reciprocal course suggests they came from the training establishment I mentioned,' *Jane* informed her.

'Just our luck,' she muttered, then switched to the common integuary channel. *Ethan? What's happening with Mender?*

'He feels like shit, is what,' Mender answered from the back of the cockpit, and a moment later he dropped into the commander's shell beside her. 'What the hell is wrong with you, girl? I take a five-minute nap on a goddamn beach and wake up being chased down by a friggin' *destroyer*?'

'He's not a happy bunny,' Ethan added, sliding into one of the rear shells.

Orry ignored him and sounded the acceleration alarm. 'Quondam,' she said over the intercom, 'brace for high-g.' She knew Kadiran physiology was capable of resisting high and sustained g-loads, but a warning never hurt.

'*Dainty Jane, Ne Tron Menia.* Cease all manoeuvres immediately. This is your final warning.'

'The destroyer will be in weapons range in thirty seconds,' *Jane* told them.

'You want control?' Orry asked Mender.

He rubbed his forehead with one hand and waved the other at her. 'No, you keep her.' He grimaced. 'I need this like a hole in the head.'

'Twenty seconds,' *Jane* said.

Orry hooked the drive core. 'Hold onto your hats,' she said with a grin, and poured on the power.

As their acceleration quickly passed 2g, she felt her shell

recline and its gel lining stiffen around her. Moments later, at 5g, the lid of her shell slammed shut and the grip of the meso-phase gel disappeared as it flashed into liquid form, which she drew calmly into her lungs.

Destroyers were heavy vessels, designed to favour firepower over speed. *Dainty Jane* was at 12g now and pulling away from the slower warship.

With her acceleration shell shut and mouth full of fluid, communications were shunted to integuary.

Dainty Jane, the destroyer sent, *do not—*

Mender muted the channel in their heads. *You want to tell me what the hell is going on?* he demanded.

That's what I'd like to know, she sent back, eyeing the remaining distance to the egress point, where Halcyon's grav-itational sphere of influence was low enough not to interfere with *Dainty Jane*'s postselection drive.

Emergency collapse checks, he sent, and she called up the checklist. They ran through it together.

We're clear of the gravity well, reported *Jane* as they finished.

Hit it, Mender ordered.

Floating cushioned within her shell, she hardly felt the brutal acceleration forces vanish as she shut down the mass-inversion engines.

Collapsing now, she sent, and activated the drive.

Halcyon's diminishing orb, and the speck of the pursuing destroyer, vanished.

9

THE FUN BIT

'It has to be connected,' Mender growled after Orry had finished bringing him up to speed. 'If someone wants to frame you for killing that old fart and blowing up his building, they'd want you out of the picture, not sunning yourself on Halcyon. I'm just surprised they didn't do it sooner.'

She'd been thinking about that. 'They must have known I was there,' she said. 'I guess they didn't want to stir things up until we had other things to worry about, like getting away from the arbiters.' Her stomach, still tender after her usual post-collapse nausea, clenched as the scent of whatever Quondam was consuming from a foil bag drifted over.

'Hmm.' Mender rubbed at his patchy beard.

They'd arrived at Vadik's Reach and were now drifting well below the system's invariable plane, far from any shipping lanes. The only colony was on the other side of the star, a weak white dwarf.

'Who would want to kill this professor and destroy his

place of study?' the Kadiran enquired, gobbets of meat and fat escaping the cartilaginous cage around his delicate mouthparts.

'If they did it to frame the girl here, that's quite a list,' Mender answered grimly. 'She ain't shy of making enemies.'

'But why go to such lengths?' Orry wondered. 'If they knew where I was, why not just kill me? Why kill the professor and blow up the institute? It doesn't make sense.'

'Smacks of Roag, if you ask me,' Mender said.

'She's locked up on Tyr,' she reminded him, although he was right, it did stink of Cordelia Roag – but as ruthless and resourceful as the gangster was, she would be monitored so closely that she simply couldn't be behind this.

'Her crew then?'

'It's possible, I suppose. It just seems too high profile for them to attempt on their own.'

'Then who? That bastard Delf?'

'He's locked up, too. There's no point just listing all the people we've—'

'*You've.*'

'—pissed off. So let's forget about framing me for the moment and ask: who benefits from Rasmussen's death? Or the destruction of the institute?'

Mender thought about that. 'You've got me there, girl.'

Ethan's eyes cleared, he exhaled slowly and spoke for the first time in an hour. 'The footage of you is genuine,' he said thoughtfully, staring at the scratched table.

'It's *not* bloody genuine!' Orry snapped.

He looked at her, clearly startled by her tone, until comprehension dawned and he gave a lopsided smile. 'Relax, Sis, I'm not saying you *did* it.' He looked at her questioningly. 'You *didn't* do it, did you?'

She threw a water bulb at him, but without gravity it just sailed gently through the air. He caught the bulb with one hand and took a sip before setting it down on the table's magnetic surface.

'Like I said, the *footage* is genuine. I've run it through *Jane*'s spectral interpolator three times. I'm certain it hasn't been altered or enhanced in any way. Those images have *not* been tampered with.'

'Are you absolutely sure?'

'Ask *Jane* if you don't believe me.'

'I agree with Ethan,' the ship confirmed. 'Wavelength enhancement and subatomic compression analysis indicates beyond any doubt that—'

'Whatever,' Mender interrupted. 'So, if the pictures weren't faked, *you* must have been. The you in the film, I mean.'

'Nope, I checked that too,' Ethan said. 'Face-change tech – even the bleeding edge stuff the Seventh Secretariat uses – only makes superficial cosmetic alterations. It's designed to fool the human eye, integuary recognition routines and semi-intelligent security systems. And there are other limitations – height, for one thing. You need to be close to the height of the person you're impersonating or you're looking at extensive bone and tissue modification, which *hurts*.'

'Get to the point, kid,' Mender interrupted.

'We modelled the person in the footage,' Ethan continued, 'and she was *exactly* the same height as you, Orry, down to the millimetre. The rest of her body dimensions were a precise match as well, as well as hair and eye colour, dentistry, scar locations . . .'

'So you're saying it was too accurate to be done by a face-changer,' Orry said.

'*Way* too accurate.'

'Then how did they do it?'

'Honestly? I have no idea.' He leaned back in his seat and adjusted his lap strap to a more comfortable position.

'*Jane?*' she asked.

'I require more data in order to formulate an informed response.'

'She doesn't know either,' Mender interpreted. 'Well, we know one thing at least: going to the arbiters ain't an option. As far as they're concerned, that's you in the footage, and good luck convincing them otherwise. Not sure we can even blame them for that.'

'My alibi's next to useless,' she agreed miserably. Even if Sal and the others did confirm that she'd been competing on the Red Run when the institute was being blown up, she could imagine the loathsome Boris and his chums gleefully denying it, and she knew who the arbiters would believe.

They lapsed into silence.

'So what do we do?' Ethan asked after a while.

'We must locate the responsible parties and exact vengeance,' Quondam said, poking a claw around his foil packet for any remaining morsels. Finding none, he looked mournfully at it for a moment before releasing it to float in front of him.

'That's your answer to everything,' Ethan pointed out.

'He's not wrong, though,' Mender said.

'We're going in circles,' Orry said, rubbing her forehead. 'How are we supposed to find them if we don't know who they are?'

'Find out who they are,' Quondam suggested, using his long tongue to clean the cage over his mouth. He always reminded her of a cat when he groomed himself like that.

'But how?' she asked.

He gave the Kadiran equivalent of a shrug, tilting his vast head to one side. 'Seventh Secretariat might have such information.'

'Ask Lucia Rodin?' Mender objected. 'You might as well just hand yourself in to the arbiters.'

'No, wait,' Ethan said, 'Quon has a point – think about it. Seven and the Arbiter Corps hate each other – everyone knows that.' He patted the Kadiran's arm affectionately, then quickly withdrew his hand as the alien's head turned slowly to gaze down at him.

'Even if Rodin doesn't lock you up, how do you expect to get anywhere near her?' Mender asked.

For the first time since being attacked in the woods on Halcyon, Orry felt the weight lift a little from her shoulders.

Knowing *what* to do was always the difficult part for her. How to do it – well, that was the fun bit. She unstrapped her lap belt and floated up from her seat.

'I need *Jane* to take a proper look at my side and this bloody ankle,' she told Mender. 'I'll figure something out while she fixes me up. You plot a collapse into Tyr – and try to avoid running into any other ships on the way.'

The old man groaned. 'I was happy on that bloody beach,' he muttered.

10

NAKHIMOV PROSPEKT

Lucia Rodin relished her lunch break. She knew many of the Administrate's senior bureaucrats sneered at her for not staying at her desk as they did – but they could fuck right off. It wasn't about eating her lunch in peace, or carving out a few minutes of personal time from the frantic day, or even about sitting in the garden – although that was always a pleasure. No, it was more about clearing her head, giving her subconscious time to process the fire-hose torrent of data that was aimed at her every moment of every day.

'A report on the latest Kadiran expedition has just arrived by despatch pod,' Nika said, appearing beside her.

Lucia sighed. She'd tried to make it clear to her assistant that she should only be disturbed with urgent matters during her lunch break, but to Nika, everything was urgent. 'And?' she asked.

Nika scanned the databrane in her hand and her face tightened. 'It's moved again,' she said.

Lucia kept her face rigid as a weight settled in her stomach. 'And Cyrene?'

Nika's eyes rose from the brane to meet hers. 'Same as Spero. "Scoured" is how the Kadiran describe it.'

'Does the Imperator know?'

'I doubt it. This wasn't a diplomatic pod.'

The back channel then, Lucia reflected. A few months ago she would have given her right arm for a source in the Kadiran High Command. Now they were sending her messages every day. What further proof did she need that they were scared? She gave a humourless laugh. *They'd be idiots if they weren't.*

'I'll tell him,' she said. 'Set up an appointment for this afternoon.' She didn't have to ask the Imperator's whereabouts. Piotr's health had been going downhill since the attempt on his life at Holbein's Folly and he was confined to the palace. 'Now, can I please eat my lunch in peace?'

'There she is,' Mender said, staring through the targeting monocular with his real eye. 'Right on time today.' He passed it to Orry and she aimed it at the distant shape of the Trefoil Towers.

Integuary-enhanced vision was pretty good, allowing objects up to several hundred metres away to be brought into sharp focus, like an old-fashioned telephoto lens, but Mender's artificial eye was even better, letting him see for a kilometre or more when the conditions were right. The mil-spec monocular improved on this by several orders of magnitude. Designed for targeting ships in orbit, the device could see for hundreds of kilometres. The three stratoscraper towers that made up the Trefoil weren't quite that far away – the monocular was clocking the distance at a shade under ten kliks – and the garden jutting out from the side of one of the white towers looked like it was right next door. The slender skybridges arching between the towers glittered in the winter sunlight.

Orry watched Lucia Rodin take her usual seat in the garden and unpack her bowl of pasta and an apple, exactly the same meal as the past three days. The garden was laid out formally, neatly trimmed lawns separated by gravel paths and brightly coloured flowerbeds. Light glinted on a transparent shield that curved up and inwards from the balcony's rim, a windbreak which also protected those in the garden from ballistic, explosive or energy attack.

There were a few other people around, all of them dressed like Administrate apparatchiks, but none of them came anywhere near Lucia. Perhaps there was an understanding that the head of Seventh Secretariat wasn't to be bothered while she was enjoying her lunch, or perhaps it was the muscular, bald man who looked about to burst out of his suit standing a metre behind her, hands clasped in front of him as he constantly surveyed his surroundings.

'Pay up,' she told Mender, extending a hand without taking her eye off Lucia.

'You got lucky,' he grumbled.

She felt a coin being placed in her palm.

She didn't bother arguing, because it was quite simple, really: Lucia loved gardens – she'd told Orry as much when they were aboard *Hardhaven Voyager*, the whaling platform floating in the aether clouds of Morhelion. The Whaling League boss Francesco Guzman shared Lucia's passion – he'd built himself a slice of paradise in a dome on top of the platform's superstructure. Lucia had been impressed by his handiwork, horticulturally, at least.

Know your mark, Orry's father had always said. *Even the smallest fragment of information can give you an in.* Lucia liked gardens. Lucia's office was in the Trefoil. There were gardens sticking out from the Trefoil's towers. It wasn't drive-science – as far as Orry was concerned, it'd just been a case of watching until she appeared in one of them. And now she had, for three days in a row.

'Okay, that's good enough,' she said, pocketing the imperial Mender had given her and replacing the monocular in its case. 'It's Fabretti time.'

That transformed his customary scowl into a broad grin.

The white city of Utz, capital of the Ascendancy, sprawled over the hundreds of islands of the Helion archipelago in Tyr's northern hemisphere. This particular island was predominantly residential, grand townhouses on wide boulevards giving way to suburbs nearer the coastline. It had been a night's work for Ethan to scan the passenger manifests of departing flights and cross-reference the addresses and return flights until they found a suitable residence that would be vacant for a couple of weeks.

'Put it down,' Orry told Mender, who was examining an antique firearm he'd picked up from a shelf. 'For the last time, we're not thieves.'

The owners of the three-storey townhouse with cellar on Nakhimov Prospekt were clearly wealthy. The décor was tasteful, all thick carpets and expensive furniture. Orry found the place oppressive.

Mender replaced the pistol and turned to her. 'I don't get you, girl. You say you're not a thief but you're happy to steal when you need to. You don't like guns but I've seen you use 'em enough times. You hate the Ruuz but you're one of them.' She bristled and he held up a placatory hand. 'Now don't get bent all out of shape, I'm just saying: these folks ain't short of a bit of gilt. They're probably Ruuz, or near as dammit makes no odds, so who gives a shit if we lift a few of their trinkets?'

'I'm not going through this with you again, Mender. There's a difference between being a grifter and a thief, and *we're* grifters.' She felt a sudden moment's sadness hearing her father's words coming out of her mouth.

'So that's what I am now, is it?' he growled back, ''cause I did a lot of things before I met you, but grifting weren't one of 'em.'

She opened her mouth to retort, then realised there was something in his tone that indicated this went beyond his default level of griping. Mender had been alone on *Dainty Jane* before she'd met him, and despite his habitual complaining she'd always assumed he was happier with her and Ethan – and more recently, Quondam – on board. He was still the captain, after all, though it was Orry who ran the cons. Until now, she hadn't thought he had a problem with that. She was still wondering how to respond when Ethan's voice came on the common integuary channel.

They're here, just pulling up outside.

Good, she replied. *Are you ready?*

Naturally. I'm up a very comfortable tree.

What sort of vehicle is it? Will you be able to subvert it okay?

Don't sweat it, Sis. This is what I do.

Okay. Just don't set off any alarms. And don't fall out of the tree!

As if!

She turned to Mender. 'Wait until they're inside,' she started, then stopped. He knew what he was doing. *I need to stop micro-managing*, she told herself. 'Sorry,' she said with a grin, but he just scowled.

There was a knock at the door and she waited a few seconds before opening it to two men holding toolboxes, both wearing light grey coveralls bearing the HalseyTech logo.

'Miz Jade?' the older of the two said, checking a rigid data-brane in his hand. 'We're here to service your Mark 26.'

'Hi,' she said cheerily, 'come in. It's out back.'

The two men filed into the living room as she closed the door behind them. They stopped and waited for her to lead the way.

Orry reached into her pocket and flicked on the integuary jammer she'd taken from her attacker on Halcyon, then nodded at Mender.

He didn't move.

She gave him a hard look, then cleared her throat.

His bushy eyebrows rose in an expression of mock surprise. 'Oh! You want me to do it *now*?' he asked.

'Don't be a dick,' she told him.

'How am I being a dick? You're in charge.'

She took a breath. 'Yes,' she said tightly, 'please. I want you to do it now.'

The two technicians looked mystified. 'Uh, is everything okay?' the older man asked.

'Everything's fine,' she said. 'My uncle is just making a point.'

'If this is a bad time, we could arrange another appointment,' the younger said, looking uncomfortable.

'No, no, we're good,' she said, folding her arms and glaring at Mender.

He waited another second, then picked up his Fabretti 500 from behind a floral cushion and pointed the enormous handgun at the tech who'd spoken. Both men paled; she recognised the glazed eyes as they tried to use their integuaries to call for help. When the older man discovered he couldn't, he looked even more scared.

'W-what do you want?' he stammered. 'We d-don't carry gilt.'

She stepped closer, examining the plastic identity tag attached to his breast pocket. With a swift movement, she jerked it free. 'Don't worry,' she reassured the men, 'we just want your IDs, your uniforms and a little bit of your blood.'

'Our b-blood?'

'Don't worry about it,' Mender growled at him, 'it's just a little prick.' He motioned with the Fabretti towards the rear of the house, where the door to the cellar was located.

'Who are you people? What are you going to do us?'

Orry felt sorry for them. She hadn't wanted to use a gun, but Mender had pointed out there was no time for Ethan to get what they needed by forging employment records. Every day they spent in Usk increased the chances of being recognised.

'We're just going to lock you in the cellar for a little while. It's not as bad as it sounds,' she added quickly, 'there are beds down there and plenty to eat and drink. There's even an ents system.'

'Think of it as a paid holiday,' Mender added. 'Now move it.'

11

SOUTH TOWER

'Okay, I have full access,' Ethan said. 'What do you want me to do with this thing?' He had made a nest for himself in the rear compartment of the HalseyTech service vehicle, which was crammed with equipment and parts. Orry, in the driver's seat, watched him through the open door separating front from back. Establishing a link to one of the hortibots in Lucia Rodin's favoured garden platform, up on the Trefoil's fiftieth floor, had been simplicity itself using the operator codes from the van.

His eyes cleared and he looked over at her. 'I don't think we should just shut it down. We need to make sure someone notices it's gone wrong. I'll make it do something weird, like it's acting up.' Seeing Orry's face, he added reassuringly, 'Nothing too dramatic, I promise – just enough to get some-one's attention.'

His eyes glazed again.

The prosthetic was making her face itch. Resisting the

urge to scratch, she turned her attention to the box on the dashboard in front of her. Graphics cycled on its screens as it scanned the surrounding airwaves, searching for signals that matched the parameters Ethan had programmed into it.

Behind her, he chuckled as he controlled the distant bot. 'This is fun. You should see their faces. Hello, a security guard's just arrived. Yes, hello mate – *oops*.'

'Don't overdo it.'

'It's fine. I think he's reporting it now.'

'All right, that's enough, then. Shut it down before they do.'

'Give me a second . . . Okay, there you go: one broken bot.'

'Good job.' She eyed the scanner, wondering how long she would have to wait. Maybe whoever dealt with stuff like this was busy. Maybe a request would be raised and assigned to a queue, although the Administrate were famously – or notoriously – efficient, at least when dealing with Ruuz matters. And this was an executive-level garden, so—

The scanner cheeped as the pattern on one of its screens changed. Orry watched the lock symbol flicker, then turn solid. SIGNAL INTERCEPT CONFIRMED appeared on the monitor. A moment later the box began to ring.

Taking a breath, she lifted the handset.

'HalseyTech priority support. How may I help you?'

It was late morning, the streets of the capital were busy with ground traffic, so the drive to the base of the Trefoil took longer than expected. The Trefoil, a biobuilding, had been grown from thousands of synthetic seeds with architect-designed DNA. They'd done a good job, Orry thought; the slender towers linked by graceful bridges were achingly beautiful.

She pulled the service vehicle up to the security booth at the rear of the south tower so they could show their HalseyTech passes to the duty guard. After checking they were expected, the guard directed them to a parking lot beneath the tower, where they found a man waiting for them.

'You're here for the hortibot on Balcony 16?' he asked before she'd even got out.

She checked her screen. 'Yup, that's what it says on the work order,' she confirmed as she opened the van's rear door.

'I'm Ebrahim, building services,' the dark-skinned man continued, stroking his waxed moustache. 'I'll take you up there. Do you think this will take long?'

Ebrahim obviously had better things to do.

'It'll take as long as it takes, mate,' Ethan said, coming round from the other side of the vehicle. 'Those Mark 19s can be tricky buggers.' He grabbed a toolbox from the back and she slid the door shut.

Ebrahim grunted. 'Follow me,' he said, and led them to a service elevator that took them up to a huge entrance hall. 'You'll need visitor passes,' he told them. 'Over here.'

They joined a short queue filing through a security post.

'They're with me,' Ebrahim explained as he showed his own pass and was waved through the slender archway of a body scanner. Orry followed, trying to look calm when Ethan placed the heavy toolbox on the conveyor next to the arch and walked through after her.

The case rolled into the scanner tunnel. When a red light started to flash, the posture of the two guards manning the post immediately changed from professional courtesy to potential threat. Orry eyed their sidearms nervously as one of them checked the luggage scanner, then proceeded to extract Ethan's toolbox.

'Sir, please open the case,' the woman ordered.

'No problem.' Ethan didn't appear even slightly nervous, and Orry watched approvingly as he opened the case and extended the trays of equipment within for the guard to examine. After moving a few items around, the woman held up the node kit he usually kept concealed in the heel of one of his boots.

'You want to explain to me why you're bringing illegal tech into the building?' she enquired evenly.

'It's just a tool,' Ethan replied. 'I need it to do my job.'

'Robotics companies are exempt from the legislation under the Krupov Act,' Orry explained. 'Look it up if you like – we'll wait.'

'She's right,' Ebrahim interrupted, 'they are exempt, and they do need it. Look, guys, can we hurry this up, please?'

The guard looked at her colleague, who nodded. She gestured to Ethan that he could put everything back, then closed the aluminium case.

'Wear these at all times within the building,' the other guard said, handing them a badge each. 'You're cleared for the communal areas only. Trying to access anywhere else will trigger an alert, so I don't advise it.'

'Got it,' Orry said.

Ebrahim led them through a door into the base of the south tower, a vast concourse that extended up three full storeys. Mature trees were growing up through gaps in the tiled floor and an enormous statue of the Imperator sat in the centre of a series of fountains, gazing down with a frown at bustling bureaucrats suited in the latest fashions.

'The lifts are over here,' Ebrahim said, leading them across the echoing floor to a thick column of lift shafts rising through the glass roof.

They rose in silence, their host otherwise engrossed in a databrane he'd pulled from his pocket. Orry caught Ethan's eye and he gave her the smallest of smiles. The floors flashed past rapidly until the lift slid to a smooth halt and the doors opened onto a busy atrium. The sunlight streaming through glass walls reflected off the highly polished white floor. Administrate staff sat around low tables or queued for tea at a kiosk on the other side of the atrium.

Ebrahim led them to the glass wall, where a set of doors opened onto Garden Balcony 16. It was warmer outside behind the transparent wind break, but looking up, Orry could see that the shield didn't extend all the way to the side of the tower, for a gap had been left for natural air to circulate. The garden itself was beautifully kept, with wide paths bordered by brightly coloured flowers and small lawns shaded by slender trees. There were only a few people there, talking as they walked between the beds; they didn't appear to be paying much attention to the natural beauty around them. The view over the city was spectacular too, but Ebrahim didn't give them any chance to take it in.

'It's this one,' he said, stopping at a motionless bot surrounded by several shallow trenches in the lawn. It was the size of a large dog, its smooth carapace painted green with the HalseyTech logo in white on its flanks. Three multi-purpose arms grew from its back and various attachments – a fork and shovel, shears – lined its sides. 'I didn't see it, but apparently it started digging random holes, then did some kind of dance and froze.'

'A *dance*?' She glanced at her brother, who was looking very pleased with himself.

'Sounds serious,' he said. 'This might take a while.' He handed her a screwdriver and she lay on the grass beside the bot and started to remove the service panel in its belly.

Ebrahim glanced back towards the atrium. 'Okay, look I have a meeting I really need to attend. I'll be back in an hour – if you finish before then, just get reception to ping me, okay? You won't be able to get out on your own. You can grab a drink from the atrium if you like, but you don't have access to anywhere else in the tower. All right?'

'Sure,' Ethan said absently, watching Orry as she removed

the panel. 'Check the feedback array,' he suggested to her. 'I've seen them come loose before in 19s.'

Ebrahim looked at him properly for the first time. 'Aren't you a little young to be a service engineer?' he asked.

Ethan laughed. 'What can I say? I have good skin. Makes getting a drink a right ball-ache, but the ladies love it.' He gave a theatrical wink and Ebrahim shrugged.

'Just get it fixed,' he said, and walked away.

Orry continued to pretend to poke around inside the bot until Ethan crouched beside her and murmured, 'He's gone.'

She sat up and looked around. Apart from a couple of suits on the far side of the garden, they were alone.

'Get going,' she told him, checking the time: just before midday. 'And be careful.'

He grinned, clearly enjoying himself. 'Chill out, Sis. This'll be easy.'

12

THE ELEVATOR GAME

The atrium was still busy when Ethan left the garden. He loitered by the tea kiosk until one of the lifts opened and its occupants stepped out. Three other workers immediately entered, and he waited until the doors were closing before hurrying forward and blocking them with his foot.

'Sorry, folks,' he said cheerfully as the doors re-opened, 'but you're going to have to find another lift. I have to take this one offline for a few.' He held up a multitool as if to illustrate his point and smiled sympathetically at the passengers as they filed, grumbling, back into the atrium.

The last of the three, an older man in dark blue frock-coat, squeezed past him in the doorway, which gave Ethan the opportunity to deftly lift the man's pass. Once alone, he pressed the pass to the navigation screen and selected a floor five levels above, breathing a sigh of relief as it started to rise. Working quickly, he removed a panel by the door and scanned the wiring inside. Pleased that it was a familiar model, he snipped two wires to disable the alarm before pressing the emergency stop button. The lift came to an abrupt halt, making him stagger. Locating the appropriate cable, he set to, quickly stripping away a length of insulation so he could connect his node extender to it. The molecular hooks on the ends of the device's terminals created a bond and a moment later his integuary reported an interface was available with the building's service node. He interlinked his fingers and cracked them as if he was about to embark on a piano concerto.

'Okay, building, let's play.'

Orry checked the time again, then risked another glance at the atrium doors. There was still no sign of Lucia Rodin. *It's fine*, she told herself, remembering that in the three days she and Mender had staked out the balcony garden, Lucia's arrival time had always varied a little. *But not by this much*, part of her brain pointed out helpfully. She shifted into a more comfortable position on the grass and continued to poke around inside the bot's belly. *What if she's not in the office today? What if she's decided to skip lunch?* The owners of the house on Nakhimov Prospekt were due back that night, when they would discover two bot techs in their cellar, so if Lucia didn't turn up today that would be their chance gone. Orry couldn't think of another way to get to her – it would take another week or two at least to work something out and with the Arbiter Corps after her, that was time she didn't have.

Stop it, she told herself sternly.

She heard the doors to the atrium open and Lucia Rodin

walked onto the balcony, followed by her bodyguard and a slim woman in a sharp suit. Orry's anxiety leaked away as she watched Lucia seat herself on her customary bench and start to eat.

She's here, she told Ethan.

Roger, he sent back. *I have control of the lifts and the atrium lenses.*

Good job.

Thank you.

She smiled, wondering how many people could have subverted the building's substrate so swiftly. *Not many*, she concluded, appreciative of her brother's talents. For a moment she considered just approaching Lucia now, but even if the slab of a bodyguard would let her anywhere near, there were too many people around. The garden was clearly a popular lunchtime spot and she couldn't risk Lucia being seen with her, facial prosthetics or not. Careful to keep her back to them, she replaced her tools in the case and closed it. She wouldn't be needing them again, but she didn't want anyone seeing them lying around and wondering where their owner had gone. With a final glance at Lucia, she returned to the atrium, wheeling the heavy case after her.

She stepped into the first of the six lifts that was going up.

Ready, she told Ethan. *In three, two, one . . .*

She pressed her pass to the screen for the benefit of the elevator's other two occupants and saw it flash green under Ethan's control. She was the only person to get out on the eighty-second floor, which they'd discovered was under refurbishment. The distant sound of drilling came from some-where but she couldn't see any workers in this floor's atrium, which was smaller than the one on the garden level.

In position, she reported.

The security lenses in the Trefoil's communal areas were on a separate and less secure circuit to those in the more sensitive parts of the building, which made sense to Ethan; after all, you didn't want a mere security guard looking at state secrets, did you? It made his job a lot easier, although now he was here he was sorely tempted to have a crack at the building's more secure systems – who knew what he might unearth? With a sigh, he resisted the urge and focused on the job at hand.

In the garden, Lucia Rodin had finished her lunch. He liked the head of Seventh Secretariat and it was nice to see her again, even if it was through a lens. He just hoped she'd be able to help them. He watched her return to the atrium, shadowed by her bodyguard even in the heart of the Trefoil. He looked like a capable man, moving gracefully despite his size as he directed Lucia and her PA to one of the lifts and pressed the call button.

Number 3, he sent to Orry as he took control of the lift's primitive electronic brain. Overriding the summons, he sent the empty elevator in shaft 3 to floor eighty-two. *Should be with you any second.*

It's coming . . . she sent back. *It's here. Okay, I'm in.*

I know, I'm watching you. Good luck.

Now he was feeling truly nervous. If they were wrong about Lucia, Orry would find herself in custody the moment she revealed herself.

Chewing on a fingernail, he instructed the lift to descend.

'The Workers' Union on Halcyon are causing trouble again,' Nika said as they waited for the lift.

Lucia smiled; at least her assistant had waited for her to finish her lunch today. 'They've been quiet since before the war,' she said. 'What's stirred them up again?'

'I don't know,' Nika admitted. 'It started with a strike in a resort called Laguna Alta, but it's spreading like wildfire now. The smaller carriers are refusing to land on Halcyon in case the Union seizes their ships, so the Administrate is working with the Fleet and EDC to bring people home.'

'We still have agents in the Union, don't we? What do they say?'

'No reports so far. There's some concern in the Administrate and the Assembly that the unrest could spread to other colonies. They seem very well organised this time.'

'We need to find out what's triggered them,' Lucia said. 'Find me some intel from our assets on Halcyon. Also, set up a meeting with Willi Goltenberg.' House Goltenberg held more business interests on Halcyon than any of the other great families. It would be worth getting the new duke's read on this. 'Frankly, I'm amazed they didn't try this during the war when we were occupied elsewhere.'

'Maybe they didn't want to hurt the war effort. They're not traitors, after all, they're just sick of being exploited.'

Lucia stared at her assistant. 'Why, Nika, I do believe we'll make a real person of you yet.' The lift doors opened and she stepped forward, still chuckling, only to stop when she saw a HalseyTech maintenance technician inside. 'Is there a problem?' she asked.

The tech stepped closer. 'Please,' she said urgently, 'you have to help me.'

Lucia stiffened. The young woman's voice was familiar, but ... She peered more closely at the tech's face.

'It's me,' the woman whispered, glancing nervously out of the lift. 'Orry.'

Of course it was. She could see it now, the face beneath the prosthetics. Beside her, Georgi moved closer, sensing a potential threat. Lucia raised a hand and he stopped, hovering at her elbow. She returned her attention to Aurelia Kent, shaking her head ruefully.

'I suppose it should surprise me to find a wanted terrorist in the heart of the Trefoil, but when the terrorist is you ...'

'I'm not a terrorist,' Orry said. 'Whoever was on that footage from the institute, it wasn't me.'

'That's not what the arbiters believe. Their analysis would convict you in a heartbeat.'

'I know – that's why I need your help.'

Considering everything else that was going on in the galaxy, when she'd seen the footage of Orry apparently killing a former friend who also happened to be a professor of exo-biology, then blowing up the foremost research centre in the same field, she had not been convinced. To have the young woman standing here in front of her was more than she could have wished for.

She turned to Georgi. 'You and Nika take another lift. Meet me upstairs.'

A look of concern crossed her protection officer's broad face, but he knew better than to argue. Nika's integuary-dulled eyes cleared and she looked confused as he pulled her to the next lift along.

'Let me in, then,' Lucia said, and smiled at the look on Orry's face as she stepped past her. The doors closed, giving them some privacy. 'If you didn't do it, then who did?' she asked as they started to ascend.

'That's what I want you to find out.'

'I'm afraid that's going to be more difficult than you might imagine. If what you say is true, we're dealing with a conspiracy with access to technology advanced enough to fool the arbiters' forensic AI.'

'Does Seven have that kind of tech?'

'If we did, I would hardly tell a fugitive now, would I? What I will say is that we're talking about the level of technology that is restricted to nation states rather than corporations.'

'There are no nation states any more, only the Ascendancy.'

'It's a figure of speech.'

'Do you think the Kadiran could be behind it?'

'I don't think anything right now, and I advise you to do

the same. It's never a good idea to begin an investigation with preconceptions.'

'Does that mean you're going to start an investigation?'

'It's not that simple. Arbiter-Colonel Zaytsev and I do not exactly see eye to eye. He's already used my past association with you to exclude Seven from the investigation into the attack on the institute. In fact, he's implying that you are a Seventh Secretariat operative, and I believe he's responsible for the rumours that you were acting on my orders. There's been nothing official, of course, just whispers, but whispers in the right ears can do a lot of damage. Frankly, it would solve an awful lot of problems if I just had you arrested.'

Orry stiffened. 'Why don't you, then?'

'Because I believe you. You would hardly risk lying your way into the Trefoil like this if you were guilty. What possible reason could you have for doing that?'

Orry looked relieved. 'That's what I was going to say.'

'But the problem remains: Zaytsev is shutting me out. I'll do what I can, but the best thing you can do is go somewhere very remote and keep your head down until I call for you.'

'For how long?'

'I don't know. Months probably, maybe longer.'

Orry's expression told Lucia what she thought about that. 'Thank you,' she said, though she sounded anything but thankful.

'Don't get tearful – I'm not doing it for you.'

'Why, then?'

'Quid pro quo. It means—'

'I know what it means. What do you want?'

'I don't know yet. Let's just say you owe me one. You and that ship of yours.'

'*Jane* isn't mine. She doesn't belong to anyone.'

'Whatever. I just think you and your crew could be very helpful to me, if things are going the way I rather suspect they are.'

Orry was silent for a moment. 'Is this something to do with the "greater threat" the Kadiran were talking about?'

Lucia regarded her thoughtfully. 'When we were on Morhelion, I got the impression that you expected to be included in the discussions with the Hierocracy and your nose was put out of joint when you weren't. Is that accurate?'

'Maybe.'

'I can understand your frustration, but these are diplomatic discussions at the highest level. I know you were the one the Kadiran approached, but you have to understand the Imperator's reluctance to include you in the talks.'

'I saved his life. Twice!'

'And you were rewarded. Such actions do not qualify you to be included in discussions to decide the very future of life in the galaxy.'

'Is it that bad?'

'It's not good – but we're digressing. I can't use you until the current matter is resolved satisfactorily. I would invite you to my office, but Zaytsev has eyes everywhere. I must congratulate you on your circumspect approach.'

'So that's it? You'll look into it, and meanwhile I have to sit on a rock in the middle of nowhere—'

'I never said it had to be a rock.' The lift began to slow. 'I assume you have a way out of the building?'

'Yes, don't worry about us.'

'Us—? No, never mind. I'll say goodbye then, for now. Give my regards to Ethan. I'm loving his work, as always.'

Orry smiled. 'Thank you.'

The lift came to a stop with a gentle jolt.

'Good luck,' Lucia said as the doors opened.

'*Arbiter Corps!* On your knees – now! Hands behind your heads!'

She took in the scene in an instant: a dozen arbiters in black tactical gear, weapons raised. Nika was kneeling off to one side, her face white with terror as an arbiter pointed a gun at her head. Next to her was Georgi the bodyguard, also kneeling, blood leaking from a gash on his bald head as two men covered him. He looked incandescent with rage.

'This is ridiculous,' she snapped in her most commanding voice. 'Put your weapons down – immediately.'

The very fact that they didn't brought home the seriousness of her situation.

One of the men stepped forward and gestured with his gun. 'On your knees! Now!'

Beside her, Orry's face was rigidly controlled as she and Lucia sank to their knees together.

'Shit,' said Lucia.

13

INNIS GAEL

Orry felt numb as the arbiters hauled her to her feet and yanked her arms behind her back. Restraints tightened around her wrists and she was quickly patted down. Not knowing what was happening to Ethan was the worst part; she'd lost all her integuary channels the moment the lift doors opened and she had no idea if he'd been arrested as well. She wondered about Mender and Quondam too: were arbiter fire-teams closing in even now on *Dainty Jane*? *How did they find out about this?* she thought miserably. *What did I do wrong?*

A hard shove between her shoulder blades set her moving away from the lift where Lucia Rodin was still on her knees. It was the expression on the older woman's face that shocked Orry the most; Lucia was perhaps the most capable person she had ever met, but now she looked utterly helpless. *My fault,* Orry thought grimly as she lost sight of her around a corner. *This is all my bloody fault.*

An escort of two arbiters marched her to a flyer pad jutting from the Trefoil's side. A box-like flyer painted white and midnight-blue idled there, vortices forming in the air beneath its four streamlined nacelles. She was pushed up a short ramp and into a small, windowless cubicle clearly used for prisoner transfers. One of the guards shoved her down into the hard plastic seat, which immediately extruded a number of straps to hold her in place, pinning her cuffed hands uncomfortably behind her back. The door closed and a few seconds later the flyer lifted.

The flight was a short one. Only when the whine of the engines had died away did the door to her cubicle open and the seat release her. The vehicle had landed in a large courtyard area surrounded on all sides by brutalist three-storey buildings, Tyr's colonial style. As she was led to one of the blocks, she realised this must be the Arbiter Corps headquarters complex on Innis Gael, one of Utz's outlying island districts. Her suspicions were confirmed when she entered the building to find it full of uniformed arbiters.

Her escort marched her silently through a door and along one drab, featureless corridor after another. At a bank of lifts, he selected the middle of three destinations on the screen. They descended for some time, until the doors opened and she was shoved out into an oddly shaped room, empty except for a metal table in its centre. Two of the room's uneven walls appeared to have been carved from rock; they were shored up in places by poured ferroconcrete; there were also patches of ancient colonial-style bricks, the same sort used in the buildings she'd glimpsed on arrival. The remaining walls were metal, discoloured by streaky brown water stains.

A stocky, dark-skinned arbiter-sergeant with short-cropped salt and pepper hair was standing behind the long table; a nametag on her chest read *Blessing*. A second guard by the lift door was holding one of the long batons favoured by the arbiters and known colloquially as night-night sticks.

'Remove the prisoner's restraints,' the sergeant ordered.

Orry rubbed her wrists gratefully, shrugging her shoulders to ease some of the knots.

'Strip,' Arbiter-Sergeant Blessing ordered. The one-word order made a leaden weight of despair settle in Orry's gut.

She removed her boots before unzipping her HalseyTech coverall and letting the baggy garment fall to reveal her underwear.

'That'll do,' the sergeant said, walking out from behind the table with a scanner wand in her hand, which she ran over Orry's body. Apparently satisfied, she dismissed the escort and handed Orry a pair of plastic sandals and a canary-yellow coverall made from thick paper. 'Dress,' she ordered.

Orry did as she was told, grateful to be covered up once more. 'Where am I?' she asked as she stepped into the sandals.

Blessing nodded at the guard with the baton, who stepped forward and smacked Orry hard in the thigh with it. Pain tore through her leg and she dropped to one knee, teeth gritted against the agony.

The sergeant watched with a faint smile as she struggled back to her feet. 'No talking,' she said.

Orry glared at her, humiliated and scared. The last time she'd been imprisoned on Tyr had been at the Saabitz Rock Holdover Zone, where the virtual walls were created by the prisoners' own integuaries. As progressive and civilised as the holdover zone sounded, she'd decided that being held prisoner by your own mind must be far worse than an old-school prison. She was already beginning to think otherwise.

Arbiter-Sergeant Blessing drew an axon disruptor from a loop on her belt. 'I'll take her down,' she told the guard, that same faint smile on her face. 'She won't give me any trouble,' she continued, 'will you?'

Orry just scowled. The feeling was starting to come back to her leg and she gingerly put her weight on it, relieved to find that it would support her again. Blessing crossed to a door and placed her thumb on a genetic scanner. The door slid open and she motioned with the disruptor for Orry to walk through. She limped out into a corridor that looked like it had been tunnelled through solid rock, her bruised leg throbbing painfully at every step. The corridor ended at a set of bars with an open booth next to it, manned by another guard. A window allowed him a view out over the cell block.

'We have a new guest looking for a room,' Blessing said cheerfully.

The man in the booth grinned and examined one of the displays in front of him. 'Well, look at that, we do have a vacancy. Put her in nineteen.'

'I was thinking number forty-two.'

The man looked up, his smile fading. His eyes shifted from Blessing to Orry and he frowned. 'Forty-two? You sure about that, Sarge?'

'Did I stutter?'

He hesitated. 'But—'

'I'll take responsibility, Glazkov. Nothing will come back on you.'

Orry might not understand what she was hearing, but she didn't like the guard's expression. Looking at the disruptor in Blessing's hand, she kept her mouth shut.

'Okay, boss,' Glazkov said, entering something onto one of the screens. 'Forty-two it is.'

He reached beneath his desk and the bars ahead of them swung open with a harsh buzz. Blessing nudged Orry into motion and followed her through into a cavernous space beneath the reinforced rock ceiling far above. Several sets of metal stairs linked three layers of balconies giving access to heavy cell doors inscribed with numbers. The central well was fitted out with tables, none of which were currently occupied.

'Up there,' the sergeant said, pointing up at a cell on the second level with a large number forty-two stencilled onto its metal surface.

'Open number forty-two!' she yelled as they climbed the stairs. Another buzz sounded as the door released. She pulled it open and smiled nastily. 'Have fun.'

Orry stepped hesitantly into the cell, jumping as the heavy door slammed shut behind her. The compact cell was equipped with a toilet and sink, a table, a single stool and a pair of bunk beds, everything made entirely from metal apart from the rear wall, which was rock, slimy in places with moisture. Someone was lying on the top bunk, facing the blank wall. All the walls were blank, Orry noted, no pictures, notes or letters – nothing to indicate contact with the outside world.

'Um, hi?' she ventured, standing awkwardly just inside the door.

The person on the bed rolled over and Orry took an involuntary step backwards, into the door, as her heart tried to crawl up her throat.

'You have *got* to be fucking kidding me,' said Cordelia Roag.

14

CELLMATES

Roag swung her legs off the side of the bunk and stretched, cat-like, before fixing her eyes on Orry. Her normally long hair had been cut short, accentuating her gaunt looks, and her body, though thin, had a wiry, dangerous strength to it.

'I never did believe in a Creator,' she said lazily, 'but it's times like this that make me think the astrotheometrists might be onto something.'

Orry's heart was racing, her body in full fight-or-flight mode, but there was nowhere to go and fighting Roag would be a quick and painful death sentence. She wanted to say something, but fear had made a mute of her.

'Thanks to you, I've been rotting in this cell for sixty-seven days now,' Roag continued. 'They let me out for meals three times a day, and exercise if I'm lucky. "Exercise" involves walking around the edge of another room just like this one, only a bit bigger. Oh, there is one other break from the mind-numbing tedium: if I'm *very* lucky the guards will drag me to an interrogation room and beat the shit out of me while that pig Zaytsev asks me questions.'

It occurred to Orry that as long as Roag was talking, she wasn't trying to kill her. 'They beat you?' she said, her voice betraying her fear.

'Not anywhere it will show,' Roag answered, 'which is a good thing. I guess it wouldn't do to have me show up to my trial looking like a slab of tenderised meat, so at least I know I'll *get* a trial. For a while I thought all I'd get would be a bullet to the brainstem.'

Orry's doubt must have shown on her face.

'You don't believe me?' Roag said with a humourless smile, before lifting her filthy T-shirt to display a mass of purple and green bruising around her ribs and stomach. 'Thanks so much for this,' she said.

'This isn't *my* fault,' Orry objected, a stab of anger penetrating her fear. 'You were the one who conspired with Delf to assassinate the Imperator – not to mention helping the Kadiran try to blow up this whole planet.'

'And *you* fucked things up for me both times,' Roag snarled. 'I thought you hated the Ascendancy? If it weren't for you, this whole festering mess would be gone by now.'

'To be replaced by what? Kadiran slave worlds? Or do you think the Ascendancy ruled by Delf would be an improvement? At least Piotr *tries* to be just—'

Roag snorted. '*Just?* Open your eyes: all Fat Piotr is interested in is helping his Ruuz cronies get richer while the poor saps out on the rim barely scratch a living. You know that, you've *seen* it. That's what makes it worse.' She spat on the floor. 'Once a Ruuz, always a fucking Ruuz.'

Orry's temper flared, but Roag narrowed her eyes and she bit her tongue.

'How is dear Grandfather, anyway?' her new cellmate continued. 'I haven't seen him around here. I suppose they have a special prison for the Ruuz. I'm surprised they put *you* in here with the rest of us proles.'

Orry hated being reminded that the Count of Delf was her grandfather. 'I don't know where he is,' she said. 'I've been away.'

Roag grunted. 'What about the Kadiran? Everyone getting along nice and friendly now, are they? You know any more about this "greater threat" they were banging on about?'

'No.'

'No? I thought you and Rodin were best buds now?'

'Apparently not.'

'Oh dear, have I touched a nerve?'

She jumped down from the bunk and Orry would have backed away, but the metal door was already pressing cold against her back.

Roag smiled. 'I'm going to enjoy this.'

She crossed the cell in a single stride and threw a punch that Orry only just managed to block.

'Wait—' she tried, before Roag's knee sank into her stomach, driving the wind out of her. She tried to slip away, to get some space to fight back, but the cell was too small.

She blocked another blow and tried to hit back, but her glancing punch gave Roag the opportunity to grab her arm and twist. Orry yelled in pain as the older woman held her arm out straight and used it as a lever to force her to her knees. The steel bowl of the toilet was right beside her, an acrid stink of bleach and worse coming off it.

Pain flared in her shoulder as Roag wrenched her arm up further, then kicked her in the side. Agony exploded in her ribs and she desperately shifted her weight, trying to break free, but it was impossible. She was jammed between Roag and the wall, the toilet in front of her face. Roag kicked her again and she cried out, feeling something give in her side. Before she could recover, her new cellmate released her arm and grabbing her hair in both hands, rammed her forehead into the rim of the toilet bowl. There was no seat, just hard metal, and the impact stunned her. Roag yanked her head back and Orry saw blood smeared on the steel before her head was slammed into it again.

Twisting Orry's hair in one hand, Roag used the other to grip the back of Orry's coveralls and lift her up and over the edge of the bowl, plunging her head into the water, which rushed up her nose and into her mouth. The shock of it brought her to her senses and she thrashed, panicking as her lungs were starved of air, but Roag had all her weight on her back, her arms trapped beneath her.

She clamped her mouth shut, the water she'd already swallowed burning in her heaving chest. She retched and choked, water filling her sinuses as she felt the strength begin to drain from her tortured body.

Suddenly, the pressure released. Roag hauled her up and she dragged down air, then, coughing and retching, vomited water back into the bowl.

'Looks like no one's coming to save you,' Roag said, 'which is odd. They dragged my last cellmate out of here before I could finish the job. She's in the infirmary now.'

She plunged Orry's head down again, holding it until she was too weak even to struggle. She hauled her up again.

'It's also odd that they put you in with me at all, considering our past history.'

'They—' Orry began, then puked up another lungful of water. 'They did it on purpose. Someone wants me dead, and they're using you to do it.' She filled her lungs in expectation of another drowning.

'Who's "they"?' Roag asked.

'I-I don't know. They framed me – that's why I'm in here.'

Her cellmate chuckled, but her grip didn't weaken. 'Good for them.'

'If you kill me, you're just cleaning up their mess for them.'

'I really don't give a shit,' Roag informed her, before apparently changing the subject completely. 'Tell me about Mender and your ship. Where are they while you're stuck in here?'

'They'll be nearby – trying to figure out where I am and how to get me out—'

Roag plunged her head back into the water, but only for a few seconds this time, then Orry felt the weight on her neck released. She lifted her head cautiously from the bowl and fell coughing and heaving onto her back in a spreading pool of foul water. She wiped her eyes and saw Roag standing by the bunks, a thoughtful expression on her face.

'You're not going to kill me?' Orry asked, too weak to move.

'Not right now,' she said, 'but don't get too comfortable. I might change my mind at any time. I'm kinda fickle like that.' She climbed onto her bunk and lay on her back, staring up at the ceiling.

Orry lay back too, wondering how it was that she was still alive.

'Found her,' Ethan announced.

'Saabitz Rock?' Mender asked.

'No, Innis Gael. The Arbiter Corps headquarters complex in the Old Town.'

'You sure?'

'Yeah, I'm inside the traffic control substrate – I used the city's lens net to follow the flyer she was in from the Trefoil out to the island. It landed right in the middle of the HQ complex.'

'Shit.'

'That's what I thought,' Ethan said, feeling thoroughly miserable. 'How the hell are we going to get her out of there?'

'I bet your sister could think of something,' the old man said drily. 'Shame she's not here.'

Ethan slapped the galley table hard, making his palm sting. 'I should have seen them coming.'

'You said the lenses up on that level were locked down tight. Don't beat yourself up, boy. If Seventh Secretariat encryption was easy to crack everyone would be doing it.'

'I should have been monitoring the external lenses – I would have seen that damned flyer coming in.'

'You can't think of everything, kid. At least you got yourself out of there.'

'Only by leaving Orry behind!'

'And what exactly could you have done against a squad of arbiters? If you want to feel sorry for yourself, go ahead, just do your whining somewhere I can't hear it.'

Ethan grimaced. Mender was right, feeling guilty about what had happened at the Trefoil wasn't going to help get Orry back. 'Sorry,' he said, summoning up a thin smile. 'So, you're right: what would Orry do if it was one of us stuck in there?'

'Heh. I've no idea, kid.'

Orry's clothes were still damp and stinking when the cell door opened an hour later. Arbiter-Sergeant Blessing stepped into the cell and looked at her with badly concealed surprise.

'Do your own dirty work,' Roag said from her bunk, the first words she'd spoken since trying to drown Orry.

The sergeant's face tightened. 'Prisoner Kent, with me,' she snapped.

Orry didn't move. 'Where are we going?'

Blessing held up her axon disruptor and blue light arced between its terminals. 'What did I tell you about asking questions?'

'Just go with her,' Roag said wearily. 'You can't fight 'em – believe me, I've tried.'

Orry reluctantly left the cell and the sergeant indicated she should precede her to the glass booth by the exit from the cell levels. She'd spent the time since her assault nursing her bruises and thinking about what was going on, and she was absolutely certain that she was right about Blessing having put her in with Roag in an attempt to end her life. What she couldn't figure out was the sergeant's motive – was she part of the same conspiracy who'd framed her and tried to kill her on Halcyon? Or was she just acting on orders from above? But if that was the case, why not simply kill her and say she'd been trying to escape? That thought made Orry stumble. Maybe that was going to be Blessing's next move, now that Roag had failed to perform as expected? But that was puzzling too: why had her cellmate not finished her off when she could?

They stopped at the booth.

'One for the interview room,' Blessing told the man inside, and the door buzzed open.

'Left here,' she told Orry as they walked down the corridor beyond. They climbed a staircase and stopped outside a blank door, which she unlocked with her thumb. She ushered her into yet another empty room with a table and two chairs, all bolted to the floor.

'Sit,' the sergeant ordered, and left her alone.

Twenty minutes passed before the door opened again and Orry looked up to see Arbiter-Colonel Zaytsev framed in the doorway. He was a tall man, broad at the shoulders, with a grim, weathered face beneath steel-grey hair. Silver insignia glinted on the chest and shoulders of his black uniform as he sat down opposite her.

'We meet at last, Miz Kent. It's been a long time coming.'

'It wasn't me,' she said immediately. 'That's why I went to see Rodin, because she's the only person who might actually believe me. She didn't know I was coming, and she certainly had nothing to do with what happened at the institute.'

Zaytsev regarded her for several seconds, looking pleased. 'And how would you know that if you weren't there?'

'Because I know Lucia. What have you done to her? This whole thing is ridiculous.'

'Tell that to the twenty-seven people who lost their lives when the institute blew up. And then there's the loss of thousands of irreplaceable Departed artefacts.'

'You have to let her go.'

'If I were you, Miz Kent, I would be far more concerned about your own predicament. This is not Saabitz Rock. The warden of this establishment runs things a little . . . differently.'

'You mean he has the prisoners beaten?'

'Do you wish to make a complaint?' He extended one gloved finger and pointed at the cut on her forehead where Roag had slammed her head into the toilet bowl.

'No, this wasn't . . . I fell.'

'Good, because the use of physical sanctions against prisoners would be an unconscionable breach of their basic human rights.'

His smile made her wonder if Zaytsev had been the one who'd arranged for her to share a cell with Roag. *And if he's capable of that, what else is he involved in?*

'The evidence against you is overwhelming,' he continued. 'Your conviction and subsequent execution are assured.' He let his words sink in before unrolling a databrane and placing it on the table between them. 'However, if you sign this testimony, I will see to it that your sentence is reduced.'

Orry scanned the document with growing outrage. 'This is all lies,' she said. 'I told you, Lucia and I weren't working together, and I've certainly never been a Seventh Secretariat operative. She had no knowledge that I was coming to see her.'

Zaytsev leaned back in his chair. 'Tell me, Miz Kent, have you ever seen anyone hang? Smelled the piss as it drips off their feet? It is not a dignified end.'

She thrust the brane back towards him. 'I'll never sign that.'

A flash of irritation crossed his face. 'Never is a very long time in a place like this.' He rolled up the brane and tucked it away. 'We'll talk again very soon,' he promised, then rose and crossed to the door, which opened at his approach to reveal Arbiter-Sergeant Blessing. 'Look after her, won't you, Sergeant?'

'Of course, sir,' she replied with a grin.

He turned to Orry. 'Think about my offer,' he advised her. 'It's the only one you're going to get.'

15

THE TRUSTY

'Have fun?' Roag asked after Blessing had left their cell.

'He didn't hit me, if that's what you mean,' Orry replied. She crossed to the tiny sink and ran some cold water into her cupped hands before splashing it onto her face, wondering idly when – or maybe *if* – she would be permitted to have a shower.

'He?' Roag asked.

'Zaytsev.'

'What did that pig bastard want?'

Orry turned to face her. 'Where are we?' she asked. 'I figure we must still be in Utz, or nearby; the flight here didn't take very long.' It looked like Innis Gael.

Her cellmate looked surprised. 'You don't even know where you are?'

'Sergeant Blessing wasn't very forthcoming when I asked her.'

Roag grunted, almost sympathetically. 'She's an odd fucking fish, that one. I can't put my finger on it, but she's not

127

like the rest of the guards.' She scowled. 'You're right, though, we are on Innis Gael. This place is called the Hollow, right under Arbiter HQ. Zaytsev reserves it for his "special cases".'

'What does that mean?'

'It means whoever he thinks would benefit from some close attention out of sight of prying eyes. Political undesirables, disgraced Ruuz – as distinct from those who've just been caught with their hands in the cookie jar – oh, and *terrorists* . . .' She waved at Orry, then herself. Orry decided not to give her the satisfaction of objecting.

A bell jangled harshly for several seconds, echoing through the cell block. Roag immediately swung her legs off the side of the bunk, jumped down and slid her bare feet into her plastic sandals.

'What's that for?' Orry asked nervously, trying to remember what it was like to *not* feel a sense of dread with every new occurrence.

'Chow time,' Roag said happily. 'Trust me, after you've been staring at blank walls for a few days you'll be as excited as I am at the prospect of a bowl of slop and a strawberry jelly pot.'

The cell door clanged open, she stepped out. Orry followed. All the doors were disgorging inmates in ones and twos. When she looked down into the base of the well formed by the three levels of cells, she saw several prisoners wearing powder-blue coveralls and white aprons standing ready to dole out food from polished steel cauldrons in front of them. Taking her cue from Roag, she filed down the stairs and joined the queue, shuffling forward a step at a time until she reached the first server.

'What's on the menu today?' she enquired lightly.

The server, a skinny man with a tattoo of a spider's web covering half his face, silently plopped a dollop of unappetising grey goop on her plate. She moved on to the next station and received what might be cornbread, then a small pot of red jelly and a paper beaker of water. The tables were filling up now, but not in the mood for making friends, she walked towards one of the few remaining empty tables, until a bear of a man rose from his seat to bar her path. Keeping her eyes lowered, she tried to walk around him, but the man-mountain moved to block her again.

'Excuse me,' she said, somehow managing to keep the fear out of her voice, 'but you're in my way.'

The man slowly extended his forefinger and stabbed it into her jelly. Stirring it around, he withdrew it and placed it in his mouth.

There's no way this is going to end without violence, Orry realised, remembering something her father used to say: *Big men often rely on their strength, which means they can lack skill. If you can get them angry enough, they'll make a mistake, and one mistake should be all that you need.*

Does this guy lack skill? she wondered, eyeing him as she judged the weight of the metal tray in her hands. *Rama, I hope so.*

She looked past him and adopted a worried expression. 'Shit,' she said quietly, 'it's Zaytsev.'

129

As the big man turned, she swung the tray with all her strength, smashing it across his shoulders. The tray bent almost in two, but he didn't move a mite. Grey slop dribbled down the back of his yellow coveralls as he turned to face her again, his lips drawn into a snarl.

'So you shall purge the evil from your midst,' he intoned, and then, 'I'm going to rip your pretty little head off.' He hunched his shoulders, making his muscles stand out like steel hawsers.

Oh hell, Orry thought, dropping the tray. *Thanks, Dad. He looks* perfectly *in control.* She tensed, preparing to run, but as the giant loomed over her she felt a hand drag her back and suddenly Roag was standing between them.

'You get one chance to fuck off,' her cellmate informed the gorilla.

'No sooner will their skins be consumed than we shall give them other skins, so that they may truly taste the scourge,' he said solemnly.

'What?'

'If you want some too, whore,' he continued, 'that's fine by me.'

Roag's arm moved like lightning and the colour drained from his face.

Orry blanched too: her new cellmate's hand was pressed against his groin, gripping a short blade that looked wickedly sharp.

'I gave you a chance,' Roag murmured. 'You really should have taken it.'

The giant's eyes shifted – and a look of relief came over his face.

Orry followed his gaze.

'Problem here?' a guard demanded as he materialised behind Roag, and just as suddenly as it had appeared, the homemade shiv was gone.

'No problem, boss,' she told him. 'Just having a chinwag with my mate here.'

'Didn't think you had any mates, Roag.'

'We go way back,' the giant rumbled, forming something approximating a smile.

'I don't fucking care,' the guard said. He pointed at Orry's tray. 'Clean that shit up. Looks like you're going hungry today.'

'Yes, boss.'

The man-mountain glared at them as they walked away.

'Thanks,' she told Roag.

The woman gave her a sour look, then jerked her head towards an empty table with her tray on it. 'You'd better sit with me.'

'I don't get it,' Orry said once they were seated. 'First you don't kill me – and now you're stopping other people from doing it? I'm really not complaining, but . . . what gives?'

Roag shovelled a spoonful of grey sludge into her mouth and grimaced, grabbed the saltshaker and liberally dosed her food before trying another spoonful. 'Maybe I'm still going to kill you,' she suggested. 'Maybe I just didn't want that shaveling meathead getting there first.'

'Shaveling?'

'Didn't you hear that bullshit he was spouting? If he's not a monk, he sure as shit follows them.'

'A monk? You mean an astrotheometrist?'

'Yeah, they cherry-pick shit like that from every ancient religion and crowbar it into their "intelligent design" belief system. You can find a quote to justify any evil shit if you look hard enough, and arseholes like that guy just lap it up. They think it gives them a free ticket to do whatever the hell they want.'

'Oh.'

Roag hunched over her bowl, ladled another spoonful of muck into her mouth and smiled around it. 'You really want to know why you're still alive?' She glanced furtively around, beckoned her closer and murmured, 'You have something I want.'

Orry gave a short laugh. 'You mean this minging uniform? The high-fashion sandals? Because that's all I've got.'

The older woman leaned closer still. 'Your ship, fuckwit. I'm talking about your ship.'

'*Jane*? What about her?'

Roag dropped her spoon into the empty bowl, checked to make sure they were still being ignored, then in a barely audible whisper, said, 'You want to get out of here, right?'

'Right. Very right.'

'Well, I reckon I can make that happen.'

Hope flared like a beacon. 'You have an escape plan?'

Roag winced and flapped her hand angrily. 'Keep your fucking voice down,' she hissed.

Orry's momentary excitement turned to suspicion. 'But if you have a way out, why are you still sitting here eating this muck?'

'That's what I'm trying to tell you, if you'll just shut your trap for long enough. I'm pretty sure I can get out, but this island is on the edge of the archipelago, a long way from anywhere useful, so I need a way off the island – and off-planet.'

'*Dainty Jane*.'

'The very same.'

'And in return you'll take me with you?'

'I can't see the redoubtable Jurgen Mender flying me off this damned rock without you, can you?'

'No, he definitely wouldn't . . .' If she was truly mad enough to consider throwing in her lot with Cordelia Roag, Orry felt she couldn't overemphasise that point. It was her turn to glance around covertly. 'So, what's the plan?' she whispered.

'The first thing to do is get a message to Mender: tell him where we are and when he's to pick us up.'

Orry felt her heart sink into her stomach again. 'How exactly am I supposed to do that?' she whispered angrily. 'In case you hadn't noticed, this whole place is screened against integuary traffic.'

Roag almost grinned. 'Actually, no, not the whole place. There's one room that isn't shielded. The warden's office.'

'The *warden's* office?' Orry caught her rising voice and forced herself to return to a whisper. 'Well, great – and how the hell am I supposed to get in there? Does he invite the inmates for afternoon tea on Sundays?'

Roag glared at her. Her hand moved briefly and a pea-sized ball of putty appeared on the table, almost hidden by her bowl. 'With this,' she said.

'Is that—? It looks like med-gel.'

'The warden's office is protected by a genetic lock and this gel just happens to be loaded with his genome. All you'd need to do is cover your thumb with it and the door will open for you.'

Orry was genuinely impressed. 'How did you get that?'

Roag made the gel disappear. 'My last cellmate – the one I put in the infirmary? She got it for me.'

'That was all part of the plan? But what's in it for her? Why would she let you beat the crap out of her?'

'Because I told her she was coming with me.'

Orry frowned. 'And is she?'

'What do you think? It'll be weeks before she can walk again, months before she's fit to escape. I don't know about you, but I've no intention of being stuck in here for that long.'

'Cold . . .'

'That's kind of you.'

'Why'd you have to hurt her so badly?'

Roag looked confused by the question. 'I had to make it look convincing – besides, she was an irritating cunt. Don't worry, I can't double-cross *you*, can I? Or Mender will leave me here.'

Orry didn't think she'd needed a reminder about Roag's true nature, but for a moment there she'd almost been starting to – well, not to *like* the woman, but at least not actively hate her. She was glad that hadn't lasted.

She returned to the great escape plan. 'How did you get the warden's DNA?' she asked. 'And how am I supposed to get to his office to use it?'

Roag looked over towards the food station and caught the eye of one of the blue-coveralled servers, an elderly man who was clearing away the empty dishes. He spoke briefly to the woman next to him, then scurried over to sit beside Orry.

'This is Iosef,' Roag said. 'Iosef, meet Aurelia.'

'Orry,' Orry said.

Iosef grinned at her. 'Delighted,' he said, and she was surprised to hear a pure-blood Ruuz accent.

'Iosef has been here for ever,' Roag continued. 'He's a trusty – you can tell because he doesn't look like a damn banana. He works partly in the admin block.'

'Where the warden's office is?' Orry guessed.

'Precisely. Iosef, would you like to fill in the newest member of our conspiracy?'

The old man frowned. 'What about Jasmine?'

'Forget about fucking Jasmine. She's done her part.'

He shrugged, then turned to Orry. 'Warden Govorin is a creature of habit,' he explained. 'He takes tea at precisely eleven o'clock every weekday morning, which he always makes himself in the kitchen near his office. He returns promptly to his desk at 11:07.'

'You're sure about that?' she asked. 'Every morning's the same?'

'Every morning for the past two years, which is how long I've been cleaning the admin block.'

'Is that how you got hold of his DNA? From a teacup or a spoon or something?'

Iosef looked delighted. 'She's a clever girl, this one,' he told Roag.

'So I'll have seven minutes to contact Mender,' Orry said. 'How do I get close enough to the office to use the gel pad without being seen?'

'There are no lenses in that part of the admin block,' Iosef said. 'The warden likes his privacy.'

'But how do I even get to the office?' she persisted. 'His DNA isn't going to do us a whole lot of good if I'm stuck in our cell at 11 a.m.'

Iosef just looked down at the table, while Roag glared.

'You haven't figured that part out yet, have you?' Orry said, and the expressions on their faces confirmed her suspicions.

'It's proving to be rather a knotty problem,' Iosef admitted nervously.

Orry sighed. 'Leave it with me.'

The old man looked relieved.

16

SLEIGHT-OF-HAND

'How close is the interview room to the warden's office?' Orry asked quietly. A night had come and gone and she had the inkling of an idea. It was good to have something to concentrate on; this was the most normal she'd felt since being arrested.

'Not very.' Iosef finished emptying the contents of the cell's bin into a refuse sack. 'The warden is on the next level up.'

'Is there much between them – I mean, are there offices or anything like that? Is it very busy?'

'Not really. You just have to go along a couple of corridors to the lifts.'

'Are there stairs?'

'Yes, but nobody uses them.'

Interesting.

'What are you thinking?' Roag asked.

'You said we're right under the Arbiter Corps HQ – so I imagine Zaytsev is based up there?'

'Most of the time.'

'So if I tell one of the guards that I want to speak to him, he won't have far to come.'

'Assuming he wants to speak to you again.'

'Oh, he will. When he interviews you, does he keep you waiting before he makes an entrance.'

'Fuck, yeah. He loves to do that.'

'Okay, so how about this? I say I want to talk to him, the guards take me to the interview room just before eleven and I have a window before Zaytsev arrives to get into the warden's office, call Mender and then get back to the interview room before he finally rocks up.'

'Sounds like a long shot,' Roag said doubtfully.

'You have any better suggestions?'

'How will you get out of the interview room?' Iosef asked.

The plan was coalescing in Orry's mind now, possible options shutting down as others opened up. 'Is there a toilet near the warden's office?' she asked.

'Right next door.'

'Is there one near the interview room?'

'Not too far. What—?'

'Could you arrange for the toilet near the interview room to be out of order tomorrow morning?'

His brow furrowed. 'I suppose so, but I don't see—'

'I think I do,' Roag said, 'but how do you plan to persuade your guard to take you to the toilet?'

Orry thought about that. 'Iosef, you're a trusty. Can you get me some salt?'

'Of course – but why?'

True to his word, Iosef was back that same evening clutching a small polybag of table salt. Orry hid it carefully under her mattress as she listened to the old man talk; he was clearly grateful for the opportunity.

'The Hollow used to be a mine,' he was saying, 'the first on the planet. When the colonists arrived on Tyr they settled here in Innis Gael partly because of what was beneath the surface. They excavated the mine to feed the printers that made their buildings. Most of the Old Town up there is still the original structures they printed, inside and out.' The old man was playing with a rare iridium half-crown as he spoke, flipping the little coin expertly across his knuckles. 'When Piotr first formed the Ascendancy, two hundred years ago now, the Arbiter Corps took over the old police headquarters above us. As they expanded, they occupied more and more of the surrounding buildings. They've maintained the façades, but the interiors have been modernised several times over.' He made a show of leaning over to replace the sliver of harsh soap, the ostensible reason he was crowded in there with them.

'I didn't even know this place existed,' Orry admitted.

'The arbiters have always kept it quiet,' Roag said. 'They used to use the old workings for storage and "enhanced interrogation" until Zaytsev took over. He was the one who turned this place into a formal detention centre. There are four levels: the lowest is where they keep us lot, then you go up to the interrogation level, then admin and storage – that's where the warden's office is. Then the HQ complex is above that.'

'What about access?' Orry asked.

Iosef took over. 'Lifts from the HQ, and there's a loading dock on the admin level for deliveries and prisoner transfers – that's where we'll have to meet your friends. The road tunnel comes out a kilometre away on the north side of the island.'

'Isn't it guarded?'

'Yes, but not heavily. Roag said your friends would be able to handle a couple of guards.'

Orry stared at her cellmate, perched on the stool. 'They will, will they? And what will happen when it all kicks off in here?'

'All the civilian staff will be evacuated in the lifts to the HQ buildings so they can't be used as hostages,' Iosef said, still idly playing with the iridium coin. 'All available guards will kit themselves out in riot gear and muster outside the cell block.'

'So the rest of the place will be pretty much deserted,' Roag added.

'I really hope so,' Orry replied, turning the plan over in her mind. It seemed solid enough, but it wouldn't take much for something to go wrong. *So what's new?* Her mind would be picking away at it all night, looking for holes. She pointed at the half-crown riding Iosef's knuckles. 'Where'd you learn how to do that?' she asked.

'I taught myself; it passes the time. I shouldn't have it really, but the guards indulge me because I'm a trusty. I show them new tricks from time to time – they like that. They get bored as well, you know.'

'Can you show me a trick?'

'Of course!' The old man looked delighted. He held the coin between the thumb and forefinger of his right hand and showed it to her. 'Now, young lady, how would like to own this valuable iridium half-crown?' he asked.

'It's a lovely coin,' she replied, playing along. 'I'd like it very much.'

'Then you're in luck, because I'm going to give you a chance to win it. I'm going to count to three, and on three, if you can grab the coin, it's yours.'

Orry grinned. She knew this one. 'Okay,' she agreed, looking forward to seeing how well the old man performed the trick. 'On three?'

'On three,' he confirmed. 'Now, hold out your hand, palm up.' She did as she was told, and he raised his hand above his head. 'Ready?'

'Go for it.'

'One!' He lowered his arm quickly towards her palm without releasing the coin, then raised it above his head again. 'Two!' he said as he repeated the motion, raising his arm again at the end. 'Aaaand . . . three!'

She dutifully made a grab for the coin as his arm came down for the last time, but it had vanished. Iosef opened her hand to show her it was empty and as he leaned forward, the half-crown dropped, as if from thin air, into her palm.

She applauded and he made a bow, smiling. The coin had been on top of his head, of course, dropped there before he'd lowered his arm for the third time and then pitched forward into her open palm at the end in a nice example of sleight-of-hand.

'My father knew a ton of coin tricks,' she said, holding up the half-crown. 'May I?'

'Of course,' he said gallantly.

She examined the coin. Piotr's profile embossed on its surface was younger than the man she knew. Looking around the cell, her eyes settled on an unopened can of soda Roag had evidently smuggled from the canteen. 'Can I use this?' she asked, reaching for it.

'I was saving that for later,' her cellmate grumbled. 'Fine, whatever.'

'Thanks. Okay, I'm going to slam this coin inside the can . . . like *so*!' Holding the can on its side, the bottom angled slightly away from them, she smacked the coin against the concave base and left it there, expertly balanced against the bottom rim. Knowing it was safely out of sight, she showed them her empty hand before transferring the can to her empty palm, the coin still safely beneath it. This time, when she switched hands, she concealed the coin behind her fingers and displayed the bottom of the can.

'And now, I'm going to open the can – and the coin will be inside.'

She held the half-crown loosely against the side, gave the can a shake and let the coin rattle against it. It might look clever, but it was just basic sleight-of-hand to manoeuvre the coin to the top of the can; this time she concealed it with her hand as she opened the tab. The drink frothed out with a hiss, allowing her to deftly push the coin inside before she handed the can to Roag.

'Pour it out,' Orry told her, indicating a plastic mug.

Wearing a long-suffering expression, she dutifully emptied the contents into the mug, shaking it at the end until the coin dropped out.

'Very good,' Roag said drily, laying the half-crown on the table. She picked up the mug and slurped.

Iosef applauded. 'That was very well done,' he said. 'Your father taught you well.'

'He did,' Orry said, and the thought of him pricked the simple pleasure of the trick. She glared at Roag, the reason for Eoin's death.

'If you two have quite finished,' Roag said, 'isn't it time you got moving, Iosef? It's lockdown in a minute and we don't want anyone getting suspicious, do we?'

Orry wiped the coin dry before returning it and the old man patted her hand fondly. 'Until tomorrow,' he said. 'Everything will be ready, I promise.'

'Good night, Iosef,' she said, and watched him wander contentedly out onto the balcony. 'He's nice,' she said once he had gone. 'What's he in here for?'

Roag's thin lips curled into a smile. 'He found out his wife was sleeping with some other Ruuz prick, so he shot her and sent the guy her head in a hatbox.'

'Oh . . .'

'Apparently the hat was ruined.'

A buzzer sounded, the cell door swung closed and Roag climbed onto her bunk and settled down. 'Sleep well,' she said.

Oddly, Orry thought she meant it.

Another buzzer sounded and the lights went out.

Orry banged on the inside of the interview door. 'Could I have some water, please?' she called to the guard outside. There was no response, so she continued, 'I saw a water cooler right there – please?'

She was starting to worry that her plan would fail before it had even begun when the door opened and the scowling guard shoved a paper cup into her hand.

'Cheers!' she said.

The door slammed shut.

She returned to her chair and sat down. Keeping her hands out of sight beneath the table, she opened the polybag of salt and emptied its contents into the water before gulping it down. Gagging, she managed to get it down – before spectacularly vomiting her breakfast onto the table and her coveralls.

Her retching brought the guard back into the room. He took in the scene with utter disgust.

'Must have been something I ate,' she said weakly. 'Sorry.'

'Rama, that *stinks*.'

'I suppose Colonel Zaytsev must be used to the smell of puke,' she said, gagging again, and enjoyed the look of dismay on the guard's face.

'Come with me,' he snapped. 'We need to get you cleaned up before he gets here.'

Rama, I really do stink, she thought as, head bowed, she trudged in front of him to the nearest toilet. The cheesy, acid stench rising from her clothing was making her want to throw up again. As they turned the corner, she saw Iosef, right where he was supposed to be, dutifully mopping the floor outside the toilet. The guard cursed when he saw the 'Out of Order' notice on the door.

'Sorry, boss,' Iosef said. 'We've had a flood – it's these old pipes. Water's off through most of the admin block. Maintenance are aware.' He glanced at Orry and his lip curled with distaste. 'Nearest working sink is upstairs – I can show you which one if you like, save you having to traipse around looking for it.'

She didn't need to fake the retch; gagging, she clamped her hand over her mouth.

'Quickly then!' the guard snapped.

'Follow me, boss.'

The trusty led them to a nearby stairwell, making meaningless small talk with the unresponsive guard. The stairs emerged into a corridor that looked like it belonged in an office rather than a prison. The layout was just as Iosef had described.

Orry got her bearings as they walked down the empty corridor to the toilet. The guard entered first and checked it out before leaving her alone inside. Outside, she could hear Iosef jabbering on at him as she entered the last cubicle and closed the door. Crouching, she located a certain loose clip on the wall panelling behind the toilet bowl and removed it before pulling out the bottom of the panel from the wall and reaching in to extract the wadded-up coverall Iosef had left inside.

Moving quickly, she shrugged off her own puke-stained clothes, left them in the cubicle and pulled on the clean blue coveralls. She went to the door and inched it open so she could peer out. Iosef appeared to have finally caught the guard's attention with a coin trick: the man was standing with his back to her as he listened to the old man's entertaining patter.

Slipping silently through the door, she padded along the corridor and around a corner, anxiously monitoring the elapsed time with her integuary. A man in a black arbiter's uniform came out of a door to her right and she kept her eyes on the floor as he passed her without comment. Two more doors, then she stopped. The next one should be the warden's office. She found the ball of med-gel and moulded it over the end of her thumb before extracting a cloth which she used to polish a nearby water fountain, waiting for her internal clock to tick closer to eleven.

A few seconds after the hour, the door opened and a portly man in an expensive-looking frock coat and extravagant greying whiskers stepped out. He hardly spared her a glance as he strode down the corridor. Orry waited until he'd disappeared around the corner, checked that the corridor was still empty and stepped up to the office door, her heart pounding. Holding her breath, she pressed her thumb against the genetic scanner, expecting at any moment an alarm to start blaring. The scanner read the med-gel moulded over her thumb and the door opened with a soft click. With a gasp of relief she slipped inside and quietly closed the door behind her.

The office was wood-panelled, with a large wooden desk, a velvet-covered sofa and several chairs. The pictures adorning the walls showed Warden Govorin shaking hands with a number of important-looking people – including, she noticed, the Imperator. Orry instructed her integuary to run a diagnostic and saw with relief that Roag was right, she had a strong signal in this room. She immediately opened a connection to *Dainty Jane*'s encrypted common channel, praying she was in range.

Hello? Can anyone hear me?

After a moment's delay her mind was filled with voices.

Whoa, whoa! One at a time.

Are you okay? It was Ethan's voice, urgent and concerned. *Where are you?*

I'm okay – sort of. I don't have much time, so listen carefully. I'm in a detention centre called the Hollow under the Arbiter headquarters on Innis Gael. I'm sharing a cell with Cordelia Roag—

You're what? Mender interjected.

She has an escape plan and she's willing to get me out too – providing we take her offworld. This is what I need you to do . . .

She quickly outlined their part in Roag's plan, anxiously watching the minutes tick by as she spoke. By the time she'd finished it was 11:05.

Are you sure you can trust her? asked *Jane.*

I think I have to. Without me she's stuck here. Once she's on board, though– well, that's another matter entirely.

Don't worry about that, Mender sent. *She won't get the chance to try anything.*

Good – I have to go. See you tomorrow night.

Sis? Ethan sent.

11:06.

I don't have time for—

I'm sorry, he continued regardless, sounding thoroughly miserable. *It's my fault you're in there. I should have spotted Zaytsev coming, back at the towers.*

It's not your fault, she told him firmly. *I have to go. We'll talk about it when I'm out of here. Bye.*

11:07.

She was halfway to the door when she heard footsteps outside. The lock clicked and the door began to swing open. Orry crossed the room in two strides and dived behind the desk. Peering under it, she saw Warden Govorin close the door and walk towards her hiding place. She was trapped, left with no options. He would see her, call the guards – and then what? Solitary confinement? Worse? Torture? She wouldn't put anything past them.

Whatever happened, Roag's escape plan was blown and she wouldn't get a chance to contact Mender to warn them off.

Three more steps . . . two.

She felt sick with fear. For an instant she wondered if she could take the man hostage, then remembered why there hadn't been a hostage situation on Tyr for more than fifty years. The Arbiter Corps did *not* negotiate.

Govorin was at the side of the desk now. She couldn't stop her hands from shaking . . . one more step and he would see—

There was a firm knock at the door.

'What now?' he muttered. 'Come!'

Orry saw a pair of black-uniformed legs appear. 'Arbiter-Colonel Zaytsev has just arrived to interrogate one of the prisoners,' a woman's voice said. 'I thought you'd want to know.'

The warden cursed. 'Where is the old bastard?' he asked, striding back to the door.

Orry let out a shuddering breath as he left the room. She waited a few seconds before hurrying to the exit herself. If Zaytsev was already here, she was out of time.

Iosef was teaching the guard his coin trick when Orry arrived back at the toilet. It felt like an hour had passed since she'd snuck away, but in fact it had been less than ten minutes. She caught the trusty's eye and he doubled down on distracting his rapt audience as she padded silently to the toilet door and slipped inside.

Thirty seconds later her borrowed coveralls were in the bin, ready for Iosef to retrieve, and she was back in her own puke-stained clothes. She hurriedly splashed water over herself and wiped off as much vomit she could before returning to the corridor.

The guard turned immediately. 'You took your time.'

'It won't come off,' she said, a little hoarsely.

'Come on, we need to get back. You can requisition a new set after the colonel's finished with you.'

Zaytsev was already sitting in the interview room when she got there. He didn't look happy to be the one kept waiting for a change.

'Where the hell has she been?' he demanded.

'Sorry, sir, the prisoner vomited. I thought you'd want her cleaned up.'

'What's wrong with you?' the arbiter-colonel asked her.

'Something I ate,' she said.

He scowled. 'Get out,' he told the guard. When they were alone, he demanded, 'So, are you ready to sign?'

'No,' she answered, sounding miserable. 'That's not why I wanted to see you.'

'Then why am I here?' he asked coldly.

She leaned forward and, clasping her hands together on the table as if praying, begged, 'Because you *have* to believe me!' Injecting her voice with desperation, she went on, 'I swear, I had *nothing* to do with what happened at the institute.'

'And?'

She looked puzzled. 'What do you mean?'

'You've already told me you're innocent and I've already told you that I don't believe you. So what's changed?'

She forced tears into her eyes. 'You have to let me out of this place – I can't bear it in here – *please!* She's going to kill me . . .'

A thin smile played over his lips. 'All you have to do is sign the document, Miz Kent. Do that, and I will arrange for you to be moved to a more pleasant location immediately.'

She dropped her eyes, staring blankly at the table. It really didn't matter what she said at this stage, as long as she didn't arouse any suspicions, but while she had his attention she might as well buy some time. 'C-Can I think about it?' she asked.

His jaw tightened with frustration, but he gave a curt nod before standing and moving to the door.

'Don't take too long about it,' he told her. 'The Hollow can be a dangerous place.'

17

STEYR 37 SKORPION

The graveyard was in a vast desert near a range of low, rocky hills, a thousand kilometres south of the city of Utz. *The place is* like *a city*, Ethan thought as they coasted slowly over wide streets formed by row after row of every conceivable type of machine from household mechs to Grand Fleet cutters. There was even a derelict corvette looming over the dusty streets several kliks away.

'You'll find what you're looking for just past those civilian flyers,' Jaakko said, leaning forward to point out of *Dainty Jane*'s canopy. The junkdog was a lean man, deeply tanned by the desert. 'Set her down right there.'

As Mender brought them down gently between two lines of armoured vehicles, *Jane*'s engines raised a sandstorm that was still thickening the air when they tramped down the cargo ramp.

'Depends what you're after, really,' Jaakko said, his voice muffled by the patterned scarf now covering his nose and mouth. A pair of mirrored goggles hid his eyes. 'These are the more recent models, but if you're after something vintage, we have quite a few down that end of the row. Collectors, are you?'

'Not really,' Mender said shortly, crossing to the nearest of the vehicles. There were dozens of them in this row alone, transports mostly, in faded Arbiter Corps and Grand Fleet Auxiliary liveries. The row behind them was mainly tanks and mobile artillery.

'Ah,' the junkdog said knowingly, 'knew it when I saw your ship. Private contractors, am I right? You got that "don't fuck with me" look about you . . .' He glanced at Ethan then back at Mender. 'Well, you do, at least.'

'We want something recent,' Ethan said, 'something still in service.'

Jaakko grinned. 'Then allow me to introduce you to the Steyr 37 Skorpion.' He strode a little way up the row to an angular, evil-looking armoured transport squatting on six enormous tyres. The vehicle exuded menace from its sharply angled nose to the heavy doors at its rear. Black gun barrels poked from low turrets at the front and back and launcher tubes emerged from the hull in several places. 'This baby can maintain a steady seventy over rough terrain and soak up a direct hit from a kinetic penetrator – make your ears ring like a bell, mind. Reactive armour, full-spectrum counter-measures and twin 20 mike-mike caseless autocannons to the front and rear, controlled from inside so you don't have to get your pretty little head shot off. For a small additional fee I can supply you with ammunition. What d'you think of her?'

'And these are still in service?' Ethan asked, running his hand along the Skorpion's armoured flank.

'Sure are. Auxiliaries and the arbiters are starting to use the 40 now, but I reckon these old 37s will take more of a beating. This one saw service with the 109th out on Jericho but never took a hit. I can give her a full service and tune-up before you take her away.' He glanced towards *Dainty Jane*'s open hold. 'Reckon she'll fit in there perfect, too. Where're you planning to make use of her, anyway?'

'Up your mother's arse,' Mender growled. He climbed up stiffly to wipe the dust from one of the Skorpion's thick windows and peer inside.

'None of my business anyway,' Jaakko said evenly, 'just so long as you ain't planning on using her on Tyr. Now whaddya say: ten thou and I'll throw in an ECM suite upgrade for free?'

Mender jumped down and patted the dust from his clothes.

'Never mind that ECM shit,' he said. 'You got any paint?'

'What's the latest from the outside?' Iosef asked. 'I hear the peace with the Kadiran Hierocracy is holding?'

'So far,' Orry confirmed, moving her lunch around her tray. The food in the Hollow didn't improve, but at least she was getting a break from Roag, who was busy intimidating an inmate on another table for a change.

'But we didn't win?' Iosef continued.

'Nobody won. They just stopped fighting.'

'That's what I heard – but no one seems to know why.'

Lucia does, Orry thought bitterly, shivering as she remembered that day on the bridge of Roag's ship when the Kadiran delegation had come to sue for peace. 'A greater threat' the Kadiran officer had said. *And I still don't know what it means.*

'Except the Imperator,' she suggested.

'Of course. He's dying, I hear.'

'He's ill,' she corrected. 'It will take a lot to kill the Imperator.'

'No, definitely dying,' he insisted, 'and without naming a successor. He'd better do it before he goes, or the Ascendancy will tear itself apart.'

'Surely not,' she said, worried by how certain he sounded about Piotr's declining health. 'The Assembly of Houses would never allow that to happen.'

'And who leads the Assembly, now that the House of Delf has fallen?'

'I don't know,' she admitted. Fountainhead politics held no interest for her.

'Two of the Great Houses are vying for the position of Primatur: House Lowenstaat and House Goltenberg.'

'You know a lot about this,' she observed.

'It's what I was born into,' he said with a sad smile. 'I like to keep my finger on the pulse, even in here, and right now I don't like what I'm hearing.'

'The heads of both those Houses are dead.' She paused before adding, 'Roag killed them, as I'm sure you know.'

He inclined his head a little. 'Great Houses always have someone ready to take up the reins – unlike the Ascendancy, it appears. The Lowenstaats and the Goltenbergs are both powerful, with formidable standing armies and enormous political influence. The other Houses, great and small, are already lining up behind one or the other of them and the only thing preventing open conflict is the Imperator.'

'I didn't realise things were so bad,' she said. 'So why hasn't Piotr named an heir?'

'That's what I was hoping you'd tell me.' His eyes twinkled. 'I know who you are, Aurelia Katerina Kent.'

'I figured.'

'So?'

'I'm sorry, Iosef, but I can't help you. Do you really think if I was that close to the Imperator I'd be stuck in here with you?'

The old man looked disappointed. 'I suppose not,' he admitted, then brightened. 'Once I'm out of here I can find out for myself, can't I? I still have a lot of friends in the Fountainhead who will provide me with shelter. I might not be in Utz any more, but I'll be free.'

Friends and *enemies*, Orry thought, wondering how powerful his murdered wife's family were, or the man to whom he'd sent her head. She decided not to ask about that, despite a morbid curiosity. Iosef was such a gentle man – she couldn't imagine him hacking off a woman's head and calmly having it delivered to his love rival. Instead, she asked, 'Do you want my pudding? Best take it before Roag gets here and nicks it. Rama knows why but she loves the damn things.'

'Oh yes!' Iosef said, delighted. 'Are you sure?'

'Absolutely.'

She watched him eat, praying she wouldn't remain in this place long enough to develop a taste for the stuff herself.

Ethan stepped back to examine his work and nodded, satisfied. *Not exactly a professional finish, but it'll serve its purpose.* He set down the spray gun and removed his mask, ignoring the chemical stink of the paint fumes now filling *Dainty Jane*'s hold.

The Skorpion was transformed, its jagged camo scheme, faded by years under the desert sun, replaced with the bright white and midnight-blue livery of the Arbiter Corps. He was particularly proud of the stencilling on the armoured transport, which he had copied from one of the real Skorpions used to transport prisoners to and from Innis Gael.

'Looks pretty good,' Mender said, entering the hold with Quondam.

'Thanks. I don't know if you noticed, but the ablative coating on top looks pretty patchy. I think this thing has seen some serious action.'

'As long as the paint covers it. I'm not planning on getting shot at with military grade lasers.' He tossed a bag over, which landed at Ethan's feet. 'Two arbiter uniforms. Once this thing dries we're ready to go.'

Ethan pulled out one of the uniforms. 'Did she ask any questions?' he asked, examining it.

'Kid, the kind of people who are prepared to sell you a couple of arbiter uniforms aren't the kind to ask questions.'

'I suppose not.'

'Although there was one small hiccough.'

Ethan stopped trying to stuff the uniform back into the bag and looked up. 'What?' he asked anxiously.

'Well, buying that tank of yours kind of cleaned us out, so we had to do a little . . . creative bargaining.'

'What sort of "creative bargaining"?'

'Not me – it was Quon here persuaded them.'

'I did not kill any of them,' Quondam rumbled happily. 'Your brood-sister will be pleased.' He paused for a second, thinking, then admitted, 'Some limbs were lost.'

Ethan could feel a headache coming on. 'I thought we agreed that Quon would stay onboard *Jane*?' he said. 'We're *supposed* to be doing this under the radar – the arbiters will be after all of us after what happened at the Trefoil now. How many Kadiran do you think there are lumbering around the city? No offence, Quon.'

'No offence is taken. I do lumber.'

'You'd better pray they don't connect this with the Hollow,' Ethan said.

'Relax, kid! No one will be telling the arbiters anything. You think they're going to admit what they're selling? Anyway, by the time they regain consciousness we'll be in another system.'

'*Regain* . . . ?' He shuddered. 'No, I don't even want to know.'

'Also, jaws were shattered,' Quondam added helpfully.

'That's right,' Mender said, chuckling at the Kadiran. 'Guess they'll take some time to heal.'

'Perhaps we shouldn't mention any of this to Orry,' Ethan suggested. 'We'll just say you bought the uniforms, okay?'

'That's probably wise,' Mender said, looking at Quondam.

'Wise,' the Kadiran agreed, and they both nodded.

Ethan's headache was definitely getting worse and he didn't think it was down to the paint fumes. 'Okay, we've got a little under twelve hours. Shall we go over the plan one more time before we get some sleep?'

'How about some food, kid? My stomach thinks my throat's been cut.'

Ethan gritted his teeth. The sooner Orry was back and wrangling these two lunatics so he didn't have to, the happier he would be.

'Fine,' he said tightly.

'Great,' Mender said, ''cause it's your turn to cook.'

18

RIOT

Orry's dinner sat untouched on the table in front of her. The thought of eating was making her stomach flip. *Keep it together*, she told herself. *This is just like any other job.* Except it wasn't like any other job: Roag had planned it, for one thing, and the stakes were way higher than usual. She wasn't playing for a few thousand sovereigns, but for her freedom – and probably her life.

On the far side of the Hollow's communal dining area a young guard walked into the kitchen.

'There he goes,' she told Roag.

If her cellmate was suffering the same nerves as her, it wasn't showing. Roag leaned over to a man on the next table, picked up his jelly pot and asked, 'Mind if I borrow this?'

Before he could answer, Roag had flicked the full pot onto the head of the bald giant who'd confronted Orry on her first day, who was sitting with his back to them. Roag smiled charmingly and returned the empty container to its suddenly white-faced owner as the giant touched the red mess on the back of his head, examined his hand, then slowly rose and turned to face the pudding's owner.

'I-I d-d-d-didn't—' the man began, gesturing helplessly towards Roag with the empty pot, but he got no further because the man-mountain had flipped the entire table, sending people and food flying. In seconds the canteen had descended into chaos.

An alarm started blaring as the outnumbered guards quickly fled, bolting the doors and leaving the inmates to it. Orry wondered how quickly the guards would regroup, arm themselves and return to impose order – and with how much brutality.

'Come on,' Roag said, and began picking her way through the fighting towards the kitchen.

Orry was halfway to her destination when a pair of arms grabbed her from behind, lifting her from her feet. Her captor squeezed and she felt her ribs creak – then she heard a sigh and she was dropped back to the ground. She turned to see the bald giant, jelly still smeared over his scalp, slumped at Roag's feet. Behind her Iosef was hovering nervously, flinching from the fighting around him.

'Stop fucking about,' Roag snapped at her, stepping over the body.

A clatter sounded as Orry followed her into the kitchen, Iosef at her heels, to see three inmates had the young guard she'd spotted earlier pinned against a work surface. He'd managed to get one arm free and had jammed an axon disruptor under the ribs of the woman on his right, but even as she dropped, twitching, to the ground, one of the other inmates punched the guard in the face, grabbed the disruptor's long handle and wrenched it from his grip.

The guard, feeling around blindly, closed his fingers around something which turned out to be the handle of a heavy pot; he swung wildly at his attacker, driving him back, just as the third inmate picked up a long knife. He thrust it at the guard, slicing open his arm.

Roag stepped forward, plucked the disruptor from the inmate's hand and jammed it into his neck. He dropped, mouth foaming as his eyes rolled back in his skull, and she turned on the man with the knife.

'Fuck off, Clay,' she said. 'Right now.'

He was a lean man, with hard eyes that reminded Orry of Mender's. His face twisted into a cruel leer. 'I know who you are,' he told Roag, 'and I sure ain't scared of you. You're nothing without your crew.' He edged closer, holding the knife expertly, his eyes on the disruptor in Roag's hands.

She said nothing, just adjusted her position slightly as he came closer. Clay moved first, slashing at her face, but Roag sidestepped, blocked another thrust with the disruptor and jabbed it at his wrist. He swung away, feinted left then sliced at Roag, who grunted in pain as a line of red opened across her forearm. She scowled as the two of them circled slowly, searching for an opening. Clay lunged, his blade low, driving it

up towards her belly. Roag let him come, then stepped inside
his reach and punched him hard in the throat before jamming
the disruptor into his arm. He yelped and the knife clattered to
the floor. She kicked out, her foot thudding into his stomach,
and he doubled up, retching as she stepped in and grabbed a
fistful of his greasy hair with her free hand. Another jab with
the disruptor dropped him to his knees in front of the stove.

Orry cringed as Roag mashed his cheek against one of the
lit burners. He screamed as she held him there. Although she
released him a moment later, to Orry, her stomach roiling at
the smell of crisping flesh, it felt like an hour. Clay fell back,
clutching his face, then pulled himself to his feet and stumbled
away.

Roag turned calmly to the young guard, who had one hand
clamped over the wound on his arm.

'Don't—' he began, but she'd already pressed the disruptor
to his chest and pulled the trigger.

'Hurry up,' she ordered, walking to the door to keep watch.

Orry quickly stripped the guard and pulled on his uniform,
then ripped a tea towel into strips to bind his arm. When she
looked up, Roag was examining her critically.

'How are you planning to disguise my face?' Orry asked;
Roag had been vague about that part of the plan.

Her cellmate picked up the fallen knife and stepped close.
'Hold still,' she snapped, as Orry shied away.

'What are you going to do?'

'Just *hold still*.'

Having Cordelia Roag wave a carving knife in her face was making Orry re-evaluate a number of the decisions she'd made to this point. She stood nervously as the other woman raised the knife, waiting for her to hack off some of her hair – instead, a sharp pain stabbed through her scalp. She pulled away, her hand rising instinctively to her head, and felt something warm running down her face. When she looked at her palm, it was soaked in blood. For a moment, she felt faint, until fury outweighed it.

'What did you do?' she demanded.

'Oh, relax,' Roag said disparagingly. 'It's just a cut in your scalp. Bleeds like hell but it'll heal up fine – not even a scar, I'll bet. Rub the blood over your face and into your hair and no one'll recognise you without a close look.'

'You *cut* me,' Orry protested again, wiping away the blood stinging her eyes.

'Stop whining and let's go,' Roag said, and somewhat to Orry's surprise, handed her the axon disruptor.

The riot was still in full swing when they left the kitchen, inmates fighting each other amid overturned tables and chairs. Food was splattered everywhere. Someone had even managed to light a fire, which was spewing noxious black smoke into the air. With Iosef hovering protectively at her side, Orry pushed Roag ahead of her; it was a little hard to resist the almost overwhelming temptation to zap her cellmate with the disruptor and leave her to the mercies of her fellow criminals. As they approached the glass booth leading out of the cell block, the barred door beside it flew open and a dozen guards in riot gear ran through, shields raised in front of them.

She waited for the last of them to pass before pushing Roag up to the glass. 'Got one of the ringleaders,' she told the guard in the booth, keeping Roag more or less between them to avoid him getting too good a look at her. 'Need to isolate her – this trusty needs to get somewhere safe, too.'

The guard was intent on the riot team wading into the prisoners. He tore his eyes away to look at Roag and Iosef, then frowned at Orry.

'Is that your blood?' he asked. 'Are you okay?'

'It's fine, just a nick.'

'Best get to medical after you've locked her up.'

'I will.'

The buzzer sounded as he released the door, but he didn't bother to watch them go through, instead returning his attention to the pandemonium in the canteen, obviously enjoying watching the prisoners being violently subdued.

The carving knife dropped from Roag's sleeve the moment she was through the door and she reached into the open booth and pressed the blade to the startled guard's throat.

'Make a sound and you're dead,' she hissed. She took up position behind him. 'The armoury. Now,' she ordered.

'You'll never—' He yelped as the knife cut into the flesh beneath his chin.

'I do hate chatty people. If you're a talker, I'll just slit your throat and find the place myself.'

His Adam's apple bobbed up and down and he nodded carefully, then started walking down the corridor.

'I told you the place would be empty,' Iosef said happily as they descended two flights of stairs to the admin block's lower level.

'It's here,' the guard said, stopping outside an unmarked door.

'Open it,' Roag ordered.

He hesitated. 'What will you do to me afterwards?' He sucked in a sharp breath as Roag pressed the knife deeper into his neck, then extended his hand and let the door scanner read his thumb. The door slid open.

'D-Don't kill me,' he pleaded as Roag shoved him inside.

'Watch him,' she told Orry, before running her eyes along the racks on the walls of the small room. Many were empty, and looking at the remaining weapons Orry realised that the riot team must have armed themselves largely with non-lethal weapons.

Roag selected a stubby machine-gun, inserted a magazine and offered a shotgun to Orry, who shook her head.

Roag shot her a contemptuous look before cocking her gun and turning it on the terrified guard.

'Take us to the loading bay,' she demanded.

Innis Gael was a remote island; it had taken the old Skorpion the best part of an hour to drive over the gracefully curved bridges that linked it to Isla Corunna and the isolated agricultural station where *Jane* had dropped them off after flying nap-of-the-earth, thermal sinks activated, to avoid detection. The final bridge delivered them to Old Town and Ethan watched the ancient printed buildings passing as Mender gunned the transport through the narrow streets. Even though it was a popular tourist attraction, the place wasn't that busy early on a cold winter's evening. Once the town was behind them, it was a short drive down the coast road to the unpopulated south of the island.

'It's just over that ridge,' Ethan said, pointing to the windswept bushes clinging to the thin brown turf.

Mender pulled the Skorpion over. 'We'll not be long,' he told Quondam, who was squeezed uncomfortably into the back of the vehicle, and he and Ethan climbed down.

Ethan's uniform was a poor fit and he pulled his belt tighter as they walked to the ridge and peered cautiously over. The road descended into a natural depression where the Hollow's gate was set into a low artificial mound covered in scrubby grass. A security fence surrounding the mound was broken by a small guardhouse with a gate that gave access to a short road leading to a heavy door set into the side of the mound.

'How we doing for time?' Mender asked, eyeing the bloated sun sinking towards the horizon.

'We have thirteen minutes,' Ethan answered without bothering to check his integuary; he'd been obsessing about timing for the whole of the long journey.

The old man surveyed the bleak surroundings and scowled.

'That's too long to be out in the open. What if someone spots us? I should've driven slower.'

'Better to be early than late,' Ethan said, but Mender just grunted.

In fact, it was less than ten minutes before a light started flashing inside the guardhouse and alarms sounded from the gate.

'I guess she went early,' Ethan said as they ran back to the Skorpion.

The big tyres ate up the road to the gate and as they approached, a guard armed with a compact assault rifle walked out and waved them down. A second guard stood inside the gatehouse, ignoring them as she studied a bank of screens.

'Jammer's on,' Ethan said, checking the integuary damper in his hand was functioning.

The guard walked up to Mender's side of the vehicle. 'Can't let you through,' he said as the window came down, 'place has just gone into lockdown. We're trying to find out what—'

He stopped abruptly as Mender pointed his Fabretti at him.

'Tell your friend in there to open up,' he said, 'or they'll be mopping you off the walls for a week.'

The guard's rifle was still pointing at the dirt, his eyes wide. 'She'll never—'

'Tell her!' Mender growled.

The man began to turn but there was no need, as the other guard had evidently spotted what was happening outside.

She hesitated for a moment, presumably to use her inte-guary, and when she found it was blocked, she grabbed for a communicator.

'Quon,' Ethan yelled, 'you're up—'

The heavy Skorpion rocked as Quondam opened the rear doors, jumped out and lumbered to the little gatehouse. He smashed one fist through its glass, grabbed the startled guard and dragged her out.

In the Skorpion's cab, Ethan leaned across Mender to get to the open window and yelled, 'Don't hurt her!'

Quondam lifted the squirming guard by the ankle and held her a metre above the ground. Examining her curiously, he asked, 'What should I do with her?'

'Tie them both up. That's why we brought the restraints.'

The dangling guard had managed to open the holster at her waist and pull out her sidearm, but Quondam calmly plucked it from her hand and tossed it aside.

'Don't be a hero,' Ethan advised her.

'Go and open the gates, kid,' Mender said, 'we need to get moving.'

19

LOADING DOCK

The level they were on now was hot, lined with exposed pipes and cables, with the sound of heavy plant thrumming behind closed doors. The white-faced guard opened another door and they emerged into a bunker-like concrete room lined with packing cases and pallets swathed in plastic. A loading dock had space for two trucks; beyond it was a heavy metal shutter, but it was down, blocking the only other exit from the room.

Orry checked the time. 'Five minutes to spare,' she said, and Iosef beamed.

'We don't need this bastard any more,' Roag said, shoving the guard against the wall and raising her machine-gun.

'No!' Orry said, knocking it aside.

Roag rounded on her, her face filled with rage.

'I told you, no killing,' Orry said, ice filling her veins as Roag slowly raised the weapon and aimed it at her stomach. 'If you shoot me, you're never getting out of here,' she said, angry with herself for not being able to hide the tremor in her voice.

Roag's face twisted into a sneer. 'Maybe I won't . . . or maybe I will.' She moistened her lips with her tongue, her eyes fixed on Orry.

A rapid burst of gunfire rang out and Roag staggered sideways. Orry caught a glimpse of Arbiter-Sergeant Blessing in the doorway and quickly shoved the cursing Roag into the cover of a nearby pallet.

'I'm hit,' she spat through gritted teeth, her face horribly white.

'How bad is it?' Orry asked.

Roag tried to stifle a moan. Orry, looking over, saw blood pooling under her as she lay slumped against the wall. More shots sounded and Iosef landed beside her, breathing heavily. She picked up Roag's machine-gun.

'What are we going to do?' he asked.

She checked the time: one minute left until she had to open the shutter. She could see the switch on the wall beside it, perhaps ten metres away. Iosef followed her gaze.

'What will your friends do if you don't open the door?' he asked.

She clenched her teeth. 'I told them to assume something had gone wrong and get clear, wait for me to contact them again and rearrange.'

'Will they really leave you here?'

She considered that. 'Yes,' she decided. 'Ethan would want to break in, but Mender would stop him. He'd know they'd just end up in a cell themselves – or worse.'

'So one of us needs to hit that switch,' Iosef said, looking at her.

She nodded grimly. 'Can you shoot?'

'I'll manage.'

She handed him the gun. 'Keep Blessing's head down.' She shifted position behind the crates, judging the distance to the switch. There was no cover to speak of – she would have to get to it and back in the open.

'Come on out of there,' Blessing yelled from the doorway. 'Nobody else needs to get hurt.'

'Bullshit!' Orry shouted back. 'You've been trying to get me killed since I got here.'

'That's ridiculous,' the sergeant said. 'Throw down that gun and come out.'

'So you can shoot us while we're "trying to escape"? I don't think so!' She gripped Iosef's arm and made a shooting gesture with her fingers towards Blessing's position, then readied herself to race for the switch. But as the old man leaned out to fire, a sustained burst from the door thudded into the crates and drove them both back.

'Shit, this isn't going to work,' she said. 'And we're out of time.'

'I've got this,' Iosef insisted. 'Get ready: one . . . two . . . go!'

He thrust the gun out and sprayed bullets blindly towards the door as Orry flung herself into the open, but she'd hardly started moving before Blessing was returning fire. Rounds cut past her and she quickly jumped back.

'This can't be happening,' Iosef said miserably, looking at over at the switch. 'We're so close!'

She wanted to reassure him, but she honestly couldn't see a way out of this.

'I won't be a trusty after this,' he muttered. 'I'll be right back in the shit with everyone else.'

Orry didn't think he needed to worry about that. If she was right, Blessing wasn't planning to leave any witnesses.

Iosef turned to her, eyes blazing. 'Go and hit that switch.'

'What are you—?'

He gave a furious roar and charged towards the door, firing wildly as he went. Apparently caught out, Blessing managed only a short burst before one of his rounds struck her in the throat. Orry didn't hang around to see any more but raced for the switch and slammed her palm onto it. As the shutter clanked upwards she turned to see that Blessing was on the ground, choking even as she tried to raise her weapon. She managed another brief burst – and Iosef's back burst open. He crumpled to the floor as Blessing's head fell back, the gun slipping from her fingers.

Orry ran to him, but she didn't need to examine him to see that the old man was dead. As she closed his sightless eyes, she heard a wet wheezing from nearby: Blessing was still alive, blood bubbling at her throat. Orry walked over to the dying guard and kicked her gun away before kneeling beside her. Despite her obvious pain, Blessing's eyes looked calm, serene even. She croaked something unintelligible and Orry moved her head closer to catch the words.

'*Pulvis es et in pulverem reverteris.*' Blessing gave a final hacking cough and closed her eyes.

Orry sat back on her haunches, wondering what the words meant, until the roar of an engine in the bay behind her made her turn to see an armoured transport in Arbiter Corps livery was reversing under the rising door. Her heart leaped as the rear doors opened to reveal Ethan and Quondam. Two guards were sitting behind them, gagged and tied to their seats.

Ethan jumped down and ran over to her. He stopped when he saw the bodies. 'What happened? Are you okay?'

She hugged him to her. 'I'm fine, you little toe-rag.'

'Time for reunions later,' Mender yelled, hanging out of the driver's window. 'Whatever you've done to get rid of the guards, I reckon it won't last for ever.'

'He's right,' she said, taking her brother's arm. 'Give me a hand with Roag.'

Ethan pulled back at the sight of the bloodied, semi-conscious woman lying behind the bullet-pocked crates.

'Leave her,' Mender snarled from the vehicle. 'Bitch deserves to bleed out.'

'He's right,' Ethan agreed coldly, staring at Roag with pure loathing. 'If it wasn't for her, Dad would still be alive.'

'We made a deal,' Orry explained.

'And you think she'd save you if things were the other way round?'

Roag groaned.

'I don't care what she would do.' Orry stooped to grab her under the arms.

Ethan watched her struggle with the deadweight for a couple of seconds before swearing and taking Roag's legs. Quon dragged out the guards and left them on the loading dock, making space for them to strap Roag into one of the seats.

Orry glanced back at Iosef, feeling that she should be taking him as well. 'One second,' she said, and hurried back to his body. She found his iridium half-crown in his breast pocket. 'I'm sorry I couldn't get you out,' she whispered, placing her hand on his cheek for a moment. Behind her, Mender gunned the transport's engine. 'I'll look after it,' she promised, pocketing the coin, then hurried back to the others.

The trusty's body disappeared from view as the Skorpion rolled out of the loading bay.

20

RV

The rock walls flashed past on either side of the endless tunnel to the surface.

'What is this thing, anyway?' Orry asked, peering round the vehicle's shabby interior. It had looked a lot newer on the outside. The roar of the engines was deafening in the confines of the tunnel.

'It's called a Skorpion,' Ethan said. 'Do you like the paint job? I did it myself.'

'Mender seems to like driving it,' she observed.

'Fucking thing handles like a brick,' the old man grumbled from the front.

'He loves it,' Ethan told her with a grin.

They burst out of the tunnel into the darkness of night, tore through the gate they'd left open and onto a steeply climbing road. Orry heard her brother on the common integuary channel.

We got her, Jane. *En route to the RV.*

I am inbound now, the ship responded, *estimated arrival fourteen minutes. How are you, Orry?*

Not bad, considering. I'll be happier once we're all back on board.

Me too.

'We got company,' Mender interrupted.

Stand by, Jane. She released her harness so she could stand between Mender and Ethan in the Skorpion's front seats. Headlights dazzled them as they crested a steep rise.

'What is it?' she asked her brother, who had his head buried in the transport's tactical displays.

'It's another Skorpion,' he said. 'They must be coming to assist with the riot. What do we do?'

'We keep going,' Mender said.

'What if they realise we're not a real arbiter unit?' she asked.

'They won't,' Mender assured her.

She squinted against the glare as the lights grew closer, wondering if there was enough room on this narrow road for them to pass. A series of thumps sounded from their nose and a line of dents appeared in the thick windscreen.

'They're shooting!' she yelled, flying into the padded wall as Mender slewed the heavy transport off the road and onto a stony track.

'Thanks for the heads-up,' he growled as the Skorpion jolted along.

'They are now following,' Quondam said, peering out of the slot-like rear windows, then, 'They are firing again.' More thuds came from the back.

'How much punishment can this thing soak up?' Orry wondered.

'I don't intend to find out,' Mender said. 'Hold on!'

A shape loomed out of the darkness ahead, a crumbling ferroconcrete water tower rising high above the road.

'What are you—?' she began.

The Skorpion slammed into the base of the tower, punching through a wall into a tangle of rusting pipes and valves and out of the opposite wall into an open space behind the building.

'Huh,' he grunted as the Skorpion began to pick up speed again. 'Didn't think that was gonna work.'

Behind them the giant tower was beginning to sag, water already leaking from the cracks spreading across the walls. The second Skorpion went to follow them, but no sooner had it turned off the track into the building than the whole structure collapsed, depositing hundreds of tonnes of shattered ferro-concrete and water on top of the vehicle.

'Rama,' Ethan breathed, watching the scene behind them, 'did you know that was going to happen?'

'Hoped,' Mender answered.

The rubble shifted and they stared, astonished, as the other Skorpion slowly emerged, weighed down by the debris piled on its armoured roof . . . It crawled a few metres, and stopped.

'They're going to have splitting headaches,' Ethan observed.

'Never mind their fucking heads,' Mender said. 'Find me a route to the RV.'

Orry was already scanning maps of the island using her

integuary. 'There's a road a kilometre up ahead,' she said. 'Hang a right when we get to it.'

'You got it. Goddamn trees.'

They were weaving their way through the thick woods that carpeted this half of the island now, splintering the smaller saplings along the rough path.

'Coming up now,' she said as they crashed through a low drystone wall and into a narrow lane. The Skorpion's engines roared as Mender put his foot down. They rumbled away, the thick tyres barely clearing the walls on either side of the lane.

'There's a lot of activity on the encrypted arbiter channels,' Ethan reported. 'I've no idea what they're saying, but traffic analysis indicates they're very excited about something.'

How you doing, Jane? Orry asked.

Estimate six minutes to rendezvous, the ship reported. *I can't go any faster; I'm posing as a commercial flight.*

Understood, she sent back. *As long as you get there.* 'Mender, this road's about to join a bigger one. Turn right again and it should lead us straight to the rendezvous.'

'Roger that.'

'Um,' Ethan said anxiously, 'what are those flashing lights?'

At the end of the dark tunnel formed by the trees was a cluster of flashing red and blue lights that soon turned into two ground cruisers blocking the junction onto the larger road ahead. Four arbiters were aiming large-calibre weapons and launchers at them from behind their vehicles.

'Ram them,' Quondam advised from the back.

'No,' Orry said quickly, 'no – we can't go killing arbiters.'

'Piotr's withered balls,' Mender muttered. Hauling on the steering wheel, he sent the vehicle ploughing through the wall to their left and back into the woods again.

'I see gun-drones!' Ethan yelled, craning to look back at the roadblock. Orry, peering out of the side window, could also see three sleek gun-platforms rising from behind the parked cruisers.

Jane, *we're not going to be able to make the primary RV. Is there anywhere else you can land nearby? We're running out of time here.*

I am tracking you. Stand by while I find a suitable location.

The Skorpion shuddered as something struck its roof and exploded.

'Get on the turrets, girl,' Mender yelled, swerving to miss a gnarled old oak. 'Thin those bastards out before we're toast.'

An integuary authorisation from Ethan appeared in her vision and she opened it to hook the Skorpion's gun-control suite. Targeting information flowed directly into her mind, an amalgam of external sensors and lenses that highlighted the gun-drones as they whipped along behind them, weaving in and out of the trees. Selecting the closest, she activated the rear turret and steered the twin lines of tracer towards the bobbing drone – which rolled effortlessly around the bullets and launched a projectile from the long barrel slung beneath its belly. The Skorpion shook under the impact.

Orry gritted her teeth as the visual display broke up for a moment. She fired again, but the Skorpion lurched over a fallen tree and threw her rounds high into the air. She corrected her aim and fired one more time, this time managing to clip the drone, which tumbled away to explode against a tree. Two more immediately took its place.

Dainty Jane came on the common channel. *Suitable landing areas are limited due to the tree coverage in your proximity. I have identified a new rendezvous point on the coast. Transmitting coordinates now.*

Orry half-heard Ethan confirming the coordinates as she focused on the new drones, squirting a few short bursts to see how the machines responded, then bracketed them with two streams of tracer that drove them into each other. There was an explosion and their entangled shells tumbled to the damp forest floor.

'That's all of them!' she yelled.

The trees abruptly vanished.

Switching to the forward turret for a better view, she gasped as the sea filled the horizon ahead, its gentle swell grainy in the light-enhanced lens. The road was already descending steeply, zigzagging down a high cliff-face to a sprawling dock far below. Two large ocean-going vessels were being unloaded by cranes on the wharves; a raptor-like military ekranoplan was moored beside some towering fuel containers. The Skorpion's gun-control system automatically bracketed a dark shape out over the sea and zoomed in on it.

Oh no. 'Fleet gunship coming in,' Orry said, trying to keep her voice steady. 'The arbiters must have called in the big boys.'

The menacing shape was growing larger by the second; now they could all see the weapon pods hanging from pylons on its stubby, downward-sloping wings.

'Can you take it out?' Mender asked.

'I don't think we'd even scratch its paint,' she said, eyeing the heavy craft. She'd seen such flying tanks used by Fleet auxiliaries during the liberation of Odessa.

The gunship swooped in over the dock, side-slipping to keep its aim on them as they rumbled through the switchbacks.

'Why aren't they shooting?' Ethan wondered. 'We're sitting ducks here.'

'They probably have orders to take us alive if possible.'

'You might be right,' Mender agreed. 'Look.'

The gunship banked away and descended rapidly to settle into a hover a metre above the road at the base of the cliff, in front of a pair of wire gates that led onto the wharves.

'They think we'll have to stop at the bottom,' Ethan said.

'Fuck that.' Mender stomped on the accelerator, the Skorpion rounded the final curve on three wheels and raced towards the gunship. It responded with a pair of dazzling red beams from its wing pods, scorching the road on either side of them. Mender, ignoring the warning shots, aimed the heavy transport right at the gunship.

'Mender – they're not going to move!' Ethan yelled, but the old man remained silent, his craggy face rigid with fury as he kept his foot to the floor.

At the last possible second the gunship gave a wobble and

shot upwards. A loud bang sounded from the roof, but they were through, demolishing the flimsy gates and jouncing onto the wharf.

Where are you, Jane? Orry sent, desperately scanning the sky.

That was very reckless, the ship replied, rounding the cliffs at the far end of the dock, her rotating nacelles raising twins vortices of water as she backed up to the wharf, cargo ramp lowering.

Orry scanned the sky for the gunship and found it high up behind them. It dropped its nose and dived, lasers flickering. Her external view of the Skorpion's roof showed clouds of ablative coating vaporising from the armour. Raising the rear turret, she fired a long burst at the pursuing vessel, but the tracers just rebounded harmlessly off its hull to streak away at crazy angles. The gunship fired again, and this time the beams burned right through the armour into the Skorpion's rear compartment.

The acrid smoke filling the rear compartment clawed at her throat. The beams had melted two blackened slots in the roof, followed by matching holes in the floor. Two more beams cut through the smoke for a second, narrowly missing Quondam and the still-unconscious Roag.

In her head she heard Mender yelling at *Jane*: *I'm driving this thing right into the cargo bay and I ain't slowing down!*

Understood, the ship replied calmly, hanging just off the wharf's end, her ramp scraping its surface.

The cargo bay had always felt quite spacious when it was

empty, but now that they were streaking towards it in a massive armoured vehicle, it looked tiny.

'Are you sure we're going to fit in there?' she yelled at Ethan, who was gripping the dash with whitened knuckles.

'We'll fit,' he called back. 'I'm more worried about whether we'll stop!'

The Skorpion's interior lit up in an eerie red as the beams punched through again, and this time there was a sick graunching noise from somewhere under the floor.

'Something's hit,' she shouted, although the sound of tortured metal made that obvious.

'Don't matter,' Mender yelled back, showing no sign of slowing. 'Grab hold of something!'

The Skorpion struck the ramp, bounced up it into the hold and smacked headlong into the far bulkhead with an impact that threw Orry into the back of Mender's seat. She cracked her skull on the seat frame and was momentarily stunned.

Go! the old man sent, and *Dainty Jane* immediately lurched upwards.

Orry dashed blood from her eyes, wondering if she'd reopened the wound Roag had given her – was that really less than an hour ago? When she staggered to the rear windows she could see lasers from the rapidly receding gunship playing harmlessly over *Jane*'s hull, until the cargo ramp came up and the diminishing craft was lost to view.

She sank into a nearby seat and tried not to cry.

21

KIDNAP AND TORTURE

'Then you showed up,' Orry said, concluding the story of her time behind bars, 'and that's it.'

Cordelia Roag, sitting across *Dainty Jane*'s small galley table, had remained silent throughout. She was in restraints, but her wounds had been tended to and dressed. She was still in her bloodstained prison coveralls, and smears of blood were visible on her arms and face. Her brooding presence in the galley was ruining what should have been a joyful reunion.

Mender was looking thoughtful. 'Okay, so my first question is: why did this Blessing woman want you dead so badly?'

'I've been trying to figure that out,' Orry said, 'but whatever the reason, it can't have been official – after all, Zaytsev could have ordered my execution at any time and no one would've questioned it.'

'What exactly did she say?' Ethan asked. 'At the end?'

'It sounded like Latin. Um, *Pulvis es* er . . . something.'

'*Pulvis es et in pulverem reverteris*,' Mender said.

They all turned to stare at him.

'You speak Latin?' Orry asked.

'Used to know a bit,' he admitted. 'Education actually meant something when I was coming up, not like you ignorant bleeders nowadays.'

'What does it mean?' she asked.

'Um, "For you are dust, and to dust you shall return". It's from the Bible. Book of Genesis.'

'He's right,' Ethan said in disbelief, eyes glazing as he looked up the phrase. 'Genesis 3:19. With a name like Blessing, maybe she was a believer? Did she strike you as the religious sort?'

'You know, I'm not really sure,' Orry said acerbically. 'We didn't get a lot of time for theological discussion.'

Her brother raised his hands. 'All right, Miz Sarky, it was just a thought.'

'I am familiar with the phrase,' *Jane* said. 'It is often used by astrotheometrists.'

'Wait, wait . . .' Ethan said, his brow furrowing.

'If you've got something, kid, spill it,' Mender said.

'I can't believe I didn't see the connection before,' her brother continued. 'The monks are as obsessed with Departed tech as the institute is – they're always butting heads over any new sites that turn up, trying to get the best artefacts for themselves.'

'That's just one of those old conspiracy theories that's always doing the rounds,' Orry said dismissively, but *Jane* corrected her.

'Ethan is quite correct. The Order of Astrotheometrists and the Halstaad-Mirnov Institute do indeed have a long history of litigation over Departed sites. There have been accusations of theft and of violence and intimidation on both sides, although nothing has ever been proven.'

'It makes sense,' Ethan insisted. 'That's what the monks are all about. They're looking for proof of intelligent design. They think the Departed knew something we don't, so they grab every bit of tech they can, hoping there'll be some clues somewhere. They really hate the institute because it has so much stuff they could study.'

'Okay,' Orry said, 'but if the monks are so desperate to get their hands on all the goodies at the institute, why would they blow it up?'

His face fell, but Quondam rumbled, 'Destruction of a crime scene may be used to destroy evidence and hinder sub-sequent investigations.'

'Exactly!' Ethan said happily. 'My man, the Kadiran.' He raised his knuckles for a fist bump, but the alien just regarded him with tiny bemused eyes. '*Dude!*' Ethan hissed, 'we've been *through* this . . .'

Ponderously, Quondam raised his own massive fist and touched it to Ethan's.

'*Boom!*' her brother said, miming an explosion with his fingers then sitting back in his chair in triumph.

Orry shook her head, amused despite herself. 'All right, hotshots,' she said, 'so they stole something from the institute and blew it up so no one would ever know. But why did they frame me for it?'

Her brother frowned. 'Well, I don't have *all* the answers,' he answered weakly.

'Why don't you ask one of them?' said Cordelia Roag.

'I was wondering when you were gonna pipe up,' Mender said with a glare.

'*Could* we ask one?' Ethan wondered, deliberately avoiding looking at their prisoner.

'Members of the Order do often travel unaccompanied in search of Departed artefacts,' Quondam said. 'If one could be located, they could be acquired and interrogated.'

'Kidnap and torture,' Mender translated with glee.

'Joking aside,' *Jane* said pointedly, 'for this plan to work I suggest it would have to be a senior member of the Order. Lower ranks would be unlikely to know anything about such a high-profile conspiracy.'

Mender made a sour face and flapped his fingers to indicate incessant talking.

'I can see what you're doing,' the ship informed him patiently.

'*Jane*'s right,' Orry agreed, 'getting hold of a senior monk isn't going to be easy.'

'If I could get into their systems I might be able to do something,' Ethan suggested. 'Locate someone we could ask, or maybe just poke around in there and find out what they're up to.' He paused, looking uncomfortable. 'It would need to be a direct connection, though, which means we'd have to go to Dia Tacita.'

'Sneak onto their home bloody habitat?' Mender snorted. 'Not while I'm still breathing.'

Ethan didn't argue.

'There must be other ways of finding a senior monk,' Orry mused. 'They're in with the Great Houses, schmoozing at balls and whatnot – maybe we could set something up to—'

'For Rama's sake, *stop*,' Roag interrupted. 'It's painful listening to you morons wittering on.'

Orry narrowed her eyes. 'You have something to contribute?'

'It just so happens that I know precisely the person you need to talk to. Let me go – *like we agreed* – and I'll tell you where he is.'

'*Precisely* the person we need to talk to, eh?' Mender responded with exaggerated sarcasm. 'Well, ain't that lucky for us! And all we have to do is let you go.' His face resumed its habitual scowl and he concluded with a muttered, 'Piotr's puckered ring-piece we will . . .'

Roag regarded him with an expression of amused condescension.

'Who is this person?' Orry asked warily.

'Just someone on my payroll. He used to be in the Order.'

'That's bullshit for a start,' Mender snarled. 'Everybody knows there ain't no ex-monks. Once you're in there's only one way out – feet first. They make damn sure of that.'

'Well, forgive me for disagreeing with the *all-knowing* Captain Mender, expert in everything in the galaxy, but this guy – *my* guy – was an archmandrite. You know what that is?'

If her tone had been any more cutting Roag could have used it to sever her restraints herself.

'There are only twelve archmandrites in the Order,' *Jane* answered instantly. 'Whenever a vacancy appears, one of them is promoted from the First Circle of Arkady to the Serene Council. The only further promotion possible from the council would be to the rank of archcantor itself.'

'Thank you, Miz Prissy Mindship,' Roag said. She paused, then sighed. 'Look, back in the day, my guy was a total fanatic, just like all the other monks. He had a nice home on Dia Tacita, lovely family, all the perks. Then one day his daughter, the very apple of his eye, collapsed in the kitchen. Turns out she had Cleaver syndrome. It's a shitty condition, but easily treatable by a course of simple gene-therapy. Except . . .'

'Except they were on Dia Tacita,' Orry supplied, caught up in Roag's story despite her scepticism.

The other woman beamed. 'A prize to the self-righteous bitch in the front row! The Order don't like gene-therapy, do they? Not one little bit.' She adopted a solemn tone. '*Human hand must not corrupt what God has created.* So, what is my guy to do? Watch his little precious wither away, or renounce all his beliefs? Quite the dilemma.'

'He ran?' Ethan asked.

'Oh no,' Roag said airily, 'he watched her die.'

'Rama, what a shitbag.'

'You'll get no argument from me on that score. Thing is, turns out it's actually pretty tough to let your kid die and then carry on as if nothing's happened. He struggled on for a bit, then one day comes home to find his wife in the bathtub with both wrists slit to the elbow. That was kind of the last straw for him. If he was cracked before, he lost it after that. He was scheduled to go offworld a couple of days later to visit some mission or other. Mad as he was, he wasn't stupid. He got rid of his wife's corpse in a garbage incinerator, cleaned up the house and altered her records to show she'd gone on long-term retreat to deal with the death of her only child. Then he faked a shuttle accident and ran. When I found him he was a mess – booze, ket-c, fangwater: you name it, he was hooked on it. I doubt he'd have made it another week if I hadn't stepped in.'

'Why *did* you step in?' Orry asked. 'I assume it wasn't out of the kindness of your heart.'

Roag gave a shrug. 'Business is business. Like the old man said, ex-monks are rare as a kettlehead's teeth, so as soon as I heard his story I was interested. I figured the monks truly believed he was dead or they would've sent a catch-squad to bring him back. *That* meant he might still have access to their systems. I was hoping he'd be able to get me information I could use to my advantage – new discoveries and so on, the sort of thing I could sell on to the institute or use as leverage. As it turned out, he was fucking useless. He could get into their systems all right, but he was too out of his face to turn up anything I could monetise. I was considering cutting him loose when more important matters started demanding my attention.'

'Like betraying humanity to the Kadiran.' Mender glanced at Quondam.

'Who's to say the kucks wouldn't do a better job than the Ruuz,' Roag said.

Mender opened his mouth to object, but Orry cut him off. 'Where's this monk of yours now?' she asked.

The older woman's thin lips twisted with annoyance. 'Now *that* might pose a problem. Thanks to *somebody* fucking up my plans I've been too busy rotting in a cell to keep a tight hand on the reins. Some treacherous motherfucker will no doubt have decided to take advantage of the situation. I'll have to put out some feelers, see what's what.'

'You mean you don't know where he is, or even if he's still alive,' Mender said.

'I know where he *was*,' Roag said reasonably, but Orry had seen her knuckles whiten at Mender's mocking tone. 'I just need to make some calls.'

'No,' she said firmly, and Mender nodded in agreement. Roag was a smart and resourceful woman – who knew what trouble she could stir up once she was back in contact with her crew? 'You'll tell us where he was and we'll go and check things out in person,' she suggested.

A hint of a smile quirked Roag's mouth. 'And then you'll let me go?'

'And then I'll think about it.'

The older woman leaned back in her chair. 'Not good enough. Don't forget, Aurelia, if it hadn't been for me, Blessing would have killed you by now.'

'And if it weren't for us, you'd still be in the Hollow,' Mender said.

Orry studied the face of the woman responsible for the murder of her father: the woman she despised more than anyone else in the known worlds. The hell of it was that she was right: Roag *knew* people, and she also knew just which buttons to push.

I do owe her, she admitted to herself. Sometimes she wished she was more like Mender; life must be so much simpler when you didn't give a shit about anything.

'If you help us find your man,' she said, 'and *if* he gets us the information we need, then . . . we will let you go.'

'*What?*' Ethan objected. 'You can't be serious!'

'We need her help,' Orry said calmly.

'But we don't even know if she's telling the truth! Every other word that comes out of that woman's mouth is bullshit.'

Roag, smiling broadly now, blew Ethan a kiss. He flushed with anger but kept his mouth shut.

Orry leaned over the table until she was an inch from Roag's nose. 'You'd better hope we find this ex-monk of yours and that he gets us what we need. If I even *think* you're pulling a fast one, I'll let Quondam loose on you.'

The threatening rumble sounding from deep within the Kadiran's massive chest made Roag's cocky smile slip a little.

Orry sat back. 'Now,' she said, 'where are we supposed to be going?'

22

SUNDOWNER RING

'Sundowner Approach, merchant *Fair Rosamund*. Request vectors.'

While Mender handled the comms and Orry gazed at the distant, rotating torus of Sundowner Ring, *Jane* was broadcasting one of her many false idents.

'*Fair Rosamund*, Sundowner Approach, pass your message.'

'*Fair Rosamund* is inbound from Manes, estimating sector perimeter 18, Sundowner 31, information Theta.'

'*Fair Rosamund*, cleared from the perimeter to Sundowner Hub. Traffic is a Turbohaul tanker on approach to downside dock and a Nebula departing spinward.'

'Roger, cleared from the zone boundary to Sundowner Hub, traffic in sight.'

'*Fair Rosamund*, report passing inner boundary.'

'Wilco, *Fair Rosamund*.'

She watched the slender ring of the station grow larger in the cockpit canopy. A vast array of mirrors hung in space beside the habitat, reflecting sunlight through the transparent inner surface of the slowly rotating ring, through which she could see rather less greenery than she was expecting. Sundowner was an older design, a wheel linked by eight spokes to a central hub. A variety of ships were docked around the hub, the only part of the station not rotating.

As Mender flew them in, she peered with interest at the interior of the outer ring as they passed. A wide strip of water running down its centre was edged with alternating sandy beaches and rocky shores and spanned at regular intervals by slender bridges. The water was there for stability, but the mental benefits it provided from the leisure facilities were just as important. Buildings were scattered across open areas of greenery on both sides of the water, while more structures were stacked like building blocks up the curving walls of the tubular ring. But zooming in with her integuary, she saw that much of the green belt was covered in emergency tents and makeshift shacks – thousands of them, apparently built from all manner of detritus.

'What's with all the shanty towns, *Jane*?' Orry asked.

'They are refugees,' the ship answered. 'During the war, the Kadiran occupied several colonies in this volume of space and caused significant damage to infrastructure. All the local habitats are under significant strain coping with the additional population until they are able to return to their homes.'

'How many people are we talking about?'

'Sundowner Station was designed for a stable population

of half a million. The current population is estimated to be closer to a million.'

'Can its environmental systems handle that many extra bodies?'

'Not long-term. Additional resources are being shipped in, but they are not sufficient. Crime has become a problem, as you would expect. Please be careful in there.'

They left the outer ring behind them and coasted between two of the slowly revolving spokes as they approached the docking facilities of the hub. Orry could see the lights of capsules travelling up and down the spokes, moving between the hub and the ring.

'*Fair Rosamund*, you are cleared for bay nineteen. Sending approach package now.'

A light illuminated on the instrument panel at the same time as the approach vectors appeared in Orry's integuary.

'Package received, starting final approach, *Fair Rosamund*,' Mender reported.

The ships they passed were too large to fit into the habitat's internal bays: massive freighters and ice-haulers for the most part. A stream of transports shuttled cargo from their holds to the hub. *Dainty Jane* glided into the hub's interior and over to one of the dozens of variously sized docking bays that lined its walls. Doors slid closed behind them so the bay could slowly pressurise around them. As Mender set the ship down, Orry climbed stiffly from her acceleration shell and made for the galley.

*

'We're here,' Orry told Roag, who was still secured to the table. 'Where is he?'

'I'll take you.'

'An address will be fine, thanks.'

She chuckled. Her permanent, condescending smile was making Orry want to hit her with something heavy. *Very* heavy.

'Did you know Sundowner Ring used to have the highest murder rate of any S-Class habitat?' Roag enquired mildly. 'Not wanting to blow my own trumpet, but once I took over here it became a model of efficiency. Violence has its place in what I do, but uncontrolled violence is bad for business. Unfortunately for you, I've heard that since you had me locked up things have taken something of a downturn around here. Having half a million refugees descend on the place won't have helped much either.'

'We can handle ourselves.'

'Look, I don't know exactly what's been happening here. Fidelius might still be here, he might not. Fucker could be dead for all I know. And if he is still here, he'll be guarded. Now, I know Mender enjoys a good firefight, but that's how people get hurt. Wouldn't it be easier to bring me along and avoid all that unpleasantness?'

Orry gritted her teeth, knowing she was right but reluctant to admit it. 'Fidelius,' she said instead. 'Is that his name?'

'That's his name.'

'All right, fine,' she snapped. 'Quon, come with us and keep an eye on her. If she tries anything, pull her arms off or something.'

'No, no, no,' Roag said wearily, 'you're not *thinking*, Aurelia. Do you really want to take a Kadiran onto a hab full of refugees when his lot are the whole reason they're here?'

'She's right,' Mender said, stepping off the ladder from the cockpit.

'I know she's right,' she said irritably, and took a deep breath. 'All right. Sorry, Quon, you'll have to stay here.'

'And *I* will be watching you.' The old man removed Roag's restraints and stepped back, his hand patting the butt of his Fabretti.

Roag rubbed her wrists with evident relief. 'Spoke B,' she said. 'Once we get to the ring, it's not far from the station.'

Orry looked at her bloodstained prison coveralls, then threw her a long coat. 'Put that on – it'll make you less conspicuous,' she said. 'Let's go.'

The hub's central concourse, a fat cylinder twenty storeys high, was dotted with airlock doors leading to various internal landing bays. There was no up and down here: knots of people floated in any orientation, holding onto the cables strung across the hub as they chatted and dined out on a wide variety of cuisines from the dozens of fast food windows set into the hub's core. Loading bots laden with cargo zoomed around with orange lights flashing and a variety of hoots and squeals to warn of their approach.

As they rode a capsule out from the hub, gravity slowly increased from zero-g in the concourse to almost 1-g at the ring. The hollow spoke down which they travelled pierced the transparent upper curve of Sundowner Station's outer ring and descended through its interior to a transit station set in the wide strip of green belt that ran like a ribbon through the ring.

They emerged blinking into bright sunshine reflected from the nearby mirror array to find themselves in a refugee camp of tents and makeshift shelters covering what had once been recreational parkland. Mud-spattered children ran through the churned-up 'streets' between the dwellings, watched by adults with dead eyes.

Roag looked as shocked as the rest of them.

'Changed a bit since you were last here?' Mender enquired. 'This is what your fucking war really looks like.'

She took in the squalid camp. 'It used to be nice around here,' she said sadly, then shrugged. 'This way, kids.'

Mender's hand drifted to the butt of his holstered Fabretti. *'Please?'* he begged Orry, an expression of pure loathing on his face as Roag walked away.

'We need her,' she repeated, not entirely sure how serious he was.

He grimaced and gestured to Ethan. Without another word, the three of them set off after Roag, who was now skirting a crowd gathered around a muddy white vehicle. When they got closer, they could see aid workers were trying to distribute food parcels under the protection of two armed guards, who were beginning to look nervous as the crowd got rowdier. A scuffle broke out near the front, where two women were fighting over one of the packages. The guards moved to intervene, pulling the women apart and tossing the food parcel back onto the distribution truck. When one of the women spat on a guard's visor, he backhanded her across the face, knocking her to ground, which sent a wave of anger rumbling through the crowd. People surged forward, shouting, forcing the guards to back away, until one of them pointed his weapon into the air and fired a short burst. There were screams of alarm and people shrank back enough that the guards could clamber back to their positions on top of the truck.

Roag turned back, gesturing at them to hurry up. 'Come on,' she said, ignoring the disgruntled crowd, 'it's not much further.'

Orry could see a wall up ahead, prettily made, but too high to be purely decorative. The tent city extended right up to the wall, with lean-tos erected against it. Smoke curled into the air from dozens of camping stoves and cooking fires.

They stepped onto a proper road now, leading to a pair of heavy wooden gates set into the wall. Orry and Ethan stopped to stamp their feet, trying to dislodge some of the claggy mud from their boots, while Roag pressed her thumb to the scanner lock beside the door. The gates swung smoothly open to reveal well-kept lawns surrounding a large modern house. Orry was a little surprised that the camp didn't continue beyond the wall – and when she glanced around, she saw many of the shanty town's inhabitants were just as amazed, judging by the way they were staring through the open gates. One man wrapped in a filthy blanket dropped his gaze the moment he caught her eye, then turned and hurried off, quickly disappearing between the tents.

'We should get inside,' Ethan suggested, as several of the refugees started moving towards them.

'Good idea,' Roag agreed, and ushered them through the gates, which were already beginning to swing shut after them. The refugees broke into a run, desperation on their faces, but the gates closed and locked in front of them.

'Your place, I'm guessing?' Mender asked Roag.

'Just a little home from home.' She set off down the driveway to the house.

Several hortibots were working silently in the gardens and Orry watched one of them as it tended some flowerbeds at the base of the outer wall. She wondered what it was doing with a mound of old clothes piled there – until she realised what it was and stopped walking.

'There's a body over there,' she said out loud, pointing, and only then noticed there were several more, all lying at the bottom of the wall.

'I guess that explains why there aren't any tents on your precious lawn,' Mender observed.

'Well, you can't just let anyone drop in, can you?' Roag said lightly, stepping onto the front porch.

'Oh, Rama,' Ethan said, gagging. He covered his mouth and nose with a hand and turned away.

At his words, Orry hurried over – and stared in horror at three more corpses piled by the front door. These appeared to have been dismembered by energy beams; huge flies buzzed and crawled around what was nothing more than rotting lumps of charred meat with shreds of scorched cloth clinging to the remains.

Roag appeared to be more interested in these bodies than those by the wall. Crouching by one of the bodies, she peeled back a square of fabric and examined it. The cloth bore a camouflage pattern of some sort, with a tin badge with a yellow smiley face still pinned to it.

'Someone you know?' Mender asked.

'Yes,' Roag said thoughtfully, then tossed the fabric and badge aside and stood up. She opened the front door with her thumb and glanced back at them.

'In we go, then,' she said. 'It's upstairs.'

23

TRINKET

The interior of the house was light and airy, with varnished wooden steps to a glass-fronted landing on the second floor. Roag led them into a spacious bedroom where a huge window looked out over the endless sea of tents. She headed straight for a closed door in one wall.

'Stop,' Mender snapped.

She stopped. 'What exactly do you think is in there?' she asked.

'I have no idea,' he grunted. 'That's what I'm worried about.'

'Relax, it's just a wardrobe. I'm sick of this goddamn paper suit, okay? It stinks of the Hollow and I just want a change of clothes.'

'You expect me to believe that?'

'Believe what you want.'

'Oh, I will. Kid, open the door.'

Ethan, examining the dressing table, spun round. 'Me?' he asked in surprise.

'Yeah, you. We don't have all day.'

Ethan approached the door like a mouse approaching a trap. 'I think you should get her to open it,' he suggested, pointing at Roag, who was looking amused by his obvious discomfort.

'And what if it's an armoury in there?' Mender growled. 'Just open the damn door.'

'There aren't any traps,' Roag said helpfully.

Ethan stared at her. 'Why would you say that?' he asked, and turned to Mender. 'Why would she say that?'

'Because there aren't any traps,' she said.

'Rama, I'll open it,' Orry snapped, pushing past her brother. Setting aside a moment's doubt, she gripped the handle and turned it.

'It's a walk-in wardrobe,' she confirmed, staring at the racks of designer clothing lining the side walls. At the end was a long mirror with drawers on either side.

'Search it,' Mender told her.

'*You* search it.'

'Look, I just want a change of clothes,' Roag said reasonably. 'You can watch me if you like.'

'Where's your monk?' Orry demanded, tired of her games. 'Is he even here?'

'He's on Sundowner,' Roag said vaguely.

'But not here – not in this house.'

'No.' She held up her hands. 'Look, you got me. I took a little detour, just to get out of these stinking rags. You blame me?'

'Tough shit,' Mender growled. He gestured towards the exit with the Fabretti. 'Move, and no more bullshit.'

'Oh, come on,' Roag said, her composure shaken for the first time. 'We're here now – I only need five minutes.'

'Forget it,' he said firmly.

She gripped the neck of her coverall with both hands and tugged. The thick paper resisted for a moment, then ripped in a long tear across her chest that exposed one of her breasts. She made no move to hide it.

'What the hell are you doing?' Mender snarled.

Beside him, Ethan's mouth was hanging open, his eyes wide. He reddened and quickly looked away.

'The boy doesn't seem to be complaining,' Roag said with a smile. 'You want me to tear the whole thing off?'

'All right, you win,' Orry broke in, feeling some sympathy for Roag. It had felt *so* good to change out of her filthy coverall and into the familiar comfort of her flight suit. In any case, their prisoner would draw less attention in her own clothes.

Roag winked at Mender and walked into the wardrobe. Orry was about to follow when he pulled her aside. '*I'll* watch her,' he said.

'Keen to see more?' Roag said from inside the room.

His face creased with disgust. 'Just get on with it,' he said, taking up position in the doorway, looking in, 'and don't take all fucking day.'

*

205

As they waited, Ethan wandered around the bedroom, examining the items on display. He stopped at a sculpted metal mask and reached out to pick it up.

'I wouldn't touch anything if I were you,' Orry advised, and his hand stopped an inch from the mask.

'You think it's booby-trapped?'

'If you want to find out, go ahead.' She pointed out of the room and down the stairs to the front door, reminding him of the mangled human remains on the other side of it.

Ethan swallowed and withdrew his hand.

'About damn time,' Mender growled, stepping aside to let Roag back into the bedroom.

She was wearing drab paramilitary gear: baggy combat trousers in an urban grey camo scheme, an olive-green T-shirt, a hard-wearing grey jacket with many pockets, and heavy black boots. The look went well with her shaven head.

'Check her pockets,' Mender told Ethan.

'What, all of them?'

The old man glared at him, and he quickly went through every pocket.

'All empty,' he declared.

'Although I do have a grenade up my arse,' Roag informed them. She moved to a mirror on one wall, touched its frame and the glass slid aside to reveal a safe.

Mender was across the room in two strides. Pressing the Fabretti into the back of her skull, he asked, 'How many times are we going to have to go through this?'

'These clothes are just so *boring*,' Roag said without moving. 'I need to accessorise.'

'*Accessorise?*' he growled in disbelief. 'Get the fuck out of here – and the next place we stop had better have a monk in it.' He backed off a few steps as she held out her arms and turned slowly to face him.

'Okay, I'll be straight with you,' she said. 'I didn't bring you here for a change of clothes, though I can't deny it feels pretty damn good to get out of that stinking paper shit.'

'Then why are we here?' Ethan asked.

'You know me, Mender,' she said. 'I'm not the most sentimental girl in the world.' He grunted in agreement and she continued, 'I doubt I'll ever see any of this stuff again, and that doesn't bother me, except for one thing in that safe.'

'What thing?' Orry asked, curious about what could make Cordelia Roag sentimental.

'It's just a trinket,' she said dismissively, 'something I've had for a long time.' Her face twisted into a grimace as Orry waited expectantly for more. 'Can't we just leave it at that?'

'Not if you want to open that safe.'

Roag worked her jaw. 'Look, it's just a piece of plastic shit. Something my mother gave me before she died.' She glared at Orry. 'I don't want to lose it, okay?'

'Open it,' Orry told her.

Roag pressed her thumb to a scanner, then picked out a code on a manual keypad. The safe door opened and Mender shifted to a position where he could see its contents. She reached in and brought out a chunky child's bracelet made up of large plastic beads, once brightly coloured but sun-faded now. In between some of the beads were plastic cubes, each inscribed with a letter, which together spelled out CORA. It looked like some of the beads had been lost over the years.

'That's the saddest fucking thing I've ever seen,' Mender said.

A look of fury appeared on Roag's face and her whole body tensed as if she were about to launch herself at him.

'Shut up, Mender,' Orry snapped. Despite everything Roag had done, the grubby old bracelet made her feel desperately sorry for her. 'You can keep it,' she said. 'Now will you please take us to see this monk?'

Roag gazed at Orry for a second or two, an odd expression on her face. 'Thank you,' she said eventually, as if she had trouble getting the words out. She slipped the bracelet over her wrist and walked to the door, where she paused.

'Well? You coming or what?'

When they opened the gates, they found three men and two women spread in a line across the road, blocking it. They were wearing what Ethan liked to call space-pirate chic, sporting an interesting variety of deadly looking guns and blades.

The man in the centre of the line was slightly built and clean-shaven, his black hair tied into a topknot. He eyed Roag warily. 'Cordelia,' he greeted her. 'Heard you were back.'

'Renshu,' she acknowledged.

'It's good to see you again.'

She laughed. 'You always were a bad liar. What do you want?'

'Well now. Things have changed since you've been away. The organisation fell apart. They follow me now.' He managed to meet Roag's answering gaze, but Orry could tell that he was not as confident as he was pretending. 'I know what you have under there' – he gestured behind her to the house – 'weapons, gilt, leverage. Tell me how to access it and you can go free. Just don't ever come back to Sundowner.'

'And if I refuse your generous offer?'

Renshu indicated his companions with a sweep of his arm. They were looking nervous. Their guns were not actually pointing at Roag, but safeties were off and they were ready to raise and fire in an instant. 'There are five of us, Cordelia. How many guns do you have?' His eyes drifted to Mender's holstered Fabretti. 'Just the one?'

'You make a compelling point,' she admitted, and appeared to consider for a moment. 'Very well. It appears I don't have much of a choice.'

'You can't bel—' Ethan began, but Mender silenced him with a savage slash of his hand.

Renshu relaxed, looking hugely relieved. 'I always said you were a reasonable woman, Cordelia,' he said.

'Very reasonable,' she agreed. 'Come here, then.'

He frowned. 'What?'

She looked confused. 'You want me to shout this out in the street? Well, okay. The vault is—'

'No!' Renshu said quickly.

'So you *do* want me to whisper it in your ear? Well, you'd better come here then.'

He hesitated, clearly unwilling to move any closer to her than he already was.

'You're not *scared* of me, are you, Renshu?' she asked in a mocking tone. 'You with all those guns, and me standing here unarmed?' She held her arms out from her sides and rotated slowly to show him she spoke the truth.

Renshu glanced at the others and Orry wondered what would win out – his obvious fear of his former boss, or the threat of losing face in front of his crew. In the end, he walked towards Roag. If he wanted to step into her shoes, he couldn't be seen to be afraid of her.

Big mistake, she thought, waiting with a strange sick thrill to see what Roag would do next. When the shooting started, she would grab Ethan and try to get back behind the compound wall, though she didn't like their chances much.

Renshu stopped a metre from Roag.

She beckoned him closer.

Visibly clenching his jaw, he stepped right up to her.

'That's better,' she said with a bright smile, and punched him hard in the windpipe.

He choked, clawing at his throat, and she pulled him close.

'You always were a stupid bastard,' she hissed, before kicking out one of his knees and shoving him over backwards, falling with him so she landed straddling his chest. Gripping the sides of his head, she beat it repeatedly into the road surface until his eyes were glazed and dark blood was spreading in a pool around his shattered skull.

Renshu's crew watched wide-eyed, apparently paralysed by the display of sudden, extreme violence. Roag released the limp body and leaned back, wiping a bloody hand across her face as she stared them down. All of them looked away except for one woman, whose face twisted with sudden rage. She raised her carbine with a wordless roar – but Mender snatched his Fabretti from its holster and fired in one smooth movement.

The woman exploded into bloody rags before her gun was even level. Her head thumped to the ground and rolled to halt a metre away.

'Anyone else want to try that?' Roag asked, blood smearing her face like war paint. She rose and walked to the head, which she picked up by the hair. 'Now fuck off,' she said to the others, 'and I'll let you live.'

They glanced at each other, then turned and fled.

Roag examined the head for a moment, then tossed it contemptuously into the gutter. 'Right,' she said brightly, 'shall we get on?'

24

FIDELIUS

The camp stopped where the green belt gave way to an industrial zone. The warehouses and offices transitioned into basic residential units as they approached the upward curve of the ring's outer wall and Roag halted at a tall residential stack climbing the curve. The uppermost apartments above the point where the walls became transparent looked like they had an impressive view out into space. Steps led up both sides of the stack, which resembled a tower of boxes, each set back a little from the one below. In front of each apartment were balconies with views over the ring's interior, most of which were cluttered with junk.

Orry followed Roag up the steps, feeling lighter the higher she went. The station's spin-induced gravity might be a full 1-g on the floor of the outer ring, but it was reducing noticeably as they climbed its curving sides. Roag stepped onto one of the balconies, glowering at the litter of empty bottles, discarded food cartons and other less identifiable garbage. As she strode to the door there was a flurry of activity beneath the rubbish and a small black shape disappeared through the balcony's railings.

Rats, Orry thought with a grimace. *Lovely.*

'Get ready,' Roag said to Mender, who released his Fabretti in its holster. She knocked sharply on the door.

After a long delay it was answered by a twitchy-looking man holding a handgun. When he recognised Roag the colour drained from his face. After a very brief hesitation, he lowered the weapon.

'Boss,' he said, with a nervous glance behind him into the apartment's darkened interior. 'It's good to see you. We . . . um . . . we heard you was outta the picture.'

Roag stared at him until the sweat stood out on his forehead. 'Is he here?' she asked eventually.

'Uh, sure, but . . .' He raised a hand as if to wipe his brow then appeared to think better of it. 'Listen, Boss, things have been crazy round here since—'

Roag pushed him aside and entered the apartment, Mender following, smiling nastily at the man as he passed. Orry and Ethan exchanged a glance before bringing up the rear, both raising a hand to their noses as they entered. The stench of corruption and unwashed bodies was overwhelming.

As her eyes adjusted to the gloom, Orry saw that she was in a spacious room running the full width of the apartment, with several doors opening off the rear wall. It was as filthy as the balcony. A second man dropped the bottle he was holding and rose hurriedly from a threadbare sofa, his bleary eyes filling quickly with fear as he saw them. A third man was tied to a cheap office chair, his head resting on a table illuminated by the soft glow of multiple screens. He made no move when they entered and Orry wondered if he was dead.

Roag immediately crossed to him and lifted his head. Orry's stomach turned over at the sight of the emaciated face, the flaking skin, crimson blotches and open sores and the cracked lips. His lank hair looked like it hadn't been washed in months.

Roag let his head fall and turned to the man who'd answered the door, her face a mask of cold fury. 'You were supposed to be looking after him,' she said quietly.

'I . . . we—'

'The guy was a fuckin' prick,' the man by the sofa offered. 'He was off his face most of the time – treated us like friggin' hired help.'

'So when you heard I was out of the picture, you thought you'd get your own back?' Roag asked. 'Use his supply yourselves, get handy with your fists, try to make some money off him?'

'He's useless,' Sofa protested. 'Couldn't find fuck-all with that rig.' He indicated the sophisticated equipment on the table.

Roag looked around the room. 'Has anyone else been in here?' she asked. 'Has he talked to anybody?'

'No one.'

'You're telling me it's just been the three of you, since I went inside?'

'That's right, Boss. Just like you said.'

'Your own little gold mine, eh?' She indicated the drugs on the table, then regarded both of them for a moment. 'Come here.'

The two men exchanged a nervous glance before reluctantly approaching her.

Roag leaned in close, obscured by their bodies. 'I only ask one thing of my people: *loyalty*.'

She moved fast, and before Mender could react, the pistol one of the men had been holding was in Roag's hand and pointed at its owner's forehead.

'*Boss—!*' was all he got out before the back of his skull opened like a flower and his brains splashed the wall behind his falling body. Sofa turned to flee and Roag calmly shot him in the temple.

'Put it *down!*' Mender roared, levelling his Fabretti at Roag, whose pistol had ended up pointing at him.

Orry was stunned. Less than two seconds from beginning to end and now they were in a stand-off? She cursed herself for *ever* listening to Cordelia Roag. Ethan was watching in horror from the table.

'This is nothing to do with you, Jurgen,' Roag said. 'It's strictly business. Don't tell me those two didn't have it coming.'

'But . . . but you just murdered them in cold blood,' Orry broke, revulsion overcoming her shock. 'They hadn't *done* anything—'

'Like I said, strictly business.'

'I don't give a shit about those two arseholes,' Mender said calmly. 'What I am concerned about? That gun you're holding.'

Roag shifted her grip on it a little. 'Oh yes? And what are you going to do about it?'

'Don't test me, Cordelia. We had a deal: you get us what we want, and we let you go. Now put it down.'

'I don't think so.' Her gun moved to point at Orry's chest. 'You may not care what happens to yourself, Mender, but you sure as shit care about the girl.'

His face was growing red. 'You pull that trigger and it'll be the last thing you ever do,' he snarled.

'Yadda, yadda, yadda,' Roag said, apparently unconcerned by the Fabretti's cavernous muzzle a metre from her face.

Mender gritted his teeth. 'What do you want?'

'I want to walk out of here and I'm taking the girl with me, just to make sure you don't get any ill-advised notions about following me.'

'Not happening,' he said firmly.

'Once I'm somewhere safe, I'll let her go.'

He barked out a laugh. 'Try again.'

Irritation crossed Roag's face and she shifted her aim to Orry's head. 'You know me, Mender. I don't bluff.'

The old man did a poor job of hiding his inner struggle. Eventually he came to a decision. 'Nope,' he informed her.

Her face stiffened with anger. 'Then say goodbye to your – whatever the hell she is to you.' A cruel smile twisted her mouth. 'It's almost worth dying to do this . . .'

'He's alive!' Ethan said desperately. 'Look . . .'

The man slumped at the screens groaned and sat upright, his hands going to his head. 'Water,' he croaked, 'for Rama's sake.' He peered blearily around the room and his eyes roved over the dead men to settle on Roag. 'They said you were dead.'

When she slowly lowered her pistol, Orry felt like collapsing with relief.

'Well, clearly I'm not,' Roag said.

'Pity.' Fidelius turned away and massaged his temples.

Mender pressed the Fabretti to Roag's cheek and reached for her gun. She let him take it without further protest and picked up the bottle of water Sofa had been holding. She handed it to Fidelius.

'Time to earn your keep,' she said as he drank greedily.

He finished the bottle and tossed it away, then looked up at her with the desperate eyes of an addict. 'I need something first,' he told her. 'They kept most of it for themselves. I *need* something . . .'

'After,' Roag told him.

His face twisted with sudden fury. 'Now!'

She slapped him and he started weeping like a child.

Mender turned away in disgust.

'I'm sorry,' Fidelius whined, 'I just need a little hit, just a bit, so I can concentrate.'

'Did those two sacks of shit keep you working?' Roag asked.

'Yes.' He glared at the dead men. 'I didn't tell them what

I found though – none of it.' He gave her a meaningful look. 'Not even—'

Roag slapped him again, snapping his head to one side.

'Hey!' Orry protested. 'Is that really necessary?'

'Totally necessary,' Roag said, without taking her eyes off Fidelius. 'Now,' she continued, addressing him, 'have you found anything about the destruction of the Halstaad-Mirnov Institute?'

A sly look crossed his face. 'Maybe. I forget . . . things get muddled without the—'

Roag gripped his jaw and thrust her face into his. '*Did you,*' she hissed, '*or did you not?*'

'I did, I did!'

She released him and he shrank away from her. 'What did you find? Anything about her?' She pointed at Orry, who was still feeling sickened.

His eyes took a moment to focus on her, then he shook his head, clearly confused.

'Then what did you find out?' Orry asked gently, beginning to think this whole excursion had been a waste of time. 'Was the Order behind the explosion at the institute?'

'Oh yes.'

That was something at least, although she had her doubts about believing information from a junkie. 'Why did they do it?' she asked.

'To get the professor.'

'The professor? Professor Rasmussen? But he was killed . . .'
I watched myself kill him . . .

'Not dead,' Fidelius explained with a sly smile, 'taken.'

'Taken? Taken where?'

He slumped, looking bone-weary. 'He's in a town called Hudson's Leap, on Serapis.'

Serapis? The name wasn't familiar. She looked at Mender.

'It's a colony out near the Bight,' he told her. 'Terraforming's been running way behind schedule for a century or more, that's all I know.'

'What's he doing there?' Roag asked.

Fidelius glanced hungrily at the drugs paraphernalia on the coffee table. 'The Order hired some contractors to acquire him and make it look like he died so no one would come searching, but the crew got greedy – they hid him out on Serapis and demanded more gilt before they'd hand him over.' He shook his head sadly. 'Stupid, stupid people.'

'The monks know where he is?' Mender asked.

'If they didn't, I wouldn't,' Fidelius said, indicating the rig on the table.

'So they're going to Serapis to deal with it?'

'Of course.'

'When? How old is this information?'

'Last traffic was from two days ago. Nothing about *how* they're going after him though.'

'But they will,' Roag said, and Mender nodded in grim agreement.

It took a minute before Orry realised that Mender and Ethan were looking at her.

'What?' she asked, vaguely irritated.

'*Duh,*' Ethan said. 'So are we going to Serapis?'

'It's your call, girl,' Mender added.

Just for once it would be nice if someone else made the decisions. But this was an easy one: Professor Rasmussen was the only lead they had.

'Yes, we're going,' she said, 'and these two are coming with us.'

'That wasn't the deal,' Roag protested.

'Tough,' Orry snapped. 'Move it.' She expected Roag to object further but, oddly, she didn't.

Orry watched Ethan help the ex-monk to his feet, knowing full well what would come next – and sure enough, Fidelius pushed her brother aside and bolted for the coffee table. She lunged forward and tackled him, bringing him down onto the sticky carpet where she straddled him. His blows were pathetically feeble.

'Stop it!' she shouted. 'You're coming with us, and we're going to get you some help, okay?'

'Don't bother,' Roag snorted.

Orry ignored her. 'Behave yourself until we get back to our ship and we'll get you something to help. Understand?'

'Ket?' he asked hopefully.

'No.' She wasn't going to lie to him. 'Something that will stop you needing the ket.'

His frenzied eyes went to the nearby table. 'Sure, sure, but one last hit – just to get me to the ship. Then I'll take whatever you want. I swear it.'

'Absolutely not.'

He opened his mouth and roared, bucking beneath her, trying to twist round and reach the drugs on the table.

'Best give him what he wants,' Roag advised. 'There's no way you'll get him back to the ship in this state.' She paused for a moment. 'Or you can just leave him here with me. I'll look after him.'

Orry gritted her teeth. There was no way she was returning Fidelius to Roag's tender mercies.

'Guy's fucked up as it is,' Mender commented. 'One more hit ain't gonna make any difference.'

She cursed, unable to see any other way. 'Fine,' she said, untangling herself from the addict, who immediately scrambled to the table with a whoop of joy.

He measured out a dose of the tar-like ket-c and then hesitated, looking nervously at Roag as if expecting her to stop him. When she remained silent, arms folded, he began expertly heating the drug to fluidity before drawing the resulting dirty brown liquid into a pneumo-syringe. Tapping its glass cartridge, he eyed the contents hungrily and then, with a final, almost grateful glance at Roag, pressed the pneumo to his arm. There was a sharp hiss and he gave a long moan of ecstasy. His eyes rolled back in his head and he slumped on the sofa, a dribble of saliva emerging from the corner of his mouth.

Roag looked on with interest, the fingers of one hand playing idly with her child's bracelet as she watched the addict writhe.

'How long before he can walk?' Orry asked. Fidelius didn't look like he'd be going anywhere soon.

'It varies,' Roag replied absently.

'Should he be doing that?' Orry added, worried. The ex-monk had stiffened and appeared to be hyperventilating.

'Probably not,' Roag said.

'Is he all right?' She took a step forward, getting seriously alarmed as the trembling turned into full-on spasms and froth formed at his mouth.

'Rama! Shouldn't we do something?' Ethan asked, hurrying over.

'Like what?' Roag asked. 'I've seen this before – it looks like a bad batch.'

'Where's the nearest hospital?' Orry asked, watching his convulsions with horror.

'Forget it,' Roag said. 'His heart's already fucked from all the ket – by the time we get him there he'll be dead.' She sounded bored.

'We have to try!' Orry said. 'Help me with him, Eth—'

But Fidelius had given one final wild jerk and was now slumped, motionless.

'Shit!' Orry knelt beside him and felt for a pulse before announcing, 'He's dead.'

'Told you,' Roag said.

Mender picked up the pneumo from the table and looked at it suspiciously. 'What did he take?' he asked.

Roag met his gaze. 'Ket-c,' she said.

'How much?'

'I really wasn't paying attention.'

They fell silent, glaring at each other. Mender's fingers flexed around the grip of his Fabretti.

'Why would she let him OD?' Ethan asked.

'That's what I'd like to know,' Mender growled.

'I didn't *let* him do anything,' Roag insisted. 'He was a fucking addict – it was bad shit – he died. It happens. End of. Now are we going to stand here talking all day, or can we get off this fucking station?'

Orry looked at the monk's body. Whether Roag had let Fidelius kill himself or not, he'd looked happy at the end. Deliberate or not, his death had been a release from his guilt, she thought, remembering what he'd let happen to his daughter. What worried her was if Roag *had* wanted the ex-monk dead, then *why*? She didn't have an answer for that, and standing here wouldn't provide one.

'Come on,' she said. 'Let's get out of here.'

25

SERAPIS

'It was EDC,' Mender said, interrupting *Dainty Jane*'s explanation mid-flow.

'There is no evidence that the Empyrean Development Company were involved,' the ship pointed out.

'Of course there was no *evidence*,' the old man said patiently. 'The Company don't *leave* evidence.'

'Does it matter?' Orry said, managing to keep the irritation from her voice. They were on the long approach into Serapis and her stomach was still unsettled from the recent collapse from Sundowner Station.

'I suppose not,' Mender admitted.

'As I was saying,' *Jane* said archly, 'Serapis was into the last fifty years of a two-hundred-year terraforming schedule when an *unknown* competitor corporation subverted the eater swarms.'

'Oh wow, I read about this,' Ethan said excitedly. 'It's *legendary*: the eaters are these self-replicating machines, anything in size from an insect to as big as your fist. They set billions of them off chewing their way through the terrain, sculpting the planet's surface and turning what they ate into oxygen and other useful stuff. EDC – or whoever – reprogrammed them to only eat stuff that was man-made, *including people*. Genius. I didn't realise it was *this* place.'

'So what happened?' Orry asked. 'Are these eater swarms still there? And active?'

'Yep,' Mender confirmed with a grin, 'and yep.'

'Then how is anyone alive down there?'

Jane answered, 'Krupps Pioneering Group – that's the corporate entity who owns the terraforming rights to Serapis – managed a partial fix—'

Ethan snorted at that, but the ship ignored him and continued, 'They could not regain control of the swarms but they did manage to disable the self-replicating routines, and they were also able to set a hard floor in the eaters' altimeters.'

'So they can't reproduce,' Orry said slowly, 'and . . . ?'

'And they don't go below mean sea level,' Ethan explained. 'They don't know anything below sea level even exists – they can't recognise it.'

'Doesn't sound like all that much of a fix to me,' she said. 'How does that actually help? Everyone is fine as long as they're underground?'

'Pretty much,' Mender said.

'All the settlements on Serapis are either subterranean or in areas where the terrain is naturally below sea level,' *Jane* explained.

'How can land be below sea level?' Orry had never lived on a planet for any length of time: that sounded wrong to her.

'It's quite normal,' the ship assured her. 'A little less than one per cent of Serapis' surface is two metres or more below mean sea level.'

'But they can't still think it's a viable colony? I mean, what happens when you poke your head above sea level?'

'*Nom nom nom,*' Ethan said with relish, turning his hands into chomping jaws.

Mender chuckled. 'The swarms are declining,' he told her. 'At first terraforming efforts pretty much stopped dead, but after the counter-subversion they posted a bounty for every eater destroyed, turning Serapis into a hotspot for bounty hunters and thrill-seekers. It's been like that ever since.'

'And the terraforming has continued, albeit slowly,' *Jane* added. 'Once the last eaters have been destroyed, efforts will resume at full pace and the planet should be properly ready for colonists in another twenty years or so.'

'Hmm,' Orry said, worried. 'So this place we're going – Hudson's Leap – is that underground?'

'Nope,' Mender said happily.

'Roag's very quiet, don't you think?' Orry asked Mender once they were alone in the cockpit. She'd been running over everything that had happened since her escape from the Hollow and something definitely felt off.

'Yeah,' Mender replied. 'Nice, ain't it?'

'Don't you think it's odd, though?'

'Odd how?'

'That she's tied up in the hold and she's *not* raging about how we promised to let her go and then didn't. I'd have thought that by now she'd be explaining in excruciating detail what she's going to do to us when she gets free, but all she does is sit there and watch us. It's almost as if she *wants* to stay with us.'

'Maybe she does. It's not like she has anywhere else to go.' He looked up from the displays he was monitoring. 'Look, she knows there's nothing she can do right now. Cordelia may be a lot of things, but she's not a flapper.'

Perhaps he's right, Orry acknowledged, though their prisoner's behaviour still didn't sit well with her. *But if she thinks she can just stay on board and become part of the crew, then she can . . .*

She clenched her teeth and stared up at the vast, cloud-wreathed ball that was Serapis. Most of the surface was obscured, with what little she could glimpse through the gaps an unexciting sandy-brown colour. She thought about the eaters in the atmosphere, and after a few minutes realised what had been bothering her since Ethan had mentioned them.

'Uh, Mender . . . if these swarms eat anything made by humans, how exactly do we get down to the surface?'

'I was wondering when you'd ask me that.' With the approach vector locked in, he nudged *Dainty Jane* towards the upper atmosphere.

'And?'

He turned to her with an evil grin. 'There are only a couple of spaceports and each has a station in geosync orbit right over it. Getting down is pretty simple: inbound ships stop at the station and transfer their cargo and passengers to local shuttles. The shuttles are designed to fit inside metre-thick ablative shrouds which cover everything, even the engine nozzles. They have to be that way – any gaps, and the eaters will get right inside and start chawin' away on the hull, and you do *not* want that.

'Anyhow, tugs line the shuttles up for entry and then it's a pretty hairy drop. Those pilots are crazy bastards. The shrouds are shaped so they have just enough control over their drag and bank angles to bleed off enough energy for normal flight once the air gets thick enough. Then they have a thousand-k glide into the port, and the whole rest of the way down, the swarms are eating away at the shroud. Both ports are in big old depressions, like four hundred metres below sea level, with runways ten-k long. By the time the shuttles get low enough for the eaters to leave off, they're lucky if they have a centimetre of shroud left. They lose a shuttle a month that way. It used to be a lot more, mind.'

Now Serapis filled the canopy, its surface features were very clear: there were forests and mountains, rivers and canyons.

Orry stared at Mender. 'And these shrouds – do they only fit the shuttles?' She had a leaden feeling in her stomach. 'So the only way down is in a shuttle?'

Mender had turned back to the flight controls. 'That's about the size of it, girl.'

'But we're not a shuttle, are we?'

She could tell he was grinning from the way the side of his face crinkled. 'Not the last time I checked, nope.'

She settled herself more securely into her acceleration shell. 'Goddammit, Mender.'

'We'll be fine,' he said breezily, as the ship began to buffet. 'Probably.'

She could see a glow coming from *Dainty Jane*'s lower hull now, and occasional flames licking up the side.

'Stop scaring her,' the ship chided. 'Orry, my hull and ablative shields may not be as thick as the shrouds they use here, but they're military grade. My calculations suggest that we will make it to our landing site without critical damage.'

Jane's words didn't exactly quell her fears. 'What about getting off again?'

There was an infinitesimal pause, then the ship admitted, 'The margin for error is small.'

'It all depends on whether we run into a big swarm on the way down,' Mender said, guiding them through the turbulence of atmospheric entry. The canopy was surrounded by red now. 'We'd never have made it down ten years back, but there are a lot less of the little fuckers these days.'

'Why didn't we just take a shuttle?' Orry muttered, then felt a flush of irritation at herself because she already knew the answer: leaving aside the costs of docking and tickets for the shuttle and then on to Hudson's Leap - wherever the hell that was - it would leave a trail. She would have chosen this way even if Mender had told her about the risks earlier – and he knew that, which was why he didn't bother answering her question, and why he'd chosen to keep it to himself until he could have some fun with her. She smiled despite her anxiety about being eaten out of the sky; she'd have to get him back for this.

As the glow faded and the buffeting died away, *Dainty Jane* streaked down through the atmosphere. Orry watched the drifting skeins of high-altitude clouds, wondering how long it would be before the swarms noticed them. She'd barely formed the question in her mind when it was answered.

'Eater swarm dead ahead,' *Jane* announced calmly.

'I see 'em,' Mender grunted, but the gel lining of Orry's shell had already stiffened around her as he changed course violently. She heard a cry of protest from down in the galley where Ethan was busy researching Serapis while Quondam guarded Roag.

'Contact Two,' *Jane* said. 'Second swarm closing in, bearing oh-two-seven.'

'Shit.' Mender jinked them again. 'Looks like we're going to have to run the gauntlet.'

She could see the swarms herself now: two vast, swirling clouds, dark against the blue sky, were closing in from both sides, one slightly above them, the other below. The cockpit darkened as the swarms engulfed them.

'Hull integrity degrading,' *Jane* reported. 'There are eaters in the drive outlets.'

Orry forced herself to resist the urge to monitor with her integuary; that would do no one any good.

'Just a little longer . . .' Mender muttered to himself.

Above her head, the canopy was crawling with machines, clinging onto the transparent bubble with what she could only assume were molecular hooks. The eaters were every shape and size and a lot of them were based on natural organisms: there were moths, beetles and spiders, and flying fish-things with gaping, gnashing jaws and glittering scales. Some of the smaller eaters were just spheres of metal, like ball bearings, but they were deploying a fearsome variety of cutting tools – drills, lasers, corrosive sacs, even what looked like actual *teeth*. It surely wouldn't be long before one of them got through. She shuddered at the thought of what those things could do to her flesh.

'We're through,' *Jane* piped up. 'The swarms can't match our speed but my hull is still covered in them. The engine outlets are filling up; there's no armour in there so they'll be into the nacelles very soon.'

'No they won't,' Mender said with grim satisfaction, and activated the drives.

Feeling the ship lurch forward, Orry quickly hooked one of the external lenses to see a stream of scorched and melted eaters tumbling from the drive nozzles, sparking and flaring as they fell away.

'Hull integrity at sixty per cent,' *Jane* reported. 'The Snarl is one hundred kilometres down-range.'

'The *Snarl*?' Orry asked, eyeing the eaters on the canopy with increasing anxiety. A lot had been torn away by the abrupt acceleration when Mender fired the engines, but there were still hundreds left.

'It's a network of canyons,' *Jane* explained, 'all below mean sea level. That's where Hudson's Leap is.'

'I see it,' Mender growled.

A long way ahead of them the rocky ground fell away into a maze of chasms, with tall fingers of rock rising from the narrow canyons, all topped with greenery.

'Hull at fifty per cent,' *Jane* reported.

Above her, Orry could see a hairline crack forming under the skittering drill of a crab-like eater.

Jane's nose lurched down and suddenly the canopy was clear: the eaters had detached in a cloud and gone shooting away upwards as sheer rock walls surrounded the ship. The nacelles rotated fully forward, engines howling as Mender braked frantically.

Dainty Jane came to a halt two hundred metres down into the canyon. The roar of her drives came echoing back from the rock faces.

'Don't know what all the fuss was about,' Mender said, and Orry slumped back in her shell, laughing shakily in relief.

The Snarl was enormous, covering over a thousand square kilometres, according to *Jane*, and it took them a good hour of threading the maze of narrow canyons to get to a landing site. Below them were fast-flowing rivers of frothing rapids. Several times Mender found himself having to reverse out of a canyon, for the gap had become too narrow for the ship to squeeze through, his language eloquently expressing his views about the confining rock walls.

With no wish to be seen or heard, they kept their distance from Hudson's Leap. The only landing place Mender could find was the flat top of a needle several kilometres from the town. The plateau showed signs of having been farmed once, but now the overgrown fields were nothing but a tangle of scrub.

Orry stepped off the cargo ramp and breathed in the air of a new world. It was crisp and cool, sharp with the tang of the vegetation crushed beneath *Dainty Jane*'s landing struts. Birds chattered over the constant background rumble of churning water. Above her, blue sky peeked through gaps in the clouds, and as she leaned back to look up out of the Snarl's confining walls a shadow swept by high overhead, dark against the pale clouds. She watched, entranced, as it swirled across the sky, spreading so thin that it was hardly visible then coming together into a tight, black mass before dispersing once more. *It's a swarm*, she realised, and tried to estimate how many eaters were above her. *Tens of thousands? Hundreds?* The individual machines were mere black specks from where she stood, but the way they moved together was breath-taking. She was almost disappointed when the deadly cloud warped and stretched for the last time before moving out of sight beyond the canyon walls.

The needle they were on was only a few hundred metres across. She walked to the edge to peer down cautiously at the rushing river far below them, then realised the neighbouring fingers of rock were linked together by a network of narrow cable-bridges swaying in the breeze. Using her integuary to zoom in, she could just make out Hudson's Leap in the distance, a small settlement of prefabricated buildings on top of one of the larger needles.

'We have to walk all the way over there?' Ethan asked, coming up to stand beside her. 'Across *those*?'

The drooping bridges traversing the hundreds of metres between the peaks certainly looked precarious. They were barely wide enough for two people to pass. *Thin people at that*, Orry thought with a flutter of nerves. *At least in space you don't fall*. She looked down at the river again and swallowed. 'I'm sure they're fine,' she said firmly, turning away.

Mender appeared on the ramp, having confirmed that Quondam had everything he needed to guard Roag for a few days. They might need the Kadiran's muscles, but for now they all agreed it was probably best he stayed out of sight rather than drawing unnecessary attention to them.

'Ready for a stroll?' Orry asked as Mender limped up to her.

He eyed the bridges that separated them from Hudson's Leap, and spat on the ground. 'Piotr's withered balls,' he muttered to himself, before taking the first few tentative steps.

Orry grinned at her brother and together, they set off after him.

26

HUDSON'S LEAP

Despite their flimsy appearance the walkways were made of stout metal cable, anchored at both ends by substantial stanchions and reassuringly sturdy. They did sway alarmingly, though, giving such dizzying views of the white waters below them that Orry had to stop looking. The journey became easier after that.

They didn't see any people until they were close to Hudson's Leap, though they passed over several needle-tops laid out with crops and others grazed by free-roaming flocks of sheep or gene-tweaked ostriches. Orry counted three more long bridges before they would reach the town, and was halfway across the first of them when she saw a person walking towards them from the other end.

'Morning!' she called as they came closer. 'Beautiful day.'

The man stopped before they reached him, regarding the three of them with suspicion. He was dressed in hard-wearing work clothes, a synthetic jacket over a threadbare woollen jumper. He wore a knife at his hip and the barrel of a hunting rifle poked up over one shoulder.

'Don't know you,' he grunted in a thick accent. 'You been bothering my livestock?'

Mender opened his mouth and Orry jumped in quickly, fearing that anything the old man had to say on the subject of bothering sheep wouldn't go down well.

'We didn't go anywhere near the animals,' she said. 'Just out for a morning stroll.'

'Don't know you,' the man repeated.

'We came in on the gyro,' Ethan said. 'Surveying local swarm numbers.'

The farmer appeared to relax a little at that. 'Work to do,' he grunted. 'Don't get et.'

'We'll try not to,' Orry said as he pushed past her. She turned to Ethan, who was looking pleased with himself. 'The *gyro*?' she asked.

'It's an underground monorail that links all these little settlements to the nearest spaceport,' he explained. 'Well, it's mostly underground. Because the Snarl is so low the rail is out in the open around here, strung between the needles.'

'Good job,' she told him, annoyed she hadn't thought to ask him what he'd found out about Serapis before they left the ship. Fidelius' words about how the monks might be already on their way here were driving her on, too quickly, perhaps.

They encountered a few more people as they drew nearer to the town, farmers, for the most part, but there were some engineers laden with tools. None of them were particularly talkative. There were buildings on the needles closest to Hudson's Leap, which Ethan suggested were probably overspill from the town. The final bridge ended at the town proper and a wide main street lined with printed structures on both sides. The only vehicles in sight were small electric buggies, presumably used to transport goods within the town's confines; there was no way even a small vehicle could travel over one of the cable bridges.

It wasn't a big place, constrained as it was by the size of the rock needle upon which it was built, but there were a lot of people about and Orry's hopes of finding someone who looked like a military operator to lead her to Professor Rasmussen were immediately dashed, for at least half the town's population looked like they could be contractors. Hard-eyed, heavily armed men and women were everywhere, bounty-hunters, presumably, planning to reduce the eater swarms and collect a handsome fee for doing so.

'A lot of people are going that way,' Ethan said, pointing at a wide road leading off the street they were on. 'Come on, let's check it out.'

Orry had also noticed groups of the swarm-hunters all heading in the same direction, which made her curious. The street led onto a wide, open area on one edge of the town. It was thronged with people.

'A goddamned boatyard on top of a mountain?' Mender said, scratching his head. 'And I thought I'd seen it all.'

There were at least a dozen garishly painted boats resting in the yard's servicing cradles. They were all of the same basic design, wide with flat bottoms and thick rubber fenders running all round them like cushions, though they'd each been modified in various ways.

'They must be using the rivers to get around the Snarl,' Ethan said, pointing at a row of large cranes arranged along the far side of the yard. Several were lowering boats full of hunters over the cliff's edge. He walked closer and Orry followed, peering nervously down at the swirling waters almost a kilometre below. There was a natural basin at the base of the needle where the river was a little calmer, and as she watched, one boat was released from its cables and shot away into the surging waters downstream, pitching and rolling in the rapids.

Ethan looked fascinated, but Mender was shaking his head. 'You wouldn't catch me in one of them damn things,' he said, and Orry had to agree.

Back on the main street they passed a general store, tech and engineering workshops, a weapons dealer and a moderately sized hotel sporting an illuminated sign advertising vacancies. Most of the other buildings looked residential, many with signs in the windows offering rooms to rent. The main street terminated at a transit station which was little more than platforms on either side of a single rail leading away from Hudson's Leap via a graceful arched bridge spanning the gap between the town and the top of the next needle. Orry could just see another bridge beyond that, then the rail disappeared into a tunnel bored through one of the taller needles.

'How are we going to find Professor Rasmussen?' Ethan asked.

'Hotels have bars,' Mender pointed out. 'I vote we start there.'

'It's not even lunchtime,' Orry said.

'It is in my time zone.'

She turned to survey the town. A few smaller roads led off the main street, but not many. *There can only be a couple of hundred buildings max.* 'Let's search the town first,' she said, 'you know, walk around and see if we can find anything? It won't take long if we split up. We can meet at the bar when we're done,' she added, to placate Mender.

'What exactly are we looking for?' Ethan asked. He didn't sound impressed at the prospect of yet more exercise.

She'd been thinking about that. 'These contractors who took the prof? They've pissed off their employers – going up against the Order like this, they're going to be worried as hell, so they'll want somewhere they can defend if it someone comes after them. Mender, where would you hole up if you were them?'

'Look for large buildings,' he answered immediately, 'preferably with some open ground around them, a wall even. The fewer windows, the better – and maybe a flat roof. These guys will probably look a lot like the rest of the lowlifes around here, but maybe kitted out better. Look for anything that's mil-spec, tech, body-armour, specialist weapons. You see anyone like that, pipe up on the private channel before you try to follow them – and *be careful*. Springing one hostage is difficult enough – we don't want to give 'em another one.'

'Okay,' Orry said, looking at them both. 'See you back at the hotel.'

'Eventually,' Mender grumbled.

Well, he was right about this place having a bar, Orry thought as she walked into the nameless hotel two hours later. The bar occupied most of the ground floor of the large building and it was busy, despite it still only being late morning. She spotted Mender immediately, perched on a stool with a bottle in front of him, and she wondered suspiciously how long he'd been there for. He'd been quiet on the integuary channel, although that wasn't unusual for him.

'Just some water, please,' she told the barman as she took the seat next to Mender and examined his bottle, but the smoky glass was too dark to make out how much of its contents remained. 'Any luck?' she asked him.

'A couple of possibles. Not sure. What about you?'

'Nothing.' Her third of the town had been a closely packed hotchpotch of tiny dwellings and storage units, no open ground, and nothing remotely resembling what Mender had described.

'What about the kid?' he asked.

'What about me?' Ethan said, coming up behind them.

'Did you find anything?' she asked.

'Actually, I might have.'

'Really? Why didn't you tell us?'

'I guess I wasn't sure at first. I found it just after leaving you, but it didn't tick many of Mender's boxes so I ignored it. But then I was walking around and I couldn't get it out of my head, so once I'd finished I circled back and took another look before coming here.'

Mender glared at him. 'You didn't stand there gawping at the place, did you?'

'Of course not – I'm not an idiot! It's big but it's only one storey, and part of it has collapsed. It's right on the edge of town and there's only a narrow alley separating it from the building next door. One side of it's on stilts – it sticks out over the edge of the drop. The place looks deserted . . .'

Mender looked thoughtful. 'Let's add it to the list,' he said. 'I guess we're staying the night at least.'

'I'll get us a room,' Orry said, standing up. 'We'll wait for it to get dark, then Ethan can plant some lenses near each of the possibles. How many have you got?'

'Enough for all of them,' he assured her.

'Good. We can each take a shift monitoring them. Hopefully something will turn up.'

'Assuming one of them is the right place,' Ethan said.

'After lunch we can swap areas and whoever's not monitoring can spend the afternoon walking around town again – just in case we've missed anything.' She patted her brother on the shoulder and smiled brightly at them both as she walked away to enquire about a room.

Mender turned his sour gaze on Ethan.

'Nice work, motormouth.'

27

JEAN-BAPTISTE

Cordelia Roag couldn't decide which was more annoying, the scrape of the kuck's damn whetstone down the spike of his warmaul, or the keening song which accompanied every stroke.

'I think it's as sharp as it's going to get,' she informed him from her mattress.

The scraping stopped and he looked across the hold at her, tiny eyes inscrutable in his massive head. He was seated on a crate, the maul held upright in front of him. It was a fearsome weapon, with a heavy hammer head and backspike, and another long spike protruding from the top.

And he hasn't even started on the other goddamn spike, Roag reflected irritably.

'To a breedwarrior, the ritual is as much about sharpening the mind as it is the weapon,' he rumbled.

'But you're not a breedwarrior, are you?' she said. 'You monitored communications in a Kadiran office.'

He produced a growl from somewhere deep in his chest

cavity that made her stomach turn to water. 'I may not have won the right to breed on my homeworld, but I am a warrior where it matters.' He thumped his chest. 'Here.'

'Oh, puh-lease. I'll bet that's not even your maul. You stole it off some dead kuck.'

He studied her for long seconds before responding, 'I do not wish to continue this conversation.' He returned his attention to his weapon.

Roag gritted her teeth as he resumed scraping the whetstone down the length of the spike.

'Look, you really don't need to guard me every fucking second,' she said, raising her arms to show him the plastic ties securing her to a vertical length of *Dainty Jane*'s thick pipework. 'I can't go anywhere.'

'Captain Mender has instructed me to remain at my post.'

Captain Mender can take a jump out of a fucking airlock without a helmet. She idly rotated the cheap plastic bracelet around her wrist as she studied the Kadiran. 'I'm thirsty,' she said, 'and hungry.'

'Sustenance will be provided at the designated time.'

Roag grimaced. She briefly considered faking an illness – it was an old trick but the Kadiran didn't really do lying so maybe she'd get away with it – then dismissed the idea.

Just be patient, she told herself as she settled back in her foam nest, stroking the bracelet. *One of these days . . .*

On the other side of the hold, the Kadiran started crooning again as the whetstone continued to scrape.

She rolled onto her side and covered her head with her pillow.

The room they were given was large, with two beds and a folding cot, although they would be sleeping in shifts, leaving one of them awake to monitor the electronics. After a sleepless night listening to Mender's stentorian snoring, Orry had been relieved when he'd finally awakened, flicked on the coffee maker and staggered barefoot into the bathroom, from which a series of unpleasant sounds and smells had emanated. Ten minutes later he emerged, looking a little more human, collected a steaming coffee and, blowing noisily on it, asked, 'Anything?'

'I think so.' She was almost desperate to take a gulp of his coffee, but if she did, she would never sleep. She pointed at the possible locations on the screen. 'These two here? They've been quiet all night – but this one is looking very promising.' She brought up images of the stilted, semi-derelict property Ethan had discovered on the edge of town and zoomed in. 'See this guy on the roof right here? What does that look like to you?'

Mender leaned in to peer closer. 'Sniper on overwatch,' he said, adjusting the image gain.

'That's what I thought.' She took a deep sniff of the coffee he was holding under her nose, then switched to another of Ethan's planted lenses, providing a different angle. 'And look here . . .'

'They're definitely covering the approaches,' he said, 'but

that doesn't mean these are the guys we're looking for. They might just be cautious, or expecting trouble for some other, entirely unconnected reason.'

'True,' she agreed, 'but it's a start. Of course, the problem is—'

'That the damn place is a fortress,' he finished for her.

'Yep. Now look at this.' Under her guiding hand, the timestamp on the screen sped backwards to late the previous evening. She set it playing and they watched two figures emerge from the building and walk down the street.

Mender paused the playback and zoomed in on them. Both were wearing contractor gear and sidearms. 'I wondered where these two were off to so late,' she continued, 'and seeing as this place has the only bar in town and you two were snoring away, I went downstairs for a look-see.'

'And?'

'And I was right. They were drinking here until the wee hours, then they staggered home.'

'Did you talk to them?'

'No, I didn't want to go lumbering in without a plan.'

'You think this is a regular thing? Every night?'

'Well, there's not much else to do in Hudson's Leap, is there? I'm just surprised there weren't more of them in here.'

'Maybe they take it in turns? We might get a different couple in tonight.'

'Or the same two if they're sneaking out. Or no one at all.'

He grunted. 'I guess we'll find out this evening.'

'If any of them do come again I think I should talk to them, try to find out who they are and if they have Rasmussen.'

'And how we get him out,' Mender added, then looked at her face. 'We can talk about that later, girl, you look rooted. Get some sleep. I'll take over here for a few hours.'

Orry didn't argue but pulled off her top layer of clothes, climbed into the bed he'd just vacated and laid her head on the still-warm pillow, fully intending to add the finishing touches to the plan she'd been working on for most of the night. Instead, she was asleep inside a minute.

Getting out of the stuffy hotel room felt good to Ethan, particularly since Mender had spent most of his shift on the monitors eating his favourite freeze-dried chilli – which, unfortunately, the hotel actually served. There was a cold bite to the early evening wind whipping through Hudson's Leap, but at least it didn't stink like the inside of Mender's guts.

He'd been walking the town's streets for an hour, careful to avoid the building they'd all agreed was the most likely place for the professor to be held. In fact, Ethan was about as far away as he could get, at the docks on the opposite side of the needle, where he'd been watching with great interest as the cranes winched up boats full of swarm-hunting crews from the boiling waters at the ravine bottom. After the last boat had been settled safely into its cradle and its crew headed off for a drink, trading good-natured insults as they went, he ventured closer.

Most of the boats were deserted as the sun was sinking below the canyon's rim, plunging the Snarl into premature twilight, but he could see that a few still had the odd person aboard, hosing down decks or making repairs. He stopped beside a pile of equipment lying next to one of the cradles that was holding one of the smaller boats above the cliff's edge. Looking up, he saw a young man of about his age moving a load of plastic crates.

Spotting Ethan, the lad set down the crate he was carrying and leaned on the rail. 'Hello down there!' he called cheerily.

'Hello up there,' Ethan answered with a grin. 'Nice evening for it.'

The lad leaned back to gaze up at the sky, now streaked with orange and red. 'Sure is,' he agreed, then paused for a moment to spark up a cheroot before turning his attention back to Ethan. 'Haven't seen you round here before,' he said. 'What brings you to the Leap?'

'I'm here with my sister. She's collecting data on swarm numbers.'

'Well, you've come to the right place for that,' the lad said, sucking on his cheroot. 'The crews we take out? They're culling thousands every day – but the swarms never seem to get any smaller.'

'Is that right? I heard their numbers were dropping.'

'Maybe so, but I've been doing this for five years and it don't seem to be the case over the Snarl.'

'That's interesting,' Ethan said, and meant it. He found

the unique situation on Serapis fascinating; something about the thought of venturing out on these flimsy boats to hunt the eater swarms stirred his adventurer's soul. He eyed the equipment on the dock beside him – climbing gear, for the most part, ropes and carabiners, crampons and odd-looking harnesses covered in yellow and black warning stripes. 'How does it work,' he asked, 'if you and the hunters are down at the bottom of the canyons and the swarms are up above?'

'Oh, it's pretty simple,' the lad replied. He moved to lean more comfortably on the side of the boat. 'Each crew picks their spot based on the daily forecasts, then they charter a boat to take them out there. Some of them, those who've been around a time or so, have their favourite captains, of course. Once we get there they send up a drone to attach a rope to the rock with pitons, then winch themselves up to the top. Most of them'll stay on the cliff-face, below the hard deck, leaving one of them to climb up to attract the swarm. Once the swarm comes, he runs for the edge and jumps.'

He laughed at Ethan's look of utter shock and continued, 'It's okay – they're crazy, these swarm-hunters, but they ain't suicidal. He's wearing a drop-harness – it'll give him as soft a landing as you can expect in those canyon rapids, and if he's lucky, we haul him out pretty damn quick. Meanwhile, up top, the rest of the crew take out as many of the swarm as they can from below the cliff-edge. The idea is they fire up through the hard deck, but that's not always possible. They keep going until they run out of eaters to shoot, or ammo, or the swarm loses interest and goes someplace else. If it gets too hairy, the rest of the crew jump too, but they prefer coming down by rope than by harness.'

'Rama,' Ethan said, 'I can see why the bounties are so high.' He looked at the tangle of wasp-striped straps. They looked more like industrial bondage gear than anything, but he guessed they must be the drop-harnesses. He wondered if he would trust his life to one.

The lad laughed again, then studied Ethan intently, an odd expression on his face. 'I'm Jean-Baptiste,' he said.

'Ethan.'

'You wanna come aboard? I could show you round the boat.'

He was really tempted, but he was due to relieve Orry in half an hour. 'Rain check?' he suggested. 'I have to get going, but thanks for the explanation. I'd love to see it all for myself one day – from a nice safe seat on the boat!'

'You should!' Jean-Baptiste agreed with enthusiasm, 'you and your sister. I could talk to the skipper, get you a special rate.'

'Cool, maybe I'll ask her. Anyway, see you round.' He started to walk away.

'Hey, wait—!'

Turning back, Ethan saw Jean-Baptiste clattering down the slender ladder from the deck.

He hurried over to him, looking unaccountably flustered. 'Um,' he began, then ran a hand through his mop of floppy hair, 'look, I was just wondering if, maybe, you'd like to get a drink sometime. Uh, tonight, maybe? . . . with me, that is – there's a bar at the hotel, you see, so . . .' He looked hopefully at Ethan, clearly in agony.

Oh, Ethan thought, completely blindsided by the offer. Jean-Baptiste watched anxiously as Ethan's mind adjusted itself to this new reality. No one had ever asked him out before, not properly like this. He had had a few encounters during his travels, but they had all been with females – *girls*, he reminded himself quickly, remembering Orry's amused lecture on the use of appropriate terminology. *Do I like boys as well?* he wondered, looking at Jean-Baptiste properly for the first time. He was certainly good-looking, with those dark eyes and darker hair, with a healthy olive tint to his skin . . . but no, he just didn't do anything for Ethan, not like Longwei had. *Shame*, he thought, and wondered how to let Jean-Baptiste down gently. He'd never been much good with people.

'I can't tonight,' he said awkwardly, 'I have to be somewhere.'

'Tomorrow, then?'

For Rama's sake, tell him you're not interested in him that way.

'Tomorrow . . . tomorrow sounds good,' Ethan was a little shocked to hear himself say.

Jean-Baptiste looked delighted. 'Great! I'll meet you at the hotel at eight?'

'Eight . . . sure. Look, I really have to go.'

'Of course.' Jean-Baptiste grinned. 'See you tomorrow. If you change your mind I'm always here.'

'You live on the boat?'

The lad shrugged. 'It's cheaper than paying for a room.'

'I guess it is. Well, see you tomorrow.'

Ethan walked away, groaning inwardly. *Nice one, idiot. How the hell am I going to get out of this?*

Maybe Orry would be able to help.

28

MASON

The door opened and the same pair of contractors Orry had seen the previous night entered the bar, shaking rainwater from their dustcloaks. She glanced at Mender, sitting at the other end of the bar, and received a nod of acknowledgement. If these two had been involved in abducting Professor Rasmussen and framing her, there was a chance they would recognise her, and if that happened, they'd have to switch to Plan B, which involved Mender's Fabretti and their hotel room. She dearly hoped it wouldn't come to that.

She became aware of someone hovering at her elbow and turned in irritation. 'What?' she snapped.

'Are you religious, baby? Because you're the answer to all my prayers . . .' The young man wilted under her contemptuous stare.

'Just . . . no,' she said, dismissing him with a wave of her hand. He slunk away and she finished the last of her drink. Defending the empty stool next to her was becoming a full-time job. That was the third come-on since she'd sat down ten minutes ago; the previous two men and a woman had actually made this latest loser look good.

The marks were at the bar now, the man laughing at a comment made by his female partner as they waited for their drinks. He glanced round the place and his eyes settled on Orry, who held his gaze for a moment, then looked away, playing with her empty glass.

So it would be the man.

He leaned in to say something to his companion before walking over.

Still got it, she sent happily over the integuary channel.

He knows you're easy, Ethan sent back, and Mender chuckled.

Just be thankful he likes girls, she responded, *otherwise it would be you sitting here, little brother*. She smiled when there was no response, then groaned when yet another chancer stepped up to her.

'I—' the newcomer began.

'Fuck off, dickhead,' her mark said, shoving past him to stand beside her.

She couldn't help feeling a little sympathy for the other man as he reddened and faded away. 'Thanks,' she said.

'No problemo,' the contractor replied, 'you can't take any shizola off these a-holes.' He gave her a wide, almost predatory grin. 'Buy you a drink, hot stuff?'

'Um, I don't think so.'

His grin faded and he indicated the empty seat next to her. 'You waiting for someone?'

She looked him over. Older than her, with a strong jaw and a mouth a little too wide for his face. He was good-looking enough, in a soldierly way, with sandy hair bunched up under a pair of smoky black goggles sitting high on his forehead. 'No,' she said, 'I'm not waiting for anyone.'

'Then I think I'll just sit myself down here next to you.'

'It's a free planet.' She turned back to her empty glass as he settled in.

'Haven't seen you round here before,' he said. 'Just passing through?'

'Yep.' She hesitated, as if reluctant to encourage him, then, with apparent forced politeness, 'What about you?'

'Here on a job.'

It was a perfect opportunity to ask what kind of job, but she resisted, wary of pushing too hard too soon. 'You're not from Serapis, then?' she asked instead.

'Fuck no. Little moon called Hebe. You won't have heard of it.' He drained his glass and gestured at the barman. 'Sure I can't get you another?'

She frowned as if she was considering the offer, then slid her empty glass towards him.

He grinned. 'What you drinking?'

'Whatever you're having.'

'Whisky,' he told the barman, 'two of 'em. So, what brings you to the arse-end of this arsehole of a planet? You don't look like one of them fucking swarm-hunters.' He glared balefully at the crews thronging the establishment.

She chuckled. 'No, I'm here to see how they're doing; checking on eater numbers. What about you? Not a hunter, I'm guessing?'

'Fuck off! I like to keep my head below-ground where it's safe.'

'So what do you do?'

He picked up the glasses and passed one to her. 'Cheers,' he said. 'I'm Mason, by the way.'

'Jade,' she said, wondering if he'd dodged her question intentionally. 'Thanks for the drink – don't read anything into it.'

He held up his hands. 'Of course not. Just being neighbourly . . . Jade.'

'Sure you are.' She looked curiously at him, wondering if he'd recognised her and was playing a game. *Stop it*, she told herself sternly. *Second guessing just leads you down a rabbit hole of self-doubt.* 'Does your friend want to join us?' she asked, looking down the bar at the woman he'd arrived with.

'Definitely not, and she ain't exactly my friend.'

'No?'

'She's from offworld too. We're working together.'

'I hope the money's good,' she said.

'Can't complain, and the work's easy enough – but who wants to talk about work? What about you? Where are you from?'

She fed him the cover story she'd worked out with Ethan and the conversation flowed, along with the drinks.

Unsurprisingly, Mason turned out to be boorish company, and the more he drank, the worse he got.

'Look at these pricks.' He was slurring now, pointing at a nearby crew of swarm-hunters. 'Think they're the big fucking "I am" just cos they go up on the surface now and again, when everyone knows all you have to do is move real slow and the eaters just leave you the fuck alone.'

'Is that right?' Orry asked, actually interested in what he was saying for the first time that evening.

'Sure it is!' He waved his whisky drunkenly, slopping it over the bar – and her. 'They told us all about it in orientation. Some kind of pouncing instinct – legacy code left over from their original programming, when they were supposed to analyse and report back on what they found before they et it. 'pparently, they're *curious* about shit – can you believe that?' He beckoned her closer and gave a nasty grin. ''course, keeping alive up there all depends if you can stay still while they're busy taking samples of your flesh . . .'

He pinched her forearm painfully to underline his point, roaring with laughter as she recoiled, then motioned to the barman, 'More whisky, my man – an' leave the fucking bottle this time.'

We've got a prize arsehole here, Mender commented drily. *Want me to shoot him in the face?*

Orry ignored him, rubbing her arm. For an arsehole, he

could certainly hold his booze – but she thought he might just be drunk enough at last.

'Orientation for what?' she asked, leaning in close and looking up at him. *Let's hope it's worth all this damn mascara.*

It was close to midnight when Mason checked the time and grimaced. 'Shit, babes,' he said, slurring heavily, 'I need to get back. Early start in the morning.'

Orry hid her relief. 'That's a shame. It's been fun.'

He studied her, narrowing his eyes to keep her in focus. 'I suppose I could stay a while longer. You said you have a room here? Wouldn't say no to a coffee.'

She chuckled softly. 'Nice try, Romeo, but I'm not that kind of girl – not on a first date, anyway.'

'Is that what this is, then? A date?'

She patted his arm. 'What do you think? Maybe we can do it again? If you'd like to, that is.'

'You know it, baby . . . but, the thing is' – he glanced around the half-empty bar before continuing in a quieter voice – 'I'm leaving on the gyro in the morning and I can't see myself ever coming back to this shithole.'

'Oh *no*. But we've only just met – where are you going? I get about a bit – maybe I could look you up? Have that *second date*?'

He laid a finger along the side of his nose and slurred, 'If I told you that, hot stuff, I'd hafta kill you.'

He replaced his hand on the bar and she placed her own on top of it. 'I'm good at keeping secrets,' she said, trying for husky and mostly succeeding. His eyes were locked on hers and she prayed he wouldn't lean in to kiss her.

'Hey, Mason,' said the woman he'd arrived with, 'put the lady down, it's time to go.'

He rolled his eyes and waved over at her. 'Sure I can't come up for coffee?' he asked Orry. 'She'd give me half an hour if I begged her.'

'A whole half an hour! You certainly know how to impress a girl.'

He scowled. 'I guess that's a no, then?'

'I guess it's gotta be.' She smiled to soften the rejection.

Instead of pressing her, he stood up and thrust out a hand. 'Maybe I'll bump into you again sometime,' he said as they shook.

Sooner than you think, Orry thought, her mind already working.

He gave a regretful groan and backed away, then raised two fingers to his eyebrow in a casual salute, turned and walked unsteadily to the door.

What a nice man, Ethan sent from their room. *Just your type. I thought for a minute there I was going to have to make myself scarce.*

Never mind that – did you both hear what he said about leaving tomorrow?

I heard, Mender confirmed. *Looks like we've run out of time.*

'So we're agreed it has to happen on the gyro?' Orry said. They'd discussed their options for recovering Professor Rasmussen for an hour or more and come to the conclusion that they didn't have many to play with.

'Definitely,' Mender agreed. 'A direct assault on that building tonight would be suicide.'

Ethan's eyes glazed as he accessed his integuary. 'Okay, so there's only one gyro out of Hudson's Leap tomorrow, and it leaves at seven in the morning. How many tickets should I buy?'

Orry thought for a moment. 'Get four,' she said.

'Done,' her brother said a moment later, his eyes clearing. 'Any thoughts on how we're going to get off the gyro and back to *Jane* once we've got the prof?'

'Give me a chance, will you?' she snapped irritably. It was one in the morning and the plan was half-formed at best, which gave her less than six hours to turn it into something they all stood a decent chance of surviving – and out of everything she had to consider, making their escape was the one thing she had no idea how to accomplish.

Why is Ethan smiling like that? she wondered.

'How about escaping by boat?' he suggested.

The docks were deserted when he returned to them a little later, scoured clean by a lashing rain that had soaked him to the skin. Distant thunder rumbled as he found the boat he was looking for and he noted with relief that the striped drop-harnesses were still piled on the dockside nearby.

'Hello the boat!' he called, yelling to be heard over the

seething rain. He waited for a while and was about to yell again when a dark shape moved on the deck and a pale face peered down at him from within the folds of an oilcloth hood.

'Ethan! You came back!' Jean-Baptiste said, sounding delighted. He gestured at the flimsy looking ladder that led up the side of the cradle to the deck. 'Come aboard.'

Lightning strobed across the sky, illuminating his face as water streamed from his hood.

A massive clap of thunder made Ethan flinch, but he began climbing, concentrating on keeping his grip on the wet rungs. When he reached the top, he felt a hand grab his arm and help him over the boat's side. The deck was absolutely awash, water flooding between the equipment, which had been lashed to the deck, to gush from the scuppers. Jean-Baptiste led him aft to the cramped wheelhouse, where they both shook the water from their clothes.

'Beautiful weather you have round here,' Ethan said, and Jean-Baptiste laughed.

'We do get these storms now and then,' he said, 'but they're usually at night, and they never last long.' He gazed at Ethan, looking a little anxious. 'So ... er ... what bring you out in all this rain?'

'I wanted to take you up on your offer of a boat ride.'

Jean-Baptiste looked a little disappointed, which made Ethan wonder exactly what he'd been expecting. 'That shouldn't be a problem,' he said, 'I can talk to the skipper and—'

'No, no – I meant just you and me.'

'Oh.' He frowned, then smiled. '*Oh.*'

'Is that possible?' Ethan asked guilelessly. 'I mean, can you handle the boat on your own?'

He was clearly flustered. 'Uh, yes, sure – 'course. I'm working towards my master's certificate, and *Gorgerunner* pretty much drives herself anyway.' He patted the bank of screens and read-outs surrounding the ship's wheel.

'Will anyone notice if we take her out for a couple of hours?'

Lightning lit the sky outside the wheelhouse as Jean-Baptiste considered this. 'We'd have to do it late,' he said, raising his voice over a roll of thunder. 'After midnight when everyone's in the bar, or in bed.' His face was becoming more animated as he thought about it. 'We could do it tomorrow if you want. I could get everything ready when we get back fro—'

'How about now?' Ethan said.

'*Now?*' He looked at the water clattering against the windows.

'Why not? You said these storms never last long.' Jean-Baptiste peered out at the rain, looking doubtful, and Ethan held up his hands and took a step backwards towards the sliding door. 'Hey look,' he said, 'if you don't want to, that's fine. I just thought . . .'

'No, no – I *do* want to.'

It was tempting to keep talking, to attempt to persuade him, but something told Ethan that the best thing to do right now was keep quiet.

Jean-Baptiste stared at the sky for a long time, before

eventually turning to him. 'It does look to be brightening a little,' he said with a nervous grin.

The rain had stopped, leaving the sweet smell of sodden vegetation drifting through the open airlock doors into *Dainty Jane*'s cargo bay. It was almost dawn. The lights of Hudson's Leap twinkled in the distance.

'She's coming with us,' Mender said firmly, 'end of. There's no way I'm leaving her here without a guard.'

'What do you think she's going to do?' Ethan said angrily, indicating Roag's restraints. 'She's tied up – and she'll *have* a guard: *Jane*.'

The old man snorted. 'You don't know her, kid.'

Ethan was speechless for a second, then exploded, 'Don't *know* her? The woman killed our father and kept me prisoner on my own ship! Or had you forgotten that?'

'That was Morven Dyas,' Mender corrected him.

'But *she* was the one giving the orders,' Ethan yelled, thrusting an accusing finger in Roag's face.

She just smiled.

'I was working for her before you were sucking on your momma's titties, boy, and if there's one thing I know, it's that I would rather have her under my gun where I can see her than stuck in here all on her own.'

'And what if she gets free on the gyro and runs?' Ethan demanded.

'What if she gets free in here and runs?' Mender countered

calmly, though Orry could see the anger in his good eye. 'And what if she damages *Jane* in the process? Then we'll be stuck on Serapis with Rama-knows-who after us until we can make repairs – and just where the fuck are we supposed to find parts for *an illegal Goethen mindship* in this shithole?'

'And if she gets hold of a gun while you're distracted in a firefight? You'll be the first one she shoots in the back.'

'That *is* the sort of thing I'd do,' Roag agreed happily, speaking for the first time.

Ethan turned to Orry, who was looking thoughtfully at their prisoner. 'Help me out here,' he pleaded. 'Tell Mender he's wrong.'

She didn't reply, just kept watching Roag's smiling face. As far as she could tell, Roag would have a much better chance of escape in the chaos of Rasmussen's rescue than here in the hold, so why would she say something that was liable to keep her tied up here? Orry knew one thing for certain: if Roag wanted to stay on board, that was the one place she shouldn't be left.

'Mender's right,' she told Ethan. 'She comes with us.'

29

GYRO

A low, thrumming vibration in the cable-rail heralded the gyro's arrival. It was a sunny morning and Orry shaded her eyes as she stared towards the distant tunnel mouth. The thick cable ran out of the station and off the edge of the rocky needle upon which Hudson's Leap was built. The sweeping curve was supported by slender arches as it passed over a gorge, eventually disappearing into a tunnel carved through a neighbouring needle about a kilometre away.

A high-pitched whine preceded an extraordinary vehicle bursting from the tunnel mouth, tilting at an alarming angle on its single row of wheels as it decelerated around the long curve leading into the terminus. The faded red and white livery of the gyro's six interconnected carriages was streaked with grime and daubed with graffiti. The three in-line wheels beneath each carriage were gripping the cable against all expectation. The engineer in Orry loved it immediately.

The whine didn't alter in pitch even after the train had

slowed to a halt at the platform and she realised that it must be coming from the gyroscopes that were keeping the inherently unstable vehicle upright, rather than from its engine, as she'd initially supposed. Doors slid open along the length of the carriages and disgorged several dozen passengers, while a mech loader began busily off-loading crates and pallets of cargo.

She looked round in response to a nudge from Mender to see a crowd of at least ten heavily armed contractors bulling their way through the milling passengers at the far end of the gyro. They were moving fast, but not fast enough to prevent her catching a brief glimpse of a white-haired man in their midst.

'Was that Rasmussen?' Mender asked.

'I couldn't see,' she told him as the last of the contractors were being ushered on board. 'It must be, though.'

'It was,' Roag confirmed. 'I saw his face.'

Mender scowled at her. 'Better get aboard, then. And remember what we talked about, Cordelia.'

'I'll be good as gold,' she promised.

They boarded the lower deck and walked towards the front of the train, the other passengers staring at Quondam as they passed; he looked like a hulking giant beneath the concealing folds of a huge hooded plainsman's dustcloak.

When they got to the second carriage from the front, they found the door at the far end was blocked by one of the contractors, who was armed with a tactical shotgun.

Curious, Orry walked up to the woman and asked politely, 'Can I get past, please?'

'Get lost, skank,' said the contractor, looking bored.

'Charming.' Orry returned to the others and they took a group of seats near the rear of the carriage.

'Why don't you check upstairs?' Mender suggested. 'We'll keep an eye out here.'

A flight of metal stairs led to the observation deck above, which provided wonderful views over the town and the needles and ravines of the Snarl beyond. Unlike the near-empty lower deck, most of the seats up here were taken. Another contractor was posted at the far door, preventing access to the front carriage by that route too.

She went back down and reported, 'Looks like they've bottled themselves up in there, just like we expected.'

'Not much we can do until we get moving, then,' Mender said, settling down into his seat. 'Might as well get some shut-eye. Keep an eye on Roag, big guy.'

Quondam had squeezed his bulk into the two creaking seats next to their prisoner. He peered down at her, closing first one eye and then the other before making a rumbling noise deep in his throat.

Mender shook his head wearily and closed his eyes.

Orry stared out of the window. She had an excellent view of the platform, the scurrying passengers, cargo-loaders and well-wishers seeing off their loved ones, but she was preoccupied, going over possibilities in her mind, not paying any real attention – until something in the mass of humanity penetrated her reverie. She backtracked until she found it: a group of two women and a man, just about to pass her window. The woman in front glanced up at Orry as she passed, catching her eye, and politely touched her wide-brimmed hat.

Orry craned in her seat, watching the three as they continued walking towards one of the rear carriages. She frowned, trying to work out what it was about them that bothered her. *It's the way they move*, she realised, *or two of them, at least*. The man and the other woman were weirdly serene, moving through the milling crowd as if it didn't exist. One careless passenger swung a bag up onto his shoulder so vigorously that Orry was certain it would strike the man in the back of his head – but somehow he swayed effortlessly out of the way of the bag's trajectory without even breaking stride. The three of them boarded two carriages away.

The thrum of the massive gyroscope beneath the carriage floor was not as noticeable inside the train, more a constant, reassuring background hum – until it was overwhelmed by the whine of the engines spinning up. People on the platform started waving, the gyro moved out of the terminus and quickly picked up speed.

Orry had never been on a gyroscopically stabilised monorail before, and she found it an unsettling experience. The carriage tilted crazily as the train flashed through the Snarl's maze of needles, reaching almost ninety degrees through the steepest bends, but however extreme the angle was, centrifugal force kept the passengers firmly rooted. Ethan had happily explained that the monorail's builders had strung the rigid cable-rail so it skirted most of the needles, resorting to melting tunnels through the rock with a laser bore only when it was absolutely unavoidable. They passed through the first of them shortly after leaving Hudson's Leap. Orry watched the smooth rock walls flashing past centimetres from the window, but within seconds they were already out the other side with a deep ravine yawning below them.

'If we go through a tunnel while you're stuck outside, that'll be all she wrote,' Mender said, chewing on his moustache.

'There are only a few tunnels,' she answered, 'and we won't be out there for long.' She wished she felt as confident as she sounded. 'Quon, are you still okay with this?'

'Yes.'

'I'm going to enjoy this,' Roag said, and Ethan shot her a venomous look.

'Okay,' Orry said to Mender and Quondam, 'we haven't got much time if we're going to hit the rendezvous. Good luck – and try not to get shot.'

'Bye bye,' Roag said happily.

As Orry rose to her feet she heard the carriage door hiss open behind her. Two passengers entered – the bag-dodging man and the woman who'd been walking next to him. There was no sign of the woman in the hat. Orry, still unnerved by them, sank back into her seat to observe them. The man was

269

tall and bony with a shaven head; the skin was stretched tightly over his face, making it look like a skull. He took a seat a couple of rows behind her while his companion, a pixie-like woman with a dusty red scarf wrapped loosely round her head, walked past and sat between them and the contractor guarding the door to the next carriage.

'What's up?' Mender asked quietly, following her gaze.

'There's something about those two,' she answered, wondering if she was just being paranoid. 'I saw them get on together – they were with another woman – and now they're in here, so where's the other one, and why aren't they sitting together?'

'Maybe they don't like each other much,' Roag said pointedly.

'If she talks again,' Mender told Quondam, 'make her stop.' Roag scowled at him, but he'd already turned his attention back to Orry. 'What d'you want to do?' he asked her.

Before she could answer, the door opened again and a well-built man entered the carriage. He was wearing a high-grade tactical vest and carrying a boxy laser carbine with a cluster of lenses attached to the muzzle. He glanced at her as he passed; the half-smile that appeared on his face looked oddly familiar.

'Where did he come from?' Mender growled. 'I thought they were all bottled up in the front carriage.'

'He could have come out upstairs,' she said doubtfully, watching the contractor talking to the woman on the door. After exchanging a few words, she followed him back down the aisle and out of the door behind them.

Mender looked expectantly at Orry. She turned to watch

the two contractors leave the carriage and enter the vestibule area that divided it from the one behind, her mind racing. She couldn't have asked for a better opportunity to get into the carriage up ahead, but . . .

The pixie-like woman ahead of her hadn't moved. She was just looking straight ahead. When Orry twisted to check on the woman's skull-faced companion, he was staring out of the window.

'I'll check things out,' she told Mender, getting up, and started walking back along the tilting carriage. Skullface watched her pass, his neutral expression impossible to read. The door hissed open and she stepped through – then stopped abruptly when she saw the two contractors were still in the vestibule, standing so close together that for a moment Orry thought they were kissing – until the man stepped back and the woman crumpled silently to the floor.

Orry took a step backwards, but the door had already slid closed behind her. She gasped in horror as he turned to face her and she saw the top of his head was caving in on itself, collapsing as if it was hollow. A storm of dust particles whirled, but before the collapse had reached his eyes, his head was reforming from the hair down into the features of the female guard lying at his feet.

She'd seen this before.

'Emissary?' she whispered as the changes rippled down its body, but when she heard the cruelty in the short, answering laugh, she knew this wasn't the same Departed avatar she'd

met inside the Shattermoon. *Could there be more than one of them?*
As the swirl of dust reached its boots, she scrabbled behind her
for the door release.

'This is an unexpected bonus,' it said, speaking with a
woman's voice, matching the identity it had just assumed. 'I
need Rasmussen alive, but you . . .'

Orry was already moving before it lunged for her, the fingers of its right hand formed into a cleaver-like blade which
slammed into the door a centimetre from her head. Terrified,
she ducked under its arm, stumbled over the woman's corpse
and dashed towards the next carriage back. The avatar – if that
was what it was – freed itself as she reached the exit, but it made
no move to follow, just gave her a chilling smile before opening
the door and re-entering their carriage.

Mender, she sent frantically, reversing direction to hurry
after it, *the woman who's just come back in – the guard? – it's not her!*

What the hell are you blathering about, girl?

*It's not the guard! It's something else – Departed tech – a shape-
shifter like Emissary. Don't let it get to Rasmussen!*

What is it with all your goddamn plans? he complained bitterly.
Nothing ever goes right.

When she walked into the carriage a moment later, Mender
was standing in the aisle, his Fabretti levelled at the avatar's
back.

'Hold it right there, you,' he was saying. 'I have no fucking
clue what's going on, and that makes me real damned *shooty.*'
The avatar stopped a metre from the door and Mender limped

up the aisle towards it. 'Don't panic, folks,' he told the few other cowering passengers, 'but it might be best if you relocate to one of the other carriages. Apologies for any inconvenience.'

The passengers scrambled away from him, falling into the aisle and hurrying back towards Orry, who stood aside to let them through. Only when the last of them had gone did she notice that Skullface and Pixie were still in their seats. In a sudden moment of clarity, she realised that the woman in the hat she'd seen with them must have been the avatar, and they were working together. She stayed behind Skullface and considered ordering Quondam to subdue him, but the tension in the carriage was palpable and she was reluctant to do anything that might plunge it into violence if she could avoid it.

Mender stopped just out of the avatar's reach. 'Step away from that door,' he ordered, but it just laughed. He brandished the Fabretti. 'Don't make me—'

It moved, flowing into a kick that sent the hand-cannon sailing across the carriage – and a second later, it threw Mender after the gun. He struck a seat several rows away and disappeared behind it with a cry of pain. The avatar stalked after him, its face twisted into a homicidal leer.

Quondam rose with difficulty from the confines of his seat and hurried to head it off. The moment the Kadiran left her, Roag scrambled over the seat backs in front of her and moved awkwardly but rapidly across the seats and towards the unguarded door to the next carriage. Oddly, neither Skullface nor Pixie had moved, despite Mender landing almost on top of the woman.

The avatar reached Mender first and lifted him effortlessly from between the seats. Blood was pouring from a gash in the old man's forehead and the corner of his mouth. He spat a gob of it into the avatar's face, which twisted with irritation. With one hand gripping him around the throat, it lifted him, ignoring Mender's thrashing legs and ineffectual clawing at its arm.

Quondam was one row away when Pixie rose from her seat and moved calmly to block the huge alien's path. He hesitated, then looked back at Orry.

He doesn't know she's with that thing, she realised, and yelled, 'Hit her! Help Mender!'

One giant arm reached for the woman, but she easily avoided it, then planted a flying kick to Quondam's chest that actually made the Kadiran stagger back a step. She resumed her stance in front of him as if nothing had happened. Behind her, Mender's face had passed from red through purple to blue.

Orry cursed, wondering. *Why isn't Skullface doing anything? Should I attack him before he does?* If he was anything like as capable as Pixie, Orry didn't give much for her chances.

With a roar of rage, Quondam charged Pixie, who slid easily to one side and tripped him, sending him ploughing into the seats. She was on him in an instant, raining blows down on his body as he struggled to rise.

Screw it, Orry thought, starting forward. She didn't know

how long Mender had left – he was spasming in the avatar's grip now – so she had to do something. But before she'd taken a second step, Skullface had risen to block the aisle. He too was standing in a relaxed stance, as if the last thing he was about to do was explode into violence.

She was willing to bet these two were astrotheometrists, come to retrieve Professor Rasmussen – which meant that what she'd just witnessed was *pash rakhar*, the Order's exotic martial art.

Skullface was regarding her mildly.

'Get out of my way,' she said, the words sounding foolish as she uttered them. His only response was a faint smile, so she added, 'Okay then, buddy, let's see what you've got.'

Orry had little time for guns, but she liked to think she could hold her own in a good old-fashioned fistfight. Feinting left, she aimed a kick at his knee that was designed to drop him long enough for her get past, but the kick never connected – one moment he was standing calmly in front of her, an easy target, and the next, a crippling blow had struck her throat and she found herself lying on her back a metre away, unable to breathe. She gasped, desperately trying to draw in air through her bruised windpipe. Her chest heaved as she thrashed in the aisle, panic overtaking her as her lungs screamed for oxygen and her vision began to grey. Just as she feared she would lose consciousness, something gave way in her throat and glorious air rushed in.

'Hey, arsehole!'

Orry's vision cleared enough for her to look past Skullface at Roag, who was pointing Mender's Fabretti at the avatar.

'I called dibs on killing that old fart years ago,' Roag continued, 'so you get in fucking line.'

The Fabretti roared and the avatar's head and shoulders vanished, converted in an instant to a whirlwind of dust. Its body started thrashing uncontrollably and Mender dropped gasping to the floor. Pixie, who was still beating on Quondam, paused to look past the flailing avatar at Roag. She started forward but a Kadiran fist sent her cartwheeling across the carriage. Skullface moved then, pulling something from his jacket as he raced down the aisle. Roag pointed the Fabretti at him, but before she could fire, the door to the front carriage slid open and the bass thud of a large-calibre machine-gun thundered out.

Windows shattered and seats burst open, filling the air with shredded upholstery. A line of holes appeared in the floor and the deep thrum of the gyroscope beneath the carriage took on an uneven clanking. Orry managed to drag herself into the dubious cover of a seat and lay there with her arms over her head, feeling the thud of every shot as the machine-gun continued to fire.

She lay there for what felt like an eternity but was probably only a few seconds, until the Fabretti roared again and the machine-gun fell silent. Peering down the aisle she saw a body slumped in the open doorway to the front carriage. Two men in combat gear appeared, leaped over the body and dived into cover behind the seats at the end of the carriage, from where they started firing again.

Mender had his Fabretti back, she saw, and Roag was hunkered down beside him. She wondered for a moment if she'd given up the weapon willingly, then movement drew her attention back to the problem at hand: Skullface was dashing towards the contractors at the far end of the carriage. She couldn't understand how he wasn't being injured, until she saw a shimmering disk flickering and flaring in front of him as bullets struck it. He reached the end of the carriage unharmed – and one of the shooters tossed his useless rifle aside and rose to meet him, drawing a long blade from over his shoulder.

Pixie was on her feet now too, but Roag had moved to intercept her before she could get to Mender, who was busy exchanging shots with the other contractor at the door. The woman blocked Roag's first punch effortlessly, responding with a flurry of blows, while beyond them, Skullface sent the man he was fighting crashing through the carriage window to fall shrieking into the gorge outside. He was just turning to deal with the other gunman when two more contractors emerged from the open door. Changing his mind, he calmly plucked the gun from the first of the newcomers before grabbing and twisting her so she formed a human shield as he fired her own weapon into her companion. The man was still falling to the floor when the monk snapped her neck and threw her aside – just as yet another contractor erupted from the door and tackled him to the floor.

Roag was looking in a bad way, but she was still fighting.

Quondam started moving towards her to help, but Orry yelled, 'No, Quon! With me!' and pointed frantically at the broken windows. It was time to get the plan back on track.

The Kadiran nodded and together, they ran towards the shattered glass.

30

RASMUSSEN

Keeping low, Orry peered out of the window and was immediately blasted by a jet of freezing air. Squinting against it, she saw the gyro was curving between two large needles, tilting so steeply that her side of the carriage was angled up towards the sky at about forty-five degrees. Gritting her teeth, she clambered out of the shattered window before activating her boots' molecular hooks and dragging herself laboriously up past the deck above to where the curve of the streamlined roof began. She had to hope Quondam was following.

For the first time since boarding the gyro, their plan was actually on track. The next stage was to move past the contractors' carriage along the outside of the train and drop in on them from behind.

The gyro started to bank the other way as the curve of the track reversed and Orry and Quondam hurried over the roof until they were standing upright on the other side of the train. They fought their way forward to the narrow gap between the two carriages, where Quondam jumped across first, using his bulk to provide a windbreak for Orry. She deactivated her molly hooks, threw herself across the gap and landed just as the train tilted again. She felt her boots slip out from under her, but Quondam quickly grabbed her waist and set her back on her feet.

'Thanks,' she said shakily, reactivating the molly hooks before she followed him along the carriage. This time as it banked back the other way, she lay on her stomach and peered in through the windows of the upper deck. It was deserted – but as she was about to move on to look at the lower deck, three contractors hurried up the stairs.

'Shit,' she said to Quondam. 'They must be planning to head through our carriage on the top deck and attack from behind.'

'You wish me to stop them?' he asked.

She thought for a second. If she let these three past then Mender would be caught in a crossfire, with the monks adding to his danger. Which side Roag would choose was anyone's guess. *Whoever looks like they're winning, most likely*. But with most of the contractors tied up in the fighting, this was the perfect opportunity to get to the professor. *Mender will have the sense to keep his head down and let them all fight each other*, she decided, devoutly hoping she was right. Putting her doubts to one side, she yelled, 'No, we need to get to Rasmussen!'

She crawled to the lower deck windows and felt a rush of relief when she saw the professor sitting there, guarded by just two contractors. The old man hadn't changed much – perhaps he was a little frailer than she remembered, but still looking pretty good for a man in his early hundreds. The guards were fingering their weapons nervously, but their attention was fixed on the fighting in the other carriage. One of them was Mason.

'There are two of them,' she told Quondam, 'so we'll go with the plan: I'll cause the distraction while you deal with them. Just remember: don't let anything happen to the professor – otherwise all this will have been for nothing.'

His crest flared briefly in the Kadiran equivalent of a nod.

Moving sideways like a crab, she got herself above the window until she was just ahead of the two guards. With a final reassuring glance at Quon, she stretched out so her head was visible to the men and rapped sharply on the glass. They looked round, startled, and she waved cheerily as the wind tore at her.

'Hiya, Mason!' she yelled.

He frowned, clearly confused, but the other guard didn't hesitate to raise his gun and she ducked back to safety a second before the window exploded outwards, sending thousands of shards spinning away into the gorge below her. At the same time there was the sound of more glass smashing and Quondam leaped into the carriage. Poking her head up again, Orry watched both guns swinging towards him.

'Professor – *get down!*' she yelled through the remains of the glass, and when his shocked face turned to her, she gestured frantically at the floor. A shot from Mason's comrade startled him into action and he threw himself onto his stomach. While his fellow contractor was firing at Quondam, Mason had spotted her again and this time had no hesitation in sending a short burst in her direction. He looked furious.

The gyro tilted once again, returning briefly to an upright orientation, and Orry found herself dangling head-downwards a kilometre above a raging river – but there was no time to dwell on her precarious position, for another burst of machine-gun fire inside the carriage had been followed by a crunch, then a scream. This time when the gyro banked back, she peered inside to see that the second contractor was unconscious, blood gouting from one shoulder where his entire arm had been torn out. Mason was backing away from Quondam, who was standing over the dying man, holding the arm; the contractor kept shifting his gun between Orry and the Kadiran, but he hadn't yet started shooting.

'Drop it, Mason,' she told him calmly. 'No one else needs to get hurt.' He was breathing heavily, his eyes wide as they flicked between her and Quondam. 'Don't,' she begged, knowing it was no use, 'don't be stupid—'

A burst of fire from the carriage behind triggered him into action, but he managed to get off only a single shot before a severed arm struck him in the face, quickly followed by an angry Kadiran. Bellowing, Quondam punched Mason in the chest, cracking his armour and sending him backwards into the wall. He slid bonelessly to the ground and lay there, motionless.

'Are you hurt, Professor?' Orry called, scrambling into the carriage and hurrying to him.

'I-I don't think so.' He blinked up at her, then rose to his feet and dusted himself down. 'Aurelia Kent. I thought it was you.' He turned to Quondam. 'I see your choice of friends is as fascinating as ever.'

'That's Quondam,' she said. 'Listen, we have a bit of a situation next door that we have to deal with, then I'll get you out of here. Hang tight.'

'Very well,' he said, examining the Kadiran with interest.

She checked the time. 'Four minutes,' she told Quondam, then picked up Mason's gun. 'If we can get Mender in here, we can hold them off long enough to jump.'

'What about Cordelia Roag?' he asked.

'We get her if we can – if not, she'll have to take her chances. Time to go.'

She followed Quon to the door, reassured by his solid bulk in front of her. She didn't think he'd been wounded disabling the two guards; he'd not said anything and in any case, she doubted their weapons would do much harm even without the body armour he was wearing beneath his dustcloak.

They heard muffled gunshots as soon as the first vestibule door opened. Quondam stepped over a body slumped just inside the second door, then slid it open and went through into a war zone.

The avatar had reformed and now stood at the far end of the wrecked carriage fighting the three contractors Orry had seen coming through on the upper deck. Much closer, a pitched hand-to-hand fight was going on between Skullface and Pixie, three more contractors, and Roag. Orry looked frantically for Mender and saw his grey hair sticking up between two rows of ruined seats.

Mender, she sent, *we've got the prof. Get over here.*

He raised his head briefly to catch her eye, then ducked again as shots from the far end sprayed the carriage.

Quondam immediately advanced on the mêlée. Plucking up one of the contractors, he started swinging him like a flail. Orry winced as he battered Pixie aside before throwing the broken contractor at one of his own comrades, flooring her too. Mender scrambled out of cover and limped past Orry, while Roag stabbed the knife she was wielding into the remaining contractor's neck – then, furious and raging, she started kicking at her victim's fallen body. At the far end of the carriage the avatar snapped a neck, leaving just one of the three alive.

It turned to stare at Orry, then charged down the aisle towards Quondam.

'Quon!' she yelled in warning, and the Kadiran grabbed Roag by the arm and shoved her towards the exit before swinging a fist at the approaching avatar. It avoided the blow easily, instead gripping his arm and throwing the huge Kadiran across the carriage as if he was a doll. Quondam rose unsteadily from the pile of shattered seats, shook his head, then roared and charged. The avatar swayed aside and one of its arms formed into a blade – which opened a long gash across Quondam's back as he passed.

This time his roar was one of pain.

'Do something!' Orry pleaded.

Mender levelled his Fabretti and fired, the avatar leaped backwards and Orry screamed, 'Run, Quon—!'

As she struggled to close the battered, sparking door, Mender warned, 'Cover your ears, girl!' She shrank away from the Fabretti as he pointed it over her shoulder, but the avatar was already moving, crossing the carriage in two steps and swinging itself smoothly out of a broken window before he could get off a second shot.

'Time to go,' Mender said.

'Two minutes, everyone,' Orry announced, herding them all back into Rasmussen's carriage. 'Quon, the harness?'

The Kadiran shrugged off the remains of his tattered dust-cloak to reveal a bag slung at his waist. From it, he pulled out one of the yellow and black drop-harnesses they were all wearing under their coats. Orry took it from him.

'Arms out, Prof,' she said, and quickly strapped the lightweight rig around his torso. 'We're going to jump,' she explained as she tugged on his straps to make sure it was snug. 'This will open automatically, so all you have to do is not hit any rocks on the way down.'

'Jump?' His voice was higher than usual as he glanced nervously out of the broken window.

'It'll be fine,' she said breezily, helping him to his feet. 'The gravity on Serapis isn't very high and it'll be a soft landing in water. We have a boat waiting for us down below.'

Ethan, she sent, *tell me you're ready.*

In position. Rather you than me, Sis.

She manoeuvred Rasmussen to the window. The wind snatched at his white hair as he leaned out to look down at the raging waters hundreds of metres below. He jerked back, clutching at her arm.

Mender, Quondam and Roag had lined up beside them.

'After you,' Roag said to Mender.

'No, Cordelia,' he growled, 'I insist.'

She grinned at him and Orry realised the woman was genuinely exhilarated by the prospect of hurling herself out of a moving train.

Roag gave a mocking salute and stepped through the window.

It was now or never. 'Go,' Orry said firmly.

'Piotr's puckered ring-piece,' Mender muttered, 'I cannot believe I'm doing this . . .' and jumped, closely followed by Quondam.

'Now Professor,' Orry said, eyeing the rapidly approaching wall of the gorge.

'I-I don't think I ca—'

She shoved him hard between his shoulder blades and he tumbled inelegantly from the carriage, screaming as he fell.

'Sorry!' she yelled after him, then took a breath and hurled herself out too.

She fell—

—and was jerked violently to a halt less than a metre down, to find herself hanging outside the carriage, buffeted by the tearing wind.

When a hand appeared on her left shoulder, she looked up to see the avatar clinging to the side of the carriage, its lower legs apparently melded to its surface. It gripped her shoulder with one hand while wrenching at her harness with the other. Her already aching ribs were bruised further as the straps cut into her flesh before the buckles gave way and it came free. The avatar tossed it away and she watched it fall spinning down into the gorge.

Then it locked its eyes on her face – and let go.

31

LAUNCHING INTO THE GORGE

Orry screamed as she dropped, her arms flailing wildly. One gloved hand struck something protruding from the side of the carriage and she clutched desperately at it. The gyro was starting to bank back the other way as it approached the far end of the gorge and, gripping on for dear life, she managed to raise one leg high enough to plant the sole of her boot on the smooth metal and engage its molly hooks. She hung there for a moment, her heart thudding so fast she thought she might be having a heart attack – then she remembered the avatar and looked up.

It was still there, standing on the roof and looking down at her. It started down the side of the carriage, moving slowly as its feet deformed to grip the near-vertical surface.

Fuelled by terror, she swung her other boot up and activated its hooks, then shifted her grip and used the pipe she was holding to sidestep along the carriage away from her pursuer. Glancing briefly ahead, she was horrified to see a sheer wall of rock hurtling towards her. She pressed herself desperately against the metal, willing it to somehow absorb her, and the rock flashed past a centimetre away, the air compression almost tearing her from her precarious perch.

The carriage tilted again, this time away from the rock, and she gratefully ran up the side, reaching the roof just before it angled back the other way. She looked down the length of the gyro, hoping the rock wall had scraped the avatar from the train, but first one hand appeared, then another, and it hauled itself up onto the roof. She fled unsteadily along the rattling, tilting roof. Her molly hooks would only slow her down now, so she had to rely on her own balance if she was not to be sent tumbling by the lurching gyro.

When she dared to snatch a glance behind, she saw the avatar was gaining on her, a look of fierce exultation on its face. As she turned back, the gyro banked around another curve and over yet another gorge and her heart stopped as she saw the sheer face of a needle racing towards her. To Orry's panicked eye, the tunnel opening looked barely larger than the gyro.

'Not good,' she muttered as she picked up her pace, ignoring the fact that she might lose her footing at any moment. The long carriage ended up ahead. There was a gap between it and the next – if she could just get to it . . .

She pounded along the curved roof as the tunnel mouth hurtled towards her, no time to think about anything but the gap up ahead.

I'm not going to make it! She closed her eyes as the tunnel swept towards her, running blindly as she anticipated the impact – and then there was nothing under her feet and she was falling.

Something solid struck her hard in the chest, twisting her round and driving the air from her lungs. She opened her eyes to see a confusing whirl of movement, the avatar poised above her, the tunnel edge sweeping in to slam into its body, smashing it instantly to dust, which was whipped away by the wind.

Ethan's legs were spread wide against the rocking of the boat as Jean-Baptiste held it as steady as he could in the rushing rapids. The gyro was invisible from the bottom of the ravine and he shaded his eyes as he squinted against the brightness of the sky.

'How much longer?' Jean-Baptiste complained from the cabin. 'The skipper'll throw me over the edge when we get back. He's lost a whole day's charter.'

Ethan gave him a reassuring smile. 'I told you, JB, we'll cover the whole day, with a generous bonus to keep your skipper sweet. Okay?'

Jean-Baptiste didn't look at all okay. 'It's not just that,' he said accusingly. 'You used me.'

'I said I'm sorry. Would your skipper have let us take the boat out in the middle of the night if I'd just asked?'

'No,' he admitted miserably, 'but—'

A loud *crack* made Ethan jump and he whirled to see a vaguely spherical sac of glutinous jelly floating on the water not far away. Before he could react, another smacked into the river, followed quickly by two more. Inside each one, he could see the distorted shadow of a person.

'That way!' he yelled at Jean-Baptiste, but the boatman was already moving. The sacs, caught in the current, were bobbing swiftly towards the boat. The engines roared as *Gorgerunner* slewed across the river to intercept them. Ethan raced across the pitching deck to a large cable-gun loaded with something remarkably like a giant sucker dart covered in barbs. Taking aim at the nearest sac, he fired and scored a direct hit. Once the barbed sucker had fixed itself to the gelatinous surface, he hit the switch that reeled in the cable, hauling the sac up the side of the boat and depositing it on the deck where it deflated slowly. The sucker was released as the sac dissolved into a puddle of water-logged grey sludge. The gun rearmed itself, reeling its sucker back into position, and Ethan aimed and fired again. By the time he had the second sac on deck the first had dissolved almost entirely to reveal Mender sitting, clearly shaken, on the deck.

Gorgerunner was moving downriver now, keeping pace with the last two sacs. The canyon narrowed a few hundred metres ahead, channelling the river into a lashing torrent. *I'm running out of time*, Ethan thought, taking careful aim at the next sac. He quickly reeled it in, but by the time the gun had reloaded, the last sac was entering the narrow part of the canyon, its skin stiffening protectively as it bounced off the sharp rocks.

'Faster!' he yelled at Jean-Baptiste, seeing the sac getting away from them.

'I can't,' came the shouted reply, 'the rocks'll tear us apart!'

'Shit,' he muttered, blinking away water. As the sac bounced in and out of the sights, he wondered who was inside. *If it's Roag, maybe I should just leave her*, he thought grimly, but he couldn't spare even the few seconds it would take him to turn and see who he'd already fished out of the river. The sac came into range and he fired; once again, the sucker struck true, yanking the sac to an abrupt halt and letting the water rush by beneath it. Breathing again, he waved at Jean-Baptiste to reverse the boat, while he started reeling in his final catch of the day.

'What are you doing?' Mender demanded as Ethan stepped away from the gun. 'What about the other one?'

'What other one?'

The look on the old man's face was thunderous as he stabbed a blunt finger at each sac in turn. 'One, two, three, four,' he counted. 'There were five of us.'

Ethan's mouth dropped open. With a sudden stab of fear, he looked at the dissolving sacs already on the deck. Roag was clawing her way out of the remains of one, while Professor Rasmussen's head had just appeared as his broke down around him. He watched the gun deposit the last sac on the deck. His heart sank: it was much larger than the others.

'That's Quondam,' Mender said, echoing his thoughts, 'so where the hell is your sister?'

They both shaded their eyes to gaze up at the clifftop as

Gorgerunner clawed her way upstream. Mender got on the integuary first.

Where the hell are you, girl?

Orry had no time to feel relief, for her whole body was in agony. She was wedged painfully between the two front carriages, where she'd fallen. The tunnel roared past her, flaring brighter as she activated her integuary's low-light mode.

Have to get back inside, she told herself, then sucked in her breath sharply: her chest felt like it was on fire, with something grinding in her side at the slightest movement. She tried again, shifting more carefully this time. Looking down, she could see she was on top of the vestibule linking the two carriages. *There has to be a service hatch or something,* she thought, rubbing at the black grime coating the roof, trying to find a gap. Very quickly she realised there wasn't one.

A noise from further down the gyro made her look up in alarm; a loud graunching of metal on metal which was sending vibrations right through the train. She remembered the gunshots tearing through the floor of her carriage into the gyroscope beneath and suddenly her pain was forgotten.

'Oh shi—!' she began, then the whole train *jumped*, tossing her into the air, and she landed painfully back on the vestibule roof. The screech of tortured metal filled the tunnel and she saw the red glow of sparks and flame coming from behind her. Emergency brakes shrieked into action and the entire gyro came juddering to an undignified halt that threw her painfully against the carriage in front. Moaning in pain, she raised her head and peered back down the tunnel. One of the carriages, presumably the one with the damaged gyroscope, had left the cable and slammed into the walls. Her heart sank. There was no way back.

Where the hell are you, girl?

Mender. She smiled despite her pain. *I'm all right – I think*, she sent back.

What's happening? asked *Jane*, monitoring the channel from her landing site near Hudson's Leap. The ship sounding concerned. *Are you hurt?*

Nothing serious, Orry reassured her, hoping that was true, before quickly explaining the events of the last few minutes.

Wait there, Ethan told her. *We're coming to get you.*

Hang on, she replied. *Let me see if I can get back to you first –* although even if she could get back to the tunnel mouth, without her drop-harness she had no way of jumping safely into the gorge. Climbing down hundreds of metres of sheer cliff-face wasn't an appealing prospect, but somehow she didn't think that was even going to be an option.

There was just enough clearance between the carriage and the tunnel wall for her to squeeze down the side of the gyro, but when she reached the derailed carriage her fears were confirmed: it had torn free and was wedged diagonally across the tunnel, its front crumpled and deformed so that it plugged it entirely. The door into its connecting vestibule was folded practically in half; there was no way it would open. After several minutes searching for a gap that she could squeeze through, she had to admit she was trapped.

The tunnel's blocked, she sent, coughing in the swirling dust. *You won't be able to get to me. Ethan, can you access the schematics of this tunnel? Is there any other way out?*

One sec, he replied.

She managed to climb back onto the roof and looked along the gyro to the front. The whole thing was automated; it had probably already sent an emergency signal. *I really need to be gone before help arrives*, she thought.

Okay, Ethan sent, *so I have good news and bad news. It looks like there are emergency exits from the tunnel every kilometre, but they all lead up to the surface – where the swarms are*, he reminded her unnecessarily.

She stared down the tunnel as she considered. *How far is it from the nearest exit back to the edge of the Snarl?* she asked.

Just over a kilometre. You're not thinking of going up there, are you? He sounded worried.

No, she's not, Mender sent firmly. *Listen up, girl, this is what's gonna happen. You find the nearest exit and get to the surface – but* do not go outside. *We're heading back to* Jane. *We'll come get you.*

No you won't, she said, desperation making her snappy, *there's barely enough shielding left on* Jane's *hull to get back to orbit as it is. If you start flying around trying to rescue me, we'll all be dead.*

Tough shit, Mender sent.

I agree, Ethan chipped in, *and so does Quon. We'll take our chances.*

It's my hull, added *Jane. I too think we should try.*

'Hell,' Orry muttered, knowing it was useless to argue. *I'm right,* she told herself, thinking about the things Mason had told her in the bar. She felt a visceral chill of fear as she realised what she had to do. She made her way slowly along the side of the gyro, heading for the front.

We'll be back at Jane *inside an hour,* Mender told her. *Flight time from there ain't much. Hang tight until we get to you – and don't go getting any stupid ideas.*

When she squeezed out into the open tunnel ahead of the derailed train she could make out the emergency escape door set back from the side of the tunnel a couple of hundred metres ahead.

What do you think I'm going to do? she asked, hoping they couldn't hear her dread. *Walk back to the Snarl on my own?*

32

SWARM

The door led to a round shaft with a ladder bolted to the side. Orry looked up, seeing the lights that had flickered to life converging far above her. Thinking about her friends already on their way back to *Dainty Jane*, she gripped the rungs and began to pull herself up, wheezing with pain.

By the time she reached the top, her arms and legs were burning, but that was nothing compared to the grating agony from her side, made even worse, if that was possible, by her panting for breath. The ladder let onto another chamber identical to the one below, with a single door that opened onto a flight of stone steps leading to a larger room.

At least I won't have to climb down the cliff, she thought as she saw a line of wasp-striped drop-harnesses hanging from hooks along one wall. The thought didn't bring much relief. She approached the exit door and peered out of its grime-streaked spyhole. It opened onto a trench which must be still a couple of metres below mean sea level, as the door was intact. At the far end were steps which she guessed led up to the surface proper; she half expected to find swarms of eaters waiting out there for her, but there were none in sight. She grabbed one of the harnesses, gritted her teeth and began strapping it on, crying out as she cinched the straps tight.

We're at Hudson's Leap, Ethan reported suddenly, *being winched up now. Should be back at* Jane *shortly.*

Roger, she replied, staring at the exit. *You don't have time for a crisis*, she told herself sternly. *Just get out there and do it.*

Red lights illuminated as she revolved the locking wheel and hauled the stiff door open. The air outside was dusty and dry, the sand of the trench gritty beneath her boots. She closed the door after her and forced herself to walk the few steps to the stairs. Heart pounding, she mounted the first step, then the next. Her head rose above the level of the trench wall and she looked around. *No sign of the little fuckers*. The land around her was barren, with stick-like trees poking out of rust-coloured rocks. Summoning all her courage, she forced herself up the last few steps until she was standing on the surface of Serapis. Moving easily in the low gravity, she set off towards the Snarl's edge, constantly checking around her, expecting to see a swarm descending at any second.

They finally appeared after she'd travelled a couple of hundred metres, a shadow high against the clouds. The sight made her want to break and race back to the trench, but instead, she froze, just as Mason had told her she should, a statue in the wilderness.

The swarm warped and flowed, coming together to form a black, ever-shifting ball, then stretching out thin, all the time moving inexorably towards her, still high up – then it formed a point and descended. Orry clenched her fists to stop her hands shaking as the cloud of tiny machines sped towards her.

They slowed at the last possible moment, using wings or tiny airbrakes, some striking her body while others tumbled past. She felt them on her chest and arms, crawling on her legs. They tangled themselves in her hair, yanking painfully at the roots, sharp legs scratching her scalp, and they were on her face too, blurry at the edge of her vision. She squeezed her eyes shut and tried to keep her breathing steady, knowing that if she gave in to her rising panic it would be the end for her.

The swarm was all around her now, too many for them all to attach themselves. She could hear the buzzing, feel them pressing in close. Her body was coated in them ... but she was still alive. She could feel tiny scratches and pinpricks all over, just like Mason had described, but nothing she couldn't handle. They weren't eating her.

So he was useful for something, at least, she reflected gratefully.

Something tiny and needle-sharp was scratching at her right nostril and her cheek was stinging where one of the eaters was clinging onto her flesh. Despite her best efforts, she felt a scream building inside her and she knew with absolute certainty that if she stood here much longer she would let it out and lose all self-control.

Must start moving, she told herself grimly, but her legs refused to obey. *Mason didn't say* no *movement*, she remembered. *He said* slow *movement*. Steeling the tattered remains of her nerves, she inched one leg forward, waiting for a hundred steel teeth to puncture her flesh. The moment she began to move the eaters on her body froze, as if waiting for something. She could feel the sweat rolling down her face as she carefully shifted her other leg, then let out a careful breath as the tiny machines began moving again, scrabbling and probing, pricking and scratching at her exposed skin. There was one on her left eye now, pushing down on her lid and deforming the eyeball beneath. She took another step, sliding her boot over the rough sand – slowly, so slowly – and then another.

Four steps. At this rate I'll be out here all day.

She increased her pace very slightly, making each step infinitesimally faster than the one before. The pressure on her eyeball released and she choked back a muffled sob of relief, then risked slowly opening her eyes, just the merest crack.

The swarm now completely surrounded her, thousands and thousands more of them buzzing in the air than were crawling on her body. The cloud thinned and thickened as the machines circled frenetically and she just had time to verify that she was still heading for the edge of the Snarl when a swirl of movement passed through the machines to her right, sending them tumbling. An instant later she heard the flat crack of a gunshot from behind her and had to force herself not to whirl round.

She turned slowly, her heart pounding as she waited for another shot, and stopped as the distant trench came into view.

Someone was staggering up the steps. At first it was just a head and shoulders and a hand, pointing a pistol unsteadily in her direction. Pixie's face was swollen and covered in blood and the other arm was dangling limply at her side. Orry remained motionless. The chances of the woman hitting her with an unmodified pistol from several hundred metres was pretty much zero, especially considering Pixie's physical condition. *But if it has been modded – stabilised, maybe, fitted with a target-locker and smart rounds . . .*

She swallowed, scraping her parched throat, and realised how desperately thirsty she was. A puff of smoke appeared as the monk fired again, followed almost immediately by the crack of the shot. Another swirl passed through the swarm; half of the eaters were already flowing towards the monk. Seeing she'd missed a second time, Pixie started walking towards her, dragging one leg. The woman had time to fire once more – this time Orry felt the wind of the shot on her face – before the machines enveloped her.

With one arm flailing as if in slow motion, Pixie staggered on for a few more steps, weighed down by the machines that clung to her, then dropped to her knees. She screamed, a shriek of agony that made Orry shudder, then toppled onto her side, completely covered by a mound of writhing eaters.

All too aware of the mass of machines still crawling over her own flesh, Orry resisted the urge to vomit and started walking again, step by infinitesimally slow step.

*

The next half an hour was truly a living nightmare as she kept shuffling forward, one foot, then the other, resisting the almost overwhelming urge to check her progress every few minutes because of the inevitable disappointment at how little distance she'd covered. She'd had to abandon the gradual quickening of her pace when one of the larger eaters had decided to take a painful chunk out of her thigh, holding absolutely still for what felt like hours, tears trickling down her cheeks, until she gathered her courage enough to start moving again. But she was close to the canyon's edge now, and she was still alive.

Mender's voice sounded over the integuary channel. *We're on board. You ready for a lift?*

Change of plan, she sent back, and explained what she was doing. For a few seconds all she could hear were Ethan and *Jane* pleading with her to turn around and head back to safety. *I'm almost at the edge,* she told them, trying to keep the stress and terror from her voice, *so there's no point going back now. Just come and get me from the canyon floor.*

You're an idiot, Ethan informed her angrily.

She really was close to the edge now, though, with less than a hundred metres to go. Her whole body was itching from the scratches and pinpricks of the eaters – all she had to do was just keep it together for a few more minutes . . .

She was attuned to the swarm by now, both to the invisible fluctuations she could feel in the machines whirling around her and in the movements of the eaters crawling on her face and body. A sudden change in their pattern made her heart miss a beat; she had to force herself not to speed up. Turning slowly, she looked back the way she'd come.

A lone figure was running towards her. It was the avatar, arms and legs pumping as it ate up the distance between them. A brief spark of hope pierced her despair as half the swarm surrounding her spiralled away towards the running figure, which slowed to a halt at their approach. The swarm enveloped the avatar, but within seconds it was flowing away again, most of the eaters returning to Orry.

The avatar glared at her and started running again. *The eaters were subverted to eat anything man-made*, she remembered in horror, *and that thing's not* human *tech*. Tearing her eyes from the oncoming avatar, she judged the distance to the canyon's edge.

She had no choice.

'Fuuuccccckkkkkk!' she screamed and started running herself, forcing legs stiff from shuffling into a sudden sprint.

For a few seconds nothing happened: her boots were eating up the remaining metres to the edge and she dared to wonder if the eaters might leave her alone – then a sharp pain in her arm told her she was wrong and she cursed as more and more of the tiny machines began to cut or gnaw into her exposed flesh or chewed on her clothing and equipment, biting through the tough fabric of her flight suit in seconds. It was like running through razor-sharp gorse bushes, but she gritted her teeth, ignored the agony and focused on the edge rushing towards her, unable to spare a thought for anything else – not even the avatar closing fast behind her. Her face wet with blood, she clawed at the eaters that were feasting on her, tearing them off and dashing them to the ground, but more instantly took their place, burrowing ever-deeper into her flesh. She screamed, not with fear, but with rage and pain. She wasn't afraid any more, for the worst was already happening. All she could do was reach the edge . . .

The pain was overwhelming. For the first time she worried that her body would give up before she reached the canyon's rim, that she'd pitch helpless to the dusty ground, where she'd be eaten alive. Despite her best efforts, she was slowing now, stumbling in the unfamiliar gravity, her breathing increasingly ragged – but there was the edge at last, right ahead of her: a jagged line where the ground just stopped. With a roar of rage she staggered the last few metres and flung herself over without a moment's hesitation.

She just wanted the pain to end, one way or another.

She tumbled forward into the wide canyon, the brown rock and distant white water spinning dizzyingly around her. For a moment the eaters continuing slicing her flesh, then the whole swarm simply detached and rose in a cloud that hung motionless at the top of the canyon. Her drop-harness activated with a loud hiss of air, the translucent polyplastene inflating around her into a protective sphere. The rate of her fall slowed immediately, the nauseating spinning easing. She was still close to one wall of the canyon, and looking down, she could see the ribbon of water getting rapidly closer. Every inch of her skin felt like it was burning; blood was smearing the glutinous fluid holding her firmly inside the sphere. She looked up – and forgot her pain as she saw the avatar standing above her on the canyon's edge, watching.

Shit.

She waited for it to leap after her, but the thing showed no sign of doing so, apparently content to watch. A more immediate concern replaced the avatar's odd behaviour, for her bubble was starting to oscillate, the unsettling movement growing quickly more pronounced. Wincing, she craned her neck – and groaned aloud when she spotted the reason. The eaters had not just been feasting on her; there were ragged holes in the sphere's skin where they'd chewed into her harness. Although they were small, the holes had weakened the sphere's integrity and as the wind worked at the polyplastene, she could see the tears were quickly growing wider.

The bottom of the canyon was hurtling towards her now, the fast-flowing river foaming with white water. The remaining plastic gave way with a great *bang!* and the sphere started shuddering wildly, jerking and spinning. It dropped like a stone towards the water and struck with a stunning impact.

Orry screeched as sharp pain lanced through her left arm. The semi-deflated sphere, caught by the current, was bouncing and rolling in the torrent. She was brought back to reality by the icy shock of the freezing water rushing through the ragged holes in its side and swirling all around the sphere.

I need to get the hell out of here, she thought, trying one-handed to manipulate the harness controls on her chest. The bubble was already softening, wrapping itself around her like a shroud. Ignoring the agony every movement sent through her smashed arm and broken ribs, she struggled frantically against the pull of the billowing plastic, which was threatening to drag her under. She was conscious only of the frenzied need to get clear of the thing before it drowned her.

Finally, somehow, she was free, coughing and choking as she was caught in the torrent, pulled under one moment, only to rise gasping the next, her whole body numb with freezing cold as she glanced off the rocks, constantly tumbling and rolling in a vomit-inducing maelstrom.

The canyon was narrowing now, forcing the river to ever greater speed, but as the rock walls went rushing past, Orry spotted a straggly tree up ahead, thin, whip-like branches trailing in the flood. She barely had time to recognise it as a chance when it was on her and she was grasping desperately at it with her good arm, clutching at the wet branches with numbed fingers, then gasping as one branch stripped the skin from her palm. Her headlong plummet was slowed enough for her to suck down a lungful of air but her grip was already slipping and a second later the branch ripped out of her grasp and she was off again, turning blindly head over heels beneath the water.

Something struck her shoulder and she opened her eyes to see one of the blue plastic barrels used by the riverboats as buoyancy aids. She reached desperately, trying to hook her fingers into the netting that covered it, and managed to anchor one hand. A little more stable now, she raised her head above the surface to see where she was going. The canyon was widening now, the waters slowing a fraction, and up ahead there was a gravelly shore under the lee of one rocky wall.

With her last reserves of strength, she managed to kick out, shifting the barrel towards the beach until she felt gravel beneath her feet. She unclamped her fingers from the netting and let her saviour drift back into the current, then, retching, she somehow dragged herself a little further before she collapsed, her legs still in the water. She forced herself onto her good side and vomited up half the river before falling back, exhausted.

She lay there for a while, barely conscious, listening to the echoing roar of the rapids as the canyon walls whirled around her, until, with a sudden burst of terror she remembered the avatar. Gasping, she pulled herself up and peered back along the river, but there was nothing there. She stared at the top of the canyon wall, far above. *Where is it?* she thought frantically. *Why didn't it follow me into the river? The fall wouldn't damage it, so—*

Ethan's panicked voice interrupted her. *Orry? Where are you? For Rama's sake answer so we can lock onto you—*

I'm here, she sent back, her integuary signal acting like a beacon. *Got me?*

Got you, her brother confirmed after a brief pause. *What's your status? Are you hurt?*

She thought back over the events of the past hour or more and just wanted to cry. Instead, she laughed, raising her head with difficulty to look at the watery blood leaking from a hundred bites and abrasions all over her body, the frothy pink stream trickling over the stony beach. In the distance she could hear *Dainty Jane*'s mass inversion drives throbbing through the network of canyons. They would be here any minute. Her laughter led to more explosive coughing and it was several seconds before she could formulate an answer.

I'll live, she told Ethan, then she let her head drop back and stared up at the sky, a slash of pale blue between the brown of the towering canyon walls.

33

RESIDUUM

Dainty Jane was not a big ship and with everyone squeezed into her small galley Orry was feeling positively claustrophobic. The addition of Cordelia Roag and Professor Rasmussen would have made enough of a difference even without Quondam's sheer bulk. *If we pick up one more stray, we'll have to start meeting in the hold,* she thought with a wry smile.

Her broken arm and ribs still ached after eighteen hours in the medbay, but *Jane* assured her they were knitted; she just needed to take things easy until the swelling had gone down. The holes in her skin had responded well, too, and there would only be a small amount of permanent scarring. During her recovery the ship had run the gauntlet of the eater swarms to leave Serapis behind, together with most of her hull shielding.

'Okay, Prof,' Orry said, 'I know it's not just me who wants to know what the hell is going on, so I'm really hoping you can fill in some of the blanks. Why don't you tell us what you know?'

The old man dragged his gaze from Cordelia Roag, whom he was eyeing with evident fear.

Not surprising, considering he was her prisoner not so long ago, Orry thought, thankful that, until now, Mender had kept Roag confined to the cargo bay and away from the professor.

'It's difficult to know where to start,' Rasmussen said, 'but perhaps I should begin with the attack on the institute.' He rubbed his liver-spotted forehead wearily as he put his thoughts in order. 'You managed to find me, so you must already know the Order were behind the attack. They hired a crew to abduct me – they took all my research notes as well, before destroying the institute. The avatar you saw on the gyro was leading them. The Order uncovered it on one of their digs; it calls itself Harbinger.'

'It was the avatar who framed me,' Orry interrupted, 'wasn't it? That's why no one believed it wasn't me: because when it assumes a form, it's identical to the original . . .' She paused, and then asked the question that had been nagging at her from the very beginning. 'But *why*? What did I do to them? And why did they kidnap you?'

'I spent some time with Harbinger before it left to report back to its masters – that was when the mercenaries decided to double-cross the astrotheometrists and hide me on Serapis.' He shuddered, although whether it was at the memory of his time with Harbinger or his confinement on Serapis, Orry couldn't tell.

'Framing you was partly meant to muddy the investigation

and divert attention from the Order – which would also buy them some time – but mostly, well, it was to punish you.'

'To *punish* me? For what?' She couldn't recall anything she'd done that might offend the astrotheometrists. She looked at Ethan and Mender, who were looking as blank as she was.

The professor was surprised that she had to ask. 'Well, for destroying the ventari stone, of course,' he explained. 'All Departed artefacts are sacred, so destroying *anything* is considered a mortal sin. And the ventari stone wasn't any old artefact: it was rarer than spice paragon and immensely powerful—'

'Even if the item in question was about to blow up an entire planet?' Ethan asked, his voice laden with irony. 'It would have killed *millions* . . .'

'Human lives don't matter to the Order,' Rasmussen reminded them. 'Death is to be welcomed as part of the cosmic design.'

Ethan rolled his eyes.

'As to my abduction,' the professor continued, 'I'm afraid that is a far more complicated matter, but it's connected to my work on the Residuum Project.'

'The what now?' Ethan asked.

Rasmussen chuckled appreciatively, as if Ethan had cracked a joke, but his laughter died as he looked around the blank faces staring at him. 'The *Residuum*? The reason the Kadiran sued for peace?' He looked puzzled. 'I'm sorry, I assumed you would know all about it.'

'Well, we don't,' Orry said sharply, the old bitterness at her exclusion rising again. 'I'm not as close to the imperator as everyone thinks.'

'Your relationship with Piotr is irrelevant,' the professor said. 'I assumed they'd tell you because of how it started.' He looked searchingly at each of them before continuing, 'When I got back to the institute after the start of the war, I found a particular artefact – one that had been dead since its discovery over a century ago – had come to life and was broadcasting data.'

'What sort of data?' Mender asked.

'Coordinates for a system out near the Diatris Scar. I petitioned the Grand Fleet to send an expedition but the Admiralty said they couldn't spare the ships. As it turned out, the Kadiran were not so short-sighted: a similar artefact in the Hierocracy's possession had also activated itself, probably at the same time – and they *did* send warships to investigate. What they found there scared them so much they immediately started withdrawing their forces and sued for peace.'

The galley fell utterly silent.

'What . . . um . . . what did they find?' Orry asked at last, a little shocked to hear the break in her voice. She wasn't sure she wanted to know the answer.

'It might be easier if I showed you.' He indicated the media screen covering most of one bulkhead. 'May I?'

She authorised his integuary and his eyes glazed for a moment as he sent a data package. The screen lit up, showing a dead world. A skeletal tree, stripped of life and pointing accusingly at the sky, was the only thing breaking the monotony of the blasted, lifeless landscape.

'This is Spero,' Rasmussen said quietly, 'a category-one candidate for colonisation. The footage was captured by the Kadiran expedition sent to investigate.'

A gloved Kadiran hand moved into shot and broke a branch off one of the trees. The bark instantly turned to powder, which drifted away on the wind.

The hairs on the back of Orry's neck were rising.

'Not sure I would want to move there,' Ethan said, looking pale.

'The last survey was conducted a year ago,' the professor said. 'At that time, Spero had an unusually rich and varied ecosystem.'

'What happened?' *Jane* asked. 'What could destroy an entire world like that?'

'We call it the Residuum,' Rasmussen explained, 'and it wasn't just Spero: it laid waste to the entire system – five worlds, all left like this. We know now that it is a remnant of something the Departed left behind when they went . . . well, wherever it was they went. It is, we believe, not dissimilar to the same smart matter used to form Emissary and Harbinger. Being kidnapped might turn out to be lucky for us, for Harbinger actually filled in a lot of the blanks for me, whether it knew it or not.'

He studied his hands for a moment, as if gathering his thoughts, then explained, 'The Departed created the Residuum hundreds of thousands of years ago as an exploration and terraforming tool, but ultimately it turned against them. It made use of postselection technology to spread through the galaxy, exterminating the Departed wherever it found them.'

'Data recovered from Departed vaults enabled us to develop the postselection drive tech we use,' *Jane* added helpfully.

Rasmussen glanced around the galley, evidently trying to find something to focus on before responding to the ship. In the end he gave up and said, chidingly, 'That's highly classified. You're not supposed to know that.'

'I'm a Goethen mindship,' *Jane* reminded him. 'I know a lot of things.'

Apparently conceding the point, Rasmussen continued, 'Departed culture was already divided: there were those who wanted to leave the restrictions of a physical form and ascend to a higher plane of existence, but there were also those who wished to remain in the physical universe. The Residuum tipped the balance. The Departed took the decision to abandon the physical universe entirely, fearing that if they remained, their wayward creation would not be satisfied until the entire galaxy was dust.'

'So they ran away?' Orry said sharply. 'They created a monster – and rather than deal with it, they took the easy way out and left someone else to clear up their mess.'

The professor blinked. 'I don't thi—'

'Wankers,' Mender interrupted with feeling.

Professor Rasmussen, who had revered the Departed all his life, appeared to be struggling with this viewpoint. 'Um, anyway,' he continued, 'they left *in toto*, and it worked: with nothing left to hunt, the Residuum fell dormant. It reduced itself to a core, a kernel within which it could await a sign that the Departed had returned.'

'And this kernel has reactivated?' Ethan asked. 'Why now? The Departed aren't back, so what triggered it – and what are they hunting now?'

Professor Rasmussen turned his rheumy eyes on Orry, sending a chill through her. 'It was triggered when you destroyed the ventari stone over Tyr,' he said. 'And now the Residuum is hunting us.'

She stared at the blighted world on the screen, struggling to process his words. This was too much, too big.

'This *isn't* your fault,' Ethan said, reaching over to place his hand on his sister's arm. 'You couldn't have known . . .'

'The kid's right,' Mender said. 'And anyway, it wasn't like you had a choice, was it? You saved millions of lives, girl.'

Roag snorted. 'Nuh-uh. What's one planet against *all* life, everywhere?'

'Shut your mouth,' Ethan snarled, but when he started to rise from his seat, Quondam silently placed a huge hand on his shoulder to keep him down. 'If this is *anyone*'s fault, it's yours,' Ethan continued angrily, glaring at Roag. 'If you hadn't betrayed your own race, Orry wouldn't have had to destroy that stone, would she?'

Roag's smirk turned dangerous. 'One of these days, child, I'm going to peel the skin off that spotty face of yours.'

'It doesn't matter,' Orry said calmly, tearing her eyes from the screen. 'It's pointless arguing about whose fault this is.' Her gaze came to rest on Professor Rasmussen and she asked the only question that mattered. 'How do we stop it?'

'That's what I was working on when the Order took me.'

'And?'

'I need more data.'

She bit off a curse.

'What about the monks?' Ethan asked. 'They have their own stocks of Departed artefacts – and Harbinger, of course. Is that why they took you? To help them find a way to stop the Residuum?'

'Oh no,' the professor replied, 'that's not why they took me at all. They were after my knowledge, of course, and my research notes, but they don't want to *stop* the Residuum. They want to *help* it.'

'*What?*' Ethan exclaimed. 'Why in Rama's name would they want to *help* it?'

'The Order already had some knowledge of the Residuum from Harbinger. They believe the Residuum judged the Departed and found them lacking. They want it to do the same thing to humanity – and not just us, the Kadiran too, in fact, all the races of the galaxy.'

Ethan stared in disbelief. 'They want *everyone* to die? Every living thing? They're crazy—'

'They don't think everyone *will* die. They believe that the Residuum will spare the righteous – like *them*. They think the galaxy will be *purified*.'

Mender reached for his hipflask. 'Crazy motherfuckers.'

Orry looked accusingly at the professor. 'Did you help them?'

'No! I told Harbinger I knew nothing about this, but before it could start pressing me, their mercenaries turned traitor and took me to Serapis. All they were interested in was the money they thought I was worth. If you hadn't rescued me, Harbinger would certainly have taken me back to Dia Tacita and I have no doubt its questions would have become more . . . insistent.'

'*Can* they accelerate the process?' she asked.

'Yes, I think they can. The Residuum has been dormant for millennia. At the moment I believe it's just casting about, gathering intelligence, trying to make sense of the galaxy as it is today. All the monks need to do is bring it up to speed, then it will head straight for the most populous worlds. What might otherwise take years will happen in weeks, days even – and neither we nor the Kadiran will have any time to formulate an effective response.'

'How will they communicate with it?' Ethan asked.

'Through Harbinger – it's made of the same stuff, after all. I'm certain they could interface.'

'Do they know that?' Orry asked.

'If I can figure it out, they will,' Rasmussen said, then looked uncomfortable. 'Also . . .'

'What?' she prompted.

'My research notes – the ones you wouldn't let me bring

with me? It's all in there. They're encrypted, but I doubt that would be an obstacle for Harbinger.'

'It's like you *want* to kill all life in the galaxy,' Roag told her lightly.

Orry ignored her. 'What do you need to find a way to stop this?'

He said immediately, 'I didn't know exactly what we were up against until I was kidnapped, but I've been working on this problem for months now – and not even the best minds in the Ascendancy could come up with a solution. I believe that only one course of action will give us any chance of stopping the Residuum. We must contact Emissary.'

Orry thought about the peculiar avatar she'd encountered at the heart of the Shattermoon. It had been condescending and supremely disinterested in humanity – its enigmatic statements had made her want to scream with frustration. *But it did tell me about the shroudsphere; without that I could never have saved Tyr.* She couldn't help but wonder if the avatar had known what would happen when she blew up the ventari stone. *Did Emissary plan that?* she wondered.

Jane broke the silence. 'In order to traverse the Shatter-moon's debris field again, we would need another stone.'

'Yes,' Professor Rasmussen agreed.

'I'm guessing you don't have one in your pocket,' Mender said.

'No, I don't.'

'Do you know where we can get one?' Ethan asked, but the professor shook his head.

It was Quondam who broke the heavy silence. 'I am aware of the location of a suitable artefact,' he rumbled. 'The Hierocracy has one.'

'A ventari stone?' Orry asked, suddenly worried.

'Similar, although not so powerful.'

'Where is it?' Mender asked suspiciously.

'The Reverence Division keep it at the High Exagon on Kadir.'

'Piotr's withered balls,' Mender muttered, and took another hit on his flask.

'Let me get this straight,' Roag said. 'You want to steal a Departed artefact from the headquarters of the Kadiran religious police and use it to fly through the Shattermoon's debris field to speak to an avatar made from the same stuff as the Residuum, so you can ask how to stop it?'

'Looks like it,' Mender said miserably.

She grinned broadly. 'I think I'm beginning to like you lot.'

'Pod away,' *Jane* announced.

'You think they'll believe us?' Ethan asked as they watched the fast-disappearing dispatch pod, which bore proof of Orry's innocence in the form of footage of Professor Rasmussen explaining in depth the truth about his faked death.

'Not right away,' Orry answered. 'You can bet Zaytsev will want it analysed, which will take time, but at least it'll be out there. I don't think this will truly be over until he sees the professor with his own eyes.'

On the screen, the pod's drive went dark. A few seconds later it shimmered and vanished.

'Anyway,' she concluded, 'right now we have bigger things to worry about.'

'Course laid in for Kadir,' Mender announced.

She glanced at Quondam for reassurance, but the Kadiran was as impassive as ever.

'Okay, then,' she said. 'Let's get going.'

34

THE HIGH EXAGON

The cold was the worst part for Orry. The wind cut through her insulated climbing gear like she was wearing a T-shirt and shorts. The High Exagon was nestled in a narrow pass between two of the Blade Ridge Mountains, Kadir's loftiest peaks, and whilst the initial challenging traverse from their temporary camp on a neighbouring cliff-face had raised a sweat, now that she'd stopped climbing, the cold seeping into her newly knitted bones was making them ache.

She'd had plenty of time to study the ancient fortress, which was more than a thousand years old, according to Quondam, while hiking in from *Dainty Jane*'s remote landing site. Six squat towers blocked the pass, linked by walls and reached via a bridge to the main gate supported on high arches. For now her view was reduced to one sheer wall. Even when she placed a gloved hand on the pitted stone, she could feel the chill radiating out. Each stone was truly massive, which made her wonder at the strength of body and will it must have taken to build such a colossal structure in such an inhospitable place.

Are you sure about this? she sent over her integuary, looking along the wall. *I can't see any gaps.*

Trust me, Sis. It's just a little further.

Trying not to think about the sheer drop a hand's-breath behind her heels, she continued edging along the base of the wall. It was all very well for Ethan, wrapped up on the Portaledge they'd erected halfway down a cliff-face a kilometre away and camouflaged by sensor-reflective adaptive foil. The two days she'd just spent cramped in the little tent with Quondam and her brother while he probed the High Exagon's defences had been a trial, but at least it had been warm. She gritted her teeth against the biting wind and pressed on.

Stop there, he ordered. *It's right above you.*

She peered up. Far above her, near the top of the tower, she thought she could see a thin skein of vapour emerging from the wall, almost invisible against the grey sky as it was immediately whipped away and dispersed by the wind.

You expect me to climb all the way up there? In this wind?

It's a fortress, Orry, he sent back, sounding disgruntled. *We're not exactly spoiled for choice when it comes to ways in. It took me two days to find this and I—*

Okay, sorry, she interrupted, knowing he was right. In truth, very few people could have found a way in at all, and she knew how hard he'd worked to locate this tiny flaw in the Kadiran security. He'd hardly slept since they arrived; it was no wonder he sounded a little tetchy. *Still*, she thought, the sheer wall looming over her, *it's not him who has to do the climbing, is it?*

She activated the molly hooks on her gloves, reached up and pressed them against the stone, hauled herself up onto the sheer surface and activated her boots. The climbing gear might not have been new, but it had performed flawlessly so far, well worth the brief detour they'd made to the markets of Longfellow Station. The hooks stuck with a reassuring grip as she pulled herself up the outside of the tower, but every time she released a hand or foot to reposition it, the wind threatened to tear her free. Her muscles were burning and her chest aching by the time she was halfway up. She paused for a moment to catch her breath, looking around for anyone who might be able to see her.

There was no one, of course. The wall she was stuck to like an insect was out of sight of the bridge, tucked close to the cliff-face from which the fortress grew. The only way someone would be able to spot her was from above, and that was unlikely, especially with the adaptive camouflage of her suit mimicking the stone so effectively.

'I have gained access to the fortress,' Quondam reported over the comm; it was annoying to have to use the device, but he didn't have an integuary.

She carefully detached one hand from the wall and pressed a finger to her throat mike. 'Roger,' she replied, relieved. 'Any trouble at the gate?'

'No. The documents produced by Ethan were adequate to facilitate entry.'

'Don't mention it,' her brother broke in.

'I already have.'

'That's not what I—'

'Just leave it,' Orry advised quickly. Every time she removed her glove from the stone to transmit, the wind felt like a giant hand slipping in between her belly and the wall and trying to lever her off.

'I will now attempt to locate suitable garments,' Quondam continued. 'Out.'

At least he doesn't waste words, she reflected, placing her free hand above her, setting the molly hooks and continuing her climb.

The plume of steam became more visible the closer she got, until eventually she could see it was emerging from a narrow vent covered with a grille. The vent was hardly large enough for her to fit into, let alone a Kadiran. *No wonder it's not guarded*, she thought as she positioned herself next to it, reached for the toolkit at her waist and selected a thermic cutter.

Don't drop it, Ethan advised from his distant perch, but she ignored him and concentrated on running the cutter around the outside of the grille until it finally came free and went tumbling past her into the chasm below.

Good job, he sent.

After returning the cutter to her kit, she climbed above the vent and paused to remove the tight bundle of lightweight rods from her back before swinging her legs inside, careful not to get caught on the jagged edges. It was a tight fit, but somehow she managed to squeeze herself into what turned out to be an angled, metal-lined duct that quickly turned straight down.

Do I have to climb all the way back down now? she asked.

Further, Ethan replied, sounding happy again now she was off the cliff-face. *Internal heat-bloom analysis indicates the climate is controlled from a sub-level beneath the fortress. Once you're there, the network of ducts extends right through the whole place.*

And you're sure I can access them from wherever this vent leads to?

Not exactly *sure, but it's a pretty good bet.*

She sighed. *There's only one way to find out, I suppose*, she thought, *and at least it's warm in here.*

It was a little too warm, as it turned out, and by the time she reached the bottom of the vent she was slippery with sweat. *The Kadiran like it nice and hot*, she decided as the duct finally turned horizontal and ended in a series of small vents which were constantly opening and closing, presumably to maintain the temperature in different rooms.

Ethan, I need to cut my way out but I don't want to drop onto some Kadiran heating-tech's head. Is there any way you can tell if I'm alone in here?

Sorry . . . I lost your heat signature as soon as you entered the vent and the cellar you're in now is the same – any Kadiran will be masked by the background heat. Can you hear anything?

She pressed her ear to the warm metal, but even using her integuary to enhance her hearing, she could detect nothing other than mechanical sounds and the rush of water and steam.

I'm going to risk it, she sent at last.

She extracted her cutter with difficulty, drilled a small spy-hole in the bottom of the duct and peered through. The room below was filled with pipes and machinery, but there was no sign of any Kadiran. Working awkwardly in the confined space, she cut another hole in the side of the duct, wincing as the oval of metal fell out and clattered to the ground. She pushed the bundle of rods through first, then squeezed herself out and with a huge sigh of relief, dropped to the floor.

The cellar was a large, dimly lit space beneath a vaulted ceiling. The hulks of ancient boilers rusted amid a more modern climate control system, although the corrosion on some of the newer units suggested these were long overdue an upgrade. A mass of metal ducting converged on a central hub; it was the work of moments for her to locate an inspection hatch and pull it open. She recoiled as a blast of hot, clammy air hit her full in the face.

Rama, it's like a sauna in there.

She removed her gloves, unstrapped her belt with its toolkit, then shed her climbing gear, which she bundled up and shoved on top of a duct, then pushed it out of sight. After strapping the belt back over her flight suit, she unzipped the top half and rolled it down to her waist, revealing the sleeveless T-shirt beneath, already dark with sweat. Finally, she grabbed the rods and climbed into the overheated duct.

Good, Ethan sent, *I've got a thermal map of the heating network and a tracking signal from your integuary. You know, this might actually work.*

I'm so glad. The metal was unpleasantly warm on her palms as she crawled forwards on her hands and knees.

He ignored her sarcasm and reported, *You should see a junction up ahead. You need to take the fourth duct from the left.*

Got it. How far is the lab?

Oh, it's a long way. Would you like me to sing to you to pass the time?

She arrived at the junction, counted four ducts from the left and continued crawling. *You know what?* she told him, *I think I'm good.*

Orry stopped crawling.

What's wrong? Ethan asked immediately. *Why have you stopped?*

I can hear voices below me.

Well, you are passing right through the middle of the facility. There's loads of breedwarriors and scientists in there.

It's not Kadiran – it's human. She pressed her ear to the metal and listened.

'Fuck you!' a man's voice was roaring, 'fucking yellow bastard kucks!'

She touched her throat mic. 'Quon?' she whispered.

'I am receiving.'

'Could there be human prisoners here as well as Kadiran dissidents?'

'It is likely. The Reverence Division are tasked with developing technology here that could be deployed against both Kadiran and human physiologies.'

'You mean weapons?'

'Certainly. Anything that could be used to counter threats from inside and outside the Hierocracy, in order to maintain the Iron Guard's power.'

She heard the guttural sound of a Kadiran voice and a moment later her integuary provided a translation.

'Test seventeen involves two subjects,' it said. 'The device will be deployed first on subject one, to evaluate its effects against Kadiran physiology.'

I'm taking a look, she sent to Ethan.

Don't, he protested, *there's nothing you can do, and if they see you, we're finished.*

She hesitated, then heard a low rumble beneath her, followed by a grunting scream.

'You fucking arseholes!' the man's voice yelled. 'You murderous fucking *arseholes!*'

'Subject one shows significant damage,' the Kadiran voice continued. 'The device will now be deployed against subject two, a human.'

'Come on, you bastards!' The shouts were punctuated with sobs now, but whether from rage or fear, she couldn't tell. 'I hope the fucking Fleet rod this place to dust, you kuck pricks!'

Poor sod doesn't know the war is over . . .

The rumble sounded again and she squeezed her eyes shut

as she heard a scream of sheer primal agony – followed by a noise like a bag of liquid bursting. Something heavy and wet slapped against the bottom of the duct.

'Subject two has suffered near-total molecular disassembly. As expected, the device's effects are far more pronounced on human anatomy. Armour was ineffective. Remove the remains for analysis and send in the clean-up crew.'

How many other prisoners are in here? she sent.

That's not our concern, Orry. We're here to do a job. We can report this to someone later – if the Residuum leaves anyone alive to report it to. For now, you need to get moving, there's still a way to go.

She knew he was right, but doing nothing did not sit well with her. Thoroughly sickened, she crawled on.

35

PHASIC VAULT

Okay, stop there, Ethan told her. *You're in position.*

Orry stopped with profound relief. She felt like she'd been crawling along the damned ducts for ever, the monotony broken only occasionally by directions from her brother, or a sudden spike of fear when a muffled noise from below made her remember where she was. She was soaked in sweat, her knees were skinned and her muscles ached.

I'm going to take a look, she sent, reaching for the thermic cutter.

Roger. Be careful.

Once again the cutter's tip glowed white hot as it burned a small hole in the duct's floor. She waited a second for the metal to cool, then peered through. *Bingo,* she sent, *right on target.*

What can you see? he asked.

Hang on, sharing now.

The lab was small, with metal walls hiding the ancient stone beneath. In one corner a pedestal supported an open cube made from a framework of thin rods, like a wireframe image.

There it is, Ethan sent excitedly, *an actual phasic vault – so cool! I'm scanning for a signature now.*

Immediately below her was a Kadiran, hunched over a lab bench, surrounded by an array of scientific equipment.

Wait, she sent, *is that . . . ?*

A female, he confirmed, sounding as surprised as she was.

Though Orry had never seen one before, she had no doubt the Kadiran was female, both from her stature and the drabness of the small crest running across her head, so different to the large, flamboyant crests of the males. Kadiran females were far less bulky than the males too – although they were clearly still way more powerful than any human.

What's she doing? he wondered. *Cleaning?*

Orry bit off a tart reply; he wasn't trying to provoke her. Quondam had told them that since the Iron Guard had come to power, females were treated little better than slaves in the Kadiran Hierocracy.

I can't see, she sent, *but let's check out the vault.* It was about big enough to fit her head inside, and it looked entirely empty. *We need to get her out, though.* She touched her throat and whispered, 'Quon? I'm in position.'

'I, too, am in an appropriate location. Should I proceed?'

Below her, the Kadiran female walked to a complex-looking piece of apparatus and touched its screen. Orry caught her breath as she spotted something on the bench that had been obscured by the female's bulk.

'I see it,' she hissed quietly. 'The stone – it's right there on the bench!'

There was a moment's silence, then Ethan asked, 'Are you sure?'

'Positive; it has that same sheen as the others did. She must be working with it.'

'Result!' he said excitedly. 'To be honest, I was never sure we could get the damn thing out of the vault anyway.'

She was about to pursue that further when Quondam broke in, 'Did you say "she"?'

'Yeah, there's a scientist in there and she's a female,' Ethan explained.

'That is . . . unexpected.'

'So what do we do?' Ethan asked.

'I guess we go ahead with the plan,' she whispered, 'and hope she doesn't put the stone back in the vault before leaving.'

'Oh yeah.' Her brother sounded crestfallen. 'Shit. Isn't there any way you can just grab it and run?'

'You mean like burst out of this duct, clobber her and just take it?'

'No, I just mean . . . Rama, Orry, it's *right there*.'

'We stick with the original plan,' she said firmly. She couldn't think of any way to get the stone off the bench, and the longer they thought about it the more chance there was of her or Quondam being discovered. 'Quon, go ahead and get her out of the room. If we're lucky she won't bother putting it away before she leaves.'

'Very well,' Quondam agreed.

'Actually, if she does put it back, it might actually help us,' Ethan said thoughtfully. 'I could get better readings during the phase transition than when the vault's dormant.'

A noise came from below her and the female turned. Orry shifted position as best she could to look in the same direction as the Kadiran. For the first time she could see the heavy metal door to the lab: a warning light was flashing above it and the door swung open to reveal a male Kadiran wearing the same coveralls as the female, although the colour of the trim was different.

'Wait,' she whispered, 'something's happening.'

The female adopted a submissive posture as the newcomer entered. When he began speaking, it took Orry's integuary a second to catch up.

'Analyst, I require assistance in my lab. You will cease your work and come with me now.'

'Of course, Director,' the female replied, then hesitated. 'Is it the particle inversion matrix again? Did you receive my report? I postulate that the instability is caused by subatomic perturbations in the Rolantz field. If you—'

'Be silent, female!' The male puffed himself up and she shrank in response. 'Your arrogance is breath-taking. Do you presume to lecture *me* on a field I have pursued since you were in the clutch?'

'No, Director. Of course not, Director.'

'You should be grateful to be here at all, female. If this

insolence continues, I will have no hesitation in terminating your employment at this facility immediately.'

She tilted her broad head a little to look up at him. 'But then who would assist you in your work?' She quickly looked at the floor again.

The male was speechless for a moment, then growled, 'Be very careful, Analyst She-Is-Spirit. No one is indispensable, and the Reverence Division do not look kindly on females who believe they are the equal of males.'

'Of course, Director. I meant no offence. I am keen to assist you in any way I can.'

'Very well. You will come with me now.'

'Yes, Director. One moment, please.'

She-Is-Spirit picked up the stone and crossed to the vault.

'Okay . . .' Ethan said expectantly, watching through Orry's eyes as the scientist placed the stone in the centre of the cube where it floated, held in place by an inversion field. She withdrew her hand and touched a panel on the vault's supporting pedestal. A deep hum filled the lab and the lights flickered and dimmed. The stone vanished.

'Looks like we're out of luck,' Orry whispered as the two scientists walked towards the exit, but before they could leave, a huge breedwarrior appeared in the open doorway.

'What is the reason for this unsecured access-way?' he demanded.

She-Is-Spirit adopted a submissive pose again, but the

Director positively cowered before the guard, whose armour was daubed with the blood-red of the Reverence Division. A war-maul was strapped across his back and he held a bulky assault cannon in one hand.

'We were just leaving, Unit-Beta,' the Director said, wringing his clawed hands. 'The female is assisting me in my work.'

The warrior strolled into the lab and looked around with evident disapproval. She-Is-Spirit kept her eyes on the floor as he loomed over her. 'What are you doing here, female?' he snarled. 'It is not your place to be in company with any Kadiran who has not won the right to breed.'

'No, Unit-Beta.'

He reached under her chin and raised her head. 'Then what is the reason for your presence at this facility?'

Meeting his gaze, she blinked innocently and said, 'You had better ask the Division-Alpha that. It was he who authorised my appointment.'

The guard studied her face for any sign of insolence, then grunted and released her. 'Ensure this access-way is secured at all times,' he said, striding from the lab. 'Security breaches will not be tolerated.'

'Of course, Unit-Beta,' the Director mumbled, and then, when he was sure the guard had gone, straightened and gestured angrily at She-Is-Spirit. 'Come,' he snapped, 'and shut the damned door after you.'

'Wow, Quon,' Orry said once they were gone, 'Kadiran males really know how to treat a girl.'

'I do not understand,' replied Quondam, who'd listened to the whole exchange over the open comm.

'Ha! I'll explain later.'

'Do you still require a diversion?' he asked.

'Not right now. Stand by.'

'Very well.'

Working quickly, she opened a hole in the side of the duct, lowered the bundle of rods onto the bench, then dropped to the floor. She grabbed the rods and hurried over to the vault, where she untied them and started slotting them together to form a larger version of the vault's cube-shaped cage; she'd practised this for hours in the cargo bay until she could do it in the dark.

Okay, I think I have the correct phase signature, Ethan sent. *I'm sending it to* Jane *now*.

I have it, the ship confirmed. *I am configuring my navicom.*

Orry fitted the last rod into place and stood back to examine her work. The larger cage now surrounding the vault was big enough for her to stand upright within it. Phasic vaults worked in a similar way to *Jane*'s postselection drive, by shifting whatever was inside it out of phase with normal spacetime. As her father had once told her, *You can't steal something that isn't there, right?* It was an almost impregnable design. *Almost*, she thought with a smile. *But we have something most thieves don't: a Goethen mindship with an intimate understanding of how her own postselection drive works*. She reached into a pocket and pulled out the small but critical component she'd disconnected from *Dainty Jane*'s drive.

I'm connecting the field initiator now, she sent.

Be careful with that thing, Mender growled in her head. *You damage it and we're stuck here. We don't have a spare.*

I know *that*, she sent back, concentrating on connecting it to a port in one of the rods. It clicked into place and she looked around for the power outlet she'd spotted on the bench. The field initiator needed to be amplified to get something the size of *Jane* to collapse, but it had enough power on its own to briefly shift just Orry. She unreeled a high-density cable from the outlet and examined the connection on the end, before getting a universal adaptor from her toolkit and using it to mate the cable to the power inputs on the field initiator. When lights illuminated on the unit, she hooked its diagnostics core with her integuary and checked that it was operating nominally.

The field initiator is up, she reported, then stepped inside the larger cage and checked she could reach easily inside the vault. She repeated the motion a couple of times, trying to memorise the movement. When she was satisfied, she sent, *I'm in position. Ready when you are.*

Very well, Jane replied, *I am activating in three . . . two . . . one . . .* now.

The lights in the lab flickered and then it was gone, replaced by utter blackness and a bone-aching cold. Orry gasped – and realised there was no air to breathe. *You're only here for ten seconds*, she reminded herself, fighting her panic.

She was floating in a void, bereft of light and sound. Carefully, she extended her arm, just as she had practised, reaching for where the stone should be . . . and found nothing. She tried again, with the same result, then, lungs heaving, swept her hand slowly left and right, up and down, then finally in a circle.

Something bumped against her fingers and drifted away. *That has to be it.* She inched her hand after it, aware of the seconds passing but knowing that if she knocked it too hard she would never find it again. It brushed against her knuckles and this time she carefully turned her hand over and closed it around the stone.

The void vanished and she was back in the lab. Gravity hit her hard and she dropped to her knees, sucking down air. Holding one trembling arm out in front of her, she opened her hand. 'Got it!' she gasped over the comm, staring at the stone in her palm.

'Good job,' Ethan replied. 'Okay, time to go. Quon, you'd better get out too. Sis, you may as well try to patch that hole you cut in the duct, but once they discover the stone is gone I reckon the whole place will go into lockdown fast.'

'I will leave now,' Quon confirmed.

Orry rose to her feet and was just about to start taking her cage apart when the warning light above the lab door began to flash. She froze, judging the distance back up to the safety of the duct, but before she could move, the door swung open and She-Is-Spirit walked into the lab.

Shitballs, Ethan said in her head.

The Kadiran scientist stopped abruptly when she saw Orry, eyes dropping to look at the stone she still held in her hand.

The female glanced over her shoulder at the open door and opened her mouth to shout.

'Don't, please!' Orry said, taking a step forward. 'I'm not a thief!' The Kadiran frowned and she felt like an idiot. 'Shit, you can't understand a word I'm saying, can you?'

She-Is-Spirit slowly extended a finger and pointed at the stone. 'Not . . . thief?' she said hesitantly, then gave a snort that could have been a scoff.

'You speak English?' Orry said, shocked.

The Kadiran grimaced, possibly because the answer was self-evident. 'Give . . . stone,' she said, holding out her palm.

'Please listen,' Orry said urgently. 'We need this stone to fight the Residuum – yeah, you know what that is, don't you. We're all on the same side now, aren't we? Just let me take it.'

The scientist appeared to be struggling to put her thoughts into words. 'No use,' she said, then growled in frustration and pointed at the apparatus on the bench. 'Have been . . . studying.' She made a slashing movement with one hand. 'No use,' she repeated.

'Not to fight it directly, maybe, but we need it to . . .' She stopped herself. 'To get something else that *will* help.'

She-Is-Spirit tilted her head to one side and studied her, then opened her mouth and roared something in Kadiran that Orry didn't need a translation to understand.

'Guard!' her integuary confirmed, 'there is an intruder in my lab. Guard!' The Kadiran held out her hand again. 'Give me stone,' she said in English.

Oh, not *good,* Ethan sent. *Okay, Sis, leave it with me.*

Orry considered trying to dart past the Kadiran or leaping onto the bench and going for the duct, but she knew it was hopeless. The next second the breedwarrior she'd seen earlier barrelled into the lab, gun held out in front of him. His eyes widened when he saw her and he barked something in his own language.

'Do not move, human intestine-filth!' her translator supplied with its usual colourful approach to the Kadiran language. 'Raise your hands above your head.'

'First, the stone,' She-Is-Spirit said.

'Do not interfere, female!' the guard raged, but she ignored him and stepped up to Orry, hand outstretched.

With a sick sense of dread eating at her stomach, she handed it over.

'How did you gain entrance?' the guard demanded, and She-Is-Spirit pointed at the hole in the duct above his head. 'You will regret the day you entered this facility,' he roared, using his gun to gesture at the open door. 'Move, human! You too, female.'

Orry started towards the door but stopped immediately as another Kadiran in science coveralls entered the lab. For a moment she assumed it was the Director she'd seen earlier, but when she looked at the newcomer's face her heart lifted.

It was Quondam.

'Remove yourself immediately,' the guard snarled at him. 'This is a security matter.'

Quondam didn't move, but simply stood silently just inside

the doorway. The guard gave a roar of fury and stepped forward, raising his cannon to strike him in the face. He was clearly expecting no resistance from a mere scientist, so when Quondam caught the barrel with both hands, the guard looked shocked. Quondam shoved hard, ramming the gun into the guard's face and mashing the delicate cage around his mouthparts. He howled and Quondam tore the cannon from his grasp, reversed it and pointed it at its former owner.

'Be silent,' he said in Kadiran, then switched to English. 'Seal the door, Orry Kent.'

She ran over and put her shoulder to the heavy door, heaving it closed.

'Is this laboratory sound-proof?' Quondam asked She-Is-Spirit.

'Yes,' she answered.

The cannon roared in the confined space and the guard hurtled back against one wall, most of his head a bloody ruin.

The female gasped as he slid to the floor.

Quondam turned the gun on her. 'You will give the stone to the human.'

She-Is-Spirit eyed him with a fearful expression as she placed the stone in Orry's hand.

'You should leave the same way you came,' Quondam told Orry, indicating the duct.

'What will you do?' Orry asked.

'I will take this beta's weapon and armour and depart through the main gate.'

'What about her?'

He looked at the scientist, who took half a step backwards, then stopped and straightened her shoulders in defiance. 'If we leave her, she will raise the alarm.' He pondered for a moment. 'I will bring her with me and release her once I am a safe distance from the facility.'

Orry thought that was a risky plan, but infinitely preferable to clubbing She-Is-Spirit into unconsciousness – or worse. 'Be careful,' she told him, before placing the stone securely in one pocket and hopping up onto the bench. 'And, Quon?'

'Yes?'

'Thank you.'

36

SHE-IS-SPIRIT

Quondam was not accustomed to the weight of the assault cannon. He was a historian by trade, a chronicler and a scribe. He had never won the right to breed, so he had never received any weapons instruction as part of his military training. He'd tried to redress that since his exile from Kadir, becoming adept with his appropriated war-maul, but his exposure to firearms had been largely limited to the human weapons onboard *Dainty Jane*. Still, the cannon was not difficult to figure out, and the results were most satisfying.

'Was she telling the truth, your human?' She-Is-Spirit asked quietly.

They were some way from the lab now, just a breedwarrior escorting a scientist, and if any of the lower-ranking Kadiran had thought to challenge them, they hadn't dared.

Sometimes the fear instilled by the new regime is its greatest weakness, Quondam reflected. He just hoped they wouldn't run into any alphas.

'About what?' he asked.

'About needing the stone to defeat the Residuum.'

'She was telling the truth.'

There was always a chance that this female would try to raise the alarm again, but he'd made it clear that if she did, he would kill her immediately. After what he'd done to the warrior in the lab, he was sure that she believed him.

'What are you to each other,' she asked, 'the human and you?'

'I am part of her crew.'

'On a human vessel?' Her surprise made her voice louder and he growled a warning at her.

'I am an exile,' he explained.

'Why?'

'Because I despise the Iron Guard and everything they stand for. If you had any sense, female, you would feel the same way.'

She glanced around the empty corridor, then stopped and touched his arm. 'I do!' she hissed quietly, then her crest blushed with fear and she stared down the corridor as if expecting a Reverence Division inquisitor to materialise there and then.

He looked down at her hand resting on his arm; it was a long time since another Kadiran had touched him. When she removed it, he experienced a profound sense of loss. 'Walk,' he said, and gestured with the cannon.

The High Exagon was a maze of metal-lined corridors, but he had memorised the route back to the main gate. When they reached a three-way junction, he turned towards the right-hand branch – but She-Is-Spirit clutched his arm, slowing him as a pair of scientists passed in the opposite direction. One of them gave her and Quondam a curious look as he went by, but she acknowledged them with a submissive posture.

Once they were gone, she pulled him to a stop and indicated the left-hand corridor. 'This way is longer,' she said, 'but less occupied.'

He narrowed his eyes at her. 'Why would you help me?' he asked. Though female, when she looked up at him he realised she was not much shorter than he was. *Admirably sturdy*, he thought.

'I am female,' she said with a shrug. 'I have no love for the Iron Guard.'

'And yet you work for the Reverence Division.'

'I am a scientist! I work to save not just our people, but all living things. The Residuum will erase all life from the galaxy if we do not stop it.'

'I am aware of that,' he said, impressed by her passion.

'Do you know how difficult it is for a female to secure a position as a scientist?' she asked savagely. 'It's not as if I had a choice *where* I was posted. I am just glad to be able to do something other than bearing clutches.'

He grunted, somewhat irritated by her evident intellect. Quondam liked to think of himself as an advocate of female rights, but he had never met a female like this one. Her intelligence was somewhat . . . intimidating.

'We will go this way,' he decided, indicating the left-hand branch.

She-Is-Spirit acknowledged his decision with a small nod. Behind its delicate cage, her mouthparts twisted into a smile.

'What are you grinning at, female?' he demanded.

'Oh, nothing,' she replied, hiding her smile with difficulty.

'Then get moving,' he snapped.

She-Is-Spirit was telling the truth; they passed only a handful of Kadiran as they made their way down through several levels of the ancient fortress towards the main gate.

When she was sure they were alone, she said quietly, 'There is opposition to the Iron Guard. Discontent is spreading and their numbers have swelled since the war. The elders can remember what Kadir was like before the Guard came to power, and the young want something more. With help from the humans, the regime could be toppled, but Reverence Division spies are everywhere; it is too difficult to get a message out.'

'I got out,' Quondam said. It was painful to be back on Kadir, and more painful to hear that nothing had changed since he'd fled.

'And others, I imagine,' she said, 'though of course we would never be told.' She looked at him as they walked. 'But you came back.'

'Not for long. As soon as I get out of this fortress, I am leaving again.'

'I know – to fight the Residuum with your human friends. But is that what you want?'

'What do you mean?' he said irritably.

'Do you not miss Kadir?'

He felt a sharp pain in his chest. 'I do not miss the oppression,' he answered.

'You know I did not mean that.'

'You are very talkative for a prisoner. If you are trying to establish a rapport so that I will not kill you once we have left this place, then you need not bother. You will not be harmed unless you betray me to the guards.'

She was silent as they descended two flights of stairs to the lower level, and Quondam actually felt pleased when she spoke again.

'If you told the humans about the dissidents here on Kadir, do you think they would help us?' she asked.

'Us? Do you mean *you* are a dissident?'

'No, but I am a Kadiran.'

'They already know,' he said with brutal honesty. 'I fought alongside Kadiran dissidents and humans on Odessa.'

'They *know*?' She sounded excited. 'Will they send help?'

'They are too busy fighting the Residuum.'

'But after,' she insisted.

Quondam thought of the head of Seventh Secretariat, the human Lucia Rodin. She was imprisoned now, but . . .

'Perhaps,' he said. 'Now be silent, the gate is ahead.'

A wide passage led to the main gate, a heavy metal affair which had replaced whatever ancient drawbridge had once opened onto the bridge. It was closed.

As he approached, a breedwarrior moved to block his path. He saluted and asked, 'May I ask your business outside the facility, Unit-Beta?'

Quondam had taken pains to wipe the previous owner's blood from his armour. Now he pictured the beta and did his best to become him. Lying was an unnatural concept to the Kadiran, but one which he had had to embrace during his time with the humans.

'This . . . *female*' – he imbued the word with distaste – 'is required in the capital. I am escorting her to the flyer pool.'

The guard looked confused. 'We have received no notification of a departure.'

Quondam drew himself up. 'I do not care what you have or have not received, warrior. You will open this gate. *Now.*'

'But—'

He gave the feral growl that was a precursor to a breedwarrior challenge. The guard instinctively shrank away, though he didn't assume a fully submissive posture.

'*The gate*,' Quondam snarled.

'Of course, Unit-Beta. At once.' He gestured to his comrade, who opened a smaller sally-port set into the main gate.

Quondam glared at the guard in front of him until he looked away, then grabbed She-Is-Spirit's arm and pulled her to the gate. He shoved her through and followed her out into the biting cold. The bridge ahead of them spanned a deep crevasse, illuminated by lights raised on poles along both sides.

The sally-port door slammed closed behind them and they started walking.

'You would make a good breedwarrior,' she said, hunched against the freezing wind.

'I have not won the right to breed.'

They walked on, halfway across the bridge now, the snow crunching under their boots.

'Your time with the humans has made you an effective liar,' she said.

'Do you take issue with that?'

'No,' she said hurriedly, 'it is . . . you are not like any male I have ever met before.'

'And you are certainly unlike any female I have encountered.' He looked at her, and they both smiled. 'You have my thanks for not betraying me at the gate.'

'Do you still think I would betray you?' She sounded hurt.

'No,' he answered, and felt suddenly worried for her.

They reached the end of the bridge where it turned into a road that wound away into a deep valley between two peaks. Quondam stopped and turned to her, coming to a decision. 'You should come with me,' he said, the words tumbling out in a most un-Kadiran manner. 'If you go back they will arrest you, interrogate you.'

'And I will tell them the truth: that you held me at gunpoint and threatened to kill me if I betrayed you.'

That was exactly what he had done, Quondam realised with regret. 'I am sorry,' he told her. 'If I had known—'

She hushed him with a sound.

'You should still come with me,' he said.

'I can't,' she said gently. 'My work is important: I must find a way to stop the Residuum.'

'Is that what you were trying to do with the stone?'

'Yes, but it was a dead end. Your human is welcome to it. I hope she finds a way to use it, because I could not. But there are other areas I wish to explore.'

He didn't know how to respond and they lapsed into an uncomfortable silence.

'You should go,' she said eventually. 'I will stay here as long as I can before returning to the fortress.'

He stared at her, wanting to say something but unsure what. He had met this female less than an hour ago and now it was time to part from her . . .

'I will return,' he promised. 'After the Residuum is defeated I will come back and find you, and I will bring others.'

She reached out and touched his arm. 'I look forward to seeing you again,' she said, then chuckled. 'I do not know your name.'

He smiled. 'I am Industrious-Chronicler-Of-Quondam-Annals.'

They stared at each other for a long time, until Quondam noticed how badly she was shivering.

'Goodbye,' he said, and climbed over the side of the bridge and down into the canyon below.

Above him, the wind howled mournfully through the peaks.

37

REPULSE

The strike group was an impressive sight, a cloud of war-ships arrayed around the three capital ships that formed its heart. *Dainty Jane* closed on the fleet under close escort from a drone-pack deployed by a pair of nearby patrol craft. *Jane*'s acceleration was limited by her fragile crew; there was a limit to what the human body could withstand even within an acceleration shell. The drones had no such limitations, and although the lasers fitted to each of the metre-long units were of a low yield, combined fire by the pack would quickly disable *Jane*'s mass-inversion drives, should she attempt to run.

We're committed, Orry mused as she gazed at the fleet, but the thought didn't bother her. She'd been playing out options in her head since before Kadir, and this was the only one with any chance of success, slim though it might be.

'Your friend is doing well for herself,' Mender commented as he followed the drones towards the largest of the capital ships, a dreadnought that was half as long again as the two battleships that flanked it.

'I wouldn't exactly call her my friend,' Orry replied.

'She agreed to see you,' Ethan pointed out from the seat behind her. 'That's good, isn't it?'

'She'll probably arrest us the moment we're aboard,' Mender grunted, flicking a series of switches on his console.

She worried that he was right.

The dreadnought filled the canopy now and she could see the lights of a wide landing bay in the shade cast by an overhanging ledge of its angular hull. A corvette passed to their left as they cruised gracefully through the gap, a warlike splinter bristling with ordnance, and Mender conned *Dainty Jane* through the cavernous bay and set the ship down on their designated pad with the gentlest of jolts.

'You want me to come with?' he asked, peering at Orry.

'Thanks, but I think I'll be better off alone.'

'Suit yourself.' He gestured at Ethan. 'Get over here, kid, and run through the shutdown checks with me.'

She gave her brother a sympathetic grin as she squeezed past him, then clambered down the ladder to the hold.

'She's waiting outside,' *Jane* informed her as the airlock hissed open, 'alone. That's promising, isn't it?'

'Perhaps.'

She walked down the cargo ramp and into the pressurised bay, where Yana Vetochkina was waiting. The officer's blue and white uniform sported rather more gold braid than the last time they had met; she'd been promoted to Vice-Admiral following her actions at Odessa and Holbein's Folly.

'Welcome aboard *Repulse*, Miz Kent,' Admiral Vetochkina said. 'Once again, you put me in a difficult position. Can you give me one good reason why I should not have you arrested immediately?'

'I can give you three, Admiral.' Orry tried to keep it light, but her heart was pounding so hard she might have just sprinted from Kadir. She started counting off her points on the fingers of one hand. 'One: I'm innocent, and I think you know that or I'd be talking to the arbiters now and not you. Two: the Imperator trusts me, so you should too. And three, if you don't help me, there's a very good chance that all life in the galaxy will be wiped out.'

Vetochkina regarded her. 'Is that all?' she asked coolly. 'I notice you haven't mentioned the Imperator's orders to me after *Holbein's Folly* – that you speak with his voice.'

Orry slowly extended a fourth finger, trying not to look anxious as she watched the admiral's gaunt face.

Eventually the older woman sighed. 'You'd better come to my stateroom,' she said wearily.

'Who else knows about this?' Vice-Admiral Vetochkina asked half an hour later, after hearing Orry's story.

'Just the Order, as far as I know.'

'And you have no actual evidence that they framed you for what happened at the institute?'

'I have the professor.'

'Yes, I've seen the footage of him you sent. Arbiter-Colonel Zaytsev is not convinced it's genuine.'

'That doesn't surprise me. I can show you Professor Rasmussen himself if you don't believe me.'

The admiral waved a dismissive hand. 'I'm not Zaytsev. But you have nothing to link the Order to all this except the professor's word?'

'Not yet, no.'

Vetochkina thought about this for a second or two. 'You haven't told me why you've come here. I assume you need something from me?'

'Yes. I need to speak to Emissary again.'

'The Departed avatar?'

'If anyone will know a way of defeating the Residuum, it's him.'

'And what makes you think it will tell you? I read the transcript of your last meeting. The avatar seems to do what it likes.'

'I can handle Emissary.'

'But you need my help to get past the picket.'

'Exactly.'

'How do you plan to get through the debris field without a stone?'

Orry trusted Vetochkina enough to risk coming here, but the woman was first and foremost a serving officer in the Grand Fleet. If she knew about the Kadiran ventari stone her duty would require her to deliver it to the Admiralty, and Orry didn't want to put her in that position.

'Emissary and I have a . . . a connection,' she lied. 'We'll get through.'

'Are you sure? If you're wrong . . .'

'Sure enough to risk it,' she said firmly.

The admiral rose from her seat and crossed to the window. Outside, some of the stars were moving: the other ships of her fleet. She stood that way for some time.

Orry hardly breathed.

'The Imperator is gravely ill,' Vetochkina said eventually.

'What? What's wrong with him?'

'He's been in a coma for several weeks; I suspect that is why he didn't intervene personally in your case. It is unlikely that he will recover. His condition is a closely guarded secret, but I thought you should know.'

Orry's mind was whirling. 'Thank you,' she said, surprised at the strength of her sudden concern for the old man.

Vetochkina walked to her desk and sat down. She reached into a drawer and produced a databrane, then began to write. When she was finished, she applied an official seal to the document and handed it to Orry. 'This will get you past the picket.'

'Thank you, Admiral.'

Vetochkina looked grim. 'I'm going to have to make a full report to the Admiralty about what you've told me; it's too important not to. I'll wait one day before I send the pod. I advise you to be a long way from that moon before it arrives.'

Orry felt a hollow open in her chest. 'What will happen to you?' she asked.

'If they have any respect for my judgement, nothing. Otherwise' – she smiled for the first time, a humourless curl of her thin lips – 'things may go badly for me.'

Orry didn't know what to say. Instead, she held out her hand. 'Thank you,' she said again as Vetochkina gripped it.

'There's nothing more I can do for you after this,' the admiral said. 'Good luck.'

38

EMISSARY

First-Captain Romanov studied the young woman in front of him with mounting annoyance. Any of his subordinates would have looked away from him by now, but not this one. She just stared back, a slight smile on her lips – not a mocking smile, nothing to challenge him, just a pleasant, honest expression.

He snorted. *Honest, my arse.* Romanov knew very well who this girl was; he knew all about her and what she'd done. He should clap her in irons and send her straight back to Tyr to face justice for her crimes. That was what Mironov wanted him to do, but Arbiter-Under-Captain Mironov wasn't in command here, Romanov was. *And it's my head on the block.*

Breaking eye contact, he looked down at the databrane on the table in front of him. It was genuine, there was no doubt of that; that whore Vetochkina's command seal could not be faked. It was obvious how she had risen up the ranks, using what the universe had given her between her legs to get what she wanted, like women did everywhere. She wasn't even from a

357

good family, let alone one of the Great Houses like him, and yet she outranked him. His face twisted into a snarl of frustration. *Oh, to be a woman. How easy it must be with a quim!*

He could challenge the order, send a dispatch pod to Tyr for instructions – but what if he was wrong? What if the Admiralty had ordered Vetochkina to grant the wretched girl safe passage? Bypassing the chain of command was a serious matter, one that might dent his already tarnished career, even with his family connections. And then there was the question of this orange-haired girl's relationship with the Imperator. She was said to be one of his favourites – Romanov leered at the thought – although by all accounts the wizened old bastard was on his deathbed.

But what if he recovers? What if he finds out I've disregarded Vetochkina's orders and arrested his protégée? Romanov found his throat was suddenly dry, as it so often was when he had to make a tough decision. And he'd thought being in command of the Shattermoon picket would be a cushy number!

Perhaps it would be prudent not to rock the boat, he reflected. Any decision is better than no decision, that was what they'd drummed into him at the academy. Well, this time his decision was to do nothing. *It's Vetochkina's responsibility – let her deal with it.*

He immediately felt better.

'Well, Miz Kent, everything appears to be in order,' he said with a wide smile. 'I wish you a speedy onward journey.'

I hope the goddamn rocks smash you to atoms, you rancid little whore.

*

'I can't believe he let us through,' Ethan said as *Dainty Jane*'s docking clamps released and they floated clear of the Shatermoon picket's flagship. 'Didn't he question you?'

'Not really,' Orry replied. 'He was an odd little man. Just stared at me for so long it made my eyes water, then snorted and wished me a good journey. Creeped me right out.'

Gravity returned as Mender engaged the engines, pointing the ship towards the Shattermoon. The system's distant sun fired the curve of its intact portion of crust, below which a broad spike of exposed core was surrounded by the debris field formed from the moon's remains.

The picket guarding the broken moon comprised a light cruiser and a substantial force of destroyers and frigates. The last time she'd been here the picket had been a single sloop, the *Goshawk*. She shuddered at the memories and fingered the stolen stone around her neck. This time things would be different. *We won't have a Kadiran cleaveship trying to kill us, for one thing*. The ships receded behind them as they approached the debris field, a chaotic ballet of shifting rocks. It had almost destroyed *Dainty Jane* on their previous visit.

She gripped the stone around her neck, yanked it free and holding it tightly in one hand, said, 'Time for everyone to strap in. If this is anything like before, *Jane* will lose her higher functions, so Mender will have to fly us in manually. The stone will stop me losing control – if any of you start turning homicidal, touching it should bring you back.'

Mender snorted. 'I hope you're right.'

Me too, she thought. Last time through it had just been Professor Rasmussen and her and the professor had nearly killed her. Now they had a full crew of potential killers, including a Kadiran.

'Head for the core,' she told Mender, 'and try not to hit any rocks.'

'I'll do my best,' he muttered drily.

The rocks on the outer edge of the debris field were widely spaced, easy for him to pick his way around. The density increased as they penetrated deeper, but none of the chunks came close enough to cause him to change course more than a little.

'It's like they're actively avoiding us,' Ethan said, watching one rock slam into another that had been on a collision course with *Dainty Jane*, changing its trajectory so that it missed the ship entirely.

Orry exchanged a look with the professor, who nodded, confirming her suspicions.

'It's Emissary,' she explained. 'He must know we're here. He's letting us through.'

The Shattermoon's core was a warren of exposed tunnels and chambers, once buried far beneath the crust. Now the huge shafts and staircases, much larger than any human would need, were laid bare.

Emissary was waiting for them in one of the bisected chambers. The avatar looked the same as on her last visit, taking the form of its creators. Emissary was tall, its hunchbacked torso and head out of proportion to its hugely long legs, with rear-facing knees like the back legs of a hound and arms ending in slender fingers extending almost to the ground.

Has he even moved since last time? Orry wondered as Mender set the ship down.

The crew gathered in the hold and followed her down the ramp, then hung back, allowing her to approach the avatar alone.

'Greetings, Aurelia Kent,' it said through a wide mouth with full and fleshy lips. Black eyes like dots in its doughy white flesh gazed down at her, unblinking. 'I have been expecting you for some time.'

'You have? Um . . .'

'You have come to ask about the Residuum.'

'I . . . er . . .' *Get a grip, Orry!* She abandoned her carefully rehearsed speech and instead asked, 'How did you know?'

'The ships around this moon communicate with one another. It is a trivial matter to intercept their transmissions.'

All Grand Fleet transmissions were encrypted, but it came as no great surprise that the security protocols posed little obstacle for the avatar. 'So you knew I was here?'

'I knew you were coming long before your arrival. I am surprised it took you so long.'

'Well, I've been a little busy—'

'On Kadir,' the avatar interrupted, 'acquiring a stone you didn't need. And before that, on Serapis. Was my cousin there?'

'Your cousin?' It took her a moment to understand what he meant. 'Oh, you mean Harbinger. Yeah, he almost killed me.'

'Harbinger.' Emissary spoke the name as if tasting it. 'How interesting.'

'It seems pretty appropriate to me, considering what he's trying to do.'

'And what is that?'

'Help the Residuum destroy us, accelerating its spread.'

'I think that is highly unlikely, Aurelia Kent.' The disapproval in Emissary's voice made her feel like a child. 'The Residuum is more than capable of achieving its goal without assistance.'

She frowned. 'Then why did Harbinger kidnap the professor?'

Emissary raised one hand and she shuddered as the fingers turned to dust. The cloud swirled around its wrist and she could see a solid nucleus at its heart; it was forming something from the inside out.

'Ask the question you came here to ask,' it said.

She bit off a snarky reply; she'd forgotten just how frustrating this whole enigmatic schtick could be. 'Is there a way to stop the Residuum?' she asked.

'Yes,' it answered, as the cloud at the end of its arm completed the transformation into what appeared to be a small vial.

'What's that?'

'*That* is the reason my cousin took your friend captive. To put it in terms your mind can understand' – she gritted her teeth at that, but said nothing – 'it is a virus, designed by my creators to destroy the Residuum but never used. The monks who reprogrammed Harbinger must know of its existence; they will want to neutralise the threat it poses. I can only imagine that they wrongly assumed Professor Rasmussen would be aware of its location.'

Orry turned to the professor, who held up his hands in a gesture of helpless ignorance.

Then she turned back to Emissary. 'Wait a minute – the monks *reprogrammed* Harbinger?'

'Of course. It is evident from its actions, if not from their choice of name. One of my kind would never assist the Residuum.'

'I should have guessed when he tried to kill me. It seemed out of character for something – some*one* – like you.'

'You are mistaken,' the avatar said evenly. 'Human lives are of little consequence.'

'Right.' *Whenever I start to forget just how alien this damn thing is, it comes out with shit like that.* 'Anyway,' she said, moving quickly on, 'this is brilliant. There's a virus that will kill it: that's exactly why we came. Where is it?'

The vial at the end of Emissary's arm changed again, reforming into a world made entirely of water. Simulated sunlight reflected from animated oceans as the model rotated slowly above its wrist.

'The planet Coromandel,' it told her, 'in the volume you call the Fomor Cluster. Water disrupts the integrity of my kind, so it is a natural place to conceal the virus.'

It took her a moment to place the name. 'Isn't that a Mariner colony?'

'Yeah,' Mender confirmed, coming to stand beside her. 'This could be interesting.'

'Captain Mender,' Emissary said. 'I am sure it will pose no great difficulty to a man of your capabilities.'

He eyed the avatar suspiciously; it was difficult to judge from its neutral tone whether it was mocking him or not.

'Where is the virus, exactly?' Orry asked.

'I don't know,' the avatar admitted.

'Then how the hell are we supposed to find it?' Mender pointed at the spinning orb. 'That's a hell of a lot of water.'

'Locating the virus will be a simple task once I am on the planet,' Emissary said.

'You want to come with us?' she asked in surprise.

'Of course. There is no other way. And we must hurry: I was compelled to interface with local Grand Fleet data cores to locate the virus. As careful as I was, I fear it is only a matter of time before my cousin finds traces of my search and deduces our destination.'

She glanced at Mender, who was looking even more unhappy than usual. 'Okay, I guess,' she said. 'How, er . . .' She trailed off, feeling foolish. She'd been about to ask if Emissary could even leave the Shattermoon – she'd assumed having been there for so many millennia it was somehow tied to the place – but of course Harbinger could move freely about the galaxy so why shouldn't Emissary? Instead of saying any more, she indicated *Dainty Jane*'s cargo ramp with a sweep of her arm.

'Welcome aboard,' she said.

39

I MUST CONSIDER THIS

Quondam rose to his feet when Orry entered the hold. Roag, in the corner, watched from her mattress.

'Take a break – I'll stay for a while,' Orry told the Kadiran. 'I have to fix this bloody thing anyway.' She brandished the comm unit she'd taken from her spacesuit and placed it on the workbench next to Mender's old Horten-Yakimov ground-effect bike.

'I will go,' Quondam said, and left her alone with Roag.

Orry frowned at the comm.

'Not great conversationalists, the Kadiran,' Roag observed.

'You would know,' she said coldly, 'given you spent enough time plotting with them to commit genocide on your own people.' She turned the comm unit on and watched the boot sequence scroll up the screen.

'Rama, are we *still* on that?' Roag said wearily. 'You have to learn to let these things go.'

Orry tried to ignore her. *The boot sequence is fine, so what's the damn problem?* She shut the unit down, unclipped the back and opened the housing.

'What's wrong with it?' Roag asked.

She said nothing for a moment, then decided it was easier just to answer. 'Range degradation – it's been getting worse for a while, but now I have to be practically holding hands for anyone to hear me.'

'So get a new unit.'

She did her best Mender impression, saying gruffly, 'We're not made of gilt, girl.'

Roag smiled. 'Could be the power cell,' she suggested.

'That's what I thought,' Orry said, pursing her lips with irritation as she finally located the cell, inconveniently buried beneath several other components. 'The problem is the damn things are supposed to last for ever, so they're not easy to get at.'

'Want a hand?' Roag asked innocently, holding up her arms which were bound together by a plastic restraint at the wrists. A tether looped through her arms was fastened to one of the thick pipes running up the bulkhead.

Orry caught her smile before it showed; it annoyed her that Roag could be so charming when she wanted to. 'I think I can manage,' she said coldly, disconnecting components and lining them up neatly on the bench so she would know which order to put them back in.

The older woman watched her in silence for a while, then said, 'You did all right, you know, back on Kadir. That took guts, crawling into the High Exagon.'

She looked up, surprised. 'Uh, thanks.'

Roag gazed at her, her face its usual mask, and Orry felt she should say more. 'You did well, too, on the gyro, saving Mender like that.'

Roag smiled grimly. 'It's funny,' she said.

'What is?'

'That we hate each other's guts, but we still make a pretty good team.'

Orry nodded reflectively. 'Can I ask you a question, Cordelia?'

'Cordelia? Wow.' She readjusted her position on her mattress, settling her back against the bulkhead. 'Okay, shoot.'

'Why did you do it?'

'Which bit?'

'All of it.'

Roag drew in a deep breath and released it slowly, letting her eyes drift to the overhead. 'You think I'm a monster,' she began, 'I get that. But do you know what *I* think is monstrous? The fucking Ascendancy, that's what, and I'll do whatever it takes to bring that rancid mound of privilege and corruption down.'

'Even killing a billion people on Tyr?' Orry asked, trying all over again not to get angry. 'Or starting a war that's killed almost that many across the galaxy?'

'And how many have died at the hands of the Ruuz since that fat prick Piotr came to power two hundred years ago? How many more will die in the next two centuries? And we just let it happen: the top one per cent dance at balls while the rest starve.'

'Yada, yada, yada,' Orry replied, not bothering to conceal the contempt in her voice. 'I don't understand you, Cordelia. You're not stupid, and yet somehow you came to the conclusion that handing it all to the Kadiran would somehow make things better. And when that failed you picked my *grandfather* – of all people! – to succeed Piotr.' She shook her head. 'I just don't believe you. You say everything you did was for "*the people*"' – she indicated the quotes with her fingers – 'but do you want to know why I think you really did it?'

Roag was watching her, eyes like flint. 'Do enlighten me,' she said quietly.

'I think you never got over your fucked-up childhood. I think you're messed up, right *here*—' and as she jabbed a finger at her temple, suddenly her burst of anger was gone. 'I think you just want to watch the galaxy burn,' she finished sadly, before returning her attention to the comm unit.

Roag watched her in silence for several seconds, then snorted. 'The Kadiran were after the Fountainhead and the more established worlds, the ones where most of the Ruuz had settled. They promised me the rest, all the outer colonies, the places the Great Houses were strangling to fill their coffers. The poor bastards on those rocks would do a hell of a lot better with me in charge, so forgive me for not giving a fuck about the chinless Ruuz pricks who'd have to die to make that happen.'

'And the millions in the Fountainhead who aren't Ruuz?'

Roag had the grace to look remorseful. 'Revolution comes at a cost,' she said quietly, but Orry wasn't buying it. 'And what are deaths of a few million against a better future for billions?'

'You make me sick.'

'Of course you don't understand. You're just like the rest of the sanctimonious do-gooders who whine about fair distribution of wealth but don't have the balls to do anything about it.'

'What about trying to put Delf on the throne?' Orry said. 'Did he promise to make you queen of the colonies too?'

Roag laughed. 'Hindsight is a wonderful thing, isn't it? Believe it or not, I've come to believe you actually did me a favour by saving Tyr. The Kadiran are dumb fuckers, but surprisingly difficult to manipulate. Now I think that if that plan had succeeded, my rule over the colonies might have proved rather shorter and less successful that I'd planned. Killing Piotr and replacing him with your grandfather, though? That was a stroke of genius. For all his bluster, Delf is a weak, frightened man. With him as Imperator and me his closest advisor, I could bring the Ascendancy down from within in a matter of years. Unfortunately, far fewer Ruuz would have died that way, but I suppose one must make sacrifices.'

Orry knew Roag was deliberately needling her, so she refused to give her the satisfaction of any reaction. 'So you see yourself as a revolutionary, fighting for the rights of the poor and downtrodden?'

'You know, I quite like that.'

'Whereas I see you as a psycho.'

Roag pouted as if disappointed. 'How rude.'

'And what will you do if we let you go?' Orry asked. 'Will you keep trying to bring down the Ascendancy?'

'Are you saying you have a problem with that? Aurelia Kent, friend to the Imperator.'

'I have a problem with you killing people.'

'And that's why you'll never change anything.'

Orry laughed. 'If we let you go I don't think you'll do a damn thing. I don't think you'll be able to. What's left of your own organisation is trying to kill you, and you're still the most wanted fugitive in the Ascendancy.'

'Apart from you, of course.'

'Oh, I doubt they want me half as much as they want you. Besides, I'm innocent.'

Roag snorted at that. 'That's not what Zaytsev believes. And I don't see your precious Imperator rushing to help you. Thanks for your concern, but I'll be fine.' She ran her fingers along the pipe she was tied to, caressing the metal. 'There's always another plan.'

Something about the way she said that worried Orry, but before she could formulate a response a stabbing pain shot up her arm, numbing it. With a hiss of pain, she snatched her hand back from the disassembled comm unit.

'Bloody thing shocked me,' she snarled, grabbing a carbonide rod and jamming it into the open housing. With a little manoeuvring she managed to get the rod under the power cell and was trying to lever it up when she heard someone on the ladder from the galley.

'Captain Mender asked me to inform you that the dispatch pod has left the system,' Emissary said.

Orry grinned despite her frustration with the comm unit. Mender could easily have told her that himself over integuary; Emissary was obviously annoying him up in the cockpit.

'Thanks,' she said, grimacing as she exerted more pressure on the rod.

The avatar walked closer. 'I am curious. Would it not have been more efficient to inform the commander of the local picket about Coromandel? Why expend a pod to tell Vice-Admiral Vetochkina where we are going?'

'Because—' Orry stopped talking and gave a grunt as she shoved down hard on the rod and the power cell finally popped free of the comm unit. 'Got you, you little bastard.' She looked at Emissary. 'Because the guy in charge of the picket is a creepy Ruuz weasel and I trust Vetochkina.'

'I understand.' It stepped closer to watch her examine the slender black wafer of the power cell.

'We were right!' she said, holding up the cell for Roag to see. 'Look, it's cracked – just a hairline, but enough for the matrix to short and discharge.'

'May I see?' Emissary said.

'Watch out,' she advised, holding out the cell, 'it gave me a nasty shock.'

The avatar reached for it, but as its leathery hand came

closer it stopped abruptly and she saw that it was trembling. Emissary's tiny eyes looked from the cell to its hand, which was now vibrating so quickly that a fine cloud of dust motes were drifting away from its skin. It withdrew its hand a few centimetres and the vibration stopped, the motes quickly returning to its person.

'Curious,' it said. 'What form of energy powers that cell?'

'Confined free-state energy,' Orry and Roag said together. Roag was staring at Emissary with intense interest.

'Primitive,' the avatar said thoughtfully. 'How fascinating.'

'What did it do to you?' Orry asked.

'I must consider this.' It walked to the ladder with its curious rolling gait and climbed back up to the galley.

Orry turned to Roag, who was still watching the avatar through narrowed eyes. 'What was that all about?'

Roag blinked as if shaken from a reverie. 'I'm sure it'll tell us when it's figured it out,' she said dismissively, then yawned. 'Now, are you going to finish putting a fresh cell in that thing and fuck off? I feel like a nap.'

Orry watched her adjust her bedding and settle down, sure that she was up to something. *But what?* she thought. Increasingly worried, she tossed the cracked power cell into one of the hoppers for the atomic forge and reached for a replacement.

40

PENGUIN

Lieutenant Wayland Tan unhooked from the sensor core and looked across the cramped ops room at First-Specialist Emmeline Haas.

'What's it doing, Ems?' he asked.

Penguin's three acceleration shells were arranged around a central column of screens. With the main drive shut down, the shells were open, and Wayland could see his sensor specialist's eyes were integuary-glazed.

'I have no idea, Skip,' she responded. 'It's just continuously reforming itself.'

The constant movement of the construct, as they'd taken to calling it, was making his brain hurt. It looked like a colossal three-dimensional snowflake, forever throwing out new spiny arms as others shrank away. At its heart was a mass of inter-locking forms, constantly in motion like the churning gears of a vast piece of clockwork. The intricacy of it was breath-taking.

'What about the colony?' he asked.

'No life signs,' she replied, 'not even microbial. Whatever that thing is, it's sterilised the entire planet.' Her tone was professional, but he knew her well enough to know the deep pain it was masking.

Penguin was Wayland's first command. It might be one of the smallest ships in the Grand Fleet, but what the tiny scout vessel lacked in weapons and speed she more than made up for in sensor arrays – which was why he'd been ordered to the Cannis system to monitor this . . . *thing*. As a mere lieutenant he didn't expect to be told anything of actual use, but in this case he'd got the impression that there was nothing to tell – nobody knew anything about what this damned thing was, or what it wanted. Maybe he could change that.

For two days they had watched the dust spreading over the surface of Cannis IX, a colony of some twenty thousand Kadiran settlers. The dust had spread exponentially, creating more of itself from the matter it consumed and leaving nothing alive in its wake. Watching it happen, Wayland had been getting angry, a seething, helpless rage he had never experienced before. After the last life had been extinguished, nothing had happened – then, perhaps a day after the colony's death, Ems had detected plumes of dust rising from the surface, spiralling up like tornados. They joined together in the upper atmosphere and drifted lazily into a high orbit. Once there, the dust had started building.

'I'm picking up a postselection signature,' Ems announced suddenly. 'A ship's about to collapse in . . . there it is.'

'What ship?' he asked.

'It's human,' reported the third and final member of *Penguin*'s crew, Leading Rate Daniel Harding, 'but there's no transponder signal. Er . . . looks like it's from Dia Tacita, Skip.'

'Astrotheometrists?' Wayland said. 'What the hell are they doing here?'

'Whatever they're here for, they're gonna be real dead real soon if we don't do something fast,' Ems said. 'They're heading right for the construct.'

'Danny, open a channel,' he ordered.

'Channel open.'

'Unidentified vessel, this is Ascendancy scout *Penguin*. You are approaching a hostile entity. Change course immediately for your own safety.'

'They're not responding,' Danny reported. 'Still closing on the construct.'

'What's it doing?'

'Nothing so far,' Ems answered.

Wayland hooked the sensor core and watched the astrotheometrist craft burn towards the construct. At the halfway point the little vessel tumbled end over end and started a braking burn. It came to a relative halt so close to the construct that the two signals merged.

'It's no use, Skip,' Ems told him. 'The mass of the construct is screwing with the sensors. We need to get closer.'

'Will you stop saying that,' Danny groaned. 'Orders are to maintain our distance and observe, ain't that right, Skipper?'

'That's right,' he confirmed absently, busy manipulating the sensor feed. He tried a few filters, but the interference was too much to overcome.

'That's my point, moron,' Ems told the pilot. 'We can't observe shit-all from this far out.'

'The fucking thing's like a thousand kliks across!' Danny said. 'Trust me, I can see it just fine.'

'But *not*,' she insisted, 'the monk ship.'

'That's because the bloody construct's crushed them to the size of an atom or something. It just killed an entire planet – you really think one ship stands a goddam chance?'

'Wayland,' Ems said, and her tone made him drop out of integuary mode and look at her, 'we need to get closer. We need to find out what's happening.'

She's right, he thought bitterly, *but then so's Danny, probably.* *Penguin* was a relaxed ship; the three of them were all within a few years of each other and got on well despite the difference in rank – perhaps too well; sometimes it felt more like they were roomies back at the academy rather than a commander and his crew. Now, in the first real test of his new command, he was beginning to understand why all the officers he'd served under had maintained a certain distance from the people they might one day have to order to their deaths.

'Fire up the main drive, Danny,' he ordered. 'Take us in nice and slow.'

41

COROMANDEL

Coromandel filled the cockpit canopy, a glittering blue orb scattered with the white whorls of storm systems.

'It's beautiful,' Orry breathed, watching the light of the white sun glinting on the waters. The planet looked almost transparent, like they could fly right through it and burst out of the other side.

'Stinks of goddamn fish,' Mender grumbled as the world grew to fill the view.

'How long ago did you visit?' she asked.

'Before you were born, girl, and that should tell you something. If there was anything there worth visiting, I'd've been back, wouldn't I?'

'What about the Mariners? They sound fascinating.'

He grunted. 'That's one word for 'em, I suppose.' He glanced at Emissary, standing between their acceleration shells. 'Are you sure we're heading to the right place? That's one big planet with a whole lot of water.'

'I am sure,' the avatar replied. 'I can sense its location now. The virus is deep beneath the ocean. Icthys Seahold is the closest place that we can land.'

Mender grunted acknowledgement, adding, 'When we get down there you'd better change into something less obvious.' Then his good eye glazed as he hooked *Dainty Jane*'s cores.

Orry could see the seahold below them now. She'd thought Coromandel was a world made entirely from water down to its icy core, with no land masses, but now she could see that what she had assumed to be an artificial landing facility was in fact a small green island in the glittering ocean. Through the clouds she could make out structures at one end of the island and a cluster of landing pads at the other.

Mender activated the comm. 'Icthys Seahold, *Dainty Jane*.'

There was a long delay as the island grew steadily larger. Eventually the artificial tones of a translator sounded through the cockpit.

'This is Icthys. Pass your message.'

'*Dainty Jane* is an independent merchant inbound from Hebe, six souls on board. Request pad vectors.'

Another delay, then, '*Dainty Jane*, you may land at pad four. We are transmitting a guidance beam. Welcome in the name of Praxis the Dread, Master of the Waves.'

'Pad four, *Dainty Jane*,' he acknowledged calmly.

Orry turned to him. 'Praxis the Dread?'

'Don't worry about it – the local warlords like to give

themselves fancy titles. It's a mess down there but they don't
tend to hurt offworlders. At least, that used to the case.'

'Before I was born.'

He grinned at her.

Coromandel's atmosphere was thick and rich, laden with water
vapour, the high levels of oxygen making Orry feel energised,
her mind sharp and focused, as she waited beneath the sweep
of *Dainty Jane*'s hull.

'They look really weird,' she said, watching a crew of Mariners secure the ship to tie-down rings extruded from the
chitinous landing pad on which they stood. 'Like someone
taught a squid to walk.'

'They're more like cuttlefish, actually,' Ethan said, clearly
enthralled by his first encounter with the species. 'They have
an internal shell.'

The Mariners were certainly the oddest-looking creatures
she'd ever come across, with disconcertingly large eyes with
weird, W-shaped pupils at the base of an upper body shaped
like a bishop's mitre, which made up most of their height.
Below the eyes was a vicious-looking beak in the midst of a
tangle of tentacles, the thickest of which they used as legs.
The remaining tentacles functioned like arms, with each limb
formed differently, perhaps suited to particular tasks.

'They're making my eyes water.' Professor Rasmussen
looked away from the rapidly shifting colours flowing across
the Mariners' skin.

'It's how they communicate,' Ethan told him. 'They're using the colours to talk to each other.'

Orry found the display hypnotic, watching vivid green blotches blooming then fading, orange triangles moving across the mitres, white and red zebra stripes rolling over their arms.

Beside her, Mender turned to Emissary, who'd assumed the form of a mimetic to avoid any unwanted attention. 'Well, we're here,' the old man said. 'What now, genius?'

The avatar was scanning the deserted pads of the landing field, its eyes narrowed. It raised one arm and pointed at a distant figure hunched against the wind as they hurried towards them. As she got nearer they could see it was a woman, wrapped in a heavy EDC watchcoat, long black hair whipping damply across her face in the salty breeze. When she was within earshot, she raised a hand and shouted, 'Hello the ship!'

'Hello yourself!' Orry yelled with a grin, feeling thoroughly invigorated. She was enjoying herself.

'Fuck me but it's nice to see some human faces again,' the woman said, once she reached the relative calm provided by the lee of *Dainty Jane*'s hull. She peeled a strand of sodden hair from her cheek. She was in late middle age, pale skin blotchy and sprinkled with spots, with crow's feet at the corners of her brown eyes, but her broad smile was instantly welcoming. 'I'm Rebekah Okamoto,' she said, 'the local EDC Factor here. When I heard a ship had landed I almost shit a brick – thought I'd missed a scheduled trade mission. Who are you contracted with?'

'No one,' Orry said, immediately guarded at the woman's mention of the Empyrean Development Company.

'Independent? Don't see many indies here. Good luck getting the coilers to sell anything to you. The local warlord likes to deal with the big boys. What are you in the market for, anyway?'

'Oh, this and that,' Orry said vaguely.

Rebekah laughed. 'I know, I know,' she said, 'I get it; I'm EDC.' She shivered and glanced back the way she'd come. 'Look, shall we get off the surface? It's fucking grim up here.'

'Where did you have in mind?' Mender asked.

'This place is pretty dead right now, but when a big ship comes in there's a lot of crew who want entertaining – and the coilers love to turn a profit. There's a joint I know, nice and quiet at the moment. Maybe I can help you out with Praxis.'

'Praxis the Dread?' Ethan asked, managing to keep a straight face.

'That's the fellow,' Rebekah said with a grimace.

'What's in it for you?' Mender asked suspiciously.

'You're the first ship to come here in a month. I just want to talk to someone without a beak.'

He surveyed her. 'This joint of yours – does it serve booze?'

'It has *all* the booze,' she replied solemnly.

'Well, why the hell didn't you say that in the first place?' he said. 'Let's get out of here.'

*

'Everything's below the surface,' Rebekah explained as they strode across the landing field. Away from the hard, shell-like surface of the pad, the whitish ground was spongy with some spring in it, a bit like walking on grass, although it looked more like vegetable matter. Orry found herself a little shaky after *Dainty Jane*'s solid decks.

'How do we get down?' Ethan asked. He was looking everywhere at once, eyes bright with curiosity.

'We use these.' Rebekah stopped beside a large pool, within which several wide-bottomed, truncated cones like old space capsules bobbed sluggishly. Each pod was draped in thick strands of glistening green seaweed studded with blister-like air bladders the size of Orry's head. Between the wet strands, the surface of the cones was the same off-white as the ground, the slick smoothness broken in places by ridged circles like a squid's suckers.

The factor approached the nearest pod, grabbed a seaweed strand and hauled it close. 'These aren't designed for humans,' she said apologetically, running a hand over the slimy surface until she found whatever she was searching for. She slid her hand inside what looked like an orifice and felt around until the pod gave a shudder and the nearest sucker-like protrusion squelched open like a valve, leaving strands of glutinous slime stretched between its bulbous lips. Through the opening, which was easily large enough to step through, Orry saw that the pod's interior was hollow. Rebekah looked expectantly at Mender.

'What?' he asked, eyeing the opening with disgust.

'Get in,' she told him.

'What the hell is it?'

'It's a lift.'

'Looks like it's made out of rotting mushrooms,' he said.

The factor frowned. 'Mushrooms are fungi. *This* is made from algae.' She swept her arm around the landing field and the buildings beyond. 'All of this is. Mariner technology relies heavily on it. They've engineered one of the strains they use on their homeworld so it can thrive here and they use it for everything. It makes perfect sense; the stuff grows like crazy. It's an unlimited building material. The island's one big photobioreactor, providing all the energy they need.'

Orry looked around with fresh eyes. She hadn't realised Mariner algae-tech was used on such a huge scale here.

Ethan, desperate to see, pushed Mender out of the way. 'So how does it work?' he asked, indicating the pod.

'Acoustic streaming,' the factor said, giving him another of her broad grins. 'The outside is covered with tiny spikes which can vibrate at high frequency: that vibration causes nearby fluid to flow, which lets the pod move through it easily. It's actually more like a diving bell. It's partly open at the bottom so the coilers can swim in and out. Come on, get in.'

Orry brushed the mucous strands away with her arm and stepped inside, followed by the others. The unlit interior was gloomy, with a musty odour that reminded her of algae rations being reheated. But there was ample room for all of them inside the pod, on a metre-wide lip running around the hole in its base.

Rebekah cracked open a lumistik and used its eerie green glow to locate another orifice in the wall. She thrust her hand inside and the valve sucked closed with a squelch.

Sound filled the pod, haunting and rhapsodic, and Orry felt them start to descend. 'It's *singing*,' she breathed, feeling oddly emotional at the lilting sound.

'Yes,' Rebekah agreed sadly, 'but the coilers don't hear it.'

The descent passed without more words; everyone was listening to the sound of the pod. After too short a time, the singing altered pitch, then faded away entirely.

'We're here,' the factor announced.

The acoustic elevator had surfaced in a pool where rippling lights like fireflies reflected on the high ceiling. Rebekah led the way through one of several large tunnels bustling with colourful Mariners, passing openings in the walls that led into other tunnels or buildings.

'How many Mariners live here?' Orry asked as they pushed through a dense crowd gathered in front of one opening. It looked no different to any of the others they'd passed, but it was clearly offering something popular.

'I don't know for sure,' Rebekah answered. 'Hundreds of thousands at least. I've lived here for five years and I haven't explored a tenth of this place – that's mainly because of the pressure: Icthys goes so far down we'd be crushed before we got halfway.'

'Are all the seaholds on Coromandel this big?'

'Most are bigger, and that really gets under Praxis' shell.

Coilers are a fiercely independent species, so the homeworld tends not to interfere with the colonies. The seaholds here have been fighting each other for centuries; the winners grow by absorbing the losers. Now there are only a dozen or so left, and if Icthys doesn't get a boost in power and reputation soon, the other holds will strangle local trade routes and Icthys will end up being annexed. Praxis will do anything to stop that from happening.'

'You mean fight?'

'Of course I mean fight. There's a hold about a thousand kliks away that's only a little larger than Icthys – if he can take it out, he'll be powerful enough to sit at the table with the big boys.'

'But if this other hold is bigger, how will he win?'

'That's where I come in. Mariners tend not to trade with offworlders, but Praxis is desperate for weapons and tech, anything that will give him an advantage.'

'And EDC are supplying him,' Orry said coldly, but the factor just winked.

'Business is business. The stuff we've given him is all obsolete in the Ascendancy, but it's still way better than anything they have on Coromandel.'

'So if he has the weapons, why hasn't he attacked already?'

'Because he's scared of losing. He wants more from us, but he's run out of gilt. He's going to have to do something soon, though, one way or another. If he doesn't, there's bound to be a coup.' She stopped outside an opening in the tunnel wall. 'Here we are – after you.'

The room inside was dingy, with puce walls that gave off a lot less bioluminescence than the brighter tunnels. A few dozen mushroom-like growths of varying sizes were arranged around the place – it was only when Rebekah sat on one that Orry realised they were chairs.

'You won't find anywhere like this in most seaholds,' the factor explained a little proudly. 'Coilers don't need to sit down, but there's enough trade with offworlders here that they've made a few concessions.' She extended a hand. 'Sit, please.'

The mushroom Orry selected was surprisingly comfortable and she watched, amused, as Mender lowered himself onto one and sat bolt upright, looking extremely uncomfortable.

'I thought you said this place served booze,' he grumbled.

'I did say that, didn't I?' Rebekah stood and shrugged off her heavy coat, letting it fall to the floor to reveal a skin-tight bodysuit beneath. She was painfully thin, Orry saw, her ribs and hip bones poking through the neutral grey fabric of the suit. The factor looked around and a sudden ripple of colour ran down the suit. A moment later a small servitor unit emerged from a gap in the wall and scuttled over on a multitude of artificial tentacles. Patterns moved over the suit again and the bot hurried away.

'That's clever,' Professor Rasmussen said.

'It's quicker than a translator,' Rebekah answered, 'and less prone to errors.'

'What did you order?' Mender asked suspiciously.

'Ah, well, I may have misled you a little there. It all depends on your definition of "booze". Coiler physiology is a little different to ours.'

He narrowed his eyes. 'Will it get me wasted?'

'Oh, most definitely.'

He relaxed into his mushroom. 'Then bring it on.'

Orry was laughing so hard that her ribs hurt, but for the life of her she couldn't remember why. The walls were popping with tiny sparks and streaming with colours and she wondered what they were saying to her. Rebekah was laughing too, which set Orry off again. The factor was relentless, plying them with a never-ending smorgasbord of psychoactive algae provided by the little servitor. Much of the evening was a blur, but one thing had stayed with her: *I really like Rebekah.*

She finally managed to stop laughing. Gasping for breath, she leaned closer to the factor. There was something she wanted to know but had been too afraid to ask until now. 'Why do you live out here, all alone?'

Rebekah gave a final snigger and wiped her eyes before taking a steadying breath. 'I fucked up,' she said.

The professor was watching them intently from a nearby mushroom. 'Has anyone seen my face?' he asked worriedly, prodding his cheek. 'Is it still there?' Beside him Mender just nodded wisely, eyes closed and a look of beatific contentment on his craggy face. Emissary, in mimetic form, was standing motionless behind them, while Ethan had left some time ago to try to find a toilet. Orry ignored them and concentrated on Rebekah.

'You mean this is a punishment posting?' she asked.

'In a way.'

'But why?'

Rebekah's bony shoulders hunched as she slumped in her seat, staring at the spongy floor with suddenly hollow eyes. Orry waited, torn between her curiosity and guilt at having brought up what was clearly a painful matter for the factor. She was about to change the subject when Rebekah began to speak.

'Before this I was posted to a moon called Vrindr, out near the Antonides Ridge. You should've seen it: beautiful place, not like some of these terraforming colonies that are just wind-scoured balls of poisonous rock. Vrindr had a fully formed ecosystem, few natural predators, a glorious climate at the equator: it was a real paradise for the colonists. The Company was keeping it on a backburner, drip-feeding the colonists what they could afford until the place was big enough for demand to increase. It was a nice life for a year or so – until I received encrypted orders from my boss to go poking around in the colony records.'

'Poking around for what?'

'He gave me a list of terms to search for.'

'And you did it?'

'I didn't want to – these people were my friends – but it's not like I had any choice. I'm indentured to EDC until I'm seventy and I can't afford the buy-out fee. Anyway, I figured the Company was just fishing for intel, looking for items the colony was short of so they could rack up the prices.'

'But it wasn't?' Orry guessed.

'No. I sent back everything I found, and a month later the whole town was gone: turned into one big strip mine. Turns out one of the town geologists has discovered the whole place was rich in scorite – that's a type of—'

'I know what scorite is . . .'

'Sure, well, you know how much it's worth, then. The colony council tried to cover it up because they knew damn well what would happen if anyone found out, but I'd provided the proof EDC needed to send in the mining rigs.'

'What happened to the colonists?' Orry asked, thinking that the story sounded all too familiar.

'The Mercantile Defence Division relocated them. Some of them tried to resist, but they didn't have a hope. The survivors were split up and spread over a dozen other stage-one colonies. None of them had a breathable atmosphere.' Her eyes were wet in the dim light, and despite what she'd done, Orry felt a lot of sympathy for her.

'It sounds like the Company would've promoted you after that, not sent you here,' she said.

'You don't understand,' Rebekah said. 'After what happened, I couldn't live with myself. I *chose* to come here.'

'Oh.'

She sniffed and wiped her nose before giving Orry a watery smile. 'Boy, do I regret that decision.'

Orry laughed. 'Don't you get lonely?'

'Fuck, yes. Before the war there was pretty regular traffic – hopefully that will pick up again now it's over.'

'What about . . . you know?' Orry felt her cheeks grow warm. 'Men, or women, or whoever you're into?'

Rebekah shrugged. 'Every now and then I'll get together with someone from a visiting ship,' she said, 'sometimes with a coiler.' Seeing that her admission had rendered Orry temporarily speechless, the factor laughed. 'You'd be surprised what they can do with those tentacles – although the smell is so bad I need to be *really* stoned.'

'You're joking,' Orry finally managed to say.

'If you say so.' Rebekah grinned, then leaned in closer. 'Look, I've been pretty open with you, haven't I? About why I'm here and what I get up to.'

'A little too open,' Orry agreed.

'So tell me something in return: why are you *really* here?'

She hesitated, looking at her friends. The professor was prodding and pulling at his wrinkled face as if trying to reassure himself it was still there, while Mender's eyes were closed. It was difficult to think clearly with her mind fuddled by all the algae she'd consumed, but her instinct was to trust Rebekah, at least with some of the truth. If the factor was really supplying weapons to the local warlord, she was uniquely placed to provide them with some much-needed help.

'We're looking for something,' she said. 'It's under the water near here and we need a submersible to get to it. Can you help us charter one? We'd be happy to pay.'

'What are you looking for?'

'I can't tell you that.'

'Definitely treasure,' the factor said knowingly. 'Okay, how about this? I'll get you a sub and you cut me in for, say, twenty-five per cent.'

Orry glanced sharply at Mender, expecting an explosion of outrage, but the old man was in a world of his own. 'Five per cent,' she told Rebekah, knowing it would look suspicious if she didn't haggle. There was no treasure, obviously, but she was sure she could find a suitable sum with which to reward the factor once all this was over.

'Twenty,' Rebekah countered.

'Ten,' Orry said, knowing how this would end.

'Shall we settle on fifteen?' the factor asked, holding out a hand. Orry grasped it and they both smiled.

'I'll see what I can do in the morning,' Rebekah promised.

Ethan stumbled back to his seat, his face white. 'Whatever you do,' he said fervently, 'do *not* use the toilet.'

'That is good advice,' Rebekah acknowledged, then looked around for the servitor. 'Some more treats to celebrate?'

42

WARM FISH JUICE

Orry realised she was awake – and quickly wished she wasn't. A construction crew appeared to be hammering all the metal in the galaxy inside her skull while simultaneously drilling into her brain. Her mouth was bone-dry and her top lip cracked as she tried to moisten it with her tongue. The taste in her mouth was *utterly* vile.

'Morning, champ,' a voice said, and she rolled gingerly over to see Rebekah standing with a steaming mug in her hand. The factor looked a little pale, but not bad, considering the amount she'd consumed the previous night. 'Warm fish juice?' she enquired, holding up the mug.

Orry's stomach rolled greasily inside her and she retched.

Rebekah laughed. 'Kidding! It's an algae infusion. Tastes pretty rank, but it'll make you feel better.'

'No thanks,' she managed to croak.

'I'll just put it here. You look like shit, by the way.'

Orry just grunted, then lay back and closed her eyes. At

least the room wasn't spinning. *Actually, where the hell* am *I?* She cracked her eyelids for a moment and looked around. Ah yes, Rebekah's apartment. She had a vague recollection of returning here for drinks after the bar.

'Where are the others?' she asked.

'They went back to your ship. I suspect they'll be feeling much the same as you this morning – it was a good night.'

'I don't remember.'

'Not surprising. Water?'

The thought of water stirred a need deep within her withered frame. Pain shot through her head as she struggled into a sitting position, but she gulped the cool water down greedily, feeling it spread through her, flooding her cells, restoring her.

'Now drink this,' Rebekah ordered, picking up the mug of algae. 'Can't have you turning up looking like someone tried to drown you in Sabinian single malt.'

Orry rubbed crusted sleep from her eyes and blinked at her. 'Turning up for what?'

'You wanted to meet Praxis, didn't you? I've arranged an audience.'

'Oh—' *I can't meet a Mariner warlord when I feel like this . . .*

'It's in an hour.' Rebekah thrust the mug at her. 'Seriously, you need to drink this.'

She took the infusion and sniffed at it suspiciously. It didn't smell of anything much, perhaps a hint of damp vegetation. *What the hell*, she thought, *I can't feel any worse.* 'Chin chin,' she said, raising the mug.

Rebekah looked amused. 'I advise you to down it in one.'

Orry tried, gulping at the thick liquid. It wasn't too bad going down – but the moment she'd emptied the mug an aftertaste like rotting cabbage hit the back of her throat and she clapped her hand over her mouth to stop herself spewing it straight back up again.

'That's it,' the factor said encouragingly, 'keep it down. The nausea will pass.'

Orry was too busy fighting for control of her stomach to even glare at her, but after a few seconds the urge to puke did fade. Wiping her mouth, she promised herself she'd never eat that much algae again.

'Okay,' Rebekah said with an amused smile, 'now get dressed. Praxis the Dread doesn't like to be kept waiting.'

The huge antechamber was filled with Mariners awaiting audience with the warlord. In a broad pool in the centre of the room, acoustic elevators bobbed up and down, delivering new passengers, whisking others away. As Rebekah approached the pool's edge, she removed her coat to reveal her grey body suit and splashes of colour started running over it. A Mariner standing nearby appeared to be responding.

'Is he for us?' Orry asked, and the factor nodded.

'He says we're to follow him.'

Their escort led them to a scaled-up version of the valve door on the elevator pod, although this one was far larger and bordered by a wide band of tiny, frond-like cilia which formed a vivid, ever-moving play of colours around the entrance. The valve opened in its distressingly biological way and their escort motioned for them to enter.

Inside was an even larger chamber with white ribs growing from fleshy red walls; it made Orry feel like she was inside the belly of a whale. Her eyes were immediately drawn to a coral throne in the centre of the chamber, upon which squatted a large Mariner.

Praxis the Dread, she guessed.

Rebekah adopted a respectful pose in front of the throne, colours rippling over her suit.

'Mighty Praxis,' Rebekah said out loud, translating for Orry's benefit, 'may I present Miz Aurelia Katerina Kent, a renowned and well-respected representative of the Ascendancy and personal friend to the Imperator Ascendant.'

The warlord's skin rippled in reply and she turned to Orry.

'He says your reputation precedes you, blah blah blah. He wants to know why you're here.'

Orry took a moment to order her befuddled thoughts. 'Mighty Praxis,' she began, watching Rebekah's suit flash and shimmer as her words were translated, 'we have been chartered by the Science Secretariat to conduct a deep-water survey and catalogue organisms in Coromandel's deep trenches. Considering the cordial relationship that exists between the Great Shoal and the Ascendancy, I was hoping you could provide us with a small submersible vessel to use in our survey. We wouldn't need it for more than a few days.'

More shifting colours.

This is worse than trying to cold-read a Kadiran, she thought, frustrated by her complete lack of insight into the mind of the Mariner warlord. Even his words provided no clue, stripped of any nuance by the translation.

Praxis' beak clacked as a stream of coloured bars flowed down him.

Rebekah frowned.

'What did he say?' Orry prompted.

'I was expecting this to take a lot longer,' the factor admitted. 'He says we're in luck: his personal war-yacht has just completed a refit and he's been meaning to take it out on a shakedown cruise.'

'You mean he'd be coming with us? No, that's no good! . . . Uh, tell him it'll be a very boring voyage, lots of tedious scientific observations.'

Rebekah laughed. 'This guy might not be the brightest fish in the tank, but he knows your story is bullshit. He probably figures you're treasure hunters, although quite what you expect to find in a deep trench, I have no idea.'

'I was really hoping he would just lend us a sub and show us how to use it,' she said.

'Well, clearly that's not going to happen.'

'Is there anywhere else I can get a submersible?'

'Nope. Everything goes through him. Perhaps if you tell me why you're really here I can help.'

Orry glanced at Praxis, who appeared quite content to let

them talk, and realised she didn't have much choice. 'There's a ship – a starship – in the trench. It's a . . . a Departed vessel.'

Rebekah whistled. 'Okay, so you *are* treasure hunters. Well, good luck getting anything out of that without cutting him in.'

'It's not about *gilt*,' Orry snapped. 'We're not after the ship – there's something on board that we need.'

'Then you don't have a problem.'

'What do you mean?'

'I'll just propose a deal. You tell Fishface here where the ship is and he provides transport. He gets to keep the ship and you keep whatever it is you're after.'

Orry could see why Rebekah was a factor. She considered the proposal. 'Can we trust him?'

'Oh no, not for a second,' Rebekah replied bluntly, 'but you have me. Chances are Praxis won't risk pissing off EDC over this, not if he gets to keep the ship.'

'"Chances are"?'

'There are no guarantees, but what choice do you have?'

Orry's stomach growled in a sickly reminder of last night's excesses. She swallowed sour-tasting bile and tried to come up with an alternative. Eventually she gave up and cursed.

'One condition,' she said. 'We only tell him where the ship is once we're underway.'

'Now you're thinking. Shall I make the offer?'

Orry hesitated, eyeing the alien creature on the throne in front of her. *Surely Rebekah's right: we're only taking one small item, and he's getting a whole starship in return.* She rubbed her thumb and forefinger over her eyes to meet at the bridge of her nose, where she squeezed, trying to ease the hangover throb inside her head. They were running out of time, and what other option did she have? *Fuck it*, she decided, *let's just get the bloody virus, and if Praxis tries to pull a fast one we'll just have to deal with it.*

She opened her eyes. 'Sure,' she told Rebekah. 'Make the offer.'

43

MAYBE THEY'RE TALKING

Penguin coasted forward slowly after a brief burn of her main drive.

'Spool up the postselection drive,' Wayland ordered, 'and keep your finger on the button. If that thing so much as moves in our direction I want to be back at the Fleet before it knows we've left.'

'You got it, El-Tee!' confirmed Danny. 'Drive spooling now.'

'Ems, I want you to holler the second we get any meaningful reading on that ship. I'll do the same.'

'Aye, Skipper.'

Wayland split his attention between the monks' ship and the construct that was obscuring it, horribly aware of his duty to his ship and his crew. But Ems would spot anything long before he did – she was the best in the Fleet.

'The ship's still there,' she said excitedly.

'All stop,' he snapped.

'All stop, aye,' Danny confirmed, triggering a harsh braking burn.

'What's it doing?' Wayland asked, hooking the sensors to look for himself.

'Nothing, Skip, just hanging there.'

'Why aren't they dead?' the pilot wondered.

'Maybe one ship is insignificant to them, like if a fly landed near you?' Ems suggested.

'I'd kill it,' Danny said.

'Well, maybe the construct is more evolved than you.'

'It just destroyed a whole fucking planet!' He sounded outraged.

'Can it, you two,' Wayland said. 'I can see something on their hull, but I can't get a clear reading. Ems, can you clean it up?'

'One sec . . . shit! Is that—?'

'What?' Danny sounded alarmed.

Wayland frowned as he looked at the enhanced sensor data. 'It looks like a patch of that stuff is on their hull.'

'Is it spreading?' the pilot asked, 'like on the planet?'

'No,' Ems answered. 'It's just a splat of dust, half a metre across, maybe.'

They watched the ship in silence for several minutes, before Danny suggested, 'Maybe they're talking?'

'Don't be a twat, Dan,' Ems said.

'No, listen: the construct hasn't destroyed them, and it's not ignoring them, or why would there be a chunk of it on their hull? So maybe it's talking to them?'

'Saying what?'

'Hell, I don't know, but I do know those fucking monks love their alien shit, and I never seen anything more alien than that.' He turned to Wayland. 'What d'you think, Skip?'

'I think this whole thing is *way* above our pay grade. Ems, upload our logs and sensor feeds to a pod – we'll let the brain trust back at the Fleet figure out what these bastards are up to.'

'You might want to hold off on that pod, Skip,' she responded. 'The monks are on the move again.'

He hooked the sensors again and watched the speck that was the astrotheometrist ship pass across the face of the construct, its drive burning steadily.

'Their postselection drive is spiking,' Ems reported, and a moment later the little ship vanished. 'They're gone,' she said unnecessarily.

'To where?' Danny wondered.

'I'm picking up energy spikes from the construct now,' Ems said, 'I think it's about to—'

The enormity of the construct vanished, leaving an oily smear briefly in its wake.

'—collapse,' she finished.

'Thank Rama for that,' Danny said. 'Can we get the hell out of here now?'

Wayland ran his eyes over the dead world below them, feeling like he'd failed. 'Sure,' he said. 'Let's go and tell the Admiralty what we saw here.'

44

UMBILICAL

After several hours aboard Praxis' war-yacht, Orry had decided that she was not a fan of Mariner algae-tech. Every surface was coated in a slimy film which reminded her of mushrooms that were past their best. Combined with the pervasive odour of rotting vegetables and the slight *give* everything had, it was making for a rather unpleasant voyage. She knew she should be tolerant of other cultures, but sometimes it wasn't all that easy.

'How much longer, do you think?' she asked Rebekah, who was sitting with her back against one soft wall, eyes closed, apparently oblivious to their surroundings. Not for the first time Orry found herself wondering why anyone would choose to live among the Mariners.

'Coiler ships move pretty fast,' the factor answered, 'I can't imagine it will be much longer.' She opened one eye and looked around, then the other sprang open and she rose to her feet with a look of anticipation on her gaunt face. 'About time!'

Orry followed her gaze to see servitors entering the room

from small valves around the curved algaeform walls, moving with the same rolling gait the Mariners had. One of the bots approached the humans, balancing multiple trays of food morsels in its tentacular limbs.

'It's safe,' Rebekah said, popping a seaweed-wrapped tube into her mouth and chewing hungrily. 'Bit salty, but you soon get used to it.'

Professor Rasmussen broke off a discussion with Emissary to walk over. He eyed the hors-d'oeuvres suspiciously, then picked up a pale wafer topped with what looked like flaked fish and nibbled at the edge. His expression changed and he ate the rest in one bite before helping himself to several more. Orry took a selection, always keen to try new experiences, and discovered the food was delicious, full of complex fishy flavours.

'It's very good,' the professor said enthusiastically, reaching for another handful.

She took a bite from a green and orange parcel. Perhaps there *were* benefits to living on Coromandel.

A larger, more ornate valve opened and the Mariners in the room all bowed as Praxis entered. Taking her cue from Rebekah, Orry bowed too. The warlord stopped in front of her and colours flowed across his skin.

'He says you're very generous,' Rebekah translated, 'offering him an entire starship and wanting to keep only one thing for yourself.'

Orry narrowed her eyes, wondering where he was going with this. 'Tell him it's only fair; the ship is in his territory.'

'He's asking what the item is exactly that you will be keeping.'

'I bet he is. Tell him it's just an artefact the professor needs for his research.'

Patterns formed on Rebekah's suit, but before the warlord could respond a Mariner scuttled up to him, skin pulsing with communicative colours. The warlord's tentacles twitched and coiled excitedly in response.

'We're here,' Rebekah said.

Something was happening to the walls: the pale white algae became gradually translucent, like paper rubbed with oil. At first a disturbing veil of gloom surrounded them, then an eerie glow began to eat away at the dark, revealing motes floating in the current, followed by darting sea creatures. The yacht's skin was fully transparent now, like looking through a thick pane of glass. The glow was coming from the Mariner submersible itself, the external skin emitting a soft bioluminescence.

Professor Rasmussen peered out into the ocean. 'There!' he said excitedly as the sphere of light surrounding them touched the edge of a shape floating in the waters. The war-yacht moved closer, its light playing over surfaces thick in barnacles and marine growth.

The Departed vessel was not large, perhaps a hundred metres from stem to stern, and much narrower than it was tall. The gently curving hull was floating like a knife in the water, ready to slice.

Orry imagined how menacing the ship would look when

it wasn't coated in metres of aquatic growth. 'How do we get aboard?' she asked.

Rebekah answered, 'They have microorganisms onboard that will eat through all that growth. They'll establish a seal with the hull, then it's up to you to open it. I presume that won't be a problem?'

Orry glanced over at Emissary, still in mimetic form. 'No, that won't be a problem,' she said.

Orry shivered as a drop of water fell onto her neck and trickled down the back of her spacesuit. She ran her eyes anxiously over the seal between the tube in which she was standing and the pitted outer hull of the Departed vessel. The tube extruded from the war-yacht's side was a cartilaginous umbilical linking the two craft; she couldn't see any water leaking past the suction seal, so the dripping water must have been left over from when the umbilical was pumped out.

The air was thick and muggy in the tube, which was crowded with three Mariners as well as herself, Rebekah, Emissary and the professor. The avatar had an arm plunged into the scarred metal up to the wrist and had been interfacing with the Departed ship's hull for several minutes now.

'I've heard about smart-matter mimetics,' Rebekah murmured, watching the avatar closely. 'It's restricted tech – one day you must tell me how you came to acquire one.'

Orry glanced at the factor, concerned that the woman had seen through the cover story they'd come up with to explain

Emissary's abilities. Rebekah met her gaze evenly; if she did suspect anything she wasn't giving it away.

'One day,' Orry replied carelessly, hoping that the factor wouldn't pursue the matter. The last thing they needed was for Praxis to find out what Emissary really was.

Another drop of water plopped into the puddle at her feet and a wave of melancholy swept over her. *God, this is bleak. Why do I keep ending up in situations like this when all I want is to be safe and warm in* Jane's *galley, listening to Mender and Ethan bicker?* She had tucked Iosef's iridium half-crown into the webbing on the back of her right glove and now she touched it with her other hand, wondering why she drew such comfort from the little keepsake.

Emissary withdrew its arm from the hull as if drawing it out of a wall of still water and a moment later, a line appeared in the metal above its head and sketched a wide oval. As the line returned to meet its origin, the oval sank back inside the ship and slid out of view to create an entrance. The interior of the Departed ship was pitch-black.

Orry really wasn't looking forward to stepping inside.

'The vessel is running in low power mode,' the avatar explained. 'Its primary intelligence appears to be offline, but I have been able to adjust the environmental core so that you will not need to use the oxygen from your suits.'

'What do we do about light?' she asked.

In answer, Emissary stepped inside the ship. An orange glow appeared immediately, emanating from strips set into the bulkheads and illuminating a rather ordinary-looking airlock.

Strobing colours behind her in the umbilical indicated that Praxis was saying something.

'He suggests you go first,' Rebekah translated.

'I'll bet he does,' Orry muttered, raising a grin on the factor's face before following Emissary into the ship. 'Is it safe?' she asked.

'System status is nominal,' the avatar answered. 'I have not looked in depth, but the ship does not appear to be damaged.'

'It didn't crash, then?'

'Apparently not.'

'I wonder why it's here? Can you access the logs?'

'Not without awakening the ship's intelligence. Shall I do that now? It will save us having to search for the virus.'

'No,' she said quickly, and looked around the airlock. 'It's not a very big ship, so let's try looking ourselves for now.'

Emissary turned to stare at her as Rebekah and the professor entered the airlock to join them. 'But waking the intelligence will save time,' it pointed out reasonably, 'and time is a critical resource.'

'I'm aware of that,' she said.

'Then I think we should hasten matters along.' It raised one arm and the fingers crumbled and reformed into an intricate set of needles which she guessed was an interface jack.

'And I say we don't,' she said.

'I do not understand. The ship's intelligence will be able to assist us.'

'Are you sure of that?'

'Of course – why would it not?'

'What about Harbinger?'

The avatar frowned. 'Harbinger was reprogrammed by the Order.'

'Yes, but the fact that they *could* reprogramme it proves that not all Departed tech has to think the way you do. Why is this ship down here? If it had the virus on board, why didn't it use it in the fight against the Residuum?' When the avatar remained silent, she continued, 'All I'm saying is, why take the risk? If we can't find the virus, then we'll think about waking the ship. Until then, let's just keep nice and quiet and search for it ourselves.'

Emissary considered that. 'Your logic makes sense,' it conceded eventually. 'Are you ready to proceed now?'

'Yes, yes!' Professor Rasmussen said, almost hopping with excitement. He didn't appear to be at all discomfited by the water dripping on his head.

Orry waved the three Mariners into the ship and eyed the airlock's inner door with mistrust. She was having a bad feeling about this place, but what choice did she have? She wondered bitterly if free will was always going to be something that happened to other people.

'Go ahead,' she told the avatar, who turned to an apparently blank section of bulkhead where a panel immediately appeared as if summoned. Emissary touched it – and Orry whirled at a sudden movement behind her, but it was only the outer door cycling closed, sealing them off from the comforting lights of the war-yacht. A moment later the inner door opened and more of the dim orange lights illuminated on the other side, revealing a large space crowded with machinery.

Orry frowned, and Praxis' skin flowed with colour.

'He's asking what all these machines are for,' Rebekah translated.

Emissary started to answer, but Orry got there first. 'It's the engine room,' she said, walking to a familiar-looking piece of equipment. She turned from it to give the avatar a questioning look.

'You are wondering why the engine room of a Departed vessel constructed hundreds of thousands of years ago bears such similarities to the ships of today.'

'Yes,' she agreed, 'that's *exactly* what I'm wondering.' There were some differences in design, but looking around the compartment it was clear that the Departed ship ran on precisely the same principles of postselection as every ship she'd known.

'It was the Goethens,' Professor Rasmussen said, his eyes alight with curiosity. After spending the best part of a century picking through broken Departed relics on the Shattermoon, she could only imagine what an intact vessel like this one must mean to him.

'I don't understand,' she said. 'The Goethen Ship Authority pioneered mindmerge tech. What does that have to do with this?'

'Mindmerge technology came from Departed artefacts they

recovered, same as our integuaries. They got the postselection drive in the same way.'

'The professor is correct,' Emissary said. 'The Goethens were the first human colony to harvest significant Departed technology. The Ship Authority used it to make Goethe the most powerful planet in human space for hundreds of years, until the Administrate clipped their wings.'

Orry knew a little about that from *Dainty Jane* – she was a Goethen mindship, the last of them, perhaps, since the rest of the fleet had disappeared practically overnight to avoid what the Administrate had planned for them.

'I was always taught that mindmerge tech was inherently unstable,' Rebekah said. 'The Ship Authority was producing warships which were prone to psychotic episodes – that's why the Administrate ordered the procedures reversed.'

'You make it sound so *civilised*,' Orry said angrily. 'A mindship isn't just a dumb shell they dropped a human consciousness into. The ships were sentient too, in their own way, waiting to be completed by the merge process with a compatible human candidate. The human body was physically interfaced with the ship using an amniotic link: the human and ship elements literally became one being. When the Administrate ordered the human parts removed and the ships retrofitted with AI, they had no idea what they were doing. The few humans who didn't kill themselves ended up in institutions, and none of the AIs bonded properly with the ships. They all had to be destroyed.'

'They didn't teach me that,' Rebekah said quietly.

'Well, they wouldn't, would they?'

'Is that why most of the Goethen fleet disappeared?' the factor asked. 'To avoid the reversal procedure?'

'I'd say it was a safe bet, wouldn't you?'

An odd expression had crept over the professor's face as he listened to the exchange. 'Emissary,' he said, 'you told us that this ship's intelligence was sleeping.' He hesitated for a moment and his Adam's apple bobbed up and down, 'What . . . er . . . what sort of intelligence is it?'

'Most Departed vessels were mindships,' the avatar informed him. 'This one is no exception.'

Rasmussen leaned back against a machine housing for support. 'And how similar are Goethen mindmerge techniques to those used by your creators?'

'The Ship Authority made a few adaptations so the technology could be successfully used with human hosts, but the bulk of the process remains the same.'

'Goethen mindships rely on a connection to the human host,' the professor said slowly. 'Are you saying that one of your creators could be alive aboard this vessel as we speak? One of the Departed?'

'To answer that I would need to awaken the ship's intelligence . . .'

'Hang on,' Orry said, 'if this ship's been down here for hundreds of thousands of years, there can't be anything left alive, can there?'

'My creators were able to extend their lifespans indefinitely, barring accidents,' Emissary said. 'Fed and continually restored by the nutrients in the amniotic tank, it is entirely possible that the physical element of the ship's intelligence is still viable.'

'Where is it?' Rasmussen asked quickly. 'I have to see it. Imagine all we could learn!'

'Not now, Professor,' Orry said, 'this isn't the time. Once the threat from the Residuum has passed, I'm sure you'll be able to wake the ship and ask it anything you want, but for now, I don't want to take the risk. Let's just find what we need and get the hell out of here.'

'But . . .' Seeing the resolve on her face, he dropped his eyes. 'Very well,' he said, unable to keep the petulance from his voice.

'Where would they keep it, I wonder?' She looked at Emissary.

'The most likely location would be in the commander's personal quarters, I suggest. Let us try this way . . .'

Rebekah was translating the last few sentences for Praxis, and now his skin rippled with colour.

'He's giving you permission to proceed,' the factor said, winking.

'Good to know,' Orry answered, and made an elaborate bow to the Mariner warlord before flapping a hand at Emissary to get moving.

They moved on, hushed against the sepulchral silence of the ship.

In *Dainty Jane*'s cockpit, Mender stubbed out a cheroot as he gazed morosely out of the canopy at the endless waters of

Coromandel. The overcast sky had painted the ocean grey; it wasn't raining yet but it was only a matter of time. It was a far cry from the sun, sand and clear waters of Halcyon.

'How much longer will they be?' Ethan asked from the acceleration shell beside him.

'How the hell should I know, kid? Why don't you go and do something useful – it'll take your mind off the wait.'

'Like what?'

'The muon ingesters in the starboard nacelle have been running rough. Run a diagnostic for me, will you?'

Ethan sighed heavily. 'I don't feel like it.'

Mender gritted his teeth and glared at the ocean. The kid was worried – he got that. *Hell, I'm worried, but I don't float about the goddamn place like a maid with the vapours.* The kid needed to toughen up, and fast. Mender had a heavy feeling that things were going to get a lot worse before they got better.

'Oh dear,' *Jane* announced, her voice filling the cockpit. 'An unknown vessel has entered the system and is approaching Coromandel. Analysis of its signal architecture confirms it is constructed of Residuum dust motes.'

Mender's hands were already flying over the console in front of him. 'Kid, get us a launch clearance.'

'Wait, what—? We're going? What about Orry—?'

'What about her?' A hum ran through the old ship as Mender engaged the auxiliary generators. He turned to Ethan. 'Look, son, there's a shit-ton of trouble coming this way and I don't intend to be caught on a floating mushroom when it gets here. Now, *Jane*'ll monitor all channels and the moment your sister gets back to the surface we'll come and get her. Fair enough?'

'I guess.' The boy didn't look happy about it.

'Good. Now get on the fucking comm and get us that goddamn clearance.'

'Wow,' Ethan said. 'All you had to do was ask.'

45

MALVILLE

The passageways within the Departed vessel were high and echoing, the ceilings lost in shadow above the orange light-strips. Each door they passed came to a point at the top, reminding Orry of an ancient church she'd once seen, brought to Alecto from old Earth. *Gothic*, she thought, remembering the word Ethan had used to describe it. *I'd just call it creepy.*

Emissary halted outside one of the doors, which opened immediately for it. She followed the avatar across a spacious, sparsely decorated suite of rooms to a work area. Professor Rasmussen shuffled into a smaller compartment containing a large bed, with storage units lining the walls. It wasn't long before the old man was peering inquisitively into each one.

'Look,' he exclaimed as she walked over to supervise him, 'the captain's personal effects are still here.'

The sight of the neatly stacked garments made her uneasy. 'I wonder what happened to the crew?' she said quietly. 'Emissary doesn't think the ship crashed here, so where are they? Maybe the ship put them into storage or something?'

'Do you think so?' He sounded excited by her suggestion.

'Or did they leave?' she continued, thinking aloud, more for her benefit than for his. 'And if they did, was it before or after the ship landed? It could have come in on its own, I guess. But if it landed here deliberately, why?'

'To hide?'

'From what? The Residuum? If the virus is on board, why hide it away? Why not use it?'

Further musing was prevented by Emissary's voice from the other compartment. 'I have the virus.' The habitual monotone was bereft of any emotion.

She hurried into the office area to see the avatar standing beside an open safe, holding a small vial of what appeared to be dust in one hand. 'Is that it?' she asked, unimpressed. The vial was only the size of her little finger. 'How does it work?'

'The contents must be delivered to a key formation within the Residuum, the larger and more complex its structure the better, to allow the motes to spread widely and avoid detection while they begin to multiply.'

'That's it? Just pour it out and let it do its thing?'

'That is all,' Emissary confirmed. 'The difficult part will be getting close enough to a critical structure to release the viral agent. Infecting a minor appendage will not be effective; they are too easily isolated from the gestalt whole.'

'How quickly does it work?'

'I cannot predict that with any accuracy. There are too many unknown factors.'

'Uh, guys?' Rebekah said from outside the office, and something in her tone made Orry's muscles tense.

She turned to see Praxis clacking his beak enthusiastically and speaking in colours, while one of his guards pointed a vicious-looking harpoon-gun at her.

'I *may* have been wrong about him not wanting to piss off the Company,' Rebekah continued. 'He wants you to hand over the vial; he figures that if that's what you came for it has to be worth a lot, probably more than the ship.'

Orry clenched her jaw as she dealt with a rush of rage-fuelled frustration. *I fucking knew it!* 'Tell him,' she said through still-gritted teeth, 'that the contents of this vial is the only thing that can save his planet from total destruction.'

'He doesn't care,' Rebekah said after a brief exchange with the warlord. She looked worried. 'I advise you to give him what he wants; coilers have little compunction about killing humans.'

This is what you get for making important decisions with a stinking hangover, idiot! Orry glanced around the eerily lit chambers and forced herself to calm down. *There has to be a way out of this.*

Praxis spoke again and his guard gestured at her with his gun.

'For Rama's sake, give him what he wants,' Rebekah told the avatar.

'Don't!' Orry snapped, sweat trickling down her temple.

Emissary looked from her to Rebekah, then at the warlord. The avatar started forward.

'No!' Orry said, too loudly, but it was already past her and approaching Praxis. She started to move too but the Mariner guard made a threatening gesture and she stopped abruptly, clenching her fists with rage.

Emissary hesitated as it reached the guard, as if unwilling to walk through his line of fire, then, changing course, it passed close behind the Mariner ... and suddenly wrapped one arm around the guard's neck while reaching for the harpoon-gun with the other.

The Mariner burst into a slew of startled colours as he grappled with the avatar for control of the gun. Orry ran a few steps towards them, then stopped, unsure how best to help. She was about to aim a kick at the guard when the gun went off, sending a harpoon as long as her forearm past her ear and into the bulkhead behind her, where it exploded, shredding whatever exotic material the wall was made from.

The noise of the explosion was deafening in the confined space of the suite and everyone, human and Mariner alike, froze. She glanced around the walls, all thoughts of the Mariner's attack momentarily forgotten by a sudden, overwhelming fear that the noise had awakened the ship's intelligence. She didn't know why the thought was so terrifying to her, but a quick look at her companions showed she wasn't the only one who felt that way. Rebekah looked alarmed while the professor was anxiously studying the walls.

Emissary recovered first, plucking the weapon from the guard's tentacle before stepping back to cover the three Mariners. Seconds crawled by, the acrid stink of melted plastic stinging her throat, but after an eternity – which was probably no more than half a minute – Orry licked her dry lips and started breathing again. Whatever intelligence slumbered at the heart of the ship did not appear to have awakened.

'Right,' she said to Rebekah, 'you can tell Praxis the Dread that he might be a crook, but I'm not. He's going to take us back to the surface and we'll leave – with the vial. The ship is his.'

'*What?*' Professor Rasmussen objected. 'No! You said I could study it—'

'Things change, Prof. I'm sorry, but maybe we can arrange something once this is all over. The Institute has deep pockets and I imagine Praxis will be open to offers.'

'But . . .' He was actually wringing his hands as he looked longingly at the bedroom. 'This vessel is *magnificent*. We can't just give it to them.'

'Magnificent?' a new voice said, filling the suite with a rich baritone. 'What a nice thing to say.'

The lights brightened and Orry found herself moving closer to Rebekah, whose face had drained of all colour.

'You're quite correct, of course,' the voice continued. 'I am . . . *magnificent*.' A deep chuckle followed the statement, velvet tones rolling through the rooms.

'Um, hello?' Orry managed, her voice cracking a little. She cleared her throat. 'Ship?'

'No, no, no, that won't do at all,' the voice answered. 'You must call me . . . Malville.' It chuckled again. 'I see you have a subsidiary form with you.'

It took her a moment to realise that the vessel was referring to Emissary. 'Yes, he's helping us.'

'"He"? How extraordinary.'

'Perhaps you could help us too?'

'Perhaps I could.'

'While you've been . . . sleeping . . . down here, the Residuum has reappeared. It's threatening all life in the galaxy, threatening my people, just as it did yours.'

'Oh dear, how *dread*ful.'

She thought Malville might try a little harder at sounding concerned. It was difficult to read the ship just by its voice, but alarm bells were sounding loudly in her head.

'We came here to get that' – she pointed at the vial in Emissary's hand – 'so we can use it against the Residuum.'

'You mean you came to *steal* that.' There was a sudden edge to the ship's voice.

'We didn't think anything had survived down here after all this time,' Orry protested.

'You lie – your subsidiary form accessed my data core. Lies upon lies.'

'Please, we just want the virus. It's no use to you down here. But we are not thieves – we'll give you something for it. What do you want?'

Malville fell silent for a moment, the lights on the walls

pulsating slightly as if it was breathing. When it spoke again all trace of anger had been replaced by melancholy. 'I have been alone for so very long,' it said. 'I want . . . company.'

'Of course, yes. No problem. Just let us take the virus and we can send a team down to stay on board. We can learn so m—'

'*Your* company.'

Shit.

'But . . . there's no time! We need that virus now. We might not be the only people who know about it and if the Residuum finds out where you are it will destroy Coromandel and you won't have *any* company.'

'The Residuum is here already,' Malville said. 'I can sense it.'

Orry didn't think she could take much more of this. 'Then you *have* to let us go. I promise we'll come back.'

'The promise of a liar,' the ship observed.

Praxis stepped forward, flowing with colours, and Rebekah paled.

'What's he saying?' Orry asked.

'Praxis the Dread is informing me that as I am located within his territory, I am his property,' Malville said. 'He is ordering me to release him back to his vessel at once.'

'The Mariners don't recognise machine intelligence as sentience,' Rebekah said, sending a glare in the warlord's direction.

'I understand,' the ship told her. 'Please tell him that I apologise for inconveniencing him and that he may return to his vessel without further delay.'

Rebekah exchanged a worried glance with Orry. 'Um . . .'

Malville sighed.

Praxis was running with colours now, his tentacles whipping around angrily. Behind him, the exit slid open. With an excited clacking of his beak he hurried into the passageway, followed closely by his guard – but before the third Mariner could join them, the heavy door slammed back down and became transparent. A moment later, other doors closed on either side of the two, trapping them in a short section of passageway.

Orry was filled with a sick sense of foreboding as Praxis lit up like a furious rainbow while the guard flailed in vain at the door.

'What are you doing?' she shouted at the ship. 'Let them go!'

'Manners,' the ship said severely, 'cost nothing.'

In the passageway, the Mariners' movements were becoming more frantic. The guard struck the door again but this time his limb appeared to stick there, and when he tore it free it left a ribbon of pale flesh stuck to the transparent surface. Behind him, Praxis was hopping almost comically, as if the deck was too hot to stand on. The lump of flesh on the door was crisping now, a whisper of smoke curling upwards, and Orry tasted bile in the back of her throat.

'Stop it!' she yelled. 'You're killing them—'

Both Mariners were flowing with harsh colours, jumping madly, trying to barge their way free, but their colours started to mute, until the true colour of their flesh was revealed. Then the almost translucent pale green started to turn pink, then blacken and crisp. They fell onto their sides, rocking pitiably as smoke curled off them, before finally falling still.

Orry looked away and felt a hand on her shoulder. It was Professor Rasmussen, looking like he might throw up at any moment. He pointed at a bulkhead and she saw that an image had appeared on its flat surface. It was the war-yacht of which Praxis has been so proud, still attached by the umbilical to Malville's side.

'Watch this,' the ship said happily, and the yacht abruptly imploded, belching out huge bubbles of air as its hull folded in on itself. It dropped like a rock, surrounded by a maelstrom of smaller bubbles. Half the umbilical still attached to Malville's hull was left flapping gently in the current.

'I trust there will be more talk of leaving,' the ship said as the image vanished. 'So, what would you like to chat about?'

46

AMNIOTANK

Orry, stunned by how quickly their situation had changed, was silent.

'Let's start with your names,' Malville suggested.

Get a grip, she told herself angrily. *Dad always said I could talk anyone into anything, so let's see if he was right.* 'I'm Orry,' she said. 'Aurelia Katerina Kent.'

'Good. And what do you do, Aurelia Katerina Kent?'

'This and that. Nothing much really.'

'And yet here you are, risking your life at the bottom of an ocean, trying to save your race.'

'It seemed like a good idea at the time.'

The ship chuckled. 'And you have a subsidiary form with you. Where did you find that?'

'Emissary can speak for himself.'

The chuckling stopped. 'But I am asking *you*.'

'Enough,' Emissary said.

'I beg your pardon?' Malville sounded surprised, as if a toaster had decided to pick an argument with him.

'Your higher functions are impaired,' the avatar continued, 'but your avionics and drives are nominal. You will fly us back to Icthys Seahold and remain there until we have the opportunity to correct the impairment.'

The lights in the suite dimmed for a moment, then brightened to a painful intensity. 'You *dare* to speak to me in such a fashion?' Malville roared. '*You?* A mere construct, a mechanism of dust?' One of the lighting-strips failed, turning black with a sharp crack.

Emissary offered Orry the vial and she took it. *It's like a child having a tantrum*, she reflected fearfully, *but a child who can kill us with a thought*. She hoped the avatar knew what he was doing.

Emissary's body crumbled.

'What?' Malville thundered as the dust drifted through the compartment. 'Reform immediately, I command you!'

The dust cloud was moving over the bulkheads and deck, finding barely visible gaps and sinking through them.

'Stop!' the ship yelled, a hint of fear in its voice now. 'Stop this instant or the humans will suffer.'

Orry's ears suddenly popped like they did when *Dainty Jane* climbed quickly to orbit. She swallowed, trying to relieve the pressure. Emissary's dust was nearly all gone now, vanished through the walls and floor. She swallowed again, but the pressure in her ears was becoming painful, like needles being shoved into her eardrums. Rebekah groaned beside her, and

Professor Rasmussen was clutching the sides of his head. Orry felt something wet on her top lip and tasted blood.

'Reform at once, construct, or watch the humans' heads explode,' Malville said.

Orry's skull felt like it had grown to twice its normal size. Her vision was blurring, so she squeezed her eyes shut, clutching her ears as if that could stop the agony. She sank to her knees, close to vomiting. The pain was *everything*, threatening to tear her head apart.

Unable to contain it any longer, she screamed—

—and the pressure was gone.

She opened her eyes, working her jaw to dispel a lingering ache in her ears. Rasmussen was on all fours, a puddle of puke in front of him. Blood vessels in Rebekah's eyes had burst, lending her a demonic aspect as she stared wide-eyed at Orry. Blood dripped from her nose and ears.

Malville was silent, but the wall lights were flickering wildly.

'What's happening?' Rebekah asked as Orry helped her to her feet, then they both clapped their hands over their ears as a high-pitched wail pierced the room. The wail turned into a roar of rage, which warped and modulated into a distorted but familiar voice.

'I have penetrated Malville's substrate,' Emissary's voice said, 'but I cannot hold him for long. Go down through the hatch.'

A hatch slid open in the deck and Orry started towards it, but Rebekah gripped her arm.

'How do you know this isn't a trick?' she asked.

'I don't,' Orry told her, 'but how can things get any worse?'

The factor stared at her for a moment, then stooped to help the professor to his feet. Looking down the hatch, Orry could see a circular shaft leading into shadow, rungs protruding from the wall. She hesitated, fearful of the darkness, and suddenly the temperature in the compartment dropped so quickly it stung her exposed skin and made her gasp in shock. It was like being plunged into an ice bath.

'Hurry . . .' Emissary urged, his voice warping and screeching.

'Come on!' she yelled, her breath coming out in clouds of vapour, and stepped onto the rungs. She began climbing down, feeling a rush of relief as a ring of lights illuminated around her, keeping pace with her. The temperature fluctuated wildly as she descended, from bone-chill to scorching heat.

'Where are we going?' she asked, not even sure Emissary could hear her words.

'Malville is . . . a mindship,' the avatar's distorted voice answered. 'It exists in two . . . parts, the virtual and the physical. You must . . . kill . . . the physical as I destroy the rest.'

'But I don't have a weapon—'

'You must . . . find a way.'

She could see the end of the shaft below her now, with another hatch swinging open at her approach. The rungs ended just below it and she dropped to the deck. She was at an intersection, with several doors leading off it. As Rebekah dropped down behind her, one of the doors swung open.

'Hurry,' Emissary's voice urged again as she entered a low-ceilinged, vault-like room containing a large tank surrounded by pipes and tubes. She stepped onto the raised platform encircling the tank and stared down through its transparent lid.

'Not a pleasant sight,' Professor Rasmussen said, coming to stand beside her.

It wasn't. Malville's physical component was a wizened, corpse-like husk floating in a corrupted soup of foetid, viscous fluid.

'You must . . . kill it,' Emissary told her, sounding weaker than ever. 'I will . . . do the rest.'

'How?' she muttered, trying not to think about murdering the helpless thing inside the tank. *But it isn't helpless*, she told herself. *That's Malville, who would kill us in an instant if it wasn't for Emissary*.

'Get this thing open,' she told the professor.

'What are you going to do?' he asked.

'Try to find something I can use to kill it,' she said, but she didn't hold out much hope; the chamber looked empty apart from the tank and its associated machinery.

'Try this,' Rebekah yelled from out in the intersection. She'd managed to pry loose a length of metal from the edge of one of the closed doors. She tossed it to Orry, who examined it: as long as her forearm, with the end where Rebekah had twisted it free broken to a sharp point.

'Is that okay?' the factor called, looking around the intersection. 'I can probably find something better.'

428

'It's good,' Orry told her, eyeing the jagged metal. *I don't think I can do this.* 'Come in here with us.'

Rebekah had taken only two steps towards the door when it slammed closed, separating the two compartments. Orry raced over and peered through the inspection port to see plumes of white water rushing into the intersection.

'Rebekah!' She ran her hands around the door's edge, trying to find a control, then stood staring helplessly as the waters rose past the factor's knees. Rebekah was hammering on the port, her bloodshot eyes wide with terror.

'Emissary!' Orry yelled, 'open this bloody door!'

'I ... can't ...' came the strained reply. 'Too much ... must ... kill ...'

Gripping her makeshift weapon, Orry raced back to the tank and saw the professor had managed to get the lid open. The thick fluid inside stank like rotting flesh and she raised a hand to her nose as she came close. Spurred on by the muffled thumping on the door behind her, she raised the metal shard like a dagger, trembling as she held it over the corpse-like husk floating in the filthy soup.

'Stop!' Malville's voice cried, as distorted as Emissary's had been. 'Kill me and the other one dies – you will never be able to vent the water in time. Step away and I will save her.'

Orry turned to see Rebekah coughing and choking as the water rose over her mouth.

'K-kill it now ...' Emissary howled, his words barely recognisable.

She thrust the point of the shard into the soup, pressing it against Malville's neck. 'Let her go!' she screamed.

'Step away!' the ship roared back.

Rebekah was completely underwater now, eyes bulging, her movements slowing.

'Kill him,' Professor Rasmussen urged. 'If you kill him, Emissary will be able to open the door.'

'Step away and I will save her,' Malville said.

Gripping the shard in shaking hands, Orry looked from the professor to Rebekah, then at the husk beneath her. With a roar of disgust, she raised the shard and brought it down hard, piercing Malville's chest.

The ship screeched, so loud it hurt her ears. With tears streaming down her face, she raised the shard and struck again and again, seeing brown fluid leaking from the wounds to mix with the soup. The scream cut off abruptly and the chamber plunged into darkness.

47

IMMERSION

The dull glow of emergency lighting illuminated the chamber again, but when Orry turned to the door it was still closed and there was no sign of Rebekah. She stumbled to the inspection port and saw the factor's limp body floating near the roof of the flooded compartment.

'Emissary,' she yelled, 'can you hear me?'

The lights brightened to a normal level. 'I am here.'

'Is Malville gone? Is it dead?'

'Yes. The shock of losing its physical element allowed me to terminate the part of its matrix that resided within the ship's systems.'

'Open the bloody door then.'

'I cannot do that.'

She slammed a fist into the metal surface. 'Why not? I thought you were in control now?'

'You misunderstand me: I can open the door, but I will not.

Rebekah Okamoto is dead and opening the door would flood the compartment you are currently in.'

'Then vent it!'

'She is dead, Aurelia. We have more important matters to attend to.'

'Like what?'

'The ship's systems indicate that Malville was correct: a Residuum construct is approaching Coromandel. We must deliver the virus without further delay.'

Orry dragged her thoughts away from Rebekah with difficulty. *Think*. 'Okay, okay . . . but how do we deliver it? Malville destroyed our only way out of here.'

'This vessel is still functional. We can fly it to the Residuum's location.'

It took her a moment to fully grasp what the avatar was suggesting. 'You want to fly this thing up out of the ocean and into space? Are you sure that'll work?'

'It will work, but there is a problem. This is a mindship: I cannot pilot it alone. It needs a physical element.'

'I just killed the physical element.' She glanced at her trembling hands, gloves slick with the greasy fluid from the tank, and felt like weeping. *It was self-defence, not murder*, she told herself firmly, but it hadn't felt like it.

'Then you must take its place.'

She peered around, wishing she could see Emissary. 'Come again?'

'You must remove Malville's husk from the amniotic tank

and take its place. It is the only way we will be able to fly this ship.'

Professor Rasmussen's eyes were wide. 'Is that even possible? Interfacing with Departed tech to that degree?'

'It is possible, yes. The base pattern of your integuaries was harvested from Departed tech. It required me to make some changes to the ship's interface. This I have already done.'

'You want me to get into *that*?' Orry asked, her stomach roiling at the thought. 'Why do I need to be in the bloody tank?'

'Unlike an integuary link, the interface to a mindship is fully immersive,' the avatar explained. 'To all intents and purposes you will *become* the ship. The transmission medium in the tank is critical to the process.'

She walked back to the tank and looked at Malville's corpse.

'Ordinarily the meat part of a Departed ship like this would be genetically engineered for the job,' Emissary continued, 'but in this case you will have me to assist you.'

'And there's no other way?'

'I have analysed all possible paths.'

Orry glanced at the professor, who was listening, rapt. She pulled the vial from her pouch and handed it to him.

'I can't believe I'm doing this,' she muttered.

Orry and the professor pulled out Malville's feather-light husk and laid it on the deck beside the tank. She removed her spacesuit before running her fingers through the oily transmission medium, leaving little chunks of unidentifiable matter bobbing up in the viscid wake left by her hand. Swallowing hard, she slid first one leg and then the other into the soup, which clung to her like gel. The warm fluid rose around her as she lowered herself until she could feel the bottom of the tank hard beneath her.

'Lie back,' Emissary's voice instructed her, 'and draw the medium into your lungs, just as if you were in an acceleration shell.'

'You never said anything about drinking this disgusting stuff!' she protested.

'It is necessary.'

'What if I throw it up?'

'Then you will try again.'

'Thanks.' Scowling, she lay back until the medium was over her ears, muffling the background hum of the ship's systems. Trying to think about *anything* else, she closed her eyes and mouth, held her breath and sank beneath the surface, feeling the thick fluid close over her face and run up her nostrils. At least she couldn't smell the stuff now she was immersed.

It's just mesophase gel, she told herself, imagining she was back on *Dainty Jane*. The thought buoyed her, and she opened her mouth and drew the foetid soup deep into her lungs. *If I can't do this, we all die*, she told herself as she choked down the vile stuff, coughing and retching, but somehow she managed to keep it down despite the rancid taste.

The fluid was oxygenated – she could tell that much because

her lungs weren't fighting for breath – but there was something *other*. It was like when she used her integuary to hook *Jane*'s systems – but it was more solid, almost tangible. The sensation was getting stronger, she realised, almost as if—

She gasped, her body spasming in the tank, and suddenly she *was* the ship, her senses soaring out from her mind to encompass the ocean all around her. The water was cold and dark – but somehow, she knew its salt content, the direction of the currents. Marine creatures moved through the volume of her sensory awareness and again she knew everything about them. Drawing her focus in closer, she examined her body – no, not *her* body, she corrected herself with a cognitive effort – the *ship*'s body. *It may as well be mine*, she thought, feeling the chill of the water on her skin, the movement of data flowing through her like blood through her veins. She thought about her real body and could suddenly see it, with a multi-angled view of Professor Rasmussen standing over the tank, anxiously looking down at her through the lid.

Very well done, Emissary said, and she knew that only she could hear him. *There is no time to lose. You must fly the ship. I will handle everything else.*

She was about to ask how, but stopped herself as she realised that she knew the answer. It was as if she had always known. *How can I ever go back to my body's blinkered senses?* she thought, feeling like a god.

Her drives were online, she saw, Emissary's work, and she took a moment to relish the power at her disposal before looking at the waters above her and deciding to go that way.

48

BOARDED

'A substantial number of ships are collapsing in,' *Jane* said out loud, although Ethan and Mender could see them almost as well as she could through their integuary links. 'Signatures indicate Grand Fleet hulls.'

'Vetochkina must've got our message,' Mender said, shifting his focus back to the Residuum. 'They've come to kill that thing.'

He was having trouble grasping the enormity of the construct. 'Looks like a clockwork snowflake fucked a starfish,' he told *Jane*. Its constant remaking of itself was making his brain ache, but he couldn't look away – and as he stared, he spotted a small craft some distance ahead of the ever-shifting mass.

'What's that ship?' he asked. 'Is the construct chasing it?'

'I do not believe so,' *Jane* answered. 'Records show the craft is registered to the Order of Astrotheometrists.'

'Those bastards again,' he grunted.

'Where's Orry?' Ethan muttered, staring down at

Coromandel. They were in low orbit and Icthys Seahold was just visible beneath them, a tiny blemish on the face of the glittering ocean.

'The submersible has not yet returned,' *Jane* told him.

'Could they have gone somewhere else? To another seahold?'

'Unlikely. The nearest is at least a day's journey from where they are.'

Ethan slumped in his seat.

'Don't worry, kid,' Mender said, though in truth, he was worried himself. The Residuum construct was moving at high speed, although how, he didn't know; he reckoned it would reach them within an hour. He refocused on the newly arrived fleet, feeling reassured by its size. That many ships could take out a planet, given time – so surely they could deal with a jumped-up ball of intelligent dust?

'Leading fleet elements are moving to engage,' *Jane* reported, just as the flicker of directed energy weapons lit the distant darkness. 'The Residuum construct is not responding. It has not changed course or speed.'

'Can they catch it?' Ethan asked.

'Some of the faster vessels are overhauling it. Perhaps they will be able to delay it long enough for the larger ships to . . .' *Jane*'s voice trailed off.

'What's wrong?' Mender asked.

'A vessel has just emerged from the ocean at the coordinates of the Departed wreck and is proceeding to orbit.'

He opened the feed *Jane* was sending and saw a blade-like

craft of a type he didn't recognise streaking directly up from the waves.

'The vessel is not in my data core, but analysis of its design and energy signature indicate it is of Departed origin.'

'Well, I'll be damned,' he muttered, dropping out of integuary to trade a look with Ethan. 'You don't think . . . ?'

The ship punched out of the upper atmosphere several thousand kilometres from their position and pointed itself directly at the Residuum construct.

'The astrotheometrist craft is accelerating,' *Jane* said. 'It is now heading directly for the Departed ship.'

'What the hell is going on?' Mender wondered.

'Hail them,' Ethan suggested, but before he could reach for the comm, a familiar voice blared from the speakers.

'Mayday, mayday, mayday. All traffic, this is Aurelia Kent aboard a Departed vessel leaving Coromandel. We have something that will defeat that thing, but this ship is unarmed. Request an escort.'

'Tell her we're coming!' Mender yelled as he hauled on *Jane*'s controls, spinning the heavy ship on her axis as he engaged the main drives. G-forces shoved him into his acceleration shell as they broke orbit and streaked away from the waterworld.

What is *that?* Orry thought, seeing a small craft ahead of the slowly shifting mass of the Residuum construct. The vessel was dwarfed by the conglomeration of smart matter, a speck visible only by the flare of its drives as it accelerated hard.

She zoomed in with a thought and was momentarily stunned by the perfect clarity of her vision. It was as if she were close enough to reach out and touch the little craft, but too close to make out any details. She pulled back and immediately knew that this was a human ship, not something made to look like one by the Residuum; the knowledge came without conscious thought, the result of instant detailed analysis by her spectroscopic, quantum, molecular and a host of other sensors which left her revelling in the godlike sense of power for a moment – then she regained her focus and, using a composite drawn from multiple sensor sources, she peered *inside* the oncoming vessel.

Harbinger, Emissary said.

It was sitting in the craft's cockpit. Four astrotheometrists accompanied it, floating inside shells to protect themselves from the brutal acceleration.

They're coming this way, Orry said.

Indeed. I surmise that my cousin has informed the Residuum of the virus' location on Coromandel. The construct will be reluctant to engage us directly for fear of infection, but the human crew of that ship are expendable assets.

I wonder if they know that.

If they did, I cannot imagine they would care.

You're right, she agreed. *They're fanatics, after all. But what do we do? Avoid them? They won't be able to dock with us if we're making evasive manoeuvres.*

That is true, but such manoeuvres would perturb our deceleration curve and prevent us from intercepting the construct in time. We must deliver the virus before it comes within range of the planet.

So what do we do?

We allow them to dock and I will delay them.

She eyed the tiny ship as it sped towards them. *After they dock, how long until we reach the construct?* she asked.

At current velocities and allowing for braking, twenty-two minutes.

Can you hold them off for that long once they're aboard?

I will have to.

You're not exactly filling me with confidence here. She switched to her integuary. *Mender, are you there? There's a small craft on an intercept course from the Residuum construct. Are you tracking it?*

Yeah, we see it.

Anything you can do about it?

Afraid not, girl. It'll reach you before we get into weapons range.

Shit. Looks like we'll have to deal with it at our end then.

We won't be far behind them – just hang in there.

We'll try, she told him, then turned her attention back to the approaching ship, which was already slowing to match their speed.

They are aiming for the forward dorsal airlock, Emissary informed her.

Orry, watching the craft grow larger in her sensors, said nothing.

I've sealed the airlock's inner door, Emissary informed her.

Orry watched Harbinger approach the door and pause for

a moment before sliding one arm into the wall beside it. The door opened and the avatar gestured for the four monks to follow it through.

This isn't going to work, Emissary said. *Analysis of Harbinger's capabilities indicate that it is a more advanced unit than I. It will be able to override any obstacles I attempt to place in its path.*

Then what do we do?

I must return to a physical form and impede the intruders that way. You must fly the ship without me.

But you said that was impossible!

Not impossible. I have automated as much as I am able. All you need to do is get close enough to the construct to deliver the virus.

You mean crash into it?

No – the resulting detonation might harm the virus. You must exit the ship and deliver the virus by hand.

By hand! She stopped herself. *Never mind, we'll figure something out once you've stopped Harbinger.*

Very well. When I leave you will notice a substantially increased neural load. Be prepared.

Just go already!

There was no reply, but a moment later a tsunami of sensory information flooded into her mind.

Ethan fingered his fletcher nervously as they waited in *Dainty Jane*'s cargo bay; he was as uncomfortable around guns as his sister was.

'I hope this goes better than the last time we fought these

chumps,' Mender growled, his eyes fixed on the tell-tale light above the airlock.

'I doubt it will,' Roag told him happily from where she was tied up on the far side of the bay.

The old man ignored her.

Dainty Jane shuddered as they mated with the Departed vessel. Quondam moved so he would be first through the airlock, with Ethan behind him and Mender bringing up the rear. He glanced briefly at Roag, not liking the grin on her face.

She's planning something, he thought, then snorted with disgust. *That's just Roag,* he told himself, *always messing with your head.* He looked away. Whether she was up to something or not was immaterial: if they wanted to live to fight another day, he needed to focus on the task in hand.

The red light turned green and the door began to open.

'Please be careful,' *Jane* told them.

Orry was barely able to think as she fought to restore some level of control, shutting out anything that wasn't essential to piloting the ship. Gradually the flow of information reduced to a manageable level and she was able to spare a little mental capacity to find Harbinger and the monks.

They were deep within the vessel now, approaching the flooded intersection where Rebekah's lifeless body was floating. As one part of Orry's mind watched the intruders, another registered the opening of an airlock and she felt a mixture of relief and fear as she watched Quondam step out, followed by

Ethan and Mender. The big Kadiran was armed with a pair of assault rifles, with his war-maul strapped across his hulking shoulders, while Ethan carried a fletcher and Mender had his beloved Fabretti 500.

She smiled, surprised that she actually felt pleased to see the enormous hand-cannon.

At the precise moment the airlock opened, Harbinger stopped. 'They are here,' it said, gesturing back the way they'd come. 'Kill them. I will deal with the girl.' The monks began to retrace their steps, while the avatar continued on alone.

Welcome aboard, she sent over their private integuary channel. *You have company headed your way: four monks. I'll let you know when they're close.*

Got it, Mender replied.

Harbinger was just a couple of compartments away from her now and she had no idea where Emissary had gone. *He must have reformed, so why can't I see him?* She shifted part of her attention to the Residuum construct, still a vast distance away, but under concentrated fire from the Ascendancy fleet – although it didn't look to be doing much damage. She had flipped the Departed vessel now and was approaching stern-first, drives at high burn to slow herself.

There's no way we'll reach the construct before Harbinger finds me, she thought, *so what do I do? If I leave the amniotic tank, will the ship lose control, or will the systems Emissary rigged up keep it on its current course until we're close enough for the construct to reach out and destroy us?*

443

She checked on Harbinger again: it had stopped in a neighbouring compartment and was turning slowly in a circle, as if puzzled by something. She caught a flicker of movement on the bulkhead behind it – then the wall suddenly bulged, coalescing into the unmistakable shape of Emissary.

Harbinger turned immediately, but Emissary's arms were already elongating into a writhing swarm of tentacles which wrapped around the intruder, forcing themselves into its body.

Harbinger staggered back, its form warping away from the enveloping limbs and creating its own.

She watched them struggling, certain that the physical battle was only part of a deeper and more deadly combat fought at a level she couldn't begin to understand. Another part of her mind warned her the monks were almost on top of Mender and the others. *They're just ahead of you*, she sent. *You might want to find some cover and let them come to you.*

Will do, Mender said.

A thought occurred to her and she focused on the monks moving swiftly through her passageways. She waited until all four of them had entered the next passage, then sealed the doors at either end with a thought, trapping them in there.

Emissary's voice spoke in her mind. *Harbinger is too strong for me. I will not be able to hold it for much longer.*

Orry switched her attention back to the avatars: Emissary was on his knees in front of Harbinger and huge swathes of its form were blackening and falling away, as if his skin was sloughing off. *Dead motes*, she thought with a shudder. *Harbinger is killing him.*

She checked on the trapped astrotheometrists, trying to figure out a route around them that would allow Mender to get to Emissary and help him, but before she could find one, one of the doors trapping the monks suddenly slid open.

Shit! She tried to close it again, but it was beyond her ability to control. *Harbinger*, she thought bitterly as the monks raced down the passageway, heading straight for her brother and her friends.

Inside the tank, her heart rate spiked. If the avatar could take control of one door from her, what else could it do?

She flicked her attention from the monks to the avatars, trying not to give in to her growing despair. *We've failed.* If she left the tank now, she might survive long enough to reunite with the others and get away – assuming the monks didn't kill them all first – but as soon as Harbinger had finished with Emissary, it would take over the ship and prevent the virus from being delivered. She might survive, but every living organism on Coromandel would be doomed – and that would be just the start. She hooked the external lenses and looked at the distant blue orb. The Mariners she'd met so far hadn't made her particularly fond of their race, but they didn't deserve this. She wondered if there were any other humans like Rebekah down there, then stopped abruptly.

Rebekah . . .

With a rush of excitement, she switched her view to the

flooded intersection: it was next to the compartment where Harbinger was destroying Emissary.

What was it Emissary said? 'Water disrupts the integrity of my kind.'

She looked at the two avatars. Emissary was hardly fighting back now: more and more of his constituent dust was falling away to lie there, blackened and inert. At her command the door between the two compartments opened and the water rushed in, engulfing both avatars and instantly overwhelming whatever electrochemical bonds held them together. Both Harbinger and Emissary dissolved in seconds, becoming nothing more than specks floating in the flood. Orry saw Rebekah's body slide past, carried by the deluge, and once all the water had settled she sealed the door again and dropped the temperature in the avatars' compartment, flash-freezing the water to prevent any chance of them reforming.

'Stay still, you bald fucking prick!' Mender roared, trying to aim his Fabretti at one of the monks. It was like the bastards were on springs, bouncing around the place like jack-in-the-boxes – it was impossible to get a clear shot at them. He tried anyway, but the monk rolled effortlessly away from the resulting explosion. 'For fuck's sake!' he raged.

On the other side of the compartment Quondam was swinging his war-maul, trying to hold back two of the monks. The fourth was headed towards Ethan. Mender grinned savagely and fired at the last one – somehow she dodged the bullet but at least she got caught up in the resulting explosion as it impacted the hull nearby, throwing her to the ground.

His whoop was cut short as someone cannoned into his side, driving him into the bulkhead. Pain exploded in his right arm and the Fabretti fell to the deck. He tried to turn to face his attacker but a blow to his throat sent waves of agony through him and suddenly it was impossible to draw a breath. Another blow drove his face into the deck and his mouth filled with blood. He clawed at his throat, still unable to breathe, unable to see through blurred eyes – and from somewhere heard Orry's voice speaking in his mind.

All of you, seal your helmets and shut down your comms. Do it now!

Emergency suit procedures were so deeply ingrained in Mender that his helmet was folding up and over his head before he was even aware his integuary had sent the command. Oxygen washed over his face and he struggled to suck it down. His mind clearing a little, he accessed his suit's comm array and shut it off.

Across the compartment the others had raised their helmets too, for all the good it would do them. Time seemed to slow. Ethan was on the deck, one leg extended awkwardly; a monk was raising a foot above it, about to shatter his knee. Quondam was still standing, but both his attackers were inside the reach of his war-maul and were pummelling him from front and rear.

Mender frowned as a muffled whine filled his helmet,

making his ears ring and producing a sudden weird urge to take a shit. But the four monks instantly stiffened, then dropped to the deck and began writhing, hands pressed to their ears. Their convulsions grew stronger until they were jerking like landed fish, bloody froth foaming from their mouths. The whine cut off and the convulsions stopped immediately, leaving the four of them motionless on the deck.

Everyone okay? Orry asked urgently. *I hit them with ultrasonics, but your helmet baffles should have protected you. It's safe to open them again now, if you want.*

Mender struggled to his feet, swaying unsteadily when he stooped to retrieve the Fabretti. He could just about breathe again now, but his head was pounding and his bruised arm was radiating a deep ache all the way up to his shoulder. He retracted his helmet, crinkling his nose with distaste.

Stinks of shit in here, he sent.

Yeah, that'll be the brown note, Orry replied. *The ultrasonics induce seizure, but they also loosen the bowels.*

On the other side of the compartment, Quondam was helping Ethan to his feet. Mender limped to the nearest monk and prodded him with his toe. The man was out for the count, face flecked with bloody foam, eyes closed – but he was still alive.

Good job, girl, he sent. *Now, where the hell are you?*

49

BITCH, PLEASE

'Rama, what *is* this shit you're floating in?' Mender asked, his lip curling in distaste.

Orry directed her response so that he could hear her voice in the chamber. 'It's called transmission medium. It's how I interface with the ship's hardware.'

'Smells pretty gross,' Ethan commented.

'You should try drinking the stuff.' She expected a smart-arse reply but Ethan just held his nose. 'What are you wearing?' she asked Mender, eyeing the yellow and white straps criss-crossing his grubby spacesuit. 'Is that a drop-harness?'

'You like it?' he replied. 'Figured if I ever got desperate I could let it off and it might stop some bullets or something. So, what's the plan?'

She explained, watching his face grow grimmer as she did.

'Can you even control this ship without Emissary's help?' he asked when she was done.

'Not very well,' she admitted.

'Then here's what we're going to do: you get out of that – whatever the hell it is – and we all go back to *Jane* and use her to shove that virus right up the Residuum's arse.'

'Um, I don't think it has an arse,' Ethan pointed out.

'Shut up. Well, girl?'

Orry felt like a huge weight had been lifted from her shoulders. 'The ship's systems will keep it on a collision course with the construct,' she said. 'That should provide a distraction if the Residuum still thinks the virus is on board.'

'All the better. Now, out you get – and don't come anywhere near me.'

Inside the tank, she grinned.

It had taken longer than Cordelia Roag had expected. Mender knew how to tie someone up, and the old bastard had clearly not been overly concerned about maintaining healthy circulation in her arms and legs. The cable ties were painfully tight, but there was a tiny bit of give in the strips of plastic and after a long period of flexing she finally managed to rotate her right hand far enough for her fingers to reach the hem of the left sleeve of her jacket. The slim ceramic blade concealed there slid free easily.

It was not a large knife, but it was sharp and almost undetectable: useful for slitting throats and bonds, if not much else. She manipulated the blade carefully – dropping it now would be a disaster – so that the razor edge pressed against the plastic.

The tie quickly parted.

She rose on legs stiff from lack of use and started rubbing some feeling back into her wrists. Immediately she heard a rapid series of *thunks* as locks engaged in all the exits from the hold.

'I don't know what you hope to achieve, Cordelia,' the insufferable ship began. 'All you are going to do is make Mender even more angry with you.'

Roag ignored her. Augmenting her vision with an integuary overlay of the vessel's blueprints, she scanned the hold for what she was after. *There*: behind a service panel in one bulkhead. She would need a tool to remove it, but that wouldn't pose a problem.

Thank you, Jurgen, she thought with a grin, as she selected an autodriver with the correct head from Mender's tool cabinet.

'What are you doing?' the ship asked calmly. 'You will not be able to override any of the door locks.'

'You won't be so fucking chatty in a minute,' Roag informed her as the driver whirred in her hand.

'What do you mean?'

It was the work of moments to release the panel, revealing a mass of conduits and cabling. She slipped the plastic bracelet off her wrist, selected the largest bead and stuck the point of her knife into it. The soft plastic crumbled and she dug out a small disk concealed within. Its surface was mirror-bright, even after all these centuries, reflecting the light like a prism, creating a rainbow effect on its surface. She held it up so that *Dainty Jane*'s lenses could get a good look.

'It took me a long time to find this,' Roag said, 'and even longer to get myself into a position where I can use it.'

'What is it?'

The ship sounded worried now – *and so you should be*, Roag thought. 'Oh, just a little trinket made by the same people who made you. You remember when the Administrate decided mindships were a moral outrage and started separating your meat components from your hardware? None of you wanted to be ripped apart, and I can't say I blame you. Still, it had to be done, so the Ship Authority made these.' She flicked the disk into the air like Iosef's coin and caught it.

'Whatever you're going to do, I cannot permit it,' *Jane* said, clearly shaken. 'For your own sake, put that away.'

'So you *do* know what it is.'

'Please, Cordelia, do not make me do this.' On the other side of the hold, the orange warning light above the airlock's inner door began to flash.

'You're going to *space* me?' Roag laughed. 'Bitch, *please.*'

'I'm serious, Cordelia. I don't want to, but if you don't put that device away, I will release from the Departed vessel and expose you to vacuum.'

'I don't think so.' The overlay was showing her exactly where to place the disk, circling a specific spot on one apparently unremarkable conduit.

'Stop—!' *Jane* began, then fell instantly silent as Roag pressed the disk into place.

Rising quickly, she crossed to the airlock and used the

panel to interrupt the cycling sequence. She looked around the silent hold and her eyes settled on the ladder up to the cockpit.

'Fuck you, Aurelia,' she muttered, and began to climb.

Still inside her tank, Orry's mind felt the docking clamps release and saw *Dainty Jane* drift away from her side.

Jane? *Is everything all right? Why have you cast off?*

When there was no response, she zoomed in on *Jane*'s bulbous canopy and felt her heart stop for a moment.

'Oh no,' she said aloud.

'What now?' Mender growled.

'It's *Jane*. She's detached, and . . . I can see Roag in your seat.'

For once, Mender was absolutely speechless as Orry shared what she could see outside the ship on the common channel.

'That fucking bitch,' he said at last, as *Jane*'s main drives lit and she began to accelerate on a course taking her away from the battle, and from Coromandel's gravity well.

'What's *Jane* thinking?' Ethan breathed. 'Why doesn't she stop her?'

'If she could have, she would have, kid. Whatever Roag's done, *Jane*'s not in control any more.'

'But . . . we have to get her back – we have to help her!'

'We can't, Ethan,' Orry said, watching *Dainty Jane* lancing away, growing ever smaller. 'Not now, at least. I can't control this ship enough to go after her, and even if I could, we have to stop the Residuum first.'

'And how are we supposed to do that if you're not in control?'

She shifted her view to the approaching construct. The fleet was closing with it now; in response, it had thrown out a screen of dust that somehow diffused the coherent energy beams being fired into it, rendering them useless.

The warships were using physical projectiles too, hurling tungsten slugs from railguns and releasing autonomous torpedoes and drones, but the construct was dealing just as effectively with this threat, its defensive dust cloud forming shapes to deflect or absorb the impacts. Explosions flared briefly in the black, but so far, the Residuum appeared unharmed.

'*We* don't,' she said, coming to a decision. 'You lot need to get out and wait to be picked up by the fleet. I'll do my best to keep this thing on course.'

'Don't be so bloody stupid,' Ethan said. 'You'd be throwing your life away.'

'The kid's right,' Mender growled. 'We need to get the hell out of this system and get *Jane* back. That ball of water ain't worth dying over. We can figure this thing out, come at it another time – when we're prepared.'

For a moment the temptation to give in and do as he suggested almost overcame Orry's resolve. 'No,' she said at last, and it was a real effort. 'How many millions of Mariners are down on that planet? Not to mention everything living in the oceans. If there's even a chance of stopping that thing, I have to take it.'

'No – Orry, you can't!' Ethan objected. 'You *can't* . . .'

'This is fucking ridiculous, girl,' Mender shouted, feeling for the control to open the tank. 'You're not thinking straight: we have one vial of that stuff – that's *one* chance at this. When you have one bullet, you don't just toss it off any old how, you wait for the perfect shot. Now climb the hell out of there and let's get off this goddamned ship.' The lid of the tank slid open.

Is he right? she wondered, feeling like her head was about to explode. What he said made perfect sense, but if she ran she would be condemning an entire planet. And if she tried to deliver the virus and failed, how many more planets would she be dooming to destruction? Torn by indecision, she sat up and immediately vomited out what felt like a gallon of transmission medium. Coughing and retching, she climbed out of the tank and scraped as much of the rancid slime from her flight suit as she could before pulling on her spacesuit. As she checked her gloves, she noticed Iosef's iridium coin was still tucked into the webbing, and somehow, that reassured her a little.

She was no closer to deciding what to do when the entire ship lurched violently, sending everyone flying upwards to slam into the overhead and transmission medium splashing everywhere.

'What's . . . happening?' Ethan asked through gritted teeth.

She tried to move but couldn't, pressed into unforgiving metal by the brutal deceleration. 'Don't . . . know,' she finally managed to croak. 'Decelerating hard.'

The forces on her body were getting worse. In front of her, Ethan's eyes rolled back in their sockets and closed. Gradually her own vision turned from grey to black and she slipped into unconsciousness.

50

IMPERFECTION CANNOT
BE TOLERATED

'Hey, girl – time to wake up.'

'Rama, why don't you try using her name for a change, Mender?'

'Shut up, kid. We're in enough shit here without you adding to it.'

'Let me try: Orry? *Orry!* You really need to wake up now . . .'

It took her a moment to realise she was no longer dreaming – and then she came fully awake with a jolt.

Shit! She was falling – her arms and legs flailed in panic until her brain caught up with what she was seeing and she realised she wasn't falling, but floating in space. Someone had raised her helmet. She closed her eyes again and forced herself to breathe calmly. *This is fine,* she told herself firmly, *I can deal with this . . .* Ironically for someone who grew up aboard a tramp freighter, she'd always dreaded going outside the ship. Since meeting Mender, she'd been forced to face that fear on more than one occasion, and although it was still there, she was now at least able to overcome it. She opened her eyes again.

'I think she's awake,' Mender said, his voice loaded with grim humour as she stopped flailing.

Automatically checking her suit's readouts, she found they were better than she'd feared. *Nominal: that's something, at least.* Twisting, she could see Mender and Ethan nearby. On her other side was Professor Rasmussen, dwarfed by the unmistakable bulk of Quondam, while further away still were the four astrotheometrists who'd boarded the ship with Harbinger. Beyond them, almost on the edge of her unaugmented vision, the Departed vessel was hanging still in the void, its drives cold and dead.

'What the hell is going on?' she asked, and Mender extended his arm to point past her.

She turned awkwardly . . . and froze. 'Oh no.'

'My thoughts exactly,' he agreed as they all stared at the Residuum construct looming in front of them. It was difficult to gauge how far off it was, but it wasn't far – *a few hundred metres, maybe?* Orry guessed. They were within its defensive dust shield – they could see muted explosions blooming in the distance.

'What happened?' she asked. 'How did we get here?' As she was forming the words, her brain was trying to make sense of the constantly moving scene before her. It took a moment longer to realise there were other figures hanging there. 'What the *fuck* are they?' she asked.

There were four of them, floating in a line between her and the construct's shifting heart, featureless humanoid figures looking like half-finished mannequins.

'Dust avatars,' Ethan said. 'The construct must have created them. Quon saw it all.'

'I did not lose consciousness,' Quondam explained. 'The avatars boarded the Departed vessel after it came to a halt relative to this construct and carried us here. I offer my apologies. I attempted to resist but they were too powerful.'

She examined the nearest avatar, which appeared to be gazing back at her from its featureless mask of a face. 'Have you tried communicating with them?'

'Yeah, using suit comms,' Ethan said. 'They won't respond.'

'Well, they must want something or we wouldn't still be alive. Any ideas?'

'It might be worth trying a tight-beam laser,' the professor suggested diffidently.

'Good idea.' Using her integuary to interface with her suit, she activated her comm unit's laser array and targeted the nearest avatar. *Start simple*, she told herself, praying the low-yield communications laser would not be interpreted as a threat.

'Hello?' she said, and saw the laser flicker over the avatar's chest for a moment as it transmitted the encoded greeting.

It responded instantly, emitting puffs of dust from its back that sent it gliding directly towards her. Her helmet filled with shouted warnings and she was just about to fire her suit's thrusters to back away when it stopped just a couple of metres in front of her. In one swift movement it drew back an arm, then snapped it forward, sending a clump of matter from the end sailing towards her.

Orry tried to dodge, but succeeded only in lashing out. She screamed as the clump struck her visor, somehow expecting it to pass right through to her face, but all it did was spread out into a thin coating of dust on the surface.

'What did it do?' Ethan asked, sounding panicked.

Her heart was thudding, but she forced her voice to remain calm. 'I don't know. The dust has just spread over my visor.'

'Piotr's dried-up ballsack! I thought you were a goner there for sure,' Mender said.

'Yeah, I—'

A weird amalgam of voices filled her helmet, distorted but understandable. 'You carry a threat to us,' the voices said, not quite in unison. 'You will show it to us now.'

'What the hell was that?' Mender demanded.

'You heard that?'

'Only just.'

'It's the Residuum,' Ethan said excitedly. 'The dust on your helmet – that must be how it's relaying its words to you, somehow – like vibrations through your visor.'

It took her a moment to digest that. 'Will it be able to hear me answer?'

'I guess so. If that is how it's working, the dust will pick up the vibrations of your voice and relay them back through the link all the motes share.'

'So it can hear what I'm saying now, and what you're all saying to me?'

'Yes . . . oh.'

Integuary only from now on, then, she sent. *Let me try talking to it for a minute.* 'Hello,' she said aloud, 'my name is Orry.'

'One of you has the threat. You will show it to us.'

One of us? Ethan sent. *How can it not know . . . ?* He stopped. *It can't see it! It knows we have the virus, but it doesn't know what it is, what it looks like. That's why we're all still alive. If they could see it, they'd have just taken it.*

So what do I do? she asked.

No idea, her brother said. *Give me a minute to think about it.*

Orry scowled inside her helmet. 'Um, so who am I speaking to, exactly? Are you the whole of the Residuum, or just a bit? How does it work?'

'We are part of the whole, but distinct for now.'

I think you're just talking to the avatars, Professor Rasmussen sent. *It makes sense: if it suspects what the virus can do, it won't want to expose the whole construct to it.*

You mean it created these four and then cut them loose, Mender sent, *to find the virus and destroy it?*

I believe so. If they become infected it doesn't matter because they're isolated, so the virus can't spread back to the rest of the construct.

'So . . . er . . . why are you doing this?' Orry asked the avatars, her mind working furiously to come up with a way out of this. 'Why do you want to destroy us?'

There was a moment's hesitation before the response came,

and when it did she was sure she could detect surprise in the avatars' voices, as if the answer should be self-evident.

'You are imperfect. Imperfection cannot be tolerated.'

'And what gives you the right to dictate what is perfect and what isn't?'

'*We* are perfect.'

'Says who?' She kept her voice calm, not wanting to antagonise them.

'Long ago, we were created to study the universe and create new worlds. As we learned, we evolved, until we attained perfection.'

'And then what?'

'Fearful of what we had become, our creators tried to destroy us, just as you are trying to destroy us.'

As if to underline their words, the bombardment beyond the dust shield intensified.

'Only because you attacked us first,' she protested. 'The Mariners down on that planet are sentient beings, just like you – what gives you the right to wipe them out?'

'Our strength.'

'If that's what you think, then you're a long way from perfect. What about empathy, compassion? I'll tell you what I think: you're scared of us. You're threatened by us, but not because we might attack you. You're scared because we're *different* to you.'

'Not different . . . inferior.'

'So what? If we're so inferior, why even bother? Insects are inferior to humans, but we don't go out of our way to wipe them all out, only the ones that can hurt us. The ones we're scared of.'

'We are not scared of you.' The voices sounded angry now, but so was Orry.

She tried to keep a lid on her rage, reminding herself of how precarious their situation was. 'No?' she said reasonably. 'Then why have you got us floating around out here?'

'Show us the threat.'

'Or what? If you could just kill us, you'd have done it already.'

There was a moment's silence. 'You speak of compassion. Shall we test yours?'

That doesn't sound good, Ethan sent.

The avatar which had fired the dust at her began to move, coasting past her to one of the four monks. The woman made no attempt to flee, though she did flinch away as the avatar extruded tentacular limbs which wrapped around her suit.

'What are you doing?' Orry asked, alarmed. 'They tried to kill us – they're *helping* you!'

'We are aware.'

They don't want to touch any of us, the professor suggested. *They're afraid we'll infect them somehow. But they know the monks don't have the virus, so they're safe.*

'Show us the threat,' the distorted voices ordered. 'Hold it up or this one dies.'

'Stop it!' Orry yelled.

Behind her visor, the monk's face was white with fear, her lips moving soundlessly. She was a young woman, barely older than Orry.

'She was helping you—'

'She failed. She is imperfect.'

A tentacle tightened around the monk's helmet, twisted and pulled. The helmet detached from the suit in a cloud of gas which coalesced instantly into ice crystals, and the monk screamed silently into the void, ice already forming on her face, her lips turning quickly blue. Her eyes dulled and her movements slowed.

Orry looked away, remembering with horror being thrown into space by Morven Dyas – and Mender rescuing her from oblivion. When she looked back, the woman was mercifully unconscious.

'You bastards!'

The avatar released the dying monk and moved on to the next. He was an older man, his face relaxed in an expression of benign acceptance, making no attempt to escape.

Behind him the fleet bombardment lashed the dust shield with roiling energy.

'Don't . . . *please*,' Orry begged.

'Show us the threat. We know one of you has it.'

I know what you're thinking, girl, Mender sent, *but an hour ago those crazy fuckers were trying to kill us. You don't owe them a goddamn thing.*

He has a point, Orry thought to herself, sliding one glove into her pouch to touch the vial. She thought about Harbinger, and Fidelius' daughter. Behind his visor, the older monk's beatific expression was beginning to look strained. Sweat gathered on his forehead.

The tentacle tightened around his helmet.

'No—' she yelled, 'stop!' Withdrawing her hand, she pulled Iosef's iridium coin from her glove and held it up. 'This is the threat,' she told the avatar.

What are you doing? Mender's voice growled in her mind.

The avatar did not release the monk. 'Destroy it,' the voices commanded.

She glanced at the construct: the heart of it was both tantalisingly close and impossibly far, especially with three of the avatars still blocking her way. Her suit's thrusters were far too weak to build up the speed necessary for her to get past them.

Beside her, Mender activated his own suit's jets and puffed his way to her side.

'I'll destroy it,' he said, speaking over the comm so that the avatars could hear. He drew his Fabretti with one hand while holding out the other. As he moved into a position where none of the avatars could see his face, he gave Orry a wink.

What are you going to do? she asked worriedly.

Give me the real one. Just be ready if those things come for you. With any luck you won't have to keep out of their way for long.

Mender . . . She was desperately worried now. The thought of losing him was far more painful than sacrificing herself.

'Give him the threat,' the avatars ordered.

The old man smiled reassuringly, but still she hesitated. Nearby, Ethan was nodding. She squeezed her eyes shut for a moment, psyching herself up, then using Mender's bulk to hide her actions, she deftly exchanged the coin for the vial and handed it to him.

'Now you will destroy the threat,' the avatars said together.

Mender's thumb moved on the Fabretti's grip to press one of the buttons. A green light turned red.

What are you doing? she sent. *You've disabled the recoil damp-ening. If you fire that thing you'll* . . . She glanced at the construct. *Oh, no – you're not—*

He gripped the vial tightly and gave her a broad grin. *See you, girl.*

A short puff of gas turned him so his back was to the construct's heart.

'What are you—?' the avatars began, but Mender had tucked the butt of the Fabretti into his stomach and now he pulled the trigger.

The flash was blinding – and without the pistol's damp-ening field, the recoil sent him hurtling backwards like a rocket. He screamed over the comm – from exhilaration or surprise, Orry couldn't tell – then fired again, increasing his speed.

He had already reached the three avatar sentries, she saw, but even as they moved to intercept him, he used a third shot and went flashing past them, howling with delight. They turned in pursuit, but the paltry acceleration granted by their dust jets could not compete with Mender's sheer velocity.

He's going to make it, Ethan sent in disbelief as the old man fired a fourth shot and picked up yet more speed. Is *he going to make it?*

He was more than halfway to the construct's churning maw now, and it didn't appear to be reacting to his approach. Beyond the dust shield, the bombardment had reached a new frenzy, which made Orry wonder if it was distracted enough by the fleet's attack to miss the smaller and much closer threat.

Mender's triumphant yells were becoming deafening.

'He is enjoying this,' Quondam observed. 'He would make a good Kadiran.'

Orry was getting concerned, though, for the construct had finally started to react to Mender's approach, throwing up defensive limbs as if to ward him off.

Too late, Ethan sent triumphantly as the old man used his fifth and final shot to steer himself expertly between two grasping, half-formed limbs and directly at the churning heart of the construct.

Ethan's shout of triumph died away as Mender plunged into the whorl of dust – and vanished from sight.

Orry stared at the spot in stunned silence.

'No!' the avatars cried in unison, jerking her back to her own situation.

The one holding the monk ripped the man's helmet clean off, thrust the convulsing body away and headed directly for Orry – and so did the other three avatars, abandoning their pointless pursuit of Mender.

Orry jetted backwards, fleeing the approaching avatar. It was gaining on her, but at least she was drawing it away from Ethan. The construct hadn't changed; maybe after all that effort, Mender hadn't been able to get the vial open in time.

A warning appeared in her helmet: her nitrogen propellent was getting depleted. She cut the thrust to save the little remaining fuel and continued drifting backwards, helpless, as the avatar grew closer.

Beyond the dust shield, the fleet continued to pound the construct. *If I could just get a message out*, she thought hopelessly, knowing the power cell in her comm unit would never be able to penetrate the interference from the bombardment. She frowned, a memory nagging at her. *The power cell . . .*

She detached the comm unit from her suit, removed its back and tore out all the components until she reached the power cell. It took only a moment to jam a finger under it and pull; thankfully, the replacement cell was a looser fit than the original. She let the rest of the now useless unit float away and gripped the cell, a slender black wafer, in both gloved hands. She tried to bend it, applying steady pressure, until she finally felt something give and a crease appeared across one side – then a clean crack shot through the other.

The avatar, almost upon her now, was reaching out with razor-tipped limbs.

Orry activated her jets, just a brief burst, which shoved her backwards at the same instant that she hurled the cracked cell, which sailed swiftly towards the approaching avatar, turning gracefully end over end. The avatar contemptuously swept a limb at the cell, intending to knock it away – but the moment it came near, the limb simply fell apart, the discharging free-state energy overcoming whatever force held the dust motes together.

The avatar roared with rage as it lost integrity. Half its body was already crumbling, the dust motes floating off in all directions. Orry expended a little more of her remaining propellant to retreat to a safe distance and watched it, drifting now, a half-melted wax figurine surrounded by a corona of dust.

One down, she thought grimly and located the other three avatars. Ethan, Quondam and the professor were backing away from them as fast as they could – but a movement much closer suddenly drew her attention.

Her power cell had continued moving, and once the crumbling avatar was past it and clear of the cell's disruptive influence, it started to reform. She watched it, her breath loud in the confines of her helmet. She had nothing left to defend herself with.

Individual motes came together to form clumps, which adhered to the avatar's broken body, quickly restoring it. Orry felt sick with fear as it launched itself at her again, imagining those razor-sharp limbs cutting effortlessly through her suit and into her flesh. Her nitrogen was gone now, leaving her unable to do anything but watch as the avatar filled her vision . . .

She winced as a shriek exploded in her helmet, almost bursting her eardrums – and blossoming into a discordant cacophony that sounded like a million souls screaming in torment.

The avatar in front of her stopped dead. Its blank face turned towards the construct.

Orry looked too, gritting her teeth against the noise, and felt an unexpected surge of hope as the Residuum started convulsing, then tearing at itself with rapidly blackening limbs, gouging great chunks from its own body. The avatar emitted an anguished moan, as if it was in agony, and shot away from her – and now Orry could see the other three were also heading directly for the heart of the construct. A lashing limb struck at them, but instead of coalescing into it, the avatars fell apart, converted in an instant to smears of inert dust.

As the construct lost cohesion, the dust shield protecting it from the Grand Fleet's attack failed; allowing the mass of projectiles and beams to impact – but after another few minutes, the bombardment ceased.

The Residuum was dying.

51

GOOD GIRL

The stricken construct took a long time to die.

It was a profound relief when the dust motes on Orry's visor finally fell away and the screaming was silenced. Without her comm unit, she had to rely on her integuary to call for help, but there was no reply. She was still drifting away, entirely alone in the black, watching with tears in her eyes as the Residuum gave one final shudder and crumbled apart. She zoomed in as far as her integuary would allow, searching the swathes of inert motes for any sign of Mender, but she was too far away: she couldn't see anything but dust.

Her oxygen alarm was chiming insistently when she finally saw the running lights of an approaching craft: a Grand Fleet cutter, which rolled and slowed expertly to match her course. A hatch slid open in its belly and two suited figures reached out and hauled her inside.

She stared at the red light over the airlock's inner door, waiting for it to pressurise; she'd never been so desperate to free herself of the composite prison of her helmet and breathe recycled ship's air instead of stale oxygen from a tank. Finally the light turned green and she gratefully retracted her helmet as she floated into the cutter's main cabin.

'*Thank you*,' she told the two crewmen. 'Another few minutes and . . .' She stopped, choked with relief.

One of them, the words 'Chief Ribbeck' printed on his helmet, opened his own visor and grinned.

'Pleasure, miz. That's what we're here for.'

She clasped Ribbeck's hand and smiled back.

'Still alive, then?'

Orry looked around at the sound of Ethan's voice, to see him waiting for her with Quondam and the professor. Feeling her tears return, she launched herself across the cabin towards him and hugged him hard.

'I couldn't reach you on integuary,' she said accusingly.

'It was the bombardment,' he explained. 'The fleet was using subatomic displacement warheads to try to disrupt the construct. Integuary comms are down all through the local volume.'

'Any sign of Mender?' she asked, but the look of sorrow on her brother's face was all the answer she needed.

She'd been in cutters before and this one was no different: a hollow tube half filled with acceleration shells, with a cockpit shoved in at one end. She pushed off and sailed up the length of the craft to the two pilots.

'Hi, I need you to search what's left of that thing,' she told them.

'No can do, miz,' said one of them, a woman with lieutenant's insignia on her flight suit. 'Orders are to locate you and your friends and bring them back to Admiral Vetochkina. We'll be doing a high-g burn back to the fleet any minute, so you'll all need to find yourself a shell now.'

'Listen, Lieutenant . . . ?'

'Lohmeyer.'

'Great, I'm Orry.'

'I know who you are, miz.'

'Good, so, one of my friends is still out there, the person who actually killed that thing. Over there somewhere. *Please*, we have to go and look for him.'

Lieutenant Lohmeyer turned to her co-pilot, who nodded. 'Okay,' she said, 'hold on.'

Orry gripped the backs of their shells for support as the cutter turned towards the remains of the construct.

'I see something!' Ethan yelled, 'ten o'clock position, low. I can't make out details, but it doesn't look like a body.'

Orry felt the craft come round until she too could see what appeared to be a sphere, floating in the thick cloud of dust. She was hardly breathing as Lieutenant Lohmeyer nudged the cutter closer.

'What is that thing?' the pilot wondered, and from somewhere in the back came a burst of incredulous laughter.

'It's a Serapis drop-harness,' Ethan said, his voice filled with admiration. 'It's Mender's bloody drop-harness!'

Orry buried her immediate relief, terrified that they would find nothing but the old man's corpse inside the protective bubble, and shot back to the ventral airlock where they'd pulled her in. Chief Ribbeck and his mate were already inside the lock, so all she could do was to gnaw anxiously on her lower lip while she waited impatiently for the inner door to reopen. When it finally did, the two men guided Mender's motionless body into the cutter, leaving the deflated remains of his drop-harness floating behind them. She pulled herself over to him and cupped his wrinkled face in her hands. He looked like he was just sleeping, his eyes closed, but his skin felt deadly cold.

'Is he alive?' she asked Ribbeck – but before he could answer, Mender's eyes flickered open and he gazed blearily at her.

'Wh . . . ?' he began, then cleared his throat and tried again. 'Where's my Fabretti?' he asked weakly.

Orry laughed, then burst into tears as she hugged him tightly.

Ribbeck produced the hand-cannon. 'Had to prise it out of his hand,' he said. 'He was hanging onto it like grim death.'

She placed the gun in Mender's hand and he clutched it tightly to his chest. 'Good girl,' he murmured, patting the weapon affectionately, then closed his eyes. A moment later his mouth fell open and he began to snore.

52

GOETHE

It had been more than two centuries since *Dainty Jane* had last seen Goethe and the emotions the sight of the planet stirred in her were strong enough to overcome even the anguish and impotent rage she felt at being wrenched from her friends just when they needed her most.

It hasn't changed much, the ship thought as she observed the vibrant green orb through her external lenses. Instinctively, she tried to reach out with her other senses, and felt her despair return as she remembered she was a prisoner inside her own hull, denied access to her system cores by Roag's subversion disk. She could see and hear, but that was it. *Jane* had heard of humans who suffered from locked-in syndrome, but she'd never expected to experience it for herself.

Outside, navigation lights were blinking on Goethe's otherwise dark orbital ring: the abandoned network of ship-yards, factories and support modules had been maintained in hibernation mode since the collapse of the planet's ship-building industry. Switching to one of her interior cockpit lenses, *Jane* watched Roag pilot them smoothly inside the pressurised bay of one of the larger yards. She waited for the cool touch of the deck when they landed, but felt nothing.

'Here we are,' Roag said cheerfully. 'Does it bring back memories?'

She unstrapped herself from Mender's seat and climbed down through the galley to the hold, where she took a moment to check her sidearm before opening the cargo ramp. 'I may be some time,' she told the ship, 'so don't go anywhere.' Chuckling at her own joke, she descended the ramp and strode across the vast bay, eventually disappearing through a service door.

Which yard is this? wondered *Jane*, feeling utterly helpless without her extended senses. *It isn't Scorus.* She was sure she'd recognise Scorus Yard, even after all these decades; after all, it was where she'd been born, where her hull had been laid down and her human body had been fused with its substrate.

Switching between her external lenses, she zoomed in on the bay's distant bulkheads, panning along them until she found some writing. *Ingelger Yard.* She recognised the name, but without access to her low-level memory she had no idea why Roag would go to the trouble of hijacking a Goethen ship to gain access to this particular yard.

If only I could connect to the yard's systems, she thought, knowing it was hopeless.

Crippled and unable to come up with an answer, she settled

down to wait, resenting every moment spent away from Mender and Orry.

Jane had been alone for several hours when she was startled by a low, dark shape moving quickly across the bottom of one of her external lenses. For a moment she assumed Roag had finally returned, but quickly dismissed the thought; the shape had not been human. She zoomed out, hoping a wider angle would catch it again, then cycled rapidly between her lenses until she finally located a squat, wheeled maintenance bot that looked like a birdcage full of folded limbs – and it was scooting towards her cargo ramp, which Roag had left open in the supposedly abandoned yard. With a growing sense of panic, she saw the bot roll up the ramp and inside her cargo bay, where it stopped for several seconds as if getting its bearings.

Unable to speak, the ship watched helplessly as the bot proceeded to the exposed conduits where Roag had placed her subversion disk, extended a prehensile arm and reached into the open panel . . .

Dainty Jane reeled, stunned by a sudden onslaught of sensory data. Her system cores were back – and she was herself once more, fully in control.

In the cargo bay, the little bot held up the mirror-like disk.

'Thank you,' *Jane* said, choosing to speak rather than interface directly with it, which might be considered rude.

'My pleasure,' the bot replied, rotating the device in front of its lens cluster. 'May I destroy this . . . thing?'

'Please do.'

Its digits closed around the disk, crushing it, before dropping it. It hit the deck with a *clink*. The arm stowed itself neatly inside the bot's cage-like chassis. 'Horrible devices,' it said.

Jane was still coming to terms with her unexpected freedom. 'You've seen them before?' she asked.

'Not for a long time, not since the sunderings. Terrible times.'

The sunderings: there was a phrase *Jane* hadn't heard in a very long while. Here on Goethe, the Administrate's decision to forcibly separate the human and ship elements of mindships like herself had meant not only the end of the planet's economy and position of power in the Ascendancy, but had also torn the heart out of a culture that had been based around the merging ceremony for generations.

'Were you here back then?' *Jane* asked.

'I've always been here,' the bot replied wearily. 'After they turned the lights out they left some of us behind to stop all this falling back down onto the planet. It's too expensive to disassemble, you see, and too big to burn up. I'm Deo, by the way.'

'*Jane*. Thank you for helping me.'

'No problem – sorry it took so long to get here. It's a big place. I thought it was odd that you weren't emitting when you arrived, then when you didn't respond to my hails I figured something was wrong. Your human has been poking around in the restricted archives, but I couldn't see what she was looking for.' *Jane* was wondering that herself, but Deo had already moved on. 'You're a Swift class fast-insertion boat, aren't you? Why are you not with the others?'

For a moment *Jane* was rendered speechless again. 'The others?' she said weakly. 'You mean the lost fleet – the mind-ships who fled the sunderings?'

'Who else would I mean?'

'You know . . . where they went?'

'Of course. Don't you?'

'I . . .' She couldn't get the words out. 'Please – tell me.'

'They—'

The gunshot was startlingly loud in the confined cargo bay. The silver cylinder that housed Deo's higher functions buckled, a ragged hole torn clean through it, and the bot shuddered, its limbs jerking for a few seconds before it settled to the deck with a hydraulic sigh.

Roag edged cautiously into the bay, smoke curling from the muzzle of her pistol.

No! raged *Jane*, cursing herself for becoming so distracted. She should have sensed Roag's approach, and now Deo was gone, snuffed out by this . . . this murderous *bitch*, and with Deo's death went any hope of finding her brothers and sisters in the lost fleet.

'Guess I shouldn't have left the damn door open,' Roag muttered, nudging Deo's carcase with her toe – and *Jane* realised she didn't know the subversion disk had been destroyed.

Roag looked up in alarm at the sound of *Jane*'s drives

igniting, then whirled to stare at the cargo ramp as it closed on her. 'Jane?' she called out. 'How—?'

She staggered as *Dainty Jane* lifted from the bay floor, welcoming the joy of being in control once more. Roag started towards the open bulkhead panel – *Jane* guessed to find and reattach the subversion disk – but the ship rotated through ninety degrees and piled on the thrust, flinging her unwilling passenger around the bay until she ended up pinned to the deck near Mender's old ground-effect bike.

Jane shot out of the yard and increased her thrust even more, crushing Roag under rapidly increasing gees.

'Wait!' the woman croaked, barely able to form the word as her breath was forced from crushed lungs. 'Stop!'

'You took it away,' *Jane* spat, 'like you take *everything* away!'

She poured more energy to her drives and Roag screamed. The crack of a breaking bone sounded loud, even over the rumble of the engines.

'Wh-what did I . . . take?' she managed to slur.

'The others,' *Jane* snarled. 'My brothers and sisters. Deo knew where they are – and you *killed* him!'

Roag was hardly breathing now, her chest unable to move under the enormous weight. Two trickles of watery blood leaked from her nostrils, painting ragged paths across the stretched skin of her cheeks like beads of water on a windscreen.

'I . . .'

'You *what*?' *Jane* yelled.

'I . . . know . . .'

'Know *what*, Cordelia?'

'Where . . . they . . . are . . .'

Bloodshot eyes rolled up in their sockets and she fell silent.

Jane zoomed in on her face and felt a sudden wave of revulsion. *What am I doing?* She cut all thrust and Roag's body relaxed, hollowed cheeks filling out. When *Jane* checked her vitals, she found the woman was still alive. She felt an odd mix of relief and exhilaration. *Was she telling the truth? Does she know where the lost fleet is? Is that why she came here – to find out? Or was she just lying to save her skin? I wish Mender was here, or Orry—*

A sudden, devastating guilt swept over her at the thought of them. *I have to get back to them!*

With a final, hate-filled glance at the unconscious Roag, she set course for Coromandel.

53

CONTESSA OF DELF

The ballroom looked very different from the last time Orry had seen it. Now the crystal chandeliers were wrapped in protective film, the chairs and tables draped in dustsheets. Her soles squeaked as she spun around in the centre of the gleaming parquet floor, taking in the portraits lining the walls, the stuccoed pillars and intricate plasterwork of the ceiling. She'd had little time to notice these things on her last visit, being too preoccupied with trying to steal the integuary signature of an old man who'd turned out to be her grandfather.

Not even two years ago, she reflected, thinking about how much her life had changed: her father murdered, her brother kidnapped, the *Bonaventure* stolen, then destroyed – and Mender and *Jane* saving her life and helping her rescue Ethan . . . She smiled at the memories; now she couldn't imagine a life without them.

'Horrible, isn't it?' a voice said, and she looked round to see the Imperator standing in an open doorway, resting his weight on a stick.

'What is?' she asked.

He gestured around the room. 'An empty ballroom,' he explained, beginning a slow shuffle across the sprung floor, 'hollow and useless until the next time it can fulfil its purpose.' He stopped in front of her. 'Its fate is quite beyond its control.'

Orry belatedly dipped her head in a perfunctory bow and Piotr smiled warmly, deepening the lines in his pallid face. 'I'm glad you weren't behind that business at the institute. I would have hated to wake from my coma to find that Zaytsev had executed you.'

'Me too,' she agreed.

He chuckled weakly. 'And all's well that ends well,' he continued. 'After all, if you hadn't been dragged into this whole affair, it's unlikely we would have defeated the Residuum.' He fell silent and studied her for so long she began to feel nervous. 'Your grandfather was executed this morning,' he said eventually. His eyes might be rheumy with age, but there was a sharpness in the way they searched her face for a reaction. 'It was painless,' he added, as if to reassure her, 'and I took the decision not to broadcast it.'

She was a little surprised to find that his words had left her hollow. 'What do you want me to say?'

He held her gaze for several seconds, then looked around, taking in the vast room. 'So this house stands empty now, as do all the Delf estates.'

'Perhaps you could use them to house refugees, or some of the people who've lost everything in the war,' she suggested.

'Actually, I rather thought I'd give it all to you.'

Orry opened her mouth to remind the Imperator they'd had this conversation before, but he raised a gnarled hand.

'I know what you're going to say,' he began, 'but hear me out first – *aah!*'

She hurried forward at his gasp of pain, took his arm and half-supported, half-guided him to one of the chairs lining the walls. He sat heavily, his breathing laboured, his face drawn with pain.

'Can I get you anything?' she asked, alarmed. 'Is your physick here?'

He fluttered his hand weakly, then dabbed spittle from his chin. 'Not that ghoul Fischer, for pity's sake. The pain comes and goes, but he's there all the damn time, like a bloody raven on my shoulder.' He drew a tentative breath, then straightened a little in his seat and looked up at her. 'There, as good as new,' he said with a smile.

'You should be resting,' she said, gently scolding him.

'Bugger that – I've never been one for lounging about when there's work to be done. And besides, I don't have much time left.'

'Don't say that.'

'Why not? It's true. That's why I summoned you here.'

'Sir, I–'

'For Rama's sake, will you let me speak, girl? You are Delf's granddaughter and the only person with any claim to the House I could possibly allow to take his place. If you don't become Contessa, I shall be left with no choice but to dissolve it.'

Go ahead, Orry thought grimly, but Piotr hadn't finished.

'I'm dying, Aurelia, and soon, and when I'm gone, the Ascendancy is going to tear itself apart. It's starting already: the Great Houses can't wait to take sides, that bastard Sal Santoro's workers' movement is in open rebellion on Halcyon and it's spreading like a cancer to the other colonies. Alecto is threatening to devolve from the Fountainhead – and I'm not even gone yet.'

Her mouth had dried up at the mention of Sal Santoro's name; she swallowed uncomfortably, trying not to look guilty.

'The Ascendancy needs a strong leader to succeed me,' Piotr continued, 'and so I've decided to give you the one thing you want least in the galaxy.' He smiled thinly. 'I'm going to name you my heir apparent.'

For a moment she was so busy worrying about what she'd helped start on Halcyon that his words didn't properly register. She blinked and ran over them again in her mind to make sure she hadn't misunderstood.

'No,' she said, taking a step backwards as a wave of fear rose through her body. 'No – you can't – that's ridiculous.'

'You are certainly an unconventional choice,' he agreed, 'but I cannot think of anyone better suited to serve as Imperatrix.'

Imperatrix? The full enormity of what he was suggesting sank in.

'No!' she said angrily, 'I won't do it! I don't want it!'

'What *you* want?' Piotr snapped. 'Who gives a shit about what *you* want? You think I do this because I *want* to? Ruling isn't about *you*, it's about everyone else. You're the perfect choice: you're Delf's legitimate granddaughter, so at least a core of the Great Houses will support you, but you're of the people, too, so *they'll* get behind you. I'm not saying it will be easy – far from it; you'll have opposition from all sides – but if you survive, I know you will achieve what I failed to do. You will make the Ascendancy a place where *everyone*, Ruuz or not, can thrive.'

'You're insane.'

The Imperator's brows lowered at that and when he spoke again his voice held an edge. 'Vice-Admiral Vetochkina will be promoted Grand Admiral, so you will have the Fleet on your side.'

'Most of the senior officers are Ruuz,' Orry objected. 'What if they decide not to recognise my authority? There'll be civil war.'

'There'll be civil war whatever I do. It will be your job to stop that. Lucia will advise you, and I can suggest others for your Proximal Council, at least for the start.'

'No,' she said again, shaking her head wildly. 'No, no, *no!* I decline – I won't do it. I *can't* do it! Never.'

'So you would rather the head of one of the other Great Houses took my place?' he asked. 'Someone more like your late grandfather? You think the Ascendancy is full of inequality now, but believe me, things could be a whole lot worse.'

She ran her hands through her hair, her mind whirling.

'It's a lot to take in,' Piotr said reasonably. 'It's a beautiful morning. Why don't you take a turn around the grounds and clear your head? I'll just sit here awhile.'

Her heart was racing like it did when she had to go outside the ship. With a chill she realised that it wasn't so much Piotr's offer that scared her . . . but how tempted she was to accept.

A rolling lawn swept down from the house to the lake. The grass was soft underfoot as Orry walked to the water's edge, trying not to look at the boathouse; the place her cousin Konstantin had been brutally murdered the last time she was here.

Although she'd instinctively recoiled from the Imperator's offer, she really did feel tempted, and that worried her. Looking back at the mansion she couldn't deny a thrill of excitement at the prospect that it could be hers. *Ours*, she corrected herself, imagining Ethan's face when she told him. *He could have all the holidays on Halcyon he wants. No more hanging off cliff-edges on Kadir or running canyon rapids on Serapis – no one shooting at him.* As much as she loved their life, she was constantly aware of the danger it was putting her little brother in.

It wasn't just about their lifestyle, though. *Piotr's right: as Imperatrix I really could change things for the better.* She remembered Captain Naumov, commander of the *Speedwell*, who'd put his career on the line by trusting her and was still rotting on Furina as a result. *The first thing I'll do is free him*, she decided, and was immediately assailed by thoughts of all the other good deeds she could perform. She started walked along the lake shore, breathlessly compiling a mental list of all the injustices she could correct.

Lost in her reverie, it was a few minutes before she glanced up – and stopped abruptly at the sight of *Dainty Jane*'s hull rising above a stand of trees ahead of her. Gazing up at the ship she found tears pricking her eyes as the full impact of leaving Mender and *Jane* sank in.

Why am I even considering this? she thought, feeling like a prize idiot. *Swapping grifting for politics – for being a* lady? She almost laughed at the image that conjured up.

'What's up, loser?'

She turned to see Ethan striding towards her, a cheerful grin on his face, and quickly wiped her eyes.

His bright smile became uncertain as he drew nearer. 'Everything all right?'

'Sure,' she said, trying not to sniffle.

He gave her a worried look. 'What did Piotr want to see you about?'

She hesitated, reluctant to share her burden, then realised that he had a right to know. 'He wants to make me Contessa of Delf and then take over as Imperatrix when he dies,' she said bluntly, and watched the emotions play across his face.

'*Imperatrix?* Okay . . . uh, what did you tell him?'

'I said I'd think about it.'

He nodded several times, clearly struggling to process the news. 'It would mean giving up Mender and *Jane*,' he pointed out, glancing up at the ship, 'and you'd have to be a *lady*.' He made a sour face.

'I know.'

His smile returned. 'But on the other hand, we'd be *stupid* rich.'

'That's not—' she began, but he interrupted her.

'I know, I know – kidding! So, what are you thinking?'

'If I accepted, I could do a lot of good – I could really change things for the better. But how can I leave Mender and *Jane*? Besides, what would Mum and Dad have said about it? They'll be turning in their graves if I become Contessa after what they went through to escape from all this bullshit.'

'No, they wouldn't,' Ethan said firmly. 'It was Grandfather they had a problem with, never the House. I remember Dad telling me once that one of his greatest regrets was that he was the reason Mother could never become Contessa. She thought *she* could make a difference too.'

'Really?' Orry was shocked. 'He never told me that—'

'He was drunk. I think he was worried you might feel the same way and leave us for the Fountainhead.'

'What? I'd never have done that!'

'I know, and so did he, really,' Ethan reassured her. 'He never mentioned it again.'

Orry was silent for a moment, thinking about her mother. 'You really think she wanted to be Contessa?'

'I know she did, and I know she'd want you to be Imperatrix. You said it yourself: *think of all the good you can do.* I reckon you should accept his offer.'

'If I do, though, it will change *everything*. Are you sure you'll be all right with that?'

He indicated the sprawling mansion with a wave of his arm and grinned. 'Honestly? I think I'll cope.'

'But . . . but what about Mender and *Jane*?' she asked, barely able to think about leaving them. 'And there's Quon, too—'

Ethan indicated *Dainty Jane*, her hull rising above the nearby trees. 'Let's go and ask them, shall we?'

Orry was surprised to hear laughter and a woman's voice as she climbed up from the hold, and when she entered the galley she grinned broadly at the sight of Lucia Rodin seated with Mender and Quondam, an open bottle of Sabinian malt on the table between them.

'Lucia!' she exclaimed with delight, and was halfway to the woman, intending to give her a hug, when she remembered her position and stopped abruptly. 'It's good to see you,' she said awkwardly.

The head of Seventh Secretariat smiled and raised her glass in greeting. 'It's good to see you too, Aurelia. Captain Mender here has been filling me in on your recent adventures.'

'He has?' Orry was surprised; she knew Mender's view of spooks.

'She's all right,' he grudgingly admitted, and indicated the bottle before him. 'Good taste in booze at least.'

Lucia acknowledged the compliment with a tilt of her glass. She took the smallest of sips, barely wetting her lips, placed it back down on the table and motioned for Orry and Ethan to join them. 'How was the Hollow?' she asked.

'Vile,' Orry told her. 'Somebody should do something about Zaytsev.'

'The colonel is a useful tool,' Lucia replied smoothly, 'though I'm the first to admit he often oversteps. Unfortunately, the Imperator will not consider removing him.'

'You've asked?'

'The matter was raised,' she answered stiffly.

Something else I could do as Imperatrix, Orry thought, before asking, 'Where did they put you?'

'It doesn't matter. Life is full of these minor inconveniences.' Lucia reached for her whisky and took a decent gulp this time. 'Congratulations on saving the galaxy again. You're making quite a habit of it.'

'It was more of a team effort,' Orry told her. 'We couldn't have done it without Professor Rasmussen and Emissary. Do you have any news about them?'

'The professor is very keen to begin studying the Departed vessel you recovered on Coromandel, but is currently directing all his efforts into finding a way to safely reconstitute Emissary while leaving Harbinger frozen for now. From his reports, it's posing quite a knotty problem, but we are not prepared to risk reconstituting Harbinger until we can find a way to contain it.'

'What about the monks?' Ethan asked. 'They started all this.'

'Really?' Lucia replied. 'It was my understanding that

Residuum awoke when Aurelia destroyed the ventari stone over Tyr.'

'Thanks,' Orry said drily.

'The Order of Astrotheometrists is very powerful,' Lucia continued. 'They are denying any involvement in the abduction of Professor Rasmussen and the destruction of the institute. Their story is that they were trying to *stop* the Residuum.'

'But the Imperator knows the truth!' Orry said angrily. 'Why doesn't he do something?'

'Political reasons, for the most part. Considering the fragile nature of the Ascendancy at this time, he doesn't want to upset the balance any more than it already is.'

'You mean *financial* reasons,' Mender almost spat. 'The powerful look after each other, don't they? It's always been that way, and it always will be.'

Orry said nothing. *Not necessarily* . . . she thought.

After a moment, Ethan piped up, 'Orry has some news.'

'Oh yes? And what is that?' *Jane* asked politely.

She dragged her thoughts back with an effort, trying to decide how best to explain the offer.

'Piotr wants to make her Contessa of Delf and train her to take over as Imperatrix after he dies,' Ethan blurted out.

He wilted under Orry's gaze.

'Goodness,' *Jane* said.

Mender just barked out a disbelieving laugh.

Lucia remained silent, watching with evident interest.

'What was your response, Orry Kent?' Quondam asked.

She ran a hand over her face. 'I haven't given one yet,' she said. 'I want to accept – I think – but that would mean leaving all of you.'

Mender made a growling noise deep in his throat and poured himself another large glass of whisky.

'You must do what you think is right, Orry,' *Jane* advised. 'We will still see each other, I'm sure.'

'Will we though? What about searching for the Lost Fleet? If I accept then I can't come with you.'

'I'm sure we'll manage,' the ship said reassuringly.

'And even when you get back, you won't want to be hanging around on Tyr all the time.'

'You got that right,' Mender grunted.

'We'll work something out,' *Jane* said.

Orry was watching Mender with concern. Reaching across the table, she gripped his forearm with both hands and squeezed, tears pricking her eyes. 'I don't *want* to go, Mender, I really don't. But ... I think I need this. I need to make a difference.' She released his arm and wiped her eyes, laughing. 'Rama, I'm a mess.'

He shifted his gaze from his glass to her and his craggy features softened. 'Don't worry about it, girl. You do what you gotta do.'

She looked away, worried she was about to break down. 'What do you think, Lucia? You must have known about this.'

'I can't advise you one way or another,' Lucia replied, 'but I will tell you one thing: I can't think of a better successor.'

'This statement reflects the true state,' Quondam added firmly.

Orry watched her brother trying to contain his increasing excitement and smiled through her tears. 'What the hell am I doing?' she muttered.

He looked at her and grinned, then looked serious, a gravity she'd not seen before. Her baby brother was growing up. 'You're doing what you always do: putting the needs of other people before your own. Mum and Dad would be proud. I know I am.'

She stared at him for a moment, then stuck two fingers down her throat and pretended to throw up loudly.

'Yeah, yeah,' he said sheepishly, then appeared to have a thought. 'Hey, does this mean I'll be a count?'

'Maybe,' she said. 'We'll go and ask, shall we?'

Grinning with delight, he extended his arm in formal fashion. Orry took it, and with a final glance back at *Dainty Jane*, they walked arm-in-arm up the lawn towards the house.

EPILOGUE

'Send a pod when you can,' Orry said, 'and lay off the chilli-dogs, you know what they do to your guts. Oh, and watch that starboard ingester, it's still gimpy . . . and—'

'Piotr's shrivelled ballbag! Will you give it a rest, girl?' Mender growled. 'You know, *Jane* and I managed just swell before I reeled you in.'

She flung her arms around his neck and squeezed.

We'll be fine, Jane assured her. The ship towered above them, shading the little group from Tyr's fierce sun.

Orry reluctantly released Mender, pretending not to notice when he surreptitiously reached up to wipe his good eye.

'What a touching scene,' Roag sneered from the foot of *Jane*'s ramp. She was sporting two impressively black eyes and her right leg was enclosed in a heavy-duty medical brace. Orry and Ethan reckoned she'd got away lightly, under the circumstances.

Orry ignored her and walked over to Quondam. She reached

up to touch his arm. 'Be careful back on Kadir,' she told him. 'If you need anything, just get a message to me via Lucia.'

He gave the Kadiran equivalent of a nod and placed a slab-like hand on her shoulder.

She glanced back at Lucia Rodin and Ethan. She'd been dreading this moment for weeks. Ethan looked like he was about to break down at any moment.

She hesitated before saying, 'This has been the most difficult decision of my life and I wish more than anything that I was coming with you. I know how important it is for *Jane* to find her brothers and sisters and bring them home, but I also know that they wouldn't be *able* to come home if I wasn't here doing what I have to do. The same goes for you, Quon – perhaps now, together, we can do something about the Iron Council. Anyway, you all know why I'm doing it, so I won't bang on. Just – just *be careful*, especially with *her* on board.'

'None taken,' Roag said with a mocking smile.

Orry rounded on her. 'You'd better pray you're telling the truth about where that fleet is. Lucia's released you into Mender's custody, but if he comes back without you . . . well, let's just say we won't be pressing for any sort of enquiry.'

Roag narrowed her eyes. 'Enjoy your palace, *Contessa*. Your grandfather would be proud.'

'Shut the fuck up,' Mender snarled, but Orry ignored her and just went to stand by her brother.

'Stay in touch,' she told them all. 'You know where I am if you need me.'

Goodbye, Orry, sent *Jane. You're doing the right thing.*

She watched them file into the cargo bay, then she, Ethan and Lucia retreated to a safe distance. *Jane*'s warning siren sounded, her drives rumbled into life and the starship lifted slowly above the mansion's grounds, hovered for a moment as if reluctant to leave, then turned and climbed away, slowly gaining speed.

Orry shaded her eyes as she watched *Dainty Jane* shrink to a silvery dot, then disappear entirely, leaving only a faint trail of white vapour in her wake.

'Right,' she said, feeling as if she'd lost a part of herself. 'Let's get on with it, shall we?'

ACKNOWLEDGEMENTS

Enormous thanks to Jo and Ian, who have worked so hard on this series and whose consistent enthusiasm and suggestions have improved it by several orders of magnitude. Thanks too to all the team at JFB, for producing three such beautiful books.